# "THIS BOOK HAS IT ALL— DYNAMITE PLOTTING, RIVETING CHARACTERS, AND GRABBING SUSPENSE."
## —*Houston Chronicle*

"Shortly after the Cold War ended, the Nazis again became thriller writers' favorite bad guys, but Katzenbach has topped them all in this tale. It is horrifying to imagine surviving the Holocaust only to be tracked again by the same monster that stalked one fifty years before."
—*San Francisco Examiner*

"A compulsively entertaining thriller . . . The pace is brisk, the quest compelling, the dialogue excellent. . . . Katzenbach knows his way around both the bright and the darker sides of Miami. Better still, he knows both the courageous good and the unspeakable evil that can be found in the human heart."
—*The Flint Journal*

"Starts off at ninety miles an hour and never slows down, leaving readers breathless at the stunning climax. With solid writing, a plot that's full of menace, and plenty of suspense, this one seems destined to be a hit."
—*Booklist*

**Please turn the page for more rave reviews . . .**

By John Katzenbach:

Fiction
IN THE HEAT OF THE SUMMER*
THE TRAVELER*
DAY OF RECKONING*
JUST CAUSE*
THE SHADOW MAN*

Nonfiction
FIRST BORN: The Death of Arnold Zeleznik, Age Nine:
  Murder, Madness, and What Came After

*Published by Ballantine Books

# THE SHADOW MAN

## John Katzenbach

BALLANTINE BOOKS • NEW YORK

Published by Ballantine Books
Copyright © 1995 by John Katzenbach

http://www.randomhouse.com

Library of Congress Catalog Card Number: 96-96354

ISBN 0-345-38630-2

Printed in Canada

First Hardcover Edition: May 1995
First Mass Market Edition: September 1996

10  9  8  7  6  5  4  3  2  1

No novel ever gets finished without some assistance. Sometimes this help is technical, as in the readers who review early drafts of the manuscript and point out all the mistakes one has made. Sometimes it is less tangible, but equally important. (The children who leave you alone when they'd much rather you came out and shot baskets with them.) To complete this book, I was greatly aided by my friends Jack Rosenthal, David Kaplan and Janet Rifkin, and Harley and Sherry Tropin, all of whom contributed comments that improved the final version.

There are many extraordinary books about the Holocaust, each more heartbreaking, more frustrating, more astonishing than the next. I do not intend to list all that I examined, but there is one work that I think worth mentioning. When I first started to nurture the seeds of ideas that ultimately became this novel, the late Howard Simons at Harvard University gave me his copy of a remarkable work of nonfiction: *The Last Jews In Berlin* by Leonard Gross. Those interested in learning about true resourcefulness and bravery would be wise to examine it.

As always, my greatest debt is to my family, so it is to Justine, Nick, and Maddy that this book is dedicated.

*History, Stephen said, is a nightmare
from which I'm trying to awake . . .*
James Joyce
*Ulysses*

# ONE

## *AN INTERRUPTED DEATH*

Early in the evening on what promised to be an oppressively hot midsummer night on Miami Beach, Simon Winter, an old man who had spent years in the profession of death, decided it was time to kill himself. Regretting for an instant that he would be creating a messy job of work for others, he walked slowly to a closet in his bedroom and removed a scarred short-barreled .38 caliber detective's special from a faded and sweat-stained brown leather holster. He cracked the cylinder open and removed five of the six bullets. These he slipped into his pocket. This act, he believed, would help remove anyone's doubts as to what his intentions had been.

Carrying the pistol in his hand, he started to search for paper and pen to write a suicide note. This took several frustrating minutes, and it was not until he shoved aside some white, pressed handkerchiefs, tie bars, and cuff links in a bureau drawer, that he was able to discover a single clean sheet of blue-lined notepaper and a cheap ballpoint pen. Well, he told himself, whatever you're going to say, you'll have to keep it short.

He tried to think if there was anything else he needed, as he paused momentarily by the mirror to inspect his appearance. Not too bad. His checked sport shirt was clean, as were his khaki trousers, socks, and underwear. He considered shaving, rubbing the back of the hand that held the gun across his cheek, feeling the day's stubble, but decided it was unnecessary. He needed a haircut, but shrugged as he hastily combed his fingers through his shock of white hair. No time, he told himself. He suddenly remembered being told when he was young that people's hair continued to grow after death. Hair and fingernails. He wished it were true. This was the sort of information that was whispered from one child to another with absolute authority and invariably led to ghost stories told in darkened rooms in hushed tones. Part of the problem with growing up and getting old, Simon Winter thought, was having the myths of childhood erased.

Turning away from the mirror, he took a quick glance around the bedroom—the bed was made, there were no piles of dirty clothes in the corner; his midnight reading, paperback crime novels and adventure stories, was stacked by the bedside table—and he thought, if not precisely neat, it was at least presentable, which was more or less the same as his own appearance. Certainly no mess that wasn't understandable for an old bachelor, or, for that matter, a young child, which was an observation that momentarily interested him and gave him an abrupt sense of completeness.

He stuck his head into the bathroom, saw a vial of sleeping pills, briefly considered using them instead of his old service revolver, but decided that would be a cowardly way of murdering himself. He spoke inwardly: You should be brave enough to look down the barrel of your gun, not merely pop a handful of pills and ooze gently into a fatal sleep. He moved into the kitchen. There was a day's worth of dirty dishes in the sink. As he stared at them, a large bronze palmetto bug crawled up on the edge of a plate and paused, as if waiting to see what Simon Winter would do.

"Disgusting beasts," he said out loud. "Glorified cockroach." He raised the pistol and took aim at the bug. "Bang," he said. "One shot. Did you know, bug, I never received less than an expert rating?"

This made him sigh deeply and smile as he put his gun and paper down on the cheap, white linoleum countertop, grabbed some dishwashing soap, and quickly started scrubbing the dishes. He talked out loud: "Let's hope that cleanliness *is* next to godliness." He supposed that it was slightly ridiculous to do the dishes as one of his final acts on earth, but then, if he didn't, he knew someone else would have to take care of them. This, he understood, was a part of his nature. He did not leave things undone for other people to finish.

The palmetto bug seemed to catch a whiff of the soap, recognized it was in mortal danger, and fled across the counter, as Simon Winter took a halfhearted swipe at it with a sponge.

"That's right. You can run, but you can't hide."

He reached beneath the sink and found a can of insect poison, which he shook hard and then sprayed in the general area where the bug had disappeared.

"I guess we'll go together, bug," he said. He remembered that ancient Vikings used to kill a dog and place it at the feet of a man about to be buried, the thought being that the warrior would want companionship on the road to Valhalla, and what better comrade than a faithful dog, who presumably would ignore the fact that its own life had been cut short by barbaric custom. So, Simon Winter thought, if I had a dog, I could shoot him first, but I don't and I wouldn't do that anyway, so my companion on the road to wherever will have to be a palmetto bug.

He laughed at himself, wondering what he and the palmetto bug would talk about and guessing that, in an odd way, their lives hadn't been that different, poking around in the unpleasant remains of day-to-day life. He swiped the sink clean with a flourish, put the sponge down on the corner, and, taking up the paper and pistol, went back into the modest living room of his small apartment. He sat down on a threadbare couch and placed his revolver on a coffee table in front of him. Then he took the notepaper and pen and, after a moment's thought, wrote:

To Whom It May Concern:
    I did this to myself.
    I am old and tired and lonely and haven't done anything useful in years. I don't think the world will miss me much.

Well, he said to himself, that's all true, but the world seems to get along pretty well regardless of who it is that dies, so you haven't really said anything. He placed the tip of the ballpoint pen against his teeth and tapped it once or twice. Say what you mean, Simon Winter insisted, like an elementary school teacher frustrated with her students' compositions. He scribbled quickly:

I feel like a guest that has overstayed his welcome.

That's better, he thought. He smiled. Now, get on to business.

I have slightly more than $5,000 in a savings account at First Federal, part of which should be used to pay to fry up these old bones. If someone would be kind enough to take my ashes and throw them in the waters off Government Cut on an outgoing tide, I would appreciate it.

Simon Winter paused, and thought: It would be nice if they did this when the big schools of tarpon that live in the cut start to roll on the surface, grunting, gulping air, and picking up speed as they get ready to feed on the pinfish and small mackerel. They are beautiful animals, huge silver scales like armor on their flanks making them seem like medieval knights-errant of the sea, with great, powerful, scythelike tails that thrust them through the water. They are an ancient tribe, untouched by any evolutionary change in centuries, and some of them are probably as old as I am. He wondered for a moment whether a tarpon ever grew tired of swimming, and if it did, what it did then. Perhaps it just slows, and doesn't run as hard when a big hammerhead stalks the school. He thought: It wouldn't be half bad to come back as a tarpon. Then he continued writing:

Any money left over should go to the Miami Beach Police Department's widows' fund, or whatever it is called nowadays. No relatives to call. I had a brother, but he died, and I haven't heard from his kids in years.
    I have enjoyed life and managed to do a few good things. If anyone's interested, there's a scrapbook with some clippings about my old cases in the bedroom.

He decided to allow himself a small conceit and an apology:

Once, I was as good as they came.
Sorry to be such a bother.

He paused, examining the note, then he signed it with a flourish:

Simon Winter. Detective. Retired.

He took a deep breath and raised his hand up to his eyes. It was steady. He glanced down at the handwriting in front of him. Not a waver there, he thought. All right. You've faced far tougher things. There's no reason to wait anymore.

He gripped the gun, placing his finger on the trigger. He could feel every part of every action, as if, suddenly, each motion took on a specialness of its own. The tension in his finger around the trigger tightened the tendon in the back of his hand. He could feel his arm muscle working as he lifted the pistol, strengthening his wrist to hold the weapon still. His heartbeat accelerated. His imagination flooded with memories. He ordered his eyes shut, trying to squeeze out any residual doubt. All right, he said to himself. All right. It's time.

Simon Winter placed the barrel of his revolver against the roof of his mouth, and wondered whether he would feel the shot that killed him. And in that short hesitation, that single, momentary delay, the silence he'd created around him was abruptly shattered by a loud and insistent knock at the front door of his apartment.

The sound crashed through his suicidal determination, startling him.

In that same instant, he became aware of dozens of small sensations, as if the world had abruptly demanded he acknowledge its presence. The pressure in his finger on the trigger seemed to threaten to slice his skin; where he had expected a quick sheet of scorching oblivion, now he tasted the metallic harshness of the revolver barrel and choked on the oily, pungent smell of the cleaning fluids that he had used on the weapon. His tongue slid up against the icy steel of the trigger guard and he could hear the wheeze of his breath.

Farther in the distance the diesel engine of a bus droned past. He wondered if it was the A-30, heading to Ocean Drive, or the

A-42, on its way to Collins Avenue. A trapped housefly buzzed frantically at a window, and he remembered an unfixed tear in one of the window screens. He opened his eyes and lowered the pistol.

There was a second knocking at the door, more demanding.

The noise had an urgency that overcame his resolve. He put the revolver down on the coffee table, on top of his note, and rose.

He heard a voice saying: "Please, Mr. Winter . . ."

It was high-pitched and frightened and seemed familiar.

It's after dark, he told himself. No one has knocked on my door after the sun's gone down in twenty years. Moving swiftly, forgetting for a moment the hesitation that age forced onto his limbs, he hurried to the sound. He called out, "I'm here, I'm here . . ." and he opened the door, not knowing precisely what it was that he was opening to, but vaguely hoping in some distant spot within him that he was allowing something of importance to enter.

Fear like a halo of light seemed to illuminate the elderly woman standing outside. Her face was rigid, pale, drawn tight like a knot, and she looked up at Simon Winter with such helplessness that for a moment he stepped back, as if struck by a sudden strong gust of wind, and it took an instant for him to recognize his neighbor of almost ten years.

"Mrs. Millstein, what is the matter?"

The woman reached out her hand, grasping at Simon Winter's arm, shaking her head, as if to say that she could not force words past fright.

"Are you all right?"

"Mr. Winter," the woman said slowly, the words creaking past lips squeezed together, "thank goodness you were home. I'm so alone, and I didn't know what to do. . . ."

"Come inside, come inside. Please, what is the matter?"

Sophie Millstein stepped forward shakily. Her fingernails sliced into the flesh of Simon Winter's arm, her grip like a climber threatened with a fall down some sheer precipice.

"I didn't believe, Mr. Winter," Sophie Millstein started softly. But then her words picked up speed, following in a torrent of anxiety. "I don't think any of us really believed. It seemed so distant.

So impossible. How could he be here? Here? No, it just seemed too crazy, so none of us believed. Not the rabbi or Mr. Silver or Frieda Kroner. But we were wrong, Mr. Winter. He is here. I saw him, today. Tonight. Right outside the ice cream store on the Lincoln Road Mall. I stepped out, and there he was. He just looked at me, Mr. Winter, and I knew right then. He has eyes like razors, Mr. Winter. I didn't know what to do. Leo would have known. He would have said, 'Sophie. We must call someone,' and he would have had the number right there, ready. But Leo's gone and I'm all alone and he's here."

She looked helplessly at Simon Winter.

"He will kill me too," she said, gasping.

Simon Winter steered Sophie Millstein into his living room, depositing her on the sagging couch.

"No one's going to kill anyone, Mrs. Millstein. Now, let me get you a drink of something cold and then you can explain what has you so frightened."

She looked wildly at him: "I must warn the others!"

"Yes, yes. I'll help you, but please, have a drink and then tell me what is the matter."

She opened her mouth to reply, but then seemed to lose her grip on the words, so no sound came out. She put a hand on her forehead, as if taking her temperature, and said, "Yes. Yes, please, iced tea if you have it. It's so hot. Sometimes, in the summer, it seems as if the air is just burning up."

Simon Winter swept up his suicide letter and pistol from the coffee table in front of Sophie Millstein and hurried into the kitchen. He found a clean glass, into which he poured water, ice cubes, and instant tea mix. He left his letter on the counter, but before taking the glass back into Sophie Millstein, paused and reloaded his weapon with the five bullets in his pocket. He looked up and saw the old woman staring blankly in front of her, as if watching some memory. He felt an odd excitement, coupled with a sense of urgency. Sophie Millstein's fear seemed thick and choking, filling the room like smoke. He breathed hard and hurried to her side.

"Now, drink this," he said in the same tones one would use to a fevered child. "And then take your time and explain what has happened."

Sophie Millstein nodded, seizing the glass with both hands, gulping at the frothy brown liquid. She swallowed hard, then put the glass to her forehead. Simon Winter saw her eyes fill with tears.

"He will kill me," she said again. "I don't want to die."

"Mrs. Millstein, please," Simon Winter said. "Who?"

Sophie Millstein shuddered, and whispered in German: *"Der Schattenmann."*

"Who? Is that someone's name?"

She looked wildly at him. "No one knew his name, Mr. Winter. At least, no one who lived."

"But who—"

"He was a ghost."

"I don't understand. . . ."

"A devil."

"Who?"

"He was evil, Mr. Winter. More evil than anyone could think. And now he's here. We didn't believe, Mr. Winter, but we were wrong. Mr. Stein warned us, but we didn't know him, so how could we believe?"

Sophie Millstein shuddered hard.

"I'm old," she whispered. "I'm old, but I don't want to die."

Simon Winter held up his hand. "Please, Mrs. Millstein, you must explain yourself. Take your time and tell me who this person is and why you're so frightened."

She took another long pull at the iced tea and set the glass down in front of her. She nodded slowly, trying to regain some composure. She lifted her hand to her forehead, her fingers stroking her eyebrows gently, as if trying to loosen a hard memory, and then she wiped away the tears that were gathering in her eyes. She took a deep breath and looked up at him. He saw her hand drop to her throat, where, for just an instant, she fingered the necklace she wore. It was distinctive; a thin gold chain that held a stamped replica of her first name. But what separated this necklace from the same type worn seemingly by teenagers everywhere was the presence of a pair of small diamonds at either end of the *S* in Sophie. Simon Winter knew her late husband had dipped into his modest pension funds and given her the necklace the birthday before his heart failed, and like the wedding ring on her finger, she did not remove it.

"It is such a difficult story, Mr. Winter. It happened so long ago, sometimes now, it seems like a dream. But it was no dream, Mr. Winter. More a nightmare. Fifty years ago."

"Go on, Mrs. Millstein."

"In 1943, Mr. Winter, my family—Mama, Papa, my brother Hansi—we were still in Berlin. Hiding out . . ."

"Go on."

"It was such a terrible life, Mr. Winter. There was never a moment, not one second, not even the time between heartbeats, Mr. Winter, when we thought we were safe. There wasn't much to eat, and we were always cold, and we thought every morning when we awakened that that would be our last night together. Every second, it seemed, the risk grew. A neighbor might grow curious. A policeman might demand your papers. Would you step on the trolley car and spot someone who recognized you from before the war, before the yellow stars? Maybe you would say something, any little thing, Mr. Winter. A gesture, a tone, some slight nervousness, something that would betray you. There are no more suspicious people in the world than the Germans, Mr. Winter. I should know. I was one of them once. That would be all it took, just a tiny hesitation, maybe a frightened look, anything that indicated you were out of place. And then it would be over. By 1943 we knew, Mr. Winter. I mean, perhaps we didn't know it all, but we knew. Capture was death. It was that simple. Sometimes at night, I used to lie in bed, unable to sleep, praying that some British bomber would drop its load short, Mr. Winter, right on top of all of us, and so we could all go together and end all the fear. I would be shivering, praying for death, and my brother Hansi would come over and hold my hand until I fell asleep. He was so strong. And resourceful, Mr. Winter. When we had nothing to eat, he could find some potatoes. When we had no place to stay, he would find us a new flat, or a basement somewhere, where there weren't any questions and we could spend a week, or maybe more, still together, still surviving."

"What happened to—"

"He died. They all died."

Sophie Millstein took a deep breath.

"I told you. He killed them. He found us and they died."

Simon Winter started to interject another question, but she held up a quivering hand.

"Let me just finish this, Mr. Winter, while I still have the strength. There were so many things to be frightened of, but I suppose the worst were the catchers."

"The catchers?"

"Jews like us, Mr. Winter. Jews that worked for the Gestapo. There was a building on Iranishestrasse. One of those awful gray stone buildings the Germans love so much. The Jewish Bureau of Investigation was what they called it. That was where he worked, where all of them worked. Their own freedom depended on their hunting us down."

"And this man you think you saw today . . ."

"Some were famous, Mr. Winter. Rolf Isaaksohn, he was young and arrogant, and the beautiful Stella Kubler. She was blond and pretty and looked like one of their Nordic maidens. She turned in her own husband. There were others, too. They took off their stars and moved about the city, just looking, like birds of prey."

"The man today . . ."

"Der Schattenmann. He was in all our nightmares. It was said that he could pick you from a crowd of people, just as if he alone could see some glow to your skin, some look in your eyes. Maybe it was the way you walked, or some smell you had. We didn't know. All we knew was if he found you, death would come knocking at your door. People said that he would be there in the darkness when they came for you, and he would be there when they shipped you out in the morning gloom on the transport train for Auschwitz. But you wouldn't know, you see, because no one saw his face and no one knew his name. If you saw his face, they said you would be taken to the basement at the Plotzesee Prison, where it was always night and everyone knew that no one came out of the basement, not ever, Mr. Winter. And he would be there, to see you die, so that the last eyes you saw on this earth would be his, Mr. Winter. He was the worst. The worst by far, because it was said that he enjoyed what he was doing, and because he was so good at it . . ."

"And today."

"Here. Here on Miami Beach. This cannot be so, Mr. Winter. This must be impossible, yet, I believe. I truly believe I saw him today."

"But—"

"Just for a few seconds. There was a door left open and they were moving us through the offices because there was paperwork. Paperwork! The Germans even had paperwork when they were going to kill you. And so the Gestapo clerk finished with us, and stamped his documents and we were being taken down to the cells to wait for transport and I happened to look in for only the tiniest time, Mr. Winter, but he was there, between two officers wearing those horrid black uniforms. They were all laughing over some joke and I knew it was him. His hat was tipped back on his head and he looked up and shouted something and they slammed the door closed and I thought it was the basement for me, for sure, but instead I was put on a train that day. I suppose he thought I would die in camp. I was so small, I was sixteen, but hardly bigger than a child, but I surprised them all, Mr. Winter, because I lived."

She stopped, catching her breath in a rush.

"I didn't want to die. Not then. Not now. Not yet."

Sophie Millstein was a tiny woman, barely five feet tall, even with the lifts that she wore in her orthopedic shoes, and slightly overweight. She was dwarfed by Simon Winter, who, even with age, still stood nearly six and a half feet tall. She wore her white hair teased into a bun, to further add to her height, an effect that usually seemed to touch the ridiculous, especially when she emerged from her apartment in brightly colored polyester pedal pushers and flowered shirts, dragging a two-wheeled cart behind her on the way to the grocery. Simon Winter knew her mostly to nod hello and dodge any lengthy conversation, which invariably centered around some complaint or another, about the city, about the heat, about teenagers and loud music, about her son who didn't call frequently enough, about growing old, about outliving her husband, all of which he preferred to avoid. But if his usual opinion of his neighbor up to this moment was one of distance and studied politeness with little shared concerns, the fear she wore in her eyes on this occasion slid him away from the usual and into a different place altogether.

He did not know precisely what to believe, feeling the detective's hesitation within him; nothing was true until he himself confirmed it.

And, he realized, the only thing he could confirm was Sophie Millstein's fear.

As he looked at her, he saw a shudder crease her body. She turned toward him with a questioning look.

"Fifty years. And I just saw him for that moment. Could I be wrong, Mr. Winter?"

He decided not to answer this question, because, in his experience, the likelihood of Sophie Millstein being correct was nearly nonexistent. He thought: This person—this Schattenmann—must have been young, no older than his early twenties fifty years ago. And now he would be an old man. His hair would have changed; the tone of his skin, the shape of his face would have sagged and loosened with age. His walk would be different, as would his voice. Nothing would be the same.

"Today, did this man say anything to you?"

"No. He just stared. Our eyes met, it was late afternoon and then the sun seemed to glow right behind him and he was gone, just like that, as if he'd disappeared into the glare—and I ran, Mr. Winter, I ran. Well, not like I could run once, but it felt the same, Mr. Winter, I was so glad to see the lights on in your apartment, because I was so afraid of being alone."

"He said nothing?"

"No."

"Did he threaten you, or make any gesture?"

"No. He just looked at me. Eyes like razors, I told you."

"And what did he look like?"

"He was tall—but not as tall as you, Mr. Winter, but thickset, strong. A young man's arms and shoulders."

Simon Winter nodded. His skepticism was gaining momentum within him. To recognize a man you saw only for seconds after fifty years was not within what he used to call the homicide detective's realms of possibility, even though these realms were very far-reaching. What he guessed was this: Sophie Millstein, whose loose grip on the ways of the world had been eroded further by her husband's death, had been walking beneath a sun that was too strong on a day that was too hot, lost in memories that were too painful, when some person had caught her eye in the midst of one of those recollections and she had become disoriented and frightened because she was old and because she was lonely. And he thought too, ruefully: Would I be that different?

But instead of saying this, he stated firmly: "I think, Mrs. Millstein, that you're going to be okay. What you need is to get some rest. . . ."

"I must warn the others," she said quickly, her voice racing ahead. "They must be told. Mr. Stein was right. Oh, Mr. Winter, we should have believed him, but what's to do? We are old. We didn't know. Who would you call? Who would you tell? I wish Leo were here."

"What others? And who is Mr. Stein?"

"He saw him too. And now he's dead."

Simon Winter instantly checked his doubts when he heard these words. He spoke slowly: "I do not understand this, Mrs. Millstein. Please explain."

Instead, she looked wildly at him. "Is that your gun? Is it loaded?"

"Yes."

"Thank goodness. All those years as a policeman, same gun?"

"Yes."

"You should keep it close, Mr. Winter. My Leo, he wanted to get a gun, because he said the Negroes—actually, he used a different word, he wasn't prejudiced, but he was scared and that made him use that terrible word—he said they liked to come over to the Beach and rob all the old Jews that are here, and that's what we were, just old Jews, and I suppose, if I was a criminal, that's what I would be thinking too. But I wouldn't let him get one, because I was too scared to have a gun around the house, because Leo, he wasn't a careful man. He was a good man, but he was, I don't know, what? Careless, sometimes. And that's not a wise thing to be around guns, and I thought he might hurt himself with it, so I wouldn't let him have a gun and now I wish I had because I would have it, and I could protect myself. I mustn't hesitate any longer, Mr. Winter. I must call the others and tell them he's here and that we must decide what to do."

"Mrs. Millstein, please, calm down. Who is Mr. Stein?"

"I must call."

"There will be time for that in a moment."

She did not reply.

Sophie Millstein was now sitting rigidly, eyes straight ahead, staring intently into the space in front of her. He remembered suddenly a shoot-out he'd been a part of, years earlier, a bank robbery that had erupted into a tangled flurry of bullets, over in thirty seconds. It had not been his own shot that had stopped the robber, but he had been the first to reach the man, kicking his pistol away from an outstretched hand, then looking down and seeing the man's eyes widen as he felt his life's blood bubbling through the hole in his chest. He was a young man, in his early twenties, and Simon Winter had not been much older, and he had looked at the detective and wrapped within that look was a cascade of desperate questions, ending, of course, with the one that mattered: Will I live? And before Simon Winter could respond, he'd seen the man's eyes roll back, and he'd died. It was that moment of losing grasp that Simon Winter thought he saw in Sophie Millstein's face, and he could not prevent some of her panic rushing through his own veins.

"He will kill me," she said blankly, her voice filled with resignation. "I must warn the others." There was a dryness, like leather stretched to cracking, in her words.

"Mrs. Millstein, please, no one is going to kill you. I won't let them."

Sophie Millstein seemed to have locked her gaze straight forward, as if Simon Winter was no longer in the room. After a moment, her body quivered, almost as if she was physically struck by some memory. She turned slowly toward the old detective and nodded.

"I was so young and I was so scared. We all were, I suppose. It was such an unlucky time, Mr. Winter. We were all in hiding and no one thought they would live much beyond the next minute or so. It's a terrible thing, Mr. Winter, when you're young and everywhere you hide, death seems to track you. . . ."

Simon Winter nodded. He needed her to keep talking, thinking that eventually she would steer herself back to the present. "Please, continue."

"A year ago," Sophie Millstein said slowly, "a man named Herman Stein who lived in Surfside killed himself." Her voice had flattened once again. "At least, that is what we were told by the police, because he shot himself with a gun. . . ."

Winter thought: Like I planned to do. "Yes?"

"After he died, after the police came and the funeral home and his relatives sat shiva and all those things took place, a letter arrived at Rabbi Rubinstein's home. Do you know the rabbi, Mr. Winter?"

"No."

"He is old, like me. Retired. And he got a letter from a dead man, mailed a few days before. And this Mr. Herman Stein, who I didn't know, I mean, why should I? He lived up in Surfside, which is how many blocks away, Mr. Winter? Seventy? Eighty? Like another world. He sends a letter to the rabbi, whom he knows just ever so little, because once he learns that the rabbi, he too once comes from Berlin, like this man, and he too lives through the camps, which is almost impossible, and this man I don't know named Mr. Stein says in his letter: I have seen Der Schattenmann. And the rabbi, of course, he knows this name, so he finds me, and a few others, Mrs. Kroner and Mr. Silver, who also were once Berliners, and that's all he can find, because we are all growing so old now, Mr. Winter, there are so few of us left, and there were so few of us to survive in the first place, and he brings us together, and we read the letter, but who knows what to do? There is no police to call. There is no one to help us, and of course we don't know what to believe anyways. Who would think he would be here, Mr. Winter? Of all places. Here. And so, months pass and every so often I go to the rabbi's house and we all sit together and talk, but this is not the things that people like to remember so much, Mr. Winter. Until today, because, just like this poor Mr. Herman Stein from Surfside who I did not know, who is now dead, I too see him here, and now he will kill me too."

Sophie Millstein's cheeks were laced with tears, and her voice was whispered fear.

"Where's Leo?" the old woman said. "I wish Leo were here."

"This man, this Mr. Herman Stein, he committed suicide?"

"Yes. No. That is what the police said, Mr. Winter. But now, tonight, right now I am thinking something different."

"And the others, the rabbi . . ."

"I need to call them."

Sophie Millstein suddenly looked about wildly.

"My book. My little book with all my numbers. It's in my apartment. . . ."

"I'll go with you. It will be all right."

Sophie Milstein nodded and gulped the remains of her iced tea down.

"Could I be wrong, Mr. Winter? You were a policeman. It's been fifty years, and I just saw him for that tiny little moment before they slammed the door closed. Fifty years and people change so much. Could I be wrong?"

She shook her head.

"I want to be wrong, Mr. Winter. I am praying I am wrong."

He did not know what to say, so he remained silent. He thought: She is probably mistaken. But the story she'd told was unsettling, and he was unsure what to make of Mr. Herman Stein's suicide. Why would an old man kill himself after posting a letter? Maybe he was simply old and feeling useless, like I was. Maybe he was crazy. Maybe he was sick. Maybe he was tired of life. Maybe a hundred reasons; when one is filled to overflowing with sorrow, they don't shed only a single tear. He did not know, but he suddenly wanted to learn. Winter felt within him a sensation that he'd thought had disappeared, erased by retirement and the steady passage of time. It was a quickening in his core, where his neighbor's words and the panicky look in her eyes became factors in an equation, and he felt compelled, like some electronic calculator being fed information, to come up with an answer.

"Mrs. Millstein, whether you're right or wrong is not important. What's important is that you've received a scare and you need to speak with your friends. Then you need to get a good night's sleep, and in the morning, when everyone is refreshed, we should get to the bottom of all this."

"You will help me?"

"Of course. That is what neighbors are for."

Sophie Millstein nodded gratefully and reached out her arm, placing her hand on Winter's wrist. He glanced down and, for the first time in all the years he'd known her, noticed the fading blue tattoo on her forearm. A 1742. The seven was in Germanic style, serpentine, with a cross mark.

Night had closed with determination.

Simon Winter and Sophie Millstein walked across the courtyard, enveloped by the relentless dark. Heat like ribbons of silk wrapped around the two of them. In the center of the courtyard there was a statue of a half-naked cherub playing a trumpet. The cherub had once graced a small water fountain, but this had been dry for years. The apartment complex was small, a pair of identical tan stucco two-story buildings that faced each other. They had been built in the Miami Beach boom time of the 1920s, and there were certain Art Deco touches—an arched entranceway, rounded windows, an almost sensuous curve to the facade—that gave the buildings a femininity, like the soft shape of a longtime lover's embrace.

Age and unrelenting sun had treated the apartments roughly; some paint flaked from the walls, air conditioners rattled rather than hummed, doors creaked and stuck, their jambs swollen by the cycles of the tropical humidity. Outside by the street was a faded sign: THE SUNSHINE ARMS. Simon Winter had always appreciated the wondrously fractured metaphor, and he had been comfortable in the familiar decrepitude of the buildings.

Sophie Millstein paused outside the door.

"You will go first?" she asked.

Winter took the key from her hand and slipped it into the deadbolt lock.

"Shouldn't you take out your gun?"

He shook his head. She had insisted he bring his weapon, which he had, but he felt brandishing it was slightly foolish, and he had enough experience to know that Sophie Millstein's fear had made him jumpy and nervous as well. Put the gun in his hand, and he would be likely to shoot Mr. and Mrs. Kadosh or old Harry Finkel, her upstairs neighbors.

"No," he said. He unlocked the door and stepped inside.

"The light switch is on the wall," she said, which he knew, because the layout of her apartment was a mirror of his own. He reached out with his hand and flicked on the lights.

"Jesus!" Simon Winter screeched in sudden surprise.

A gray-white shape raced between his legs.

"What the hell . . ."

"Oh, Mr. Boots, you naughty thing!"

Simon Winter turned and saw Sophie Millstein admonishing a large, fat cat, which was, in turn, rubbing against the old woman's leg. "I'm sorry if he startled you, Mr. Winter."

She lifted the cat up into her arms. The animal eyed Winter with irritating feline complacency.

"No. It's fine," he said, feeling his heart thump away within his chest.

Sophie Millstein hung in the doorway, caressing the cat in her arms while Simon Winter inspected the apartment. A quick glance told him that they were alone, save for a parakeet in a cage in a corner of the living room, which made an irritating scratching sound as he passed by. He called out: "Everything's okay, Mrs. Millstein!"

"Did you check the closet? Under the bed?" she responded from the hallway.

Simon Winter sighed and said: "I'll do that now." He went into her small bedroom and surveyed the scene. He felt an odd embarrassment, being in the room that Sophie Millstein had shared with her husband. He saw that she was a woman of organization; an off-white nightdress and robe were arranged at the foot of the bed. Her bureau top was clean. He saw a picture of Leo Millstein framed in black, and another photograph of what he immediately took to be Mrs. Millstein's son and his family. It was a studio shot, everyone wearing jackets, ties, Sunday-best frilly dresses. He noted a small jewelry box on the bureau, a finely wrought brass container that some artisan had spent time over. A family heirloom? He suspected so.

Winter went to the closet and opened the door, revealing no intruder, but seeing that Sophie Millstein had kept Leo's supply of stolid dark brown and navy-blue suits, each one like the next, hanging next to what seemed to be a stockpile of flower-print dresses. There was also a silky brown mink coat hanging in the corner, which Simon Winter thought was not the sort of item that gets a helluva lot of wear on Miami Beach, but which probably was worth its weight in memories. He saw that Sophie Millstein's shoes were carefully lined up on the floor, next to her late husband's.

Simon Winter turned away, looked once toward the picture of Leo Millstein, apologized under his breath, "Sorry, Leo. Don't mean to intrude, but she asked . . ." quickly bent down on one arthritic knee that immediately complained, and saw that no one was lurking beneath the bed. He noted, as well, that there were no little dust balls or ancient magazines shoved out of the way, as he might have found in his own apartment. Sophie Millstein, he considered, probably greeted a speck of dust or a smudge of dirt with the same scorn as a commanding general inspecting a slovenly soldier.

He called out again: "Everything's okay, Mrs. Millstein . . ." and walked into the kitchen area. There was a sliding glass door just opposite the sink, which led to a small tile patio in the back. The patio was perhaps ten yards from a fence, and a back alley, where the garbage cans were located. He rattled the doors to make sure they were locked, and then walked to the living room.

Sophie Millstein met him there, still carrying the cat. The color had returned to her face, and relief covered her words.

"Mr. Winter, I can't say how much I appreciate this."

"Think nothing of it, Mrs. Millstein."

"I should call the others now."

"I think that would be wise."

He watched the old woman move across the living room, and thought that amongst her own knickknacks and photographs, with her cat and frilly pillows on a sofa, her own furniture and furnishings, probably the feeling of threat that had overtaken her was eroding quickly.

"I always keep my telephone numbers right here," she said as she slid into a large easy chair. There was a yellow telephone on a small side table, next to the chair. She opened the single drawer in the table and produced a cheap red leather-bound address book.

He felt, abruptly, as if he were intruding.

"Would you like me to leave?" Simon Winter asked. "While you make your calls."

She shook her head as she dialed the first number. She paused, then grimaced. "It's the rabbi's answering machine," she whispered. Then, a second later, she said in a loud, firm voice: "Rabbi? It's Sophie. Please call me back. As soon as you can."

The words themselves seemed to restore some of her urgency. She was breathing hard when she hung up the telephone. She turned and looked up at Simon Winter, who continued to stand awkwardly by her side.

"Where could he be? It's dark. He should be at home."

"Perhaps he went out for a bite to eat."

"Yes. That must be it."

"Or a movie."

"Possibly. Or a meeting at the synagogue. Sometimes he still goes to the fund drives."

"There you have it."

The innocence of these explanations did not seem to relieve her anxiety.

"Are you going to call the others?" Simon Winter asked.

"I have to wait," Sophie Millstein responded nervously. "It's Tuesday. On Tuesdays, Mr. Silver takes Mrs. Kroner to the bridge club over at the senior citizen center. He does this ever since we started our meetings with the rabbi."

"Perhaps you want to make another call?"

"To who?"

"Your son? Maybe speaking with him would help you feel a bit better."

"You're very thoughtful, Mr. Winter. I will do that in just a moment."

"Do you have something to help you sleep? You've had quite a fright, and it might be difficult. . . ."

"Oh, yes, I have some little pills. Not to worry."

"How about something to eat. Are you all set?"

"Mr. Winter, you're too polite. Yes. I will be fine. I feel much better now that I'm home and safe."

"I thought you might."

"And tomorrow, you will help me? And the others. To . . ."

". . . get to the bottom of all this. Of course."

"What will you do?"

This was a good question, and he wasn't precisely certain of the answer. "Well, Mrs. Millstein, I think the least I can do is check out the circumstances surrounding Mr. Stein's death. At the same time, perhaps, we can all consider what it is exactly you want to do. Perhaps your friends and I can get together and we can map something out."

This prospect seemed to cheer Sophie Millstein. She nodded rapidly.

"Leo," she said, "Leo was like you. He made decisions. Of course, he was a haberdasher, not a detective, so what would he know about solving this mystery, right, Mr. Winter?"

"I'll leave you, then. Make sure you lock the door after I go out. And don't hesitate to call if you're still frightened. But I think a good night's sleep would be best. Then a fresh start in the morning."

"Mr. Winter, you are a complete gentleman. I will take a pill as soon as you leave."

She rose and walked with him to the door. He saw the cat leap up into her chair, curling down into the spot made warm by her body.

"Lock the door," he said.

"I could be wrong," she said hesitantly. "It's possible. I could have been wrong, correct?"

"Anything is possible, Mrs. Millstein. The point is, we will sort it all out."

"Until tomorrow, then," she replied, nodding gratefully.

He stepped into the hallway and turned back just long enough to catch his neighbor's wan smile as she closed the door behind him. He waited until he heard the sound of the dead-bolt lock clicking shut.

Simon Winter walked out into the courtyard of the Sunshine Arms and let the sticky night air cover him. A weak street lamp from beyond the apartment's entrance threw a thin shaft of light onto the statue of the cherub, making it glisten as if wet. The darkness surrounding him seemed rich, thick as coffee. He had an odd, droll thought: Well, if you're not going to kill yourself, you might as well get something to eat. Will it be death or chicken tonight?

He did not think himself particularly amusing, and decided to head out, rapidly considering potential places to get some food. He took a step forward, then another, then he paused. He turned and looked back at Sophie Millstein's apartment. The curtains were drawn. He could hear the sound of a television playing loudly coming from another apartment. This mingled with some laughing voices coming from down the street. He could hear a motorcycle accelerate in a high-pitched whine from several blocks away. Everything was, he insisted, as it should be. Not perfect, but familiar. It is a night like any other. It is hot. There is a breeze that cools nothing. The tropical sky blinks with stars.

He insisted to himself that there was nothing unusual in the world at all except for an old woman's memories of nightmare. But we all have those, he thought. He tried to reassure himself with the ordinariness of the world around him, but was only partly successful. He found himself peering into the shadows, looking for shapes, listening for telltale noises, behaving like a man suddenly afraid he was being watched, worried that he was being pursued. He shook his head to dislodge the sensation of dread that overcame him, chastised himself for showing the uncertainty of age, and strode determinedly past the cherub in the dry fountain. He was overcome suddenly with the desire to walk, to try to put distance between him and his neighbor's fears.

He stepped forward quickly, wondering, for just an instant, if death, when it arrived, was like the night.

# TWO
## SLEEP

Sᴏᴘʜɪᴇ Millstein peeked around the edge of the curtain, watching Simon Winter disappear into the darkness of the courtyard. Then she turned away and slumped down into her easy chair. Almost immediately the large gray and white cat leapt into her lap.

"Mr. Boots, did you miss me?"

She stroked the soft fur on the nape of the cat's neck as it settled in.

"You shouldn't get too comfy," she warned. "I've still got things to do."

The cat, as cats will, ignored this and merely began purring.

Sophie Millstein rested her hand on the cat's fur and suddenly thought herself exhausted. She told herself that it would be all right for her to just shut her eyes for an instant, but when she did, she found herself enmeshed in a tangle of nervousness, as if closing her eyes reawakened fear, instead of bringing comfort. She put her hand to her forehead and wondered if she were perhaps coming down with something. She thought she felt hot, and she cleared her throat several times harshly, as if checking for telltale signs of congestion.

She took a deep breath.

"You've had an easy life, Mr. Boots," she said to the cat.

"Someone has always taken care of you. Warm and dry home. Plenty of food. Entertainment. Affection. Anything a cat could want."

She abruptly slid her hand beneath the cat and pushed him from her lap. She forced herself to rise.

She looked down at the cat, which despite its abrupt ejection, rubbed itself up against her leg.

"I saved you," she said bitterly, surprising herself with her own anger. "That man put you and all the rest of the litter into that bag and was going to throw you into the water. He didn't want kittens. No one wanted kittens. There were too many kittens and everyone in the world hated kittens and no home would have any of you and so he was going to kill all of you, but I stopped him and took just you out of the bag. I could have chosen one of the others. I had my hand around one of the others, but I let it go because it scratched me. So it was you I grabbed, and so you've had an easy life, and all the others, they went into the bag and the bag went into the water and they drowned."

She pushed Mr. Boots away with her foot.

"Lucky cat," she hissed sharply. "Luckiest cat in the world."

Sophie Millstein walked into her kitchen and began to straighten the shelves, making certain that every label on every can was face forward, lined up by size, ordered by group, so that a tin of olives wouldn't be next to a can of tomato soup. When those goods were properly placed, she did the same to the perishables, imposing military precision on the refrigerator. The final item she inspected was a flounder fillet which she had earlier intended to broil for her own dinner, but she was no longer hungry. For a moment she hesitated, fearful that the fish would not keep. She decided that she could cook the fish in the morning and have it for the next day's lunch.

The cat had followed her and meowed. The noise irritated her.

"All right. All right. Coming."

She opened a can of cat food. Manipulating the opener was difficult for her, and her hand stung with sudden soreness. She told herself to march down to the discount hardware store in the morning and purchase an electric opener. She set the food out for the cat and left it eating.

In her bedroom, she stared at the picture of her late husband.

"You should be here," she said, reproaching him. "You had no right to leave me alone."

Sophie Millstein marched back into the small living room and sat down again. She felt abruptly as if she were caught out on the street in the moments before a thunderstorm crashed down, when impetuous, sharp surgical gusts of wind sliced through the humid stillness, assaulting her from all sides.

"I'm tired," she said out loud. "I should take a pill and go to bed."

But instead she rose, tramped into the kitchen, seized the telephone, and dialed her son's number on Long Island. She let the phone ring once before hanging it up, instantly deciding that she didn't want to speak with her only child. He will just insist again that I move out into some old people's home where I don't know a soul, she told herself. This is my home.

Sophie Millstein went to the tap, filled a glass with water, and took a long drink. It tasted brackish, metallic. She made a face. "Miami Beach special," she said. She wished she'd remembered to purchase some bottled water at the store. She poured some back in the sink, then took the remainder in and filled up the water container in the bird cage. The parakeet chirped once or twice. She wondered briefly why she'd never bothered to name the bird, as she had her cat. She wondered if this was somehow unfair, then doubted it, and returned to the kitchen to rinse out her glass and place it on the drying rack. There was a small window above the sink, and she glanced out into the night. She told herself that she was familiar with every shape and shadow that she could see; everything was in exactly the same spot that it had been the night before and the night before that and every night for more than ten years. Still, she continued to examine the darkness, watching each corner of the backyard for movement, like a sentry on patrol.

She turned off the faucet and listened.

There were a few distant sounds of traffic. Upstairs, Finkel was shuffling about. A television was on too loud; that would be the Kadoshes, she thought, because they are too stubborn to turn up their hearing aids.

She continued to look out the window. She let her eyes read each shaft of light, study each dark spot. For a moment she was astonished at the number of places she thought someone could hide without being seen: the corner where the orange tree lurked next to the old chain-link fence; the shadow where the garbage cans were placed.

No, she told herself, it is all as it always is.

Nothing different.

Nothing out of place.

She breathed in hard and went back to the living room. Television, she told herself. She flicked on her set and settled into a chair. A situation comedy was on, and for a few minutes she tried to follow the jokes, and forced herself to laugh at the same moments that the canned laughter did. She let her head drift down into her hands, and as the program continued in front of her, she shivered, as if cold, but she knew that wasn't the reason.

He's dead, she said to herself. He's not here.

She wondered, for a moment, whether he had ever really existed. Who was that I saw? she asked herself. It could have been anybody, especially with that hat pulled down over his forehead and the dark overcoat. And they shut the door so quickly after he yelled, I hardly had a chance to see.

But she knew this was untrue. It was him.

She felt herself fill with bitter anger. It was always him. Day after day. Hour after hour. He had been there, even when they had thought they were relatively safe. But they weren't. He'd stalked them like some particularly patient and coldhearted hunter, waiting, biding his time, until the right moment. And then he'd taken their money first, then their freedom, and with it, their lives.

Sophie Millstein felt hatred reverberate within her. She spoke out loud:

"I should have killed him then. If I had known . . ."

She stopped and realized she'd had no chance. She told herself: You were only a child—what did you know of killing?

She answered her own question harshly: not much then. But you learned soon enough, didn't you?

On the television, an advertisement for a beer came on the screen, and for an instant she watched muscular young men and nubile young women cavort around a pool. No one really looks like that, she thought. She realized when she was the same age as the models in the advertisement, she weighed less than seventy pounds and resembled someone that had already died.

But I didn't die, she reminded herself.

He must have thought we would all die, but I didn't.

She put her head down in her hands once again.

Why didn't *he* die too? she wondered.

How could he have lived through the war? Who would save him? Not the Germans he worked for. When he was no longer useful, they would have shipped him off to Auschwitz as well. Not the Allies or the Russians, who would have prosecuted him as a war criminal. Certainly not the Jews whom he so eagerly helped along the road to death. How could he have lived?

She shook her head at the impossible thoughts that filled her.

He had to die. They all did, and he died right alongside the rest of them. It had to be that way.

She repeated this to herself: He had to die. He had to die. Then she shortened it, mentally, simply to: He's dead. He's dead. He cannot be alive. Not here. Not on Miami Beach. Not surrounded by the few people who managed to survive.

For an instant she thought she might become ill.

Sophie Millstein, filled with an old and misshapen fear, stood up. The characters in the television show were all laughing and the audience was laughing at them.

"Leo," she said out loud. She walked to the telephone and swiftly dialed the rabbi's number. When she heard the voice on the answering machine respond, she hung up. She looked down at her wristwatch and thought: still too early for Mr. Silver and Frieda Kroner. They won't be back until after midnight. Her finger hesitated above the dial, and then she punched in Simon Winter's number. She expected he would pick up the phone immediately, and she tried to think what she could say beyond the fact that she was still frightened, but all she could think of was Simon Winter's pistol and how it might protect her.

The phone continued to ring, unanswered. After a second an answering machine clicked on: "You've reached Simon Winter. Leave a message at the beep."

She waited, and after hearing the electronic signal, said:

"Mr. Winter? It's Sophie Millstein. I just wanted . . . Oh, it's just . . . well, Mr. Winter, I just wanted to thank you again. I will speak with you tomorrow."

She hung up, slightly relieved. He will have some good advice, she thought. He is a very nice man, with a level head and plenty of smarts. Maybe not as much as Leo, but he will know what to do.

She wondered where he'd disappeared to. He probably just went out to get a bite to eat, she explained to herself. He'll be back shortly. He's out just the same as Rabbi Rubinstein. Everything tonight is normal. Just like any other night.

Sophie Millstein wondered abruptly: Mr. Herman Stein, who were you? Why did you write that letter? Who did you see?

She took a deep breath, only to have it repair her nervousness.

She thought in sudden panic: I'm all alone.

Then, just as swiftly, she insisted to herself that she was mistaken. The Kadoshes, old Finkel upstairs, and before too long Simon Winter would be back from his meal; they would all be surrounding her, and she would be fine.

She nodded to herself as if insisting on the safety of her observation. She took a step back toward the television. The comedy had been replaced by a darker drama.

Who else could it have been? she suddenly demanded.

The question made her breathe in sharply again. It stung her imagination, and she swiftly tried to anesthetize her feelings with complacencies.

Why, it could have been anyone. Another old man on Miami Beach—why, the place is positively thick with them. And they all look alike too. And maybe he thought you were someone he knew, because of the way he stared, and that's why he looked back so carefully. And when he realized you weren't familiar, why, to save you the embarrassment, he just walked away. Happens all the time. Go through life meeting hundreds of folks, and so it's not unreasonable to get mixed up every once in a while.

But she did not feel mixed up.

Why here? she asked.

I don't know.

Why would he come here?

I don't know.

What will he do?

I don't know.

Who is he?

She knew the answer to this question, but she would not articulate it to herself.

She tried to take charge of her emotions as they catapulted about the small apartment. She decided that in the morning, she would go over to the Holocaust Center and speak with the people there. They were always so kind, even the young ones, and so interested in everything she had to say, she was sure they would listen to her once again. They would know what to do.

She felt immediately better.

That's a good plan, she told herself.

Sophie Millstein picked up the telephone and dialed the Holocaust Center number. She waited until the taped answering machine had completed its recitation of operating hours, and then, after hearing the signal beep, said into the phone: "Esther? This is Sophie Millstein. I need to talk to you, please. I will come by today, in the morning, and talk a bit about how I was arrested. Something has happened. I was reminded . . ."

She stopped, not knowing how much she could explain. In her hesitation, the tape machine ran to its end, beeping and disconnecting her. She held the phone out, considering calling and adding to her message, then deciding not to.

She hung up, feeling better.

She went to the front window and just slid a corner of the curtain back, peeking out once again, as she had earlier when she'd watched Simon Winter depart. She saw the lights were off in his apartment. For a moment she watched the courtyard, straining her eyes to see past to the street. A car went by rapidly. She caught a glimpse of a couple walking swiftly down the sidewalk.

She abandoned the front, then walked to the rear patio door, checking, just as Simon Winter had, to make sure it was locked. She gave the sliding door a little shake. Lamenting the flimsy lock, she decided another thing she could do in the morning was to call Mr. Gonzalez, the owner of the Sunshine Arms. I'm old, she thought. We're all old here, and he really should install better locks and maybe one of those fancy alarm systems like the one my friend Rhea has over at the Belle Vue. All she has to do is push a button and the police are called, just like magic. We should have something like that, she thought. Something modern.

She glanced outside again, but saw nothing save darkness.

Mr. Boots was at her feet.

"See, kitty. Nothing for you to worry about."

The cat did not respond.

She felt exhaustion battling with fear within her. For a moment she allowed herself to think that perhaps the elderly complex her son was trying to persuade her to move into wouldn't be such an awful idea.

But like everything else, she decided it could wait until the next day. She reassured herself with a mental list of the things she would have to do in the morning: call Mr. Gonzalez; purchase a new can opener, an electric one; call her son; visit the Holocaust Center; talk to the rabbi and Mr. Silver and Mrs. Kroner; and meet with Simon Winter and make a decision. A busy day, she thought. She stepped into the small bathroom and opened her medicine cabinet. Lined up at attention were a number of medications. Something for her heart. Something for her digestion. Something for her aches and pains. In a small container near the end of the shelf was what she was searching for: something to help her sleep. She poured a single white pill into her hand and swallowed it without using any water.

"There," she said to her reflection in the mirror. "Now, maybe ten minutes and you'll be out like a light."

She hurried into the bedroom and slipped out of her clothes, taking the time to carefully hang her dress in the closet and drop her undergarments into a white wicker hamper. She slipped on a rayon nightgown, adjusting the frilly part near her neck. She remembered it was one of Leo's favorites, and that he'd teased her and called her sexy when she wore it. She missed this. She had never thought herself sexy, but she'd liked it when he'd teased her, because it made her feel desired, which was pleasurable. She glanced at her husband's picture one last time, then slid under the thin covers. She could feel a warm, dizzying sensation moving through her body as the sleeping pill took effect.

The cat jumped up on the bed next to her.

She reached out and stroked it.

"I was mean to you," she said. "I'm sorry, Mr. Boots. I just need to sleep." He curled next to her.

She closed her eyes. It was all she wanted in the entire world, she thought: a single, restful evening of comforting, dreamless sleep.

Night like a box closed around Sophie Millstein. She did not even stir several hours later, when Mr. Boots suddenly rose up, back arched, spitting and hissing in hasty cat-fear at the harsh and heartless sounds of intrusion.

# THREE
## THE ACCOUNTANT
## FOR THE DEAD

It was already nine minutes after midnight and Miami Beach 911 operator Number 3 was irritated that her shift replacement was delayed for the third time that week. She knew Number 17's toddler had been ill with bronchitis, but still, nine minutes was nine minutes, and she wanted to get home so that she would not be completely exhausted when her own son awakened her as he did almost every morning by banging his way around the small bathroom and kitchen of her home in Carol City. One of the advantages, she knew, of teenage, was a certain obliviousness to racket. So she counted the minutes, adding Number 17's tardiness to the drive across the Beach, over the causeway, past downtown and up onto the expressway, skirting Liberty City, until finally reaching the small house she owned in a dusty part of the county that was neither city nor suburban, a lower-middle-class enclave that offered modest safety and slightly less heartbreak than the world barely a mile or two away. The trip would take her just under an hour in her eight-year-old Chevy.

To her right and left, numbers 11 and 14 had already settled into the nightly routine. Number 11 was moving a hook and ladder company to a third-story apartment fire just off Collins Avenue, and Number 14 was patching a state trooper through to wants and warrants as he chased a big BMW across the Julia

Tuttle Causeway. It had been a tiring night: a convenience store robbery, a reported rape, a fight outside a nightclub. Plenty for her to do, nothing that she thought would make the papers in the morning. Number 3 looked up, craning her neck away from the bank of phone lines, looking for Number 17.

She was still looking when the light on the board in front of her blinked red, and without thinking, she punched the connection and spoke, sounding machinelike and well drilled.

"Miami Beach Fire, Police, and Rescue."

As she heard the first words, she knew it was an old person's voice:

"Ohmigod, please send the police right away! Somebody's killed her! Oh, poor Mrs. Millstein! An ambulance! Send help! Please!"

Cutting through hysteria was her job.

"Yes, ma'am. Right away. Give me an address."

"Yes, yes, oh, the Sunshine Arms, 1290 Thirteenth Court. Hurry, please . . ."

"Ma'am, what sort of assistance do you need? What has happened?" Number 3 remained perfectly even-toned in her questions.

"We heard a noise, my Henry and I, and he went down to check it out and Mr. Finkel went too and she was dead! Oh my goodness, what's the world coming to? Send the police. Please. Someone's killed her. Oh my Lord, what are we coming to?"

"Hold the line, please. . . ." Number 3 left the woman on an open line while she punched another button: "Any officer. Possible ten-thirty, 1290 Thirteenth Court. Code is Three. People on scene. Patrol sergeant, please respond . . ." She punched a second button, connecting herself to an ambulance crew. "We have a ten-thirty at 1290 Thirteenth Court, but there are elderly people involved. Drive by. See if any need assistance." This wasn't precisely procedure, but Number 3 had been a 911 operator on the Beach for over a decade, and she knew that more than once the sound of sirens and excitement strained fragile heart muscles.

Number 3 then calmly reconnected herself to the frantic woman on the open line.

"Ma'am, help is on the way. An officer should be right there. And I've notified Rescue as well."

"He saw him, my Henry did, running out the back. A black man and Henry chased him to the alley, he did, but then he got away and I called. Oh, poor Mrs. Millstein!"

"Ma'am, is the perpetrator still on the scene?"

"What? The who? No, he ran down the alley."

"Ma'am, hold on. I will need your name and address. . . ."

Again she left the caller on an open line, as she dialed another number.

"Beach Homicide. This is Detective Robinson."

"Detective? This is Operator Three down at 911. I do believe your slow night is about to pick up. We just got a call, possible ten-thirty at an apartment complex called the Sunshine Arms in South Beach. Uniforms are en route, but maybe you want to send someone over there before they make a mess of things. . . ."

Walter Robinson recognized the voice. "Lucy," he said, "my night wouldn't be complete without a call from you."

Number 3 smiled, wished for an instant that she were younger and sexier, and that her husband wasn't at home snoring in the big double bed they owned, then replied: "Well, Detective, it's complete now. I've got a hysterical old woman on the open line, saying the perpetrator just fled the scene. Maybe you can hurry and get lucky."

"Luck," Robinson answered, "is something in short supply in this world."

Number 3 nodded. She looked up and saw Number 17 entering the phone room, looking sheepish and apologetic for being late.

"Well, Detective, if you don't need luck . . ."

"I didn't say I didn't need it, Lucy. I just said there wasn't much of it available. Especially late at night in the city."

"Amen," said Number 3 as she disconnected the detective and heard a distant siren come over the open line, its insistent wail rising above the teary sobs of the elderly woman.

Walter Robinson put the phone back on its cradle and wrote down the address on a piece of scratch paper, thinking to himself that it was hot outside, a nasty, thick, clutching, oily heat that threatened to rob his lungs of air. He knew already what he would find when he exited the cool, sterile interior of the homicide offices. A world compacted by stifling humidity, weighing on his chest like a tight jacket. He took a deep breath and shoved the legal textbooks he'd been studying into a drawer, then reached for a portable radio phone resting in an electric charging device on the corner of his desk. He said to himself: This is an awful night for anyone to have to die.

Robinson, aged less by years than a steady dosage of street cynicism, twenty credits shy of a law degree which he thought was his ticket out of police work, drove fast through the pale yellow sodium vapor lights that gave the city its otherworldly nighttime glow. Although he did not think of himself as a native Miamian—that was a category reserved for slow-drawling crackers and rednecks from the southern part of Dade County—he had been born and raised in Coconut Grove, the son of an elementary school teacher.

His middle name was Birmingham, though he never used it. It was too difficult to explain to the primarily white and Hispanic membership of the Beach force why he had been named, at least in part, after a city. His mother was a distant cousin to one of the children killed in the Birmingham church bombing in 1963, so, when he was born shortly thereafter, she had vented some of her frustration by naming him after the Alabama city, giving him a reminder, she often informed him, so that he would not forget where he had come from.

Forgetting where he had come from, however, did not seem such a terrible thing to Walter Robinson. He had never been to his namesake in Alabama, and didn't particularly like returning to the part of the city where he'd grown up. The Grove is a curious section of Miami. By accident of time and development, one of the city's worst slums butted directly up against one of its most affluent areas, creating a constant ebb and flow of fear, anger, and envy. Robinson had lived with all those sensations, and didn't particularly enjoy reminding himself of them.

And, despite eight years in the Miami Beach department, first in uniform and then three with a gold shield, he didn't consider that home either. He thought his rootlessness unusual, was slightly bothered by it and generally tried to ignore it.

He pulled down Thirteenth Court and spotted the cruisers parked outside the Sunshine Arms. He was pleased to discover that uniformed officers had already stripped ubiquitous yellow police-line tape around much of the area. He got out of his unmarked car and walked past a small group of elderly people gathered into a corner of the courtyard. A patrol sergeant greeted him by name as he approached the apartment building, and he nodded his response:

"So, what have we got?"

"Elderly victim, in the bedroom. Signs of forced entry in back. A patio door, you know, one of those sliding ones that my six-year-old could break in . . ."

"I know the type. Signs of struggle?"

"Not too much. But looks like the perp grabbed everything he could before the neighbors got there. He must have run when he heard them come poking around. One of them, a Mr. Henry Kadosh, upstairs apartment, chased the perp out to the alley, got a pretty fair look. His wife called 911."

"And?"

"Black male. Late teenage to mid-twenties. Five feet ten to six feet. Slight build, maybe 175 pounds. Wearing high-top sneakers and a dark T-shirt."

"Sounds like me," Walter Robinson said. "I know somebody's gonna say 'But they all look so much alike' before I clear this scene." He imitated an elderly person's voice as he spoke.

The patrol sergeant grinned. "When you walk over there, someone's gonna yell: 'There he is!'"

Robinson laughed. "Probably. Wouldn't be the first time."

The patrol sergeant continued. "I put out a BOLO. Maybe we'll get lucky."

"You're the second person to say that to me in the last half hour. I don't feel lucky tonight."

The patrol sergeant shrugged. "I guess she didn't either." He jerked his head in the direction of the apartment.

"You think the witness could work with an Identikit technician?"

"He said he got a good look. Maybe. But, hey, after he said that, his wife handed him his eyeglasses."

"Great. They over in that bunch?" Robinson pointed at the collection of elderly people.

"Right in front."

"All right, let me take a look inside first. . . ."

"I've already called forensics. And the medical examiner. They're on their way over."

"Good going. Thanks."

The detective stepped up to the front of the building. He hesitated for a moment, and then walked slowly into Sophie Millstein's apartment. With each step he shed a bit of the easygoing camaraderie that he'd employed outside, replacing it with an attention to detail. Another uniformed officer was standing in the living room, next to a covered bird cage, writing in a notebook. He nodded and pointed toward the back, needlessly, because Walter Robinson was already headed in that direction. He was glad that he'd arrived before the forensic team, heartened, as well, that the first police on the scene were not milling about the body, as they tended to do. He preferred to have a moment alone with every victim; it was a time when he could let his imagination play out the dead's final seconds. If there was a moment when he could hear the murdered person's voice speaking to him, it would be then. In the sturdy, fact-driven world of the homicide detective, this he knew was romance. But it helped him along the path of understanding, and he had long ago recognized that anything that spurred the steady progression of comprehension was useful.

As he quietly sidled into the bedroom, moving like a parent careful not to awaken a sleeping child, he thought, as he always did, that he hated being a homicide detective. It was an endless succession of hot nights, dead bodies, and paperwork. Heat, stench, and drudgery. Although he was still a young man, he had long before given up the fanciful notion that he was somehow linked with Sherlock Holmes or Hercule Poirot, nor did he see himself, as some of the more experienced men in his office did, as society's surrogate avenger, dedicated to righting the seemingly never-ending succession of wrongs that people committed against each other. He had come to see himself as an accountant for the dead. It was his job to tidy up and organize their last, awful moments and present the truth of those seconds to a subsequent authority, be it grand jury or court of law.

The body was spread-eagled on the bed, twisted about unnaturally, tangled in a knot of torn bedclothes. He thought: She must have kicked hard against the weight holding her down, killing her.

He believed he performed his job in a routine, dogged fashion, preferring not to focus on the moments of electric recognition and surging imagination when he centered on a killer. He preferred to consider the excitement he felt as the inevitable result of mere tenacity, where others, who watched him work, would have spoken about artistry. Regardless, his style created results. He cleared as many cases as any other detective on the force, and was held in high regard by his shift commander, a man who cared little for how crimes were solved, but who valued the power of statistics, and thus Walter Robinson was considered a man of potential by the hierarchy of the Beach department.

He, on the other hand, ignored labels, thought potential something similar to a disease, and preferred to work alone.

Robinson approached the victim slowly, taking care with where he put his feet, keeping his hands close to his body. He made a quick notation of the strident red marks on her throat, and saw that her eyes were open wide in death; there was an old myth that a murdered person's eyes would print a vision of the killer as death snatched them. He had more than once seen a victim's eyes ripped from their skull postmortem by superstitious killers. He wished the myth were true. Make things a lot easier, he thought.

He wanted to ask: Who killed you? But all he saw was terror. This did not surprise him; what awakened her was the pressure around her windpipe. If the noise of the break-in had aroused her, then the killing would have taken place somewhere else. He glanced around, looking for sleeping tablets. Check the bathroom, he told himself, knowing that he would find them on a shelf.

Robinson let his own eyes move from the body, surveying the room like an appraiser in the moments before an auction. Drawers were torn open, their contents dumped out. A bedside lamp was smashed to the floor. At first he thought: struggle. But then he appended this idea. No, he told himself. The struggle was on the bed, in the knot of sheets and ripped nightgown, and it was over quickly. This was hurry. Someone who knew he didn't have much time, and so he ransacked the room as fast as possible. He saw that a pillow was lying on the floor, without a case. An old woman sleeping on freshly laundered sheets without a matching pillowcase? No, that's what he grabbed to hold what he was stealing. He made a mental note, memorizing the floral pattern of the sheets. Are you smart enough to throw that away? I doubt it.

The detective gave a long sigh, slowly letting his breath slide from his body. It was hot in the room; the warm air from the broken patio door, and from the front door left open for the medical examiner and the forensic teams, was overcoming the airconditioning. He could feel a line of sweat starting to form on his forehead, unpleasant stickiness beneath his arms.

He shook his head slowly.

It was all so terribly, horribly familiar, he thought.

An elderly woman. Alone. A garden apartment without a good lock on a patio door. A neighborhood filled with shadows and alleys, and old folks who cashed social security checks. Just enough jewelry and twenty-dollar bills to hold out the promise of a quick and easy score, not nearly affluent enough to warrant alarm systems, security guards, and Dobermans. The fringe world, he thought.

Typical urban routine nightmare, he said to himself.

It happened somewhere, every night. Little variations on a common theme. You're old and vulnerable and trying to hold on to what little you have left of this world, and there's someone younger, stronger, and more desperate who's going to come and take it from you. If you're lucky, he just knocks you down, or hits you in the head. You survive with a concussion, a fractured arm, a broken hip. If you're unlucky, you die. He tried to imagine how many cases like this one he'd seen. A dozen? A hundred? Did she have any idea when she went to bed that she was prey?

He spoke softly, out loud, addressing the killer:

"So, you broke in, that wasn't too hard, and then you caught her in her bed asleep, and you strangled her, but killing her made too much noise, and so you jumped up and grabbed what you could and then ran, but not fast enough, you bastard, because somebody saw you."

He heard voices coming from the living room, and realized that the processors of violent death had arrived. He heard a police photographer's voice call out, "Hey! Walter, where you at?" and he answered: "In here."

He glanced at the body again. Something struck him as out of place, and he couldn't quite identify it.

Still vaguely bothered, he moved to meet the men coming into the bedroom. He immediately retreated into the forced jocularity that protects all the people who are charged with sorting out violent death.

"Hey, Walter," said a diminutive technician, lugging a huge leather case. "What's shaking?"

"Not much. She lived alone, Ted. Should be prints. Make sure you get those drawers good. Bobby, you shoot everything, including all the stuff in piles where the perp threw it. And then get shots of the forced entry. Is Doctor Death here yet?"

"He was just pulling up. Actually, it was one of the assistants. The chief must be sleeping in tonight."

"Nah, he's probably working that triple over in Liberty City," the photographer interrupted as he adjusted his light meter and flash bar. "Little problem at a crack house, so I heard on the scanner driving over. You know: 'That's my pipe!' 'No it ain't!' Bang, bang, bang. That's what's gonna grab headlines tomorrow. That's where he'll be."

Robinson knew that the county's chief medical examiner liked to attend the deaths that would preoccupy the *Herald* and the local television stations. But he shook his head. "He may start out over there, but you watch. He'll get here before we're finished. And so will the papers and the TV stations. So he'll be here, probably right about the same time they show. I'd like to say he's working himself to death, but that doesn't sound quite right."

The other policemen crowding into the room laughed. There was a popping sound as the photographer started taking his shots. It mingled with the activity that immediately enveloped the room as technicians working fibers, fingerprints, and searching for other evidence began doing their jobs.

He decided he would go outside and speak with the people who'd chased the killer away. They're old, he thought, and it's late, and pretty soon the hour will catch up with them. Get their story while it's still fresh.

From the doorway, Robinson scanned the room again, trying to discover why he felt unsettled. He glanced over at the body another time. He still did not form her name in his mind; that, he knew, would come soon enough. For the moment, she was just another item to be catalogued.

# FOUR

## _HOPE_

$W$HEN he saw the flashing strobe lights of the police vehicles from the end of the block, Simon Winter stopped short, his feet suddenly rooted to the pavement, his jaw dropping open in abrupt astonishment.

He took a single step toward the lights, his imagination racing through a series of nightmares. He told himself: There's been a fire. A break-in. A heart attack. An accident. With each possibility, his pace picked up, so that by the time he reached the yellow police tape, he was running hard, his shoes slapping a cadence of worry against the cement. He would not allow himself to form the words he feared most in his head: There's been a killing.

He stopped at the entrance to the Sunshine Arms, breathing hard. There were at least a half-dozen cruisers pulled up on the narrow street; their lights bathed the area in strident blues and reds. There were a pair of television station vans, and he saw camera crews jawing by the sidewalk. He noticed a station wagon marked with the county medical examiner's shield, and saw several uniformed officers standing next to the empty fountain in the courtyard. He realized immediately that there was no urgency in anyone's actions, and this made him inhale sharply. People work fast when there's a heartbeat. They take their time when there isn't.

He swallowed once, his throat abruptly dry, and ducked beneath the yellow tape. This motion caught the eye of one of the officers, who waved at him.

"Hey, pops! No entry here."

"I live here," Winter replied. "What's happened?"

"What's your name?" the policeman asked, approaching him. He was a young man, with the artificial bulk of a bulletproof vest making him seem larger than he truly was.

"Winter. I live in 103, right there. What's happened?"

"You live alone, Mr. Winter?"

"That's right. What happened?"

"There was a break-in. Old lady got killed."

Simon Winter choked on the name. "Sophie Millstein?"

"That's right. You know her?"

"Yes." He stumbled over the word. "Just tonight. I saw her tonight. Helped her lock herself in . . ."

"You saw her tonight?"

Winter nodded. He felt his stomach clench with pain. "I want to talk with the detective in charge," he said.

"You know something, Mr. Winter? Or you curious?"

"I want to talk to the detective in charge." He fixed the young patrolman with a long look, one that covered up the turmoil he felt ricocheting about within him.

The patrolman hesitated, then said, "I'll take you to him."

He started to steer Simon Winter across the courtyard, when the old man saw the other members of the complex standing in their nightclothes in a knot to the side of the fountain. Mrs. Kadosh instantly began waving at him.

"Mr. Winter! Mr. Winter! My God, is terrible!" Mrs. Kadosh burst out. Simon Winter walked quickly toward them. Mr. Kadosh was shaking his head back and forth.

"Terrible is right," he said, echoing his wife.

"But what happened?" Winter asked. "I went out to eat, and then I took a walk, and I only just returned and—"

Mrs. Kadosh interrupted swiftly. She was a plump woman wearing her frosted blond hair beneath a hair net large enough to trap most species of fish, and sporting a bright red quilted bathrobe that had a huge flower embossed on the breast and surely was sweltering to wear on this humid night.

"Is almost midnight, and Henry is readying for bed after watching just a few minutes of Jay Leno, just the jokes part, not so much the talk, talk, talk, and I am sitting up waiting, when I am hearing a scream, maybe, more like a shout of fear, just sudden, coming from where I do not know, but after I think about it, I am thinking it is poor Mrs. Millstein, and think maybe this is night-mare because she no longer sleeps so good, and sometimes I hear her calling for Leo, may he rest in peace. So, I am not paying too much attention, but my Henry, he comes in and saying 'You hear that?' and of course I say 'Yes.' And he says right away maybe we better need checking on Mrs. Millstein."

"Is right," Henry Kadosh muttered. "Need checking, Mrs. Millstein."

Simon Winter wanted to urge them to hurry their story, but he knew the Kadoshes were Hungarian—Henry had once been Hen-rik—and between their age and their fractured use of language, hurry was not something they ever really managed. So he simply nodded.

"So, my Henry, he goes and finds his slippers, and then he finds his robe and goes to the kitchen and finds the flashlight and then he goes next door and knocks hard for old Finkel to come too. . . ."

Mr. Finkel nodded his head in agreement. "This is true," he said.

Mrs. Kadosh shot him a quick glance, as if to say that she was accustomed to interruption by her husband, but that her neighbor should wait his turn. Then she continued:

"So, Finkel, of course, he has his hearing aid out, and so he doesn't know from nothing, but he gets his robe too, and the two men, they go downstairs and knock on Mrs. Millstein's door. Knock, knock. But there is no answer. 'Mrs. Millstein, Mrs. Mill-stein, are you okay?' But nothing. So Henry and Mr. Finkel, they trudge back upstairs and he says to me, 'What should we do? There is no answer.' I tell them to go around the back and look in the patio door, and so, back they go, to do that. And you know what?"

"Patio door is broken in. Pulled right off," Henry Kadosh answered.

"So," Mrs. Kadosh continued, "Henry and Mr. Finkel come rushing back to the front, where it is I am waiting, and saying, 'Maria, Maria, calling police, 911 dialing. Right away!' And, as he is saying this, we are hearing another noise, right from the back. This noise, it comes from the patio. Around we all run, and Henry, he sees quick—"

"Is not cats or dogs in garbage. Is nigger running out of Mrs. Millstein's apartment!"

Mrs. Kadosh shook her head. "Henry, he chases man to alley. And old Finkel and I, we stick our heads in the door. And inside, is poor Mrs. Millstein. Murdered dead."

Winter's head reeled and he felt a rush of heat rise through his gorge, flooding him with a disorienting dizziness. The young patrolman touched his back, and Winter turned toward him.

"Come on, old-timer. Now you know what happened. You still wanna talk to a detective?"

"Yes," Winter replied. "The victim ..." He stumbled and stopped, thinking to himself: The victim *what*?

His mind raced with a blistering equation. An old woman arrives at your door, afraid that she is going to be killed. And then she is killed, but by someone totally unexpected?

He thought he needed time to think, but then realized that he was walking across the courtyard, following the young patrolman, heading toward the entrance to Sophie Millstein's apartment. He walked past the trumpeting cherub. The figurine was hit every few seconds with a shaft of red light, so that it appeared to be bathed in blood. He paused at the doorway, staring inside at the activity that seemed to energize the interior. He saw a man with a fingerprint case working the kitchen. Another was taking carpet samples. The young patrolman walked up to a wiry black man who was loosening his tie against the building, thick humidity of the room, gesturing toward Simon Winter. The old detective paused, waiting for the younger man to approach him. He studied the activity within the apartment. He clamped down hard on emotions that seemed to dash about heedlessly within him, trying to concentrate, steadying himself with memory. You have been here many times before, he told himself. Process the scene. It will tell you everything, if only you take your time and let it converse in its own way, in its own voice, speaking in the ancient language of violent death.

For a moment he watched Simon Winter, and saw the way his eyes scoured the room. He mistook this attentiveness for nervousness. Walter Robinson turned to the uniformed officer who'd escorted the old man into the apartment.

"So, what's the geezer's story?" he asked.

"Name is Winter, lives across the courtyard. Says he saw the deceased this evening. Probably the last person to see her before the break-in. Heard her lock herself into the place. Thought you might want a statement."

"Uh-huh," Robinson replied. "Yeah. You take it."

The patrolman nodded. "Maybe he could do the ID for us?"

Robinson considered this, and thought: Why not?

"Good idea." Making a short gesture, he and the patrolman walked over to Simon Winter. Walter Robinson quickly introduced himself as the detective in charge.

"We'd like this patrolman to take your statement," he said to the old man. "And, if you're willing, we'd like to have you make a tentative identification for us. If you're up for it, of course. Just for paperwork, you know. And we like to be completely certain before we call the next of kin. But only if you're willing. It's not pretty. . . ."

Simon Winter kept his eyes darting about, then finally turned and fixed them on the detective.

"I've seen it all before," he said quietly.

"What?"

"I've seen it. Twenty-two years with the City of Miami Police Department. The last fifteen in homicide."

"You were a cop?"

"That's right. Retired. It's been a while since I was at a crime scene. At least a dozen years."

"You're not missing much," Robinson said.

"That's right," Winter said quietly. "I don't miss much."

Robinson ignored the double entendre, extended a hand, and

they shook. The younger man did this out of professional courtesy. "Things must have been different back then," he said.

"No," Winter replied. "People die in much the same fashion. What was different was the science. We didn't have a lot of the stuff you young guys have today. Scientific profiles. DNA testing. Computers. We didn't have computers. Are you good with computers, Detective?"

"Yes, I am."

"Think they can solve this crime?"

Robinson shrugged. "Maybe." Then, after thinking for an instant, he added, "More than likely."

For a moment he watched Winter, whose eyes had once again started to sweep the crime scene, absorbing what he saw there. The young detective had two quick thoughts. First, that he wasn't sure he liked Simon Winter, and second, that he was sure he didn't want to end up an abrasive old man, retired to the Beach, existing on memories of years on the force. Dozens of killings, rapes, and assaults remembered in advanced age as the good old days. His mind abruptly wandered to a torts law problem discussed in a class two nights earlier. He had written a mock brief on the issue, and it had been his effort that the professor singled out for praise.

Walter Robinson was determined not to simply trade in his badge and revolver for a briefcase and a slightly more expensive suit and work the other side of the criminal street, as had many of the other policemen he'd known who went on to law school and become criminal defense attorneys or prosecutors. He told himself that he would land in some corporate firm, shaking hands with executives and businessmen, and soon enough would forget about crime scenes and the helplessness of sudden death.

"Okay," he said, shaking the pleasant images of the future out of his awareness, "let's make the ID, then you can tell your story to the patrolman."

Simon Winter followed the young detective through the apartment, remembering that he had taken the same path earlier that evening. But the small space was crowded with technicians and policemen, every light was turned on, and strobe patterns from the assembled squad cars outdoors marked the walls, disorienting

Winter, almost as if the apartment he entered while Sophie Millstein waited at her door was someplace different and distant, like
a memory from childhood. The angles, the colors, the smells, all
seemed alien to him. He looked about for the cat, but it had disappeared. He followed the detective into the bedroom.

Sophie Millstein lay on her back on the bed.

Her nightclothes were torn from her struggle, the flaccid curve
of her breast exposed. Her hair had come unpinned, and fanned
out haphazardly from her head, as if she was underwater. Her
nose had been bloodied and her upper lip was stained brown
where the blood had dried. One knee was thrust over the other,
almost coyly, and the flesh of her hip was bared. The sheets on
the bed were tangled around her feet. He had an urge to reach out
and pull the off-white nightgown over Sophie Millstein's ala-
baster skin.

Simon Winter glanced quickly around. He saw a photographer
taking a picture of her purse, which had been ripped open and discarded on the floor. Another was dusting the bureau for fingerprints. The drawers had been torn open and clothes were strewn
about. Winter remembered the small jewelry box next to the picture of Leo on the bureau top. But the picture was now in a corner, glass shattered, and the jewelry box missing.

He turned to Walter Robinson.

"She had a box, you know, a little metal thing. It was sort of
reddish brass with a little design carved on the top. She kept her
rings and earrings and stuff in it. Right up there."

He pointed, and the detective took notes.

"It's gone," Winter said redundantly.

"You would recognize it?" Robinson asked.

"I think so," Winter replied.

He turned back to Sophie Millstein.

A second fingerprint technician was working on her neck, carefully dusting her skin.

"Bodyprint?" Winter asked.

"Yeah," Robinson replied. "Shot in the dark, really. Maybe lift
a usable print about one time out of a hundred. Still, worth
trying."

"We used to try, occasionally. But it never worked for us."

"We've got new paper. And the lifting tape is much better. Sometimes use an ultraviolet technique as well. And, you know, they're developing this laser that reads the print ridges. Still . . ." He shrugged.

The technician bent over Sophie Millstein, obscuring her from Simon Winter's view. He had a small piece of tape in his hand, which he pressed to the old woman's skin, then lifted carefully. He placed the tape against a sheet of special white paper, depositing the print. "Maybe," the technician muttered. "Looks okay."

The technician stepped back, moving aside.

"You want to do the ID now?" Walter Robinson said.

Winter stepped forward and looked down at Sophie Millstein.

Strangled, he thought immediately. He fixed the red and blue-black bruise marks on the old woman's neck in his memory. The skin by her windpipe was crushed, deformed by the force that had encircled her. Mentally, he measured the distance between the marks.

Large hands, he thought. Strong hands.

"Is that Mrs. Sophie Millstein?" Robinson asked.

Simon Winter continued to stare. The woman's eyes were still wide open, staring sightlessly up toward the ceiling. Winter saw the fear in his neighbor's face. She must have known, if only briefly, that she was dying then and there. He wondered if he'd worn the same look earlier in the evening, when he lifted his own pistol to his mouth. He wondered if she'd managed to think of Leo in her last panicked moments.

He looked at Sophie Millstein's eyes again. No, he thought. All they saw was terror.

Winter took note of a scratch, really a long frayed slice of skin on her neck, oddly unaccompanied by blood. He remembered the gold necklace she wore. It was gone. Ripped from her post-mortem, he thought. That's why the cut to the skin didn't bleed.

"Mr. Winter?" Walter Robinson's voice was questioning.

Simon Winter quickly glanced down at his neighbor's fingers. Did she fight back? Did she scratch and flail away and try to win her remaining years back from the man who sought to steal them? Her killer's flesh should be beneath the fingernails. But he saw Sophie Millstein kept hers cut close.

His eyes moved up to Sophie Millstein's right forearm. He could just make out the number tattooed there in faded blue.

Winter felt something touch his sleeve, turned and looked hard at the young detective.

"Of course," he said slowly. "It's Sophie Millstein. Her necklace is missing. A single strand, gold chain, but it had her name stamped in a charm at the center. The same kind that kids like to wear, but hers was distinctive. There were two diamonds, not big ones, at either end of the *S*. Her husband gave that to her about eighteen months ago, and she never took it off."

He took a deep breath, watching Walter Robinson make a notation in his book. "You'd recognize the necklace?" the younger man asked.

"Yes." He continued, "You might try taking samples from beneath her fingernails. . . ."

"They do that at the morgue," Robinson replied. "Standard procedure. Do you know her next of kin?"

"Yes. She has a son named Murray Millstein, who's an attorney on Long Island. She has an address book in a drawer in the living room. The little table that holds the phone. A little leather address book. That's where she said she always kept it."

"In the living room?"

"That's right. I'll show you."

Robinson started to lead Winter from the room. "Thank you for your help on this, Mr. Winter. We really appreciate it. . . ."

"She was scared," Simon Winter said abruptly, under his voice, to the detective. "That's why she came to me."

"Scared?"

"Yes. She'd had a fright. Today. She saw someone. She was scared and threatened. . . ."

"You think this person that scared her had anything to do with the crime?"

"I don't know. It was unusual. She was very frightened."

"It was unusual for her to be frightened?"

"No," Winter replied, slightly exasperated. "She was old and alone. She was always frightened."

"That's what I would have thought. Well, just give your statement to the patrolman. Tell him what happened."

"This person was someone—"

"He'll take your statement. I need to secure this scene and contact the family."

"But the person—"

"Mr. Winter, you were a detective. What do you think happened here?"

Simon Winter didn't look around. Instead he eyed Walter Robinson. "I'd say someone broke in, killed her, robbed her, and ran when he heard the neighbors. That's the obvious explanation, isn't it?"

"That's right. And we even have several witnesses who saw the perpetrator fleeing. Mr. and Mrs. Kadosh and Mr. Finkel. Your neighbors. So what is obvious is also true. Now, let the patrolman take your statement. Tell him who she was scared of."

He didn't finish his thought out loud, which was: *Whoever it was, it was the wrong damn person.*

The two men paused in the center of the living room. Simon Winter wanted to get angry, but felt himself searching instead for a grip on the events. He cursed his age and indecision inwardly.

"Now, where's that address book?"

"In the drawer."

Winter pointed, and Walter Robinson stepped across the small room and opened the drawer beneath the phone.

"It's not here."

"I saw it there earlier. That's where she always kept it."

"Not here now. What did it look like?"

"Red leather. Not expensive. About four by five. Gold-embossed 'Addresses' in script on the front. The sort of thing you'd get in a drugstore."

"We'll look for it. Not the sort of thing a junkie looking for cash is likely to grab. It'll show up."

Winter nodded. "She had it out, tonight, when I left her."

"Well, give your statement to the patrolman, Mr. Winter. And don't hesitate to call if you can think of anything else."

Robinson handed Simon Winter a business card. The old detective put it in his pocket. Then the younger man turned away, leaving Winter to be led outside by the patrolman. Winter started to say something, but stopped, and keeping the surge of thoughts to himself, reluctantly followed the patrolman, leaving Sophie Millstein behind. He glanced back over his shoulder once, back into the bedroom, and saw that her last moments were being documented by a police photographer's camera. The photographer dipped and swayed, dancelike, around Sophie Millstein, his camera popping with each flash of light, taking another series of shots while the morgue team waited patiently in a corner, talking quietly amongst themselves. One man idly worked the large brass zipper on the shiny black rubberized body bag, making a small tearing sound.

Walter Robinson looked on the floor in the bedroom for the address book, but could not find it. He made a note of this as well. Then he went back to the telephone in the living room and dialed directory assistance on Long Island. Sophie Millstein's son's number was listed in Great Neck. But before calling the victim's son, he dialed the twenty-four-hour service for the Dade County State Attorney's Office and received the number for the assistant with homicide duty that night.

He dialed and waited through a half-dozen rings before a sleepy voice staggered across the line:

"Yes?"

"Is this Assistant State Attorney Esperanza Martinez?" he asked.

"Yes."

"This is Detective Robinson. Beach homicide. We haven't met. . . ."

"But we're going to meet now, right?" the sleepy voice replied.

"That's right, Miss Martinez. I've got an elderly victim, killed by an unknown assailant inside her apartment, twelve hundred block of South Thirteenth Terrace. Crime could fit the profile of a series of break-ins we've had out here, except this time the perp strangled the old woman. We have a witness who got a look at the suspect. Tentative description: black, late teenage to early twenties, slight stature, about five-ten, maybe 175 pounds, and moving fast."

"You think I need to be there?" the prosecutor asked. "Is there some legal issue you need advice on?"

The young woman's voice had gathered an edge of irritation. Robinson ignored it.

"Well, no. No legal issue that I can see. The crime itself is pretty cut and dried. But what we have is an elderly white, Jewish victim and a young black perpetrator, and it's my guess this will be high-profile real quick, what with this being an election year for your boss and there being at least a half-dozen reporters and cameramen outside who are gonna be damned after waiting around all damn night if they don't make this into something that lands 'em on the front page, or maybe the top of the newscast. . . . You hear what I'm saying?"

"You think—"

"I think you've got race and murder, and that's a cocktail that don't mix too good in this county, Miss Martinez."

This was standard police procedure in Dade County: invoke the riots of the 1980s, and instantly obtain people's attention. There was a momentary silence on the line before the woman's voice, considerably more alert, answered:

"I hear you loud and clear, Detective. I'll be right over and we can wave the flag together."

"Sounds like fun."

He hung up the phone, grinning. Occasionally waking up hotshot young prosecutors was one of the homicide detectives' job perquisites. He figured at least a half hour before she arrived and got tossed in front of the press. He decided he could wait while inspecting the progress of the search team working the alley behind the Sunshine Arms. Maybe they've found something, he thought. The jewelry box. It had to be close by. The perp probably threw it in the first trash can he could, after conveniently covering it with fingerprints and the unmistakable scent of panic.

Esperanza Martinez went by the nickname of Espy to her friends, which were few. She dressed swiftly in the semidarkness of her bedroom, first pulling on jeans, then discarding them in favor of a more fashionable loose-fitting dress, when she considered she might have to face a camera crew. Although she was alone in her apartment, she was careful to be quiet; she lived in a duplex, half of which was occupied by her parents, and her mother was uncannily sensitive to her daughter's movements, and was probably, despite the wallboard, wooden frame, and insulation material that separated them, lying awake in bed, listening.

She double-checked her appearance in a small mirror that hung next to a crucifix by the front door. She made certain that she had her State Attorney's Office badge and a small .25 caliber automatic pistol in her pocketbook, and exited into the sticky nighttime. When she started the engine on the modest, nondescript compact car, she glanced up and saw the light flick on in her parents' half of the house. She put the car in gear and maneuvered quickly out into the street.

Late at night in Miami in the summer, it seems as if the day's heat leaves a residual glow, like the musty warmth that rises from a recently extinguished fire. The huge office towers and skyscrapers that dominate the downtown remain lit, shedding darkness like it was so many droplets of black. But for all its tropical smoothness, the city has an unsettling pulse, as if, when one slides down from the brightly illuminated highways that crisscross the county, one descends into a basement. Or perhaps a crypt.

Espy Martinez feared the night.

She drove rapidly, slipping from quiet suburban streets onto Bird Road, then up Dixie Highway, heading fast toward Miami Beach. There was little traffic, but just as she maneuvered onto the four lanes of Route 95, a red Porsche with ink-black tinted windows flew past her, screaming by in excess of a hundred miles per hour. The velocity of the sports car seemed to suck her along, as if she'd been buffeted from behind by a sudden strong gust of wind. "Jesus Christ!" she swore out loud—and felt fear sear through her for just one nasty instant, then flee as she watched the car rapidly disappear, momentarily glistening in the yellow-tinted sodium vapor lights of the highway before being enveloped by the night. A quick glance into the rearview mirror warned her of the state trooper's car coming up equally fast behind her. The trooper was traveling without lights or siren, trying to close on his quarry before the speeder knew he was there. She understood this went against established procedure, and she guessed the trooper would lie about it in a court hearing, if he got asked. But she also knew it was the only way he could hope to catch the Porsche, which was faster and more maneuverable, so, mentally, she forgave him as he roared past her.

"Good luck," she said. "You'll need it." She hoped the driver of the Porsche would turn out to be some middle-aged doctor or lawyer or developer trying to impress a date who was half his age, and not a twenty-one-year-old coked-up drug smuggler, brain-fried from narcotics and machismo, who kept a machine pistol on the seat beside him.

The night, she thought, was dangerous. Anger hid so successfully after dark, lurking, obscured by the warmth and the rich black air. Espy Martinez pushed her hair away from her face nervously and kept driving.

She spotted the flashing lights and haphazardly parked television trucks from a block away, and quickly turned into a parking spot. She hurried down the sidewalk, ducking under the yellow crime-scene tape before she was spotted by the dozen reporters and cameramen milling about, waiting for someone to come talk to them.

A patrolman started to wave at her, but she swiftly produced her badge.

"I'm looking for Detective Robinson," she said.

The patrolman inspected the badge. "Sorry, Miss Martinez. But I made you for one of those television reporters. Robinson's inside."

He pointed, and she stepped across the courtyard without noticing the cherub. She paused, almost as if she were abruptly out of breath.

This was only the third homicide scene she'd been required to visit. The other two had been anonymous narcotics assassinations; in each instance, young Hispanic men lacking identification, probably illegal immigrants from Colombia or Nicaragua. Each had a single gunshot wound to the back of the head, administered by a small handgun. Murder at its neatest and cleanest. Almost delicate. Their bodies had been discarded with little ceremony in vacant lots—gold jewelry, wallets stuffed with cash, expensive clothing—all intact. In many jurisdictions the similarities would have had press and public buzzing, questioning whether these were the work of a serial killer.

Not in Miami. Prosecutors in the Dade State Attorney's Office termed such homicides *felony littering*. There was a macabre theory among prosecutors and police that the closer to the center of the city each body was found, the less important the particular victim was. The truly significant narcotistas ended up dead, decomposing beneath the swampy muck of the Everglades or sinking chained to a cinder block in a thousand fathoms of Gulf Stream waters. So, these two men that Espy Martinez had merely glanced at were nobodies who amounted to nothing. Their deaths probably resulted from a single unfortunate flight of ambition, wherein they crossed some invisible but uniquely deadly line. Murder as organizational housekeeping. Even their assassins couldn't be bothered with the lengthy, messy, and bothersome effort required to dispose of their corpses where they wouldn't be discovered. No arrests were expected. No trials. Just a pair of numbers tallied on an unfortunate set of statistics.

Espy Martinez hadn't even had to approach either body. Her attendance had been requested only by homicide detectives eager to make sure the state attorney understood the inevitability of the failure attached to the investigation of those crimes.

This case, she knew, was different.

A real person, with a name. A history. Connections. Not someone who simply dropped in and out of life.

She hung in the doorway of the apartment, collecting her fears. A crime scene analyst pushed past her carrying an armful of scrapings and other samples. He muttered "Coming through" as he passed her, and to avoid standing in his way, Espy Martinez stepped into the apartment. Another policeman glanced at her, and she took the time to fasten her badge to her pocketbook. When she looked up, she saw the policeman jerk his finger toward the bedroom. Taking a deep breath, she walked through the apartment, trying to see nothing and everything at the same time.

She lingered for a second on the edge of the activity in the bedroom.

Her view was blocked by several men standing at the foot of

the bed. One moved slightly, and she saw Sophie Millstein's foot. The toenails were painted with a confident red. She bit her lip at the sight. Espy Martinez took another deep breath, and despite fearing the croaking sounds she thought would emerge, tried her voice:

"Detective Robinson?"

The wiry young black man turned, nodding. "You must be Miss Martinez?"

"That's right. Can you fill me in?"

She thought her voice wavered, and she thrust her shoulders back hard, her eyes meeting the detective's.

"Sure," he said. He pointed down at the body: "This is Sophie Millstein, white female, sixty-eight years. Widow. Lived alone. Apparently strangled. Here, look at these marks. . . ."

Detective Robinson gestured, and Espy Martinez stepped forward. She narrowed her gaze, as if by looking at parts of the victim—her throat, her hands, her legs—not all of her at once, she could minimize the fear she felt.

"Best as I can tell, he pinned her down, like one knee to the chest, and simply throttled her. Couple of bruises on the forehead, here and there, like he hit her a couple of times. But he must have got his fingers round the windpipe real quick, this is probably where he had his thumb, because it's all pushed in and crushed, and the neighbors only heard one little scream."

Walter Robinson saw the color drain from Espy Martinez's face. He stepped swiftly into her line of sight. "Come on, let me show you where the perp made his entry. . . ."

He grabbed the young prosecutor's arm and turned her out of the bedroom.

"Wanna glass of water?" he asked.

"Yes," she replied. "And some fresh air."

He pointed at the patio door ripped from its moorings. "Wait right out there. I'll get you a drink."

When Walter Robinson found Espy Martinez, after rinsing a glass and filling it with tap water, she was breathing deeply outside, as if she could swallow the night air. She took the water from his hands and gulped it down. Then she let out a long sigh and shook her head.

"I'm sorry, Detective. It's kind of a cliché, isn't it? The young woman upset at the sight of violent death. Let me get a grip, and then we'll go back inside and you can finish."

"It's all right. There's no need, really. I can fill you in here."

"No," Espy Martinez replied. "One more look. It's my job too."

"It's not necessary. . . ."

"Yes it is."

Without waiting for the detective, she reentered the apartment and stepped through the living room, into the bedroom. She tried to blank her mind of all thoughts, but this was impossible. Questions, fears, angers all ricocheted about within her, a racket of passions. She told herself: *This is why you became a prosecutor—this woman, right here.* The two morgue technicians were getting ready to lift Sophie Millstein from her bed.

"Just a second," Espy Martinez said. She approached the corpse and looked down into Sophie Millstein's eyes. What an awful way to meet someone, she thought. Who were you? She continued to stare at the murdered woman, and saw the same fear that Simon Winter did, and this infuriated her. *Coward,* she said to herself, as if addressing the killer. *Punk coward.* Steal an old woman's life just like it was a pocketbook that you ripped from her shoulder. I'm going to see you go to Hell. She held her gaze still for a moment, then nodded.

The two men from the morgue glanced at each other. What was special to Espy Martinez was the stuff of daily drudgery to them. Still, they lifted Sophie Millstein slowly and carefully.

"Jesus!" one of the morgue men shouted. He almost dropped the body back on the bed.

"Holy shit!" his companion said brusquely.

Espy Martinez gasped and had the presence of mind to slap a hand over her mouth to keep from crying out.

"Goddamn, look at that!" the other morgue man whispered. "Hey, Detective! You might wanna picture of this!"

Walter Robinson had darted to the side of the bed. He looked down at what had been uncovered. He held his gaze for a moment, then gestured to the police photographer, who was setting up for yet another series of pictures. Then he turned to Espy Martinez. She had taken a step back, but held her position.

Their eyes met. He shrugged.

"I'm sorry. I didn't know," he said.

She nodded, not eager to try her voice for an instant or two.

Walter Robinson looked down at the bed again. He stared at the small white fangs bared in terror.

"I've never seen a strangled cat before," he said quietly.

"Neither have I," Espy Martinez said grimly.

Simon Winter stood outside next to the young patrolman, but his eyes caught the sight of Detective Robinson and Espy Martinez, heads together in discussion, standing in Sophie Millstein's living room.

"Who's that?" he asked.

"That's the assistant state attorney. Martinez, I think."

"What's she doing here?"

"Policy, you know. There's an ASA assigned to every recorded homicide, but the reality is, they're only called in on the ten percent or so that the detectives think are gonna make the evening newscasts or land on the local front of the *Herald*."

"Sophie Millstein?"

"Yeah, more'n likely. News for a day or so, at least until something else happens."

"I guess so. You're probably right."

"So," said the patrolman, "I bet you want to head in and get some sleep. Right, old-timer? Me, I've got four more hours on this shift. Tell me your story."

"What do you mean?"

"You saw the victim tonight, right?"

"You want my statement?"

The patrolman had a small pad and pencil in his hand. He looked exasperated. "Yeah. That's right."

Winter organized his thoughts and spoke rapidly. "Early this evening, perhaps seven P.M., Mrs. Millstein knocked on my apartment door. Number 103, right over there. She had been frightened after doing some shopping, and she wanted me to accompany her through her place, to make certain it was safe."

"So you did?"

"That's right. The apartment was empty, and I checked the doors and windows and they were all securely locked. But what frightened her—"

"You didn't see anyone hanging around. Especially anyone who fits the suspect's description?"

"No."

"Like out back, when you checked the patio door? Nobody hanging back there?"

"I told you, no. There was no one that I saw. There was nobody there when I was in the apartment. But she described this person she saw earlier."

"Okay, tell me about that."

"She said it was someone she had seen during the war. . . ."

"What war?"

"World War Two. In Berlin. In 1943."

"Berlin?"

"Germany."

"Oh. Okay. So, this someone she saw, he wasn't a young black male, was he?"

Simon Winter stared at the patrolman as if the man had just asked the stupidest question he'd ever heard, which was undoubtedly true.

"No," Winter said carefully. "He wasn't a young black male. He was an elderly man, but she described him as singularly intense. She called him Der Schattenmann. . . ."

"Someone shot a man?"

"No. It's German. Der Schattenmann. It's a title, not a name."

"A title? Like what? Mayor? Or County Commissioner?"

"I'm not sure what it means."

He saw the young patrolman's pencil pause above his notepad, then scribble down something swiftly.

"She didn't know the guy's name?"

"No. He was someone connected to her arrest and subsequent deportation. To Auschwitz. He was someone—"

"Yeah, a lot of the old folks here on the Beach got busted back then and did time."

"Auschwitz wasn't doing time. It wasn't a prison. It was an extermination camp."

"Right. Right. I know that. So this guy she recognized . . ."

"She wasn't sure."

"She wasn't sure she recognized him?"

"Correct," Simon Winter said. "Fifty years had passed."

"Okay, so she was frightened by this Shotinmin guy. If it was the guy, after all. You're not sure, and neither was she. Okay. You think it had anything to do with her murder tonight?"

"No. I don't know. It's just unusual. Maybe a coincidence."

"Was Mrs. Millstein ever scared? I mean, like other days?"

"Sure. She was old and alone. She was frequently nervous. She changed her schedule so she wouldn't be out at night."

"Okay. But, like you didn't see anything strange or different tonight. And her behavior wasn't *that* different, correct?"

Winter froze the patrolman with a stare. "Yes. That is correct."

The younger man flipped his notebook closed. "Okay. I think I got it. You remember anything else, you call Detective Robinson, okay?"

Winter swallowed several nasty retorts and nodded. The patrolman smiled.

"Okay, you can head on home now, Mr. Winter. This crew will be wrapping up shortly. Might be some attention around here for a couple of days. News guys might bug you, but just tell 'em to go to Hell if you want. Usually works. I'll make sure the detective gets a report of everything you said."

Then the young patrolman turned and headed back toward the street, leaving Simon Winter alone, his face bathed by flashing police strobes.

In the kitchen, Espy Martinez watched as Walter Robinson picked up the telephone and carefully, double-checking each digit, dialed a number.

He finished and cupped a hand over the mouthpiece. "Middle of the night, phone rings. Your mother's murdered. What a nightmare." Then he shrugged, as if to distance himself from the pain he was preparing to deliver.

Espy Martinez watched, slightly ashamed with herself for her own fascination, the same commonplace guilt one feels when one turns and gawks at the accident that has left the highway bejeweled with broken glass and stained with blood.

Robinson mouthed the word "ringing," and then straightened slightly when he heard the telephone receiver lifted.

"Yes?"

"Murray Millstein, please."

"This is he. What—"

"Mr. Millstein, this is Detective Walter Robinson of the Miami Beach police, down in Florida. I'm sorry, but I have some bad news."

"What? What?"

"Mr. Millstein, your mother, Mrs. Sophie Millstein, died earlier tonight. She was the victim of a robber who broke into her apartment shortly before midnight and apparently killed her before looting her valuables."

"Oh my God! What? My mother what?"

"I'm sorry, Mr. Millstein."

"What are you saying? My mother what? I don't—"

"I'm sorry, Mr. Millstein. Your mother was killed earlier tonight. That's what I'm saying."

Robinson hesitated, while the voice on the telephone seemed to gather itself. He could hear another voice in the background, penetrating the night, shrill questions, edgy panic. The attorney's wife, Robinson thought. She's sitting up in bed and she's turned on the lamp on the table where she keeps her alarm clock and a picture of her children, and now she's reached out and grabbed her husband's arm, pinching it tightly, and she's demanding to know why he's swung his feet out of bed and is sitting there, frozen in place, pale, rigid, terrified.

"Detective, uh . . ."

"Robinson. Do you have a paper and pencil, Mr. Millstein? I want to give you a telephone number."

"Yes, yes, but—"

"This is the number of my office at police headquarters."

"But what happened? My mother—"

"We do not have a suspect in custody yet, Mr. Millstein. But we have a description and a significant amount of physical evidence gathered from your mother's apartment. We are really just initiating our investigation, but we have complete cooperation from the state attorney and other forces in Dade County, and I'm hopeful we'll make an arrest."

"But my mother, how, she always locked—"

"The perpetrator apparently forced a patio door open."

"But then, I don't understand. . . ."

"Preliminary investigation suggests she was strangled. But final determination rests with the medical examiner."

"She's . . ."

"Yes. Her remains will be transported to the county morgue. But after their examination, you will need to contact a local funeral home. If you call the morgue in the afternoon, a secretary there will give you some numbers."

"Oh my God."

"Mr. Millstein, I'm sorry to have to deliver this news. I have to warn you, you might hear from the local media. I'm sure you'll want more details, and I'll provide these as best as I can, but right now I have work to do. Please telephone me at your convenience at the number I gave you. I should be there by eight this morning. You could call me then."

The attorney seemed to answer with a half sob and grunt, and Robinson hung up the telephone.

Espy Martinez was watching him closely. She felt, in part, like some voyeur, fascinated and repulsed, everything happening in front of her in some oddly slowed-down time. She saw a look of helpless discouragement pass across the detective's eyes, stopping for just a moment, just long enough to play a single note, before it disappeared, echo fading. She abruptly thought: We are both very young.

But what she said, quietly, was: "That must be hard to do."

Robinson shrugged, with a small, wry look on his face, and shook his head.

"Well, you get used to it," he replied in a tone of voice that helped her recognize he was not anywhere near to telling the truth. And that he knew this.

\* \* \*

The detective and the prosecutor walked outside. Espy Martinez thought the darkness seemed to have thinned, and she glanced down at her wristwatch and saw that morning was closing fast. She spotted a clutch of elderly people standing to one side of the small courtyard, but before she could ask, Walter Robinson anticipated her question.

"Those are the folks that live here. Kadosh is the name of the old guy who got a look at the perp running away down the alley. His wife called 911. The tall guy is Winter. He walked Mrs. Millstein home earlier, and double-checked her locks. Apartment owner is Gonzalez, but he's not here yet. On his way. You know the damnedest thing? One of the neighbors told me he'd already put in new locks on half the apartments and was scheduled to come back this weekend to do Mrs. Millstein's place. I don't think it would have made much difference, but you never know. That's what's gonna be in all the papers tomorrow."

Walter Robinson gestured toward the group of reporters and cameramen. He gave them a quick wave, to let them know he was on his way over. Then he lowered his voice and said to Espy Martinez, "Okay, what we're gonna hold back is anything about that gold chain with her name on it, and we're not gonna talk about the print the tech lifted from her neck, at least until we see if we can make a match with it."

Robinson lifted his eyes and saw a pair of detectives and several patrolmen coming around the corner of the Sunshine Arms, from the back.

One of the detectives waved and approached the pair. From about five feet away he said: "Hey Walter, you called that shot."

Robinson introduced the detective to Espy Martinez and then said, "Down the alley?"

"That's right. In a trash container. We took pictures and then the lab guy bagged it. We might be really lucky; I think I saw a little bit of blood on one corner."

"What is it?" Espy Martinez asked.

"A brass jewelry box," Robinson said. "We're not gonna mention it to the press either. Okay?"

"No problem. I'd rather you did the talking anyway."

Robinson nodded. "All right. Let's go." He smiled again and made a joke: "Hey, no worse than going to the dentist."

He touched her elbow for just an instant, and then the two of them together walked into the sudden glare of the television mini-cam lights.

# FIVE
## HUNTERS AND
## HUNTED

SIMON Winter sat in his apartment, one finger hesitating over the push buttons on his telephone. Although midday sunlight filled the air, he had the sensation that he was about to step into a darkened room without knowing where the light switch was. What little sleep he'd managed had been fitful and nightmarish. Exhaustion mocked his movements. He took a final look outside his window, across the courtyard, where a slight breeze riffled the yellow police tape. Along with a red CRIME SCENE DO NOT ENTER sign posted on Sophie Millstein's door, it was the only outward, remaining indication of what had taken place the night before.

He did not know whether he was beginning something or ending it, but he thought himself obliged to make the call. He felt dizzy, almost as if he were sick, but then dragged himself to attention as the telephone started ringing on the other end.

It was answered by a distant "Hello?"

"Is this Rabbi Chaim Rubinstein?" Winter asked.

"Yes. Rabbi once, but now retired. And who is this?"

"My name is Simon Winter, I'm a . . ." He paused, trying to think precisely what he was, and then answered, ". . . a friend of Sophie Millstein."

"Sophie is dead." The rabbi's voice was singularly cold. "She

66

was killed. Last night. By some intruder. A man searching for money for drugs. That is what the paper said."

"I know. I'm her neighbor."

"So. You know more than I. You know more than was in the papers. What is it you want?"

"She came to me yesterday. Only hours before her death. She was frightened, and she felt she had to tell you something. You and two friends. A Mr. Silver and a Mrs. Kroner. She didn't speak with you last night?"

"No. No, I did not speak to her. Tell us? Tell us what?" The rabbi's voice had risen slightly, pushed by stress and sudden fear.

"That she had seen—" He stopped, correcting himself, ". . . that she believed she had seen a man she called—"

The rabbi interrupted: "Der Schattenmann."

"That's right."

Silence gripped the phone line.

"Rabbi?" Winter asked.

There was another hesitation before the rabbi spoke ice words.

"He will kill us all."

Rabbi Chaim Rubinstein lived in a modest older building on the wrong side of Ocean Drive, its view of the sea mostly blocked by two larger, more imposing condominiums. From the best apartments, Winter saw, there would be just a sliver of pallid blue available to the eye. Otherwise, there was nothing to distinguish it from dozens like it up and down Miami Beach, stretching into Fort Lauderdale, Delray, up to the Palm Beaches, save its name: The Royal Palm. There was, of course, nothing royal about the building, nor did he see any palms, except for a single, unassuming potted tree drooping in the lobby.

Winter rode the elevator up to the sixth floor and stepped into the hallway. A blandly irritating Muzak played through tinny speakers in the ceiling. The corridor itself employed a depressing uniformity: a beige carpet, flower-print wallpaper, a seemingly endless series of white doors, notable only for the gold-plated numerals in the center of each.

He knocked at number 602 and waited. He could hear locks

being disengaged, and the door opened partway, still secured by a chain.

"Mr. Winter?"

"Rabbi?"

"Could you show me some identification? With a picture on it?"

Simon Winter nodded, reached into his wallet, and produced his driver's license. He held this up for the rabbi to inspect.

"Thank you," the man said after a moment. He closed the door to release the chain, and then opened it wide. "Please come in. Thank you for coming."

The two men shook hands. Rabbi Rubinstein was a short, thin man, but without the bony, cadaverous look of an aesthete. He sported a shaggy, curly mane of gray hair that toppled over his ears, and black-rimmed eyeglasses that were perched at the end of his nose. Through these he examined Simon Winter for an instant, then, with a wave, he directed Winter into the living room.

Winter saw the elderly couple sitting on a white couch, behind a glass coffee table, waiting for him. They rose as he entered.

"This is Mr. Irving Silver and Mrs. Frieda Kroner," the rabbi said. Winter stepped forward and shook hands. Mrs. Kroner, thickset, wearing white slacks and a bulky sweater that made her seem twice the rabbi's size, immediately sat back down and poured him a cup of coffee. Mr. Silver was a small, round man, nearly bald, who nervously drummed his fingers against his knee when he returned to his seat on the couch. Winter glanced around for an instant. He saw a bookcase and quickly read titles. There were some works on Judaica, a great number of histories of various aspects of the Holocaust, and a smattering of contemporary thrillers and horror novels. The rabbi caught his eye and said:

"So, most of the time I study and learn, Mr. Winter. I try to understand these events that I was a small part of. It is what I have devoted my retirement to. But sometimes I, too, like to read something by Stephen King. This is not terrible. All the supernatural monsters and evil things he writes about, they cannot truly exist, can they? They are not real, and yet, he makes it seem as if they are, and that is most interesting, isn't it? We all like a good scare once in a while, do we not? It's entertaining."

"I suppose so," Winter answered.

"It is much easier, some nights, Mr. Winter, to read of terrors that jump from a man's imagination, that are fantasy, than to study horrors that truly happened." He pointed at a row of books examining the Holocaust.

The detective nodded.

". . . Or still happening," the rabbi added.

The rabbi swept him into a chair with a gesture. Mrs. Kroner handed him the cup of black coffee. She did not ask whether he cared for sugar or cream. He saw Irving Silver shift in his seat, leaning forward. His hands shook slightly as he rattled his cup into the saucer on the table in front of him. Winter saw a pale restraint in Irving Silver's face as he looked toward the rabbi with nervous need. The rabbi nodded, and then asked:

"So, tell us, Mr. Winter. Tell us about what Sophie told you."

The rabbi had an odd voice, one that started with a gravelly, deep tone, and then rose sharply with each word, so that at the end of his question, it was high-pitched and insistent.

"I can only repeat what I told you on the phone, Rabbi. She came to me in a panic. She believed that she had seen this man that she remembered from fifty years ago. She felt it was her responsibility to warn the three of you. And then later last night, she was killed—"

"Yes. Yes. The junkie." Mr. Silver interrupted. His voice was shrill. "Isn't that what they still call some addicts? We read about that in the paper. It was on the noon news too. He broke in and then he killed her and stole some things! The police are searching for him now! There was no mention of Der Schattenmann!"

Rabbi Rubinstein glared at Irving Silver, and asked Winter: "So, how sure was Sophie, may she rest in peace, of the man she saw?"

Winter hesitated before replying, looking at the frightened eagerness in the three faces in front of him. He had the feeling that he was entering in the midst of an argument that had been going on for weeks, which he suspected was precisely the case.

"At first, when she knocked on my door, she seemed afraid enough to be certain. As she calmed down, she seemed less sure."

He stopped abruptly.

"See?" Irving Silver insisted sharply. "She didn't know for sure! None of us know for sure!"

The rabbi shook his head slowly. "Irving, please. Let Mr. Winter finish. Bear with us, Mr. Winter. We do not want to believe this man is here. Now. Today."

"He should be dead!" Mr. Silver interjected swiftly. "How could he not be dead? And why here? Why now? No, he must be dead! He could not have survived!"

Frieda Kroner frowned at Mr. Silver. Then she spoke for the first time. Traces of German hid in her accent.

"He is here, you old fool! And where else would he be?"

"But we are the people he once . . ."

"That is correct," she said coldly. "He killed many of us once. And now, he is doing it again. This is to be expected. Why are you so surprised? Does a man who hates so much ever really stop? Poor Sophie. When he saw her, she didn't have a chance. Nobody ever did."

A large tear dropped down her round cheek. She sat back hard, folding her arms across her ample bosom, making no effort to wipe the tear away.

Simon Winter held up a hand. "Mrs. Kroner . . . there's no indication that someone other than the suspect the police are searching for is involved in Sophie's death. . . ."

"If he saw her, he wouldn't hesitate. He would act swiftly. And she would die. And this is what happened."

The woman spoke with a bitter finality, forcing Winter to pause, his mind racing with questions, as he told himself to move slowly.

"There was a letter. Sophie told me about a Herman Stein who killed himself. He allegedly saw this man as well?"

Again there was a small silence in the room.

Rabbi Rubinstein nodded his head gently. "We talked, but we could not agree. It is hard to believe."

"You have the letter?"

"Yes." The rabbi reached down and picked up a copy of Raul Hilberg's *The Destruction of the European Jews*, which was resting next to the coffee service. The letter was inside the book. He handed it to Simon Winter, who swiftly read:

Rabbi:

I know of you through Rabbi Samuelson at Temple Beth-El, who gave me your name and told me that you were once a Berliner, as I was, many, many years ago.

You, perhaps, will remember a man we knew in those sad times only as Der Schattenmann. This was the person who found my family, when we hid out in the city, in 1942. He saw to our deportation to Auschwitz.

I hoped that this man was dead, along with the others. But it is not so! Two days ago I attended a large meeting of the Surfside Condominiums Association and accidentally saw him in the audience, sitting two rows behind me! He is here. I am certain of it.

Rabbi, who am I to call?

What am I to do?

It is wrong that this man still lives and I feel I must do something. My mind is black with questions, clouded with fears. Can you help me?

The letter was signed by Herman Stein, who also gave his address and telephone number.

Simon Winter looked up from the single sheet of paper and the handwritten message.

"The letter arrived?"

"Three days after Mr. Stein's death. All the way from Surfside, this is not far, it is not Alaska or the South Pole, but the postal service does not deliver the letter until three days after it was written. Such a thing."

The rabbi's lip quivered slightly.

"I was too late to help this poor Mr. Stein."

"And?"

"I contacted the police. And I called Mr. Silver and Mrs. Kroner, and of course your neighbor."

"What did the police say?"

"I spoke with a detective who made a copy of the letter, but who told me that Mr. Stein, whom I didn't know, had lived alone for many years and all his neighbors had been worried for him of late, because he seemed so sad. Moping about. Talking to himself—"

"Acting crazy, just as if death was standing beside him," Frieda Kroner interjected.

The rabbi nodded. "The detective told me Mr. Stein had written a suicide note before he shot himself and that was that, he could not help me further. He was a nice man, this detective, but I think he was busy with many other things and not so interested in my problems. He showed me Mr. Stein's suicide note."

"Do you remember—"

"Of course. How can you forget such a thing? I can still see the words, right in my memory. It was one sentence only: 'I am tired of life, and miss my beloved Hanna and so I go to join her now.' That was all. He shot himself. The detective told me. One time, right in the forehead."

"The forehead?"

"That is what the policeman said." The rabbi tapped the space just above his eyebrows as he spoke.

"You're sure? Did you read the detective's crime scene notes? Did they show you any of the crime scene photographs? Did you see the autopsy protocol?"

The rabbi arched a single eyebrow upward at the quick array of questions.

"No. He just told me this. He showed me nothing. A protocol?"

Simon Winter started to ask another question, then stopped. He thought: *the forehead.* Not the temple. Not the mouth, as he had selected for himself in what seemed years beforehand. In his mind's eye he tried to envision holding a pistol in that position. Awkward. Not impossible. Not even improbable. But awkward, and why would anyone make their own suicide awkward? His immediate answer to this question was that the rabbi had misunderstood the detective.

The rabbi looked over at him sharply. "You know of such things, Mr. Winter?"

"Yes. For two decades I was a policeman for the City of Miami. I retired to the Beach a number of years ago. So, yes, it has been a long time, but I still know of such things, Rabbi."

"You were a policeman?" Mr. Silver asked hurriedly. "And now?"

"And now I'm just another old person on the Beach, Mr. Silver."

Rabbi Rubinstein snorted. "This is why Sophie went to you."

"Yes. I suppose so. She was afraid, and she knew I had a gun." Winter took a deep breath. "She thought I could help her."

"I am going to get a gun too," Irving Silver said defiantly. "And I think we should all go get one and be able to defend ourselves!"

"What do I know of guns?" Frieda Kroner interrupted. "And what do you know, you old fool? More than likely, you will shoot yourself, or your neighbor, or the delivery boy who brings your heart medicine from the pharmacy."

"Yes, but maybe I will shoot *him* first, when he comes for me!"

This statement brought a silence crashing into the room.

Simon Winter looked at the three faces in front of him. The rabbi seemed exhausted by fear and sadness; Mrs. Kroner's eyes captured a combination of despair and defiance; while Mr. Silver covered the terror he felt with anger. The rabbi spoke first.

"You must forgive us, Mr. Winter. Sophie was our friend and we are in mourning. But we are also upset, and now, I think, we are afraid as well."

"There's no need to apologize, Rabbi. But why is it that you are so convinced that she was killed by this man? The police have a witness, another neighbor, who saw the perpetrator fleeing the murder scene. A young black man."

"You believe this?" Irving Silver demanded.

"An eyewitness," Winter replied sharply. "He chased the man into an alley."

The rabbi shook his head. "I am confused, Mr. Winter. And confusion only seems to make me more uncertain and afraid. Mr. Stein says he sees Der Schattenmann and then he dies. A suicide. Sophie says she sees Der Schattenmann and then she dies, killed by some unknown black man. This is a mystery to me, Mr. Winter. You are the detective. Tell us: Can such odd coincidences occur?"

Simon Winter paused before replying. "Rabbi, for many years I was a homicide detective—"

"Yes, yes, but answer the question!" Irving Silver interrupted. He opened his mouth again, but Frieda Kroner snapped an elbow into his ribs.

"Let the man speak!" she whispered harshly.

Winter let quiet fill the room while he considered his response. "Let me say this. Coincidences do occur. Fantastic, unbelievable coincidences. All detectives remember remarkable events, things that no one could have anticipated in a million years. In homicide work, these things are, if not commonplace, at least familiar. But, that said, you should understand that the vast majority of deaths are perfectly routine and straightforward. It is important to always search for the simple answer first, because in almost every case, that is the truth of the death."

"So what you're saying is—" Irving Silver broke in.

"Let him finish!" Frieda Kroner said, exasperated. Again she jabbed at Irving Silver's ribs. "You rude old man!" she chastened him.

"Thank you, Mrs. Kroner, but I have."

The rabbi was nodding his head. "You're saying yes—it could be exactly what it seems. A suicide. A murder by some animal off the street."

"Correct."

Again silence occupied a chair.

"Do you have an opinion, Mr. Winter?" Frieda Kroner asked.

"I have questions, Mrs. Kroner," Simon Winter replied. "And, I think, it is wise to remove doubts where there are so many. Regardless of how Sophie and Mr. Stein died, I think it will be difficult for the three of you to go about your business if every second you think you are being stalked by this fellow. If he exists."

She nodded, as did the rabbi.

"I still want a gun," Irving Silver muttered.

They all remained silent. Winter watched tears form in the corner of Irving Silver's eyes, and the man started to shake his head, slowly, almost imperceptibly, as if trying to loosen and discard all the thoughts that had emerged.

The rabbi leaned forward, pushing the fingers of each hand

through his tangled mass of hair. He puffed out his cheeks and let his wind slowly seep through pursed lips. Then he looked up at Simon Winter.

"You will help us, Mr. Winter?"

Winter felt a rigid toughness within him. He looked at the three faces of the elderly people in the room, and he remembered the shaky hand his neighbor placed on his own, as he'd interrupted his own death to let her enter his apartment. He took a quick glance and saw a similar blue tattoo on the rabbi's forearm, and suspected that beneath Mrs. Kroner's bulky white sweater and Mr. Silver's loose, checked shirt, he would find the same. He thought: I promised to help her, and then I didn't. He realized that promise was still lingering about within him, and so he replied:

"I will try, Rabbi. I'm not certain what I can do. . . ."

"You know things we do not. Many things."

"It has been a long time."

"Does one ever forget these things? These techniques?"

"No."

"Then, you will be able to help."

"I hope so."

The three elderly people took quick glances at each other.

"I think we are in need of help," Mrs. Kroner said. "Maybe even more than we want to say out loud, Mr. Winter."

"I still want a gun," Irving Silver muttered. "If we'd had guns back then—"

"Then the Nazis would have shot us on the spot!"

"Maybe that would have been better!"

"How can you say that, you old fool! We lived! And now the world does not forget!"

"Maybe it doesn't forget, but what has the world learned?"

Irving Silver and Frieda Kroner glared at each other. The rabbi sighed.

"They are frequently like this," he said to Winter. "We were all once, when we were so young, caught up in these immense events, and now we argue. Even the scholars argue. But we were there, and we were a part of something that is maybe more than just history."

"So was *he* . . ." Irving Silver grunted.

The rabbi stopped speaking, and looked at the others.

"That is true. He was as much a part of it as any of those who either died or survived."

"And *he* hasn't forgotten either," Irving Silver added.

"No. I think not."

Frieda Kroner started to dab a napkin at the corners of her eyes. "If *he* is here . . ."

"And he finds us . . ." Silver joined in.

"I think he will kill us."

Simon Winter held up a hand. "But why? And why would he kill or want to kill Sophie and this Mr. Stein? You haven't explained this."

As soon as he asked this question, Winter realized he had entered a realm ruled by history and memory, dark at the edges, pitch-black at its core.

"Because," the rabbi started after a moment's silence, "because we are the only people who can rise up and point him out."

"Bring him to justice," whispered Frieda Kroner.

"If he's here! I don't believe it! I don't believe any of it!" Irving Silver slapped his palm against his knee. The others looked at him sharply, but it was Winter who spoke first.

"But if he is here, you would recognize him?"

It took Irving Silver several seconds to answer. The old detective saw his chest heave with deep breaths as he struggled with the question.

"Yes," Silver said. "I saw his face too. For just a few seconds. He took money from my brother and I."

"It was my father," the rabbi said quietly. "It was my father that he recognized, when we were riding on the trolley. My father turned my face away, but I saw too. I was so young."

Frieda Kroner shook her head. "I was young too. Like the rabbi and Sophie, little more than a child. He caught us in the park. It was spring, and the city was filled with rubble and death, but still, it was spring and I remember so many people were outside, enjoying the fine day, and so my mother and I, we went out too, because it was so important to behave like all the others. Before the war they called it Führer weather, as if Hitler himself could rule the heavens!"

Again a silence creased the room.

"It is difficult to speak of these things," the rabbi said.

Simon Winter nodded. "Yes," he said slowly. "But I think I will need to know more if I am to help you."

"That is not unreasonable."

"And, there is something I do not understand."

"What is that, Mr. Winter?"

"Why would he kill you? Why not simply hide? It would not be difficult. He would not face a risk. Why not simply disappear?"

"I can answer that," Frieda Kroner said quickly.

Winter turned toward her.

"Because he is a lover of death, Mr. Winter."

The two others nodded in agreement.

"You see, Mr. Winter, what made him different from the others, why we were all so frightened of him, was that we knew he did what he did not because he believed some Nazi lie that by helping he could stay alive! He didn't do it to protect his family—that was another excuse we heard. He did it because he enjoyed it."

She shuddered hard.

"And because he was better at it than anyone else."

"Iranischestrasse," Rabbi Rubinstein added. This time his voice did not rise, but remained low and harsh. "The Jewish Bureau of Investigation. That was where the Gestapo watched the catchers, who then watched for us."

"They took off their stars," Irving Silver said. "And then they hunted us down."

"Berlin, you see, it was Himmler himself who came on the radio and promised that the city would be *Judenfrei*!" the rabbi added, his voice gathering momentum. "But it wasn't! It never was! When the Russians came, there were still fifteen hundred of us hiding in the rubble. Fifteen hundred out of 150,000! But we were still there when the tanks thundered in and all the Nazis were swept up in their own fire! Never was Berlin *Judenfrei*! Never! If there had been only one of us left, it was never *Judenfrei*!"

Simon Winter nodded. "But this man—"

Frieda Kroner spoke quickly. "Der Schattenmann covered his tracks better than any other catcher. It was said that if you saw him, then you died. If you heard his voice, then you died. If he touched you, then you died. . . ."

She hesitated, then added: "In the basement at Plotzensee Prison. A terrible place, Mr. Winter. A place where horrible death was the norm and the Nazis created even worse. Racks and meat hooks and guillotines and garottes, Mr. Winter."

"We were told that his would be the last living eyes you saw," Irving Silver said flatly. "His breath on your cheek would be your last memory."

"How did you know?"

"A word here, a conversation there," Frieda Kroner said. "It got around. People would talk. A shopkeeper to a customer. A policeman to a landlord. An idle word overheard at a park or on a trolley. And then mothers told their daughters, as mine did. Fathers told their sons. That was how we knew of Der Schattenmann." She breathed out deeply, as if the very words were painful.

"But the three of you. And Mr. Stein. And Sophie. You all survived. . . ."

"Luck," said the rabbi. "Accident? Mistake? The Nazis were so efficient, Mr. Winter, sometimes now, in history, we think of them as superhuman. But so many of them were bureaucrats and clerks and little men pushing pencils! And so, instead of the basement, some of us rode the trains to our deaths."

At that moment Irving Silver burst out in a sob.

They turned toward him and saw his eyes had reddened and he had clapped a hand over his mouth, as if to prevent the words he spoke from tumbling out. He was breathing hard again, battling with his breath.

"My brother," he choked out, behind a clenched fist held to his lips, "he went to the basement."

The others were silent.

"Oh, poor Martin," Irving Silver moaned. "My poor brother Martin."

After a moment his eyes swept around to the others.

"I'm sorry," he said. "It is hard to remember, but remember we must."

Irving Silver took a deep breath.

"This is all remembrance," he continued. "We remember. And so does Der Schattenmann. He must have thought he had killed us once, and now he will try again. We were all just slightly more than children then, Mr. Winter, and this must have been what saved us from him. My older brother, he was a threat, so . . ."

"My father," murmured the rabbi.

"And my mother," Frieda Kroner added.

"Surely, Mr. Winter, this cannot be so surprising," the rabbi said. "Just as Frieda says. If we know no peace because of what lives on in our memories, why would he be any different?"

Irving Silver reached out and squeezed Frieda Kroner's hand. She nodded.

Simon Winter felt as if he were suddenly caught in a strong current, pulling him into a deepening sea, dragging him away from the shoreline. He thought: All detectives work from memory; one crime resembles another. A third is reminiscent of a fourth. Even within the most exceptional, there are common threads: a motive, such as greed; a weapon, like a gun or knife; evidence—fingerprints, bloodwork, fiber or hair samples, whatever. And all those threads strive toward a commonality of crime. But this, what the three old people in front of him were speaking of, was a sort of crime that defied characterization.

He paused before replying. Silence swept the air.

"I think I will need to know more about this man. Who was he? Surely someone knew his name, where he came from, something about his family . . . ?"

There was another momentary silence before Frieda Kroner replied: "No one knew anything for sure. He was different from the others."

"He was different," Rabbi Rubinstein added quietly, "because he was like a knife in the dark. The others, people knew, you see. If the catcher knew you, then you might know the catcher too. Maybe from the synagogue, or the apartment building, or the doctor's office or the schoolyard, from somewhere before the race laws were put in effect. So, if you were alert, you could perhaps stay . . . what? One jump ahead? You might be able to hide. Or run. Or bribe them. They were traitors, but some, even near the end, some still had some feelings. . . ."

The rabbi breathed out slowly.

". . . But no one knew who he was. It was like the Nazis just invented this golem. A wraith."

"Can you describe him?"

"He was tall, like you—" Frieda Kroner started, but Irving Silver shook his head and waved his hand.

"No, Frieda, no. He was a tiny man, like a ferret. And older. More mature . . ."

"No," the rabbi interrupted angrily. "He had to be young in order to survive. Young and strong and smart and ambitious."

They looked at each other and fell into quiet.

"We were little more than children," the rabbi started. "Our memories . . ."

"I was small, like Sophie," Frieda Kroner said. "All men looked large to me."

"My poor brother Martin was still strong and tall, and so I thought everyone not like him was short. . . ."

"You see, Mr. Winter," the rabbi said. "Der Schattenmann was better than any Gestapo. He was like a ghost. Wherever he walked, there was darkness, even in the daytime. Just like a . . . what is it, Irving?"

"A will-o'-the-wisp."

"And we all knew," the rabbi said coldly, "that if he found you, then you could not hide."

"But couldn't he be bribed?"

"Yes and no," Irving Silver said. "Perhaps you would hear a voice in some dark alleyway, and you would promise your money and you might deliver it all to him. But then the Gestapo would come anyway, and the person Der Schattenmann had touched would be taken to the basement and the rest of his family put on the next train for the camps. He covered his tracks. If he found you, then it was like the world had never seen you."

Frieda Kroner gasped at a sudden memory. She shuddered hard, but held up her hand and did not speak when the others turned toward her.

"But Sophie. The three of you. Mr. Stein. You're suggesting . . ."

"Mistakes. Mistakes," the rabbi said. "No one was ever supposed to live, but sometimes we did. This was a mistake. And now, fifty years later, are those mistakes not being erased from the board?" Irving Silver shivered and Frieda Kroner dabbed her eyes.

Simon Winter nodded. He was having trouble understanding the fear he saw before him, but knew that it filled the room. He looked around for a moment at all the simple, ordinary things that filled the rabbi's apartment. A large brass menorah. Photographs of friends and family. A finely embroidered tablecloth. But it was as if all these items were obscured by smoky memory, and the air filled with a noxious smell.

Rabbi Rubinstein leaned back heavily. "It is hard now, to be old and to be remembering these things," he said. "It is like discovering a new pain." He sighed. "I had forgotten what it was like to be hunted."

The others nodded in agreement.

Simon Winter wanted to reach out and touch the man, but could not. Instead, he said slowly: "I do not understand something. Why would this man be here? On Miami Beach, where there is a great concentration of survivors. Wouldn't this be the place where he would most likely be recognized? Why wouldn't he be in Argentina or Romania or someplace safer?"

Irving Silver shook his head. "This is where he'd be safest."

"But how?"

"You do not understand, Detective Winter," Rabbi Rubinstein said, starting slowly but rapidly accelerating his words as he spoke. "Der Schattenmann was not a Nazi! He wasn't Gestapo! He wasn't S.S.! He was a Jew, like all of us! There was no Odessa organization or Iron Cross group to help him find freedom and safety after the war! There was just himself!"

"But certainly there were organizations. The Red Cross. Groups that helped displaced persons . . ."

"Of course! That was how I arrived here."

"And me too," said Frieda Kroner.

"Not me. I had distant relatives who helped," Irving Silver

said. "But who would help Der Schattenmann? Not the Russians. They would have shot him. Bang! No trial. So who?"

"Tell me," Simon Winter asked.

"His own people. The same people he'd betrayed," Silver said.

"But not if they knew who he was, right?"

"Of course. Were not the Kapos in the camps turned over to authorities?" Silver replied. Rabbi Rubinstein nodded in agreement.

"But *he* would have known of that danger," the rabbi added.

"So what are you saying he would do?"

The three old people turned and looked at each other. For a moment Winter could hear them all breathing. It was as if they were conversing, arguing, debating, assessing this question, but without words, without gestures. Simply letting their imaginations blend together and come up with a single conclusion.

The rabbi wiped a hand slowly across his face. "He would need to become one of us. A survivor."

Frieda Kroner nodded her head. "Of course. How else?"

"But how could he fake that?"

Irving Silver frowned. "He was Der Schattenmann! He could do what he wanted!"

"But . . ." Winter hesitated. ". . . surely there were others like him. And they were caught?"

"Really? Not like him. I do not think so."

"But why here?"

"Because we are his people!"

"No one knew us better than him! That was how he was so successful. Why would he be frightened of us?"

Rabbi Rubinstein rose, but as he did, he lifted the volume of *The Destruction of the European Jews* from the table. Stein's letter fluttered to the floor, but no one moved for it. The heavy book swayed in his hands. He did not open it, and Winter realized the old rabbi could recall what was in the book by memory.

"If you remember the times," he started, "remember the times. Confusion and depravity. The Holocaust, Detective, it was like a great machine devoted to the murder of the Jews. But for the Nazis to accomplish this task—they kept talking, over and over, in all their speeches and propaganda and writings of the 'monumental' task—they had to have help. All sorts of help, from all sides . . ."

"From the Pope, who did not condemn them . . ." Irving Silver said.

"From the Allies, who did not bomb the camps or the rail routes into Dachau and Auschwitz . . ." Frieda Kroner added.

"From the non-Jewish people, the Poles and Czechs and Romanians and Italians and French and Germans who watched. Really, from the whole world, Detective, in one way or another, everyone helped. Including some of the very people they were trying to destroy."

Simon Winter sat quietly, listening.

"So, consider Auschwitz, Detective. After the Nazis did the selecting, someone had to close the doors on the gas chambers and someone had to remove the bodies afterward. Someone had to stoke the fires of the ovens and someone had to keep the whole thing working smoothly. And oftentimes those someones were ourselves."

The rabbi sat down heavily, the book in his lap.

"We helped, you see. Just by living, by doing whatever it took to stay alive, it helped perversely, to keep it all going. . . ."

He looked at Mrs. Kroner and Mr. Silver.

"Could it have been more right, more moral, just to die in the face of all that evil, Detective? These are questions that haunt philosophers. I am just an old rabbi."

He stopped, shaking his head, breathing in hard before continuing.

"It is crazy, all of it you see, Detective. Look at the world we live in today. Some days you think this is all so far away and back in the past that it cannot really have happened, but others, well, then you know that it is right there, still alive today, just as evil and terrible and waiting to rise up again.

"Der Schattenmann, he was the worst of all of us," the rabbi continued. "He was worse than the Nazis. Worse even than those strange evil things that Mr. King likes to write about."

"And now, he's here, right amongst us," Irving Silver said bitterly. "Like an infection."

"Is there not always someone like Der Schattenmann amongst us?" the rabbi asked quietly. This question went unanswered.

"Can you find him, Detective?" Frieda Kroner asked quietly.

"I do not know."

"Will you try?"

"If he's here. If what you suggest is true . . ."

"Will you search for him, Mr. Winter?"

Simon Winter felt a vast echoing sadness within himself. The answer seemed to well up through that personal darkness.

"Yes, I will try."

"Good," Frieda Kroner said. "Then I will help you, Mr. Winter."

"I too. I will help," said Irving Silver.

"Of course, I will join in as well," said Rabbi Rubinstein. "We will do whatever we can."

Frieda Kroner nodded, then reached forward and poured herself another cup of coffee. Simon Winter watched as she took a long pull at the dark cup, letting the bitter taste cascade through her. She smiled, but coldly.

"Good. And when you find him, Detective, with our help, then you will kill him."

"Frieda!" Rabbi Rubinstein interjected. "Think of what you say! Our religion speaks of forgiveness and understanding. That has always been our way!"

"Maybe so, Rabbi. But my heart speaks for all those he betrayed and who died. Think first of them, Rabbi, then talk to me of forgiveness."

She turned to Simon Winter.

"I would rather speak of justice," she said. "Find him and kill him."

Irving Silver leaned forward. "I will help. I will do whatever I can. We all will. But Frieda is right. Find him and kill him, Mr. Winter." He took a deep breath, then added: "For my dear brother Martin. And my parents and all my cousins . . ."

Frieda Kroner joined in softly. ". . . And my sister and her husband and my two little nieces and grandparents and my mother who tried so hard to save me and all the others . . ."

Simon Winter didn't reply. He stared over at the rabbi, who

was looking at the other two. He saw Rabbi Rubinstein's hand
seem to quiver as it tightened around the book in his lap.

Irving Silver spoke bluntly: "Kill him, Detective. And then
there will be one less nightmare in the world. Kill him."

And then the rabbi, too, nodded.

# SIX
## *PRAYERS FOR THE*
## *DEAD*

Simon Winter shifted about uncomfortably on a gray steel folding chair while a young rabbi spoke at the gravesite. Although the gathering was collected beneath a dark green canopy provided by the funeral home, the insistent heat of midday forced its way unbidden and unwelcome amidst the mourners. They were mostly older people, and the dark woolen suits they wore seemed to steam under the noontime sun. Simon Winter urgently wished he could loosen his tie, snugged tightly beneath the starched white collar of the sole remaining dress shirt he owned. As he looked about, he thought: We all look like we're ready to join Sophie Millstein in her coffin. He was slightly ashamed at the irreverence of his opinion, but forgave himself with the wry notation that it would not be too long before it was himself dressed out in some box or stuffed in some urn, with someone else whom he didn't know and didn't care about droning on above his head.

The rabbi, a short, rotund man, battling hard against the sweat collecting at his tight collar, raised his voice:

"This woman, Sophie Millstein, was thrust into the inferno, only to rise and through goodness and devotion, like a phoenix, become the beloved wife of Leo and the adored mother of a brilliant son, Murray . . ."

The young rabbi's voice was high-pitched, needlelike. The

words seemed to prick the still air. Winter's eyes swept up into the expanse of eggshell-blue sky, searching the horizon for gathering clouds that might carry the promise of an afternoon thundershower and the momentary relief of a steady downpour. But he saw none, and he inhaled sharply, breathing in air as hot and thick as smoke.

As he sat alone, near the rear of the gathering, he berated himself for allowing the heat to distract him.

*He* could be here, he insisted.

Over there, just beyond your eyesight, obscured by those trees. Or sitting, head down, in a row to the side, acting like a professional mourner. If he's hunting, this would be the first place he'd look, right amidst Sophie's old friends.

What he doesn't know, Winter thought, is that someone is looking for him.

Then he stopped, and let some doubt creep into his thoughts: If *he* exists at all.

To his side, Mr. Finkel and the Kadoshes paid rapt attention to the rabbi's words. Mrs. Kadosh clutched a white linen handkerchief in her hand, which she alternately dabbed at the corners of her eyes and then used to wipe the heat from her forehead. Her husband held a printed program in his hands, rolling it tightly, then spreading it out, smoothing the pages. He occasionally, surreptitiously, fanned the paper in front of him, trying without success to move some of the warmth away.

The other residents of the Sunshine Arms were spread about the gathering. Winter saw that Mr. Gonzalez, the landlord, kept his head bowed throughout the rabbi's eulogy. His daughter had accompanied her father to the service. She was as tall as her father, and wore a slim, black dress that Simon Winter thought would have served equally well at an opera's opening night as it did at a funeral.

Simon Winter sighed. For six months Mr. Gonzalez's daughter had occupied the empty apartment next to Sophie Millstein. She had enthusiastically and energetically entertained a number of boyfriends there, usually failing to close the curtain in the living room, permitting Winter to watch her. He thought she had been aware that he watched, thought, too, that she left the curtains open as an unspoken favor. He shook his head. When she had moved to fancier digs on Brickell Avenue, she had taken much of the energy out of the Sunshine Arms.

Before taking her seat next to her father, she had glanced back over her shoulder, and her eyes had met his, for just an instant, just long enough for her to pass along a small, sad smile, coupled with a slight nod, as if to remind him of what he missed in her; and this, despite the solemnity of the occasion and his troubled thoughts about his murdered neighbor, managed to bring a somewhat distracting, but altogether pleasurable, internal laugh to Simon Winter's heart.

"And so today we all feel the loss of this woman . . ." The rabbi's speech continued predictably.

He pulled his eyes off of Mr. Gonzalez's daughter's back and once again swept them across the seated mourners. If *he*'s here, he'll be looking hard, Winter thought. He'll be searching the faces, as he ransacks his own memory.

Winter centered on one man, off to his right. The man was staring hard at the rabbi. The old detective felt a quick surge within him. Why are you so curious? he wondered.

But then, just as swiftly, he saw the man turn and whisper something to an elderly woman at his side. The woman touched his arm.

No, Winter thought. You'll be alone. Aren't you always alone? If you exist.

Winter inclined his head slightly, dropping his chin toward his chest in thought. He had told Irving Silver, Frieda Kroner, and Rabbi Rubinstein not to attend the service. He did not want to give the man they feared the advantage of seeing them before he had had time to consider his own course of action. They had objected. He had insisted.

He surveyed the crowd again, looking for faces that he didn't recognize, but there were too many. Sophie Millstein had belonged to too many women's groups, bridge clubs, synagogue assemblies. There were nearly a hundred old people shifting about on the steel chairs.

The rabbi's words seemed to shimmer in the heat.

"To go through so much, only to be robbed of life near the end, is a tragedy almost too great for the heart to bear . . ."

Winter glanced about, trying to spot Detective Robinson or the young woman from the State Attorney's Office, but he did not see them. He suspected that there was someone from the Miami Beach police mingled in amidst the mourners; this had been procedure on any homicide specified as nonsubject, when he was a detective—even when the prime suspect was a different age and different race. There was still no telling who might show up, curious. He suspected that Robinson had sent a subordinate; his own skin color would have made it impossible for him to remain hidden, watching the people beneath the canopy.

Of course, whomever the detective had sent might be searching for the wrong person altogether.

Simon Winter breathed out slowly, and wrapped his fist around the printed program. He felt an unruly anger, a frustration pounding around within him.

I don't know anything, he said to himself.

All I have are some odd coincidences and a trio of frightened old folks and a nightmare from a different era.

He looked up into the sky again. He felt his anger slide away into guilt. Can you really remember how to do it? How to take some suspicions and turn them into something hard and cold and true?

He gritted his teeth.

Start acting like what you once were, he demanded.

You want them to call you Detective again? Then behave like one. Ask some questions. Find some answers.

In the front row, next to the grave, a young child of four or five fidgeted nervously, trying to speak over the rabbi's words, only to be swiftly shushed by his mother. The rabbi paused, smiled at the child, then continued:

"So who was this woman, this Sophie Millstein, who gave so much of herself, who achieved so much in her life? I feel I should learn more about this remarkable woman, so that the lessons of her life can teach me, as they have taught her son and her daughter-in-law and her beloved grandchildren . . ."

Simon Winter could only see the back of Murray Millstein. But as the rabbi spoke, he saw the attorney slide his arm around his wife's shoulders and reach all the way to his son, where his hand remained. The rabbi continued, finally switching effortlessly into Hebrew, speaking the kaddish over the coffin, but Winter no longer heard the words, and no longer felt the oppressive heat. All he saw was the hand of the young father, lingering on his son's shoulder, and the son gently leaning his head toward the hand, resting his cheek there, reassured, all the terrifying child fears of death and dying destroyed in that instant by his father's firm touch.

Winter hung near the end of the reception line, following the service, waiting for a moment when he would have more than a second, because he wanted to do more than simply murmur a few words of solace and head off. As the gathering thinned and he saw the young attorney start to search for his wife and children, he stepped forward.

"Mr. Millstein, I'm Simon Winter. I was one of your mother's neighbors. . . ."

"Of course, Mr. Winter. My mother spoke of you often."

"I am sorry for your loss. . . ."

"Thank you."

"But I was wondering, have the police—"

"They say they're making progress, and that they'll keep me informed. You were once a policeman, true? I seem to remember my mother—"

"Yes. Here in Miami. I was a detective."

"My mother spoke highly of you. She spoke highly of all her neighbors. What was your specialty?"

"Homicide."

Murray Millstein paused, as if measuring the weight of Simon Winter's one word response. He was a short man, slight, but with a wiry appearance, like a distance runner, and an alertness that seemed to speak of attention to detail. The old detective thought that whatever tears Murray Millstein was destined to shed over his mother's murder would be dispensed in private. He eyed Winter carefully before responding quietly.

"The Miami Beach police seem quite capable. Is that your impression?"

"Yes. I'm sure they are. It's just, well, is there somewhere I could ask you a few questions? Somewhere away from this?"

Winter gestured, and as he did, he saw the rabbi and the funeral director moving toward the two of them.

"We plan to sit shiva back in Long Island. We're supposed to fly out tonight. Is there something specific you wanted to ask about?"

"No, I just, it was something your mother said to me, shortly before her death."

"Something she said?"

"Yes."

"Which you think has some connection . . ."

"I'm not sure. It bothered me. Maybe I'm simply old, with an overwrought imagination. It probably wasn't anything important. You should trust the Miami Beach police. I'm certain your mother's death will be a high priority case."

Murray Millstein hesitated, then responded quickly.

"This afternoon, I'm meeting some movers at my mother's apartment. Four P.M. Why don't we speak then?"

Winter nodded, and the younger man turned away from him in order to address the approaching pair.

Simon Winter was waiting by the cherub in the courtyard of the Sunshine Arms when Murray Millstein, accompanied by a man wearing an ill-fitting tan suit, arrived. The murdered woman's son took a quick glance around before walking to the apartment door. There was a large red printed sign posted there: CRIME SCENE NO UNAUTHORIZED ENTRY. Winter saw the younger man stop, with a key poised in the air. The attorney turned to the man in the suit and said: "I don't want to go in. Just walk through the place quickly, and remember not to touch anything. Then we can talk."

The man in the suit nodded, and Murray Millstein unlocked the door. Then he turned toward Winter and sat down heavily on the front steps.

"I wanted her to move into a retirement home. You know, one

of those places up in Fort Lauderdale that specialize in elderly people. Especially ones that are alone. A planned community. Twenty-four-hour security. Bingo games. A recreation center."

"She mentioned that once."

"She wouldn't do it. She liked it here."

"Sometimes, when you get older, change is more frightening than whatever threat is out there."

"That's probably true. But it's only relevant if all those things that are out there don't show up one night and murder you in your sleep." Murray Millstein's voice was heavy with bitter guilt. "Are you the same, Mr. Winter?"

"Yes. No. Who knows? I wouldn't want to move into one of those developments either. Of course, when I finally got there, I'd probably like it. . . ."

"That's the problem, isn't it?"

"I guess so." Winter sat down on the steps next to Murray Millstein.

"I can't go in," the younger man said. "I thought I could. I thought I needed to. You know, see where it happened. But I don't want to." He took a deep breath. "Is there blood?"

Simon Winter shook his head. "No. Not really. It's a bit of a mess. All crime scenes are. Fingerprint dust on the furniture. Signs of people tramping in and out. Your mother would have been embarrassed. She kept a clean home."

Murray Millstein smiled. "She would have been mortified to think that she died in disarray." Sadness rode every word, despite the upturn at the corners of his mouth.

"True enough."

The younger man exhaled slowly. "It's unbelievably hard," he said quietly. "You have this relationship that's filled with all the mundane and difficult parts of life. Trying to get your mother to do something she doesn't want to do. Complaining to your wife. Then having her defeat all that irritation by sending presents to her grandkids. I knew she was getting old. I suppose I knew there wouldn't be a lot of time left. And there were so many things I needed to say. When my father died, I saw it, you know. I saw how terrible it was to want to say things and then not have the chance. So I was determined to make sure I told my mother everything I wanted to. But one thing, then another, and I was so busy and time slips away so quickly, Mr. Winter. It just races away, no matter what you do. And then it gets cut short because some fucking animal needs ten bucks or twenty bucks so that he can buy himself another pipe of fucking crack or whatever and he thinks it's worth my mother's life to get that. . . ."

Murray Millstein's voice had risen, like a river of anguish flooded by storm waters, until his words were reverberating about the courtyard.

"Some fucking junkie. An addict. That's what they think. Shoots my mother's life into his fucking arm or smokes her future in some fucking pipe. I hope when they catch the fucking beast they'll let me tear his heart out."

He paused for a breath of air.

"Fucking animal . . ." he added caustically.

Then he stopped, as if he was uncomfortable letting his emotions fly about the courtyard with such unbridled intensity. He stared out straight ahead for a moment, before turning to Winter and asking:

"Do you think they'll catch the bastard?"

"I don't know. Their techniques have improved. Maybe."

"But maybe not, right?"

"Maybe not. Most of the homicides that get solved are ones where you know right away who did it. A husband. A wife. A business partner. Another drug dealer. Whomever. When two lives just touch randomly . . ."

"It's harder."

"That's correct."

"Did you talk to the detective? The black guy?"

"Yes. He seemed quite competent."

"I hope so. We'll see."

"Keep the pressure on," Winter said.

"What?"

"Don't stop with the phone calls. Letters to the state attorney. Write the damn newspaper, the television stations. Keep reminding them. It will help. It will keep the case at the top of someone's file cabinet, instead of getting buried under all the other crap that starts to build up."

"You know about that? Cases that just slip away?"

"Every detective does. Keep them thinking about this case. Maybe you'll get some results."

"That's good advice."

They were both silent for a moment, and then Murray Millstein swept his arm in front of them in a wide gesture.

"I'm thirty-nine years old and I want to get the hell out of here and never come back. I want this goddamn moving man to finish his estimate and I want to get on a plane and go back to my home. . . ."

He half turned toward Winter.

"So, ask me your questions."

"On the day that she was killed, your mother came to me. She had been scared. She saw someone from her past. Berlin, 1943."

"Really?"

"Does the phrase *Der Schattenmann* mean anything to you?"

Murray Millstein paused, then replied: "No. Not that I recall." He said the name, as if by repeating it he might clarify it: "Der Schattenmann? No. It doesn't ring a bell."

"Did your mother talk about her wartime experiences much?"

Murray Millstein shook his head. "Do you know much about the relationships between Holocaust survivors and their children, Mr. Winter?"

"No."

"They are, uh, problematical." He placed a hand over his forehead, as if wiping away some difficult thought, before continuing.

"She would not talk about the camps. Or her life before the camps. Or her life up until the time she met my father. When he brought her to the U.S., she used to say that was when her life started. Do you know she couldn't speak English when she came here? Not only did she learn the language, but she was equally determined to erase—just totally and completely eradicate—any trace of her German accent. My father said she would stay up late at night, practicing in front of a mirror."

Simon Winter shrugged. "I see," he said.

"No, you don't," Murray Millstein replied, as if irritated. "No German cars. No German products. No German anything. If a story came on the goddamn television about Germany, she shut it off. You've got to understand that even if it was never spoken about, her survival dominated our house. Everything my father did. Everything I did, as a child, growing up, right up to the day she was murdered, had some connection, unspoken, unsaid, shit, I don't know, with what happened to her. It was always there. Always."

Murray Millstein shook his head.

"I grew up with ghosts," he said flatly. "Six million ghosts."

"But she didn't speak of her experiences. . . ."

"Not to me. But she made a videotape. Last year. For the Holocaust Center Library here on the Beach. I haven't seen it, but she made it."

"How did—"

"I found out because they sent me a solicitation. Fund-raising. They wanted a contribution. I sent them money. I called her up and said I wanted to see the tape, and we argued. Probably the only real argument we'd had in years. She forbade me—until after she was gone."

"Will you go see it now?"

"No. Yes. I don't know."

Murray Millstein stood up. The man in the tan suit emerged from the apartment. "How much?" the young lawyer asked.

"To Long Island. Total contents? Twenty-two hundred, packed up and marked. That's our special move service," the suit replied.

"Fine," Murray Millstein said. "I'm sure it's very special." He handed the man the key. "It may be a couple of weeks before the police release the apartment. . . ."

"Don't worry, Mr. Millstein. You just call, and we'll come right over. I'll send you a contract.".

The young man nodded, then looked down at his watch. "I'm leaving now," he said to Winter. "You go."

"What?"

"You go to see the tape, Mr. Winter. Then let me know about it."

Murray Millstein turned and took a couple of steps into the courtyard before stopping and looking back over his shoulder at Simon Winter. "I took German, you know."

"I'm sorry?"

"I studied German. In high school. We had a language requirement and I took German. She hated that. Hardly spoke to me for an entire academic year. She wouldn't even allow a German dictionary into the house. I had to do all my studying at school. I got an A."

Winter didn't know what to reply. He thought that sometimes the world seemed to accumulate an awful array of pain and hurt and deliver it unfairly, unequally, right on the heart of the unlucky.

Murray Millstein appeared to be thinking hard, for just an instant, before adding: "Do you know what it means?"

"What?" Simon Winter looked up, almost startled, as if all his thoughts had been suddenly carried into the vortex of a strong wind and he was only brought back to earth by the sound of the younger man's voice.

"Der Schattenmann," Murray Millstein said, shrugging his shoulders. "Do you know what it means?"

Simon Winter shook his head. He had not thought to translate the phrase.

"It means the Shadow Man." He paused, then said: "I wonder what she meant by that?"

But Murray Millstein did not wait for a reply. Simon Winter watched the young attorney turn and walk quickly through the courtyard, past the trumpeting cherub, whose music, the old detective imagined, was on this occasion a dirge.

# SEVEN
## URGENCY

**W**HEN Espy Martinez arrived at the Dade State Attorney's Office the morning after Sophie Millstein's funeral, there were a pair of messages waiting for her: one from Walter Robinson, and the other a summons to meet with the chief assistant in the felony division. She knew instantly that he would want to know what progress was being made on the case, so, despite the fact that he'd marked his note with a red ink IMMEDIATELY, she hurried through the warren of prosecutors' cubicles to her own and swiftly dialed the number for the homicide department at the Beach police.

Walter Robinson came on the line after a moment's delay.

"Miss Martinez," he said, "glad you phoned."

"Detective, I'm about to be called in front of the chief assistant and asked to give a status report on the Millstein killing. What can you tell me?"

"Well, the first thing I'd say is to not worry that much about Abe Lasser. He may look like Dracula, but he's not really all that terrifying. Especially during the daytime."

Espy Martinez wanted to smile at the detective's description of her boss, but instead imposed a rigidity on her words to mask her own nervousness. "He's going to want to know where we stand. Where do we stand, Detective?"

Robinson started to say one thing, then paused, and asked: "Are you getting some heat on this case?"

"No," she replied. "Not yet. But I think I'm about to."

Robinson nodded, though she couldn't see his head moving. "I thought you might. Well, I got the preliminary autopsy and crime scene reports this morning. Here's what we have. Death was by manual strangulation. Bruising to the larynx and carotid artery areas suggests that the distance between the killer's thumb and index finger is five point seven inches. There was no sign of sexual assault. Preliminary blood toxicology showed traces of Dolmane. That's a commonly prescribed sleeping agent. There were some signs that she was beaten about a bit, but I think that happened only in the first seconds. The sleeping pills must have had her pretty knocked out, so much that probably the first thing she was aware of was the guy choking her to death. Not much time to fight back. There weren't any significant defensive wounds on her hands or arms . . ."

Robinson traveled through the minutiae of Sophie Millstein's final seconds of life with a practiced, routine tone. Espy Martinez listened, trying to attach the words of the clipped, official reports to the real-life terror that engendered them, but found, after a few moments, that she could not.

"Actually, that sort of bothers me," Robinson said quietly.

"What?"

"Well, guy breaks in, murders a sleeping woman, then ransacks the place as fast as he can and splits. You see the glitch?"

"No."

"Why kill a sleeping woman? Why not just take what you want real quiet-like and get the hell out?"

"She woke up."

"Yeah. Probably. But wouldn't she have really screamed? Or fought hard?"

"The neighbors said they heard a noise."

"Yeah, but not a real scream. More like a shout. And what about the cat? Mr. Boots? Why kill the damn cat?"

"Maybe the cat was making noise?"

"A cat? Maybe Fluffy or Fido or some silly little barking toy poodle or something, but a cat? Come on. The stupid thing would just hightail it right out the patio door and never be seen again."

"So, what are you saying?" she asked impatiently.

"Nothing. It just bothered me."

Espy Martinez remembered the stiff body of the cat, its eyes bulged out, teeth bared, frozen in death. She shuddered. It bothered me too, she thought, but what does it have to do with anything? She ignored this and spoke out with a false bravado:

"Okay. So?"

"So, nothing," the detective said.

"Keep going, then."

Robinson sighed, and turned his attention back to the sheaf of reports on his desk. He thought sometimes that he was spending the majority of his adult life either reading reports or preparing them. "Okay, let's see. Oh, there was one postmortem cut on the victim's neck."

"Yes. And?"

"Well, there have been a number of break-ins throughout Sophie's neighborhood in the past coupla weeks. Robbery is sending over case summaries. Maybe I can tie the perp into them."

"Makes sense. What else?"

"What else?"

Espy Martinez glanced at the clock, and knew that the chief assistant would be looking for her. "Detective . . ."

"Actually, you can call me Walter. Most of the prosecutors in your office do."

"I've got to talk to Lasser."

"You want to know if I'm optimistic. Well, the answer is no. I'm never optimistic about this sort of case, Miss Martinez. Statistically, well, nationally we solve maybe one in three. Locally, we might be a bit worse. But I'm trying. Lasser knows the score. Don't let him muscle you."

"Okay, Walter, I'll try . . ." She laughed, just a small amount. ". . . but it's the blood dripping from his fangs that gets me disconcerted. So, please tell me something that's gonna help put the guy who killed Sophie Millstein on Death Row."

"You want to know how we're going to convict her killer, huh?"

"Yes." Espy Martinez couldn't hide the remaining nervousness in her voice.

"Well, more bad news is this: no gun to trace. That makes things more difficult. Guns are great. They make noise, leave a mess, they're easy to match up in a laboratory, and people aren't generally smart enough to dispose of them where we can't find them. No knife either. Did you know that strangulation is a remarkably efficient way of murdering someone? It generally leaves little connective tissue between killer and victim. But on the plus side, forensics came up with two prints from her dresser, and a third from the jewelry box we found down the alleyway. They also managed to lift a partial thumbprint—just a small fragment, can't really tell if it's usable or not—from the victim's neck. That's a rarity, Miss Martinez. But if we can get a match, well, even the most incompetent prosecutor will nail the sonofabitch."

"I'm not incompetent, Detective."

"That's not what I meant. . . ."

There was a momentary silence between the two. Walter Robinson thought it would have been hard for him to say something stupider to Espy Martinez.

"Okay, Detective. So, now I see how we get a conviction. Great. One problem, though: How are you going to go about catching the killer?"

"Well, first we're going to check the best of the prints we've got against those obtained at the other break-ins and robberies around the Beach in the last few months, see if we can't pick up the bastard's pattern. Then I'm gonna work some of the pawnshops and fences, see if we can't find some of that jewelry. Sophie's son gave me a pretty good description of some of the pieces stolen. I've already sent out a flyer to some places. Gonna look hard for that necklace with Sophie's name on it."

Espy Martinez was going to remark on the offhand way the detective referred to the victim by her first name, but stopped herself. "And then what?"

"And then hope we get lucky. We'll run the print through the county's Gotcha Computer, but I don't know—"

"The what?"

"The Gotcha Computer. The fancy one they got last year with all that federal money. Supposed to be able to match crime scene prints with prints stored in the computer's memory."

"Will it work?"

"It has before. But only if our bad guy has been arrested and printed in the last year or so. We'll see."

Espy Martinez stood up at the side of her desk. "Is there anything else you can tell me, before I talk to Lasser?"

"How about, I've got six other open cases."

"How about, this one stays at the top of the list," she replied before hanging up.

Walter Robinson cradled the telephone against his ear, listening to the dial tone. He wondered what Espy Martinez was like when she wasn't frightened, and then he wondered whether she was ever not frightened.

Abraham Lasser was a thickset man with a drooping mustache and a wiry mane of gray-streaked black hair that seemed to explode from his scalp in an uncontrolled wildness. This was contradicted by his penchant for wearing sleek, Italian double-breasted suits and shoes always polished to a reflective sheen. Stalking through the maze of offices on the sixth floor of the Metropolitan Justice Building, he seemed like some fashion designer's nightmare. When he made an appearance in one of the fourth-floor courtrooms, he showed a snarling, sarcastic side that was routinely mocked and just as routinely feared by criminal defense attorneys. He was a man who placed great value on intimidation, both of his opponents and the people who worked for him.

Espy Martinez had been assigned to his felony division for eight weeks. In that time she had met with him only a half-dozen or so times, and on each occasion it was merely to get his authorization for a plea bargain. This was standard procedure in the office, and had been since one unfortunate assistant had agreed to an unauthorized plea in a weak case of spouse against spouse assault, and the accused had walked directly from the courtroom to the automatic rifle he kept in his car, which he turned on himself, after gunning down his ex-wife and her two sisters outside the Justice Building. The wags in the office suggested it would have been better for the assistant who offered the plea bargain if he'd been assassinated as well, death preferable to facing Abe Lasser's volcanic anger.

She took a deep breath outside his office and knocked and entered.

Lasser's secretary looked up at her and smiled. "Go on in. He's been waiting for you." Then she pointedly glanced at her wristwatch.

"I needed to speak with a homicide detective," Espy Martinez said.

"Go right on in, dear," the secretary said.

Espy Martinez marched into the office. Lasser was behind his desk, on the telephone. He waved her into a seat and continued talking. She let her eyes wander about the room. There were several framed diplomas and Bar Association memberships. There were also the obligatory photographs of Lasser and various county and state politicians, including an enlarged color snapshot of the chief assistant and the governor, tanned, grinning, in T-shirts and shorts, standing on the edge of a dock, each holding up a large dead fish.

Separated a short distance from these photos were seven other pictures, each carefully matted and framed in glossy black steel. No politicians in these photos; they were full-face and right and left profile mug shots taken at the county jail. Espy Martinez stared at the faces that looked sullenly out at her. Four of the seven were of black men, two apparently Hispanic, one with a teardrop tattoo beneath one eye and the other sporting a scar running through the hair of his eyebrow. There was one white man, who stared out with an unsettling malevolent insouciance. She looked at this face, then over at one of the black men. He had a sleepy, almost nonchalant appearance, eyes partly closed, as if being photographed in jail were the stuff of daily routine for him.

Abe Lasser suddenly started speaking loudly:

"Look! Goddammit! If you print that before I get into court, the bastards will walk. Walk, understand? You want that on your conscience?"

He cupped a hand over the receiver, smiled at Espy Martinez, and whispered: "The fucking *Herald* got hold of the grand jury testimony in the Abella beating."

Espy Martinez nodded. Enrique Abella was a drunken motorist who took a half-dozen policemen on a high-speed chase and then, when finally cornered, surrendered loudly and abusively and arrived at the county lockup some forty-five minutes later with three fractured ribs, multiple contusions, a broken jaw and six missing teeth, a second-degree concussion, and an eye that might not regain its sight.

He swiveled rapidly in his seat.

"No, damn it, you listen. You hold off until after the indictments are handed down—they're gonna be sealed, I promise. I'll make sure you—and only you—know when those bastards are gonna turn themselves in for prints and mugs. You'll have the only camera there, got it? That's the deal."

He paused, listening, before shouting a response:

"No, you fucking don't have to talk to any goddamn editor! We've known each other for ten years! And if after all that you can't make a deal where you end up getting two fucking exclusives just by holding off . . ."

Abe Lasser started to nod. He was smiling. His voice instantly went smooth.

"Of course I trust you. And you trust me. Everyone trusts each other. And you get something and I get something and everyone's happy, right?"

He suddenly leaned forward and spoke quietly, without bombast, but cool and menacing.

"But screw me on this and you won't see another story out of this office for the next hundred years. And neither will the new asshole the *Herald* replaces you with. Or his replacement. And you'll all end up in Opa-Locka covering all-night meetings at the zoning board of adjustment."

There was a momentary pause, then Abe Lasser leaned back abruptly, bursting into laughter.

"Well, hell, you're probably right about that. Point well taken."

He cupped his hand over the phone again and said: "The sonofabitch says I'll be lucky if I end up prosecuting jaywalking and litterbug cases in what's left of Homestead."

He turned back to his conversation.

"So we have a deal? Good. Wanna have lunch sometime? My treat? Hell, maybe it ought to be your treat. Call my secretary."

He hung up the telephone.

"Can you do that?" Espy Martinez asked. "I mean, promise him that he'll be the only reporter around when those cops turn themselves in . . ."

"Of course not," Abe Lasser replied.

Lasser smiled and shifted some papers about on his desk. For a moment he swiveled away from her, looking out his window, which had a view of Miami's inner city, stretching out beyond the stolid, squat architecture of the county jail.

"So, Espy, do you know where I live?"

The question took her by surprise. "No, sir. I don't believe I do. . . ."

"We've got a real nice house right on the La Gorce Country Club golf course right in the middle of Miami Beach. Old, built in the Twenties. You know the type: high ceilings, Cuban tile floors, Art Deco window frames. My wife spends most of her time fixing it up because something breaks every damn week. Plumbing. Roof leaks. Air-conditioning. The A.C. went out yesterday morning. You know how fucking hot it was last night?"

"Yes. But—"

"So, I'm sitting there, Espy, worrying mainly about how I'm gonna put the slam to these four cops and thinking how lucky I am that Enrique fucking Abella isn't black so we're not having a riot, but also thinking that maybe because he's Cuban those bastards are gonna make all sorts of political trouble over the case, and it's ten million degrees in the house and it's gonna cost me three grand to fix the damn central air unit and there's sweat dripping off my forehead onto the sports section I'm trying to read and guess who calls me on the telephone?"

Espy Martinez didn't reply. She didn't think she was supposed to interrupt her boss's soliloquy with anything so mundane as a question.

Abe Lasser leaned forward, smiling, but without pleasure. "My fucking rabbi calls me."

"I beg your pardon?"

"My rabbi. Rabbi Lev Samuelson, Temple Beth-El. This guy that I don't talk to except once a year when he's raising money for State of Israel bonds. But last night he's not selling bonds. You know what he wants to know?"

"When we're going to arrest Sophie Millstein's killer."

"Precisely. Apparently his fellow rabbi, from some other temple, one down in South Beach, called him, because somehow he's figured out that Rabbi Samuelson knows me, and guess what?"

Abe Lasser slammed a hand down on the desk.

"And I couldn't tell him. So you tell me: When are we going to make an arrest? Who's the detective on this anyhow?"

"Walter Robinson."

Abe Lasser smiled. "Good. At least he has some idea about what he's doing and he's not a complete and total fuckup. And he says?"

"He's working on it."

Lasser shook his head. "Do better than that."

"The forensic and autopsy reports suggest that—"

"I don't care. You just find me her killer. Then I can go to my rabbi and tell him that the Dade State Attorney's Office follows the same principle established in Exodus, 21:12. You know that passage, Espy?"

"No, sir."

"Look it up." Lasser stood and gestured toward the door. "First real case, right?"

"Well, I handled the Williams prosecution, sir, the home invasions. That was in the papers. . . ."

"I know. That's what got you assigned to my division." Lasser moved out from behind the desk and walked to the wall where the seven photographs of prisoners were hung. "You were looking at these. You know who they are?"

"No, sir."

"These are the seven men I've personally put on Death Row. Now I ought to take this guy down, because he was executed last year. A gentleman named Blair Sullivan, who killed so many people I've lost count. Twenty-two-hundred volts courtesy of the State of Florida and yours truly. Went to meet his Maker cursing, foul-mouthed, and unrepentant, not an approach I particularly recommend. Anyway, I keep him up there with his compatriots for sentimental reasons."

Espy Martinez couldn't imagine what those reasons might be, but she was certain that the one thing they weren't was sentimental.

"You find Sophie Millstein's killer and then you can put a mug shot on the wall of your office and I can call my rabbi and everyone will be happy. Except for the killer, of course. And Sophie Millstein."

He looked at Espy Martinez.

"Exodus, 21:12. I'll want another report by the end of the week. And make sure there's some progress, okay? Jump on Walter Robinson, and jump on him today. And for Christ's sake don't listen to him complain about all the other fucking cases he's got. Tell him he's only got one case. My rabbi's case."

Then, with a chopping wave of his hand, the chief assistant dismissed her, returning to the paperwork on his desk.

Espy Martinez quickly exited the office, but after closing the door behind her, she turned to Abe Lasser's secretary.

"Do you keep a Bible handy?" she asked.

The woman nodded, reached into a drawer, and produced a leather-bound copy of the Bible, handing it to Espy Martinez.

"Page seventeen," the secretary said, turning back to her work.

Espy Martinez flipped the thin, crinkly pages quickly. It wasn't hard to find the proper passage. It had been marked with a yellow highlighting pen:

> He that smiteth a man, so that he die,
> shall be surely put to death . . .

Walter Robinson ignored the thick pressure of the evening humidity as he stood in the alleyway behind the Sunshine Arms adjacent to the trash canister where Sophie Millstein's jewelry box had been discovered.

He spoke steadily and quietly to himself as he dissected the crime, occasionally pausing to make a small notation on a pad of paper. He walked back to the spot where Kadosh, the neighbor, stood and saw the perpetrator. He thought: Kadosh must have seen him as he turned and discarded the box. Eye to eye for just a second. Face lit up by that streetlight over there. Then he ran. Did he know he'd been seen? Yes. So: panic. No thinking. No nothing. Just gotta-get-outta-here panic.

Walter Robinson moved from the end of the alley to a side street.

Well, my man, your blood pressure must have been soaring, ripping a hole in your chest, adrenaline hammering away inside your ears. Breathing short and shallow, just excited, afraid, and juiced all at once, didn't even have time yet to think about the bag of crack you'd be able to buy. You wanted to just get the hell out of there, didn't you? You were scared as hell, and you just wanted to make tracks. Get safe.

So, what did you do?

His eyes swept down the block toward Jefferson Avenue.

Did you have a car? Possibly. Something old and nondescript. But maybe you sold it a few weeks ago, because you needed the money, didn't you? So maybe it was something you borrowed? Who would lend a junkie a car? Did you get a friend to drive you? Another crackhead looking for an easy score? Maybe. But I doubt it. Crackheads don't make for lasting partnerships.

In the distance the diesel whine of a bus coming down the avenue filled the air. Walter Robinson listened carefully, still thinking hard.

Did you ride our nice, safe public transportation system here and then home again? Did you take the J-50? That would have carried you to Forty-second Street. And then you could transfer to the G-75. That would take you right across the Julia Tuttle Causeway, right back into the heart of Liberty City, and you'd be home and feeling safe.

Walter Robinson felt the night starting to gnaw away at the remains of the day.

Is that what you did, my man? he asked himself. Did you use a goddamn bus to escape from a murder?

If Sophie Millstein's killing was simply an afterthought to robbery, then yes, absolutely, Robinson told himself.

He slowly walked back to where he'd parked his car. He felt

there was something terribly wrong in a world where killers rode public transportation. And then he thought how crazy that idea was. Murder is as routine as anything else, he told himself, as ordinary as a bus stop. He got behind the wheel and, after checking his watch, put the unmarked car in gear and headed to the Beach's bus terminal.

Exhaust fumes seemed to blend with the remains of the day's heat, creating a thick, sticky, noxious concoction. Walter Robinson felt as if he was walking into a basement or attic, fighting through a tangle of cobwebs. He wondered how anyone could breathe inside the terminal, even though it was constructed like a covered parking area, with huge gaps where walls should have been, ostensibly to let the air breeze through, though Robinson thought that no self-respecting gust of wind would ever volunteer to enter the poisonous space.

Inside a small office the night dispatcher turned through the pages of a logbook. She was a gruff, middle-aged woman, with carrot-red hair teased into a helmet upon her head, who talked interchangeably to herself and to him. As she searched for the proper log page, Robinson spied a pinup calendar on the wall. August was illustrated by a not particularly pretty bleached blonde, slightly overweight, with pendulous breasts that were offered toward the camera with a slightly dopey expression on her face. The detective wondered why the dispatcher allowed August to stay on the wall, almost mocking her.

"Here it is. Jesus, why can't those dumb drivers ever fill this stuff out right? I've got what you need, Detective."

He leaned toward the logbook, and the dispatcher continued speaking.

"These are the routes closest to your homicide. Christ, what's the world coming to, anyway, little old lady, Jesus, I saw it in the papers, Christ, and we were running a single shift on that night, but there was one trainee too, riding in the number six. Ahhh, no one reports any incidents, except one guy, right here, says he kicked a pair of teenagers off near Jefferson, because they were playing a boom box too loud. I hate that kinda music, what do they see in it anyway? Country and western for me. Not this rap shit. That's surprising. . . ."

"Why is that?" Walter Robinson asked.

The dispatcher looked up at him as if he were crazy. "Two teenagers. Boom box. You know the kinda weaponry those kids mighta been carrying? I'm gonna stop my bus and kick them off and maybe get a bullet in my chest from some angry punk? No thank you, Detective. Just gonna let 'em ride, and listen to that crap loud as they like. . . ."

"But nothing else?"

"Nah. Not that night. But you know, these damn incident forms take damn forever to fill out, why'd they ever come up with them, triplicate for Christ's sake, I dunno. So, maybe somebody remembers something, maybe helps you out. Bus drivers see a lot, you know. We see a lot."

He nodded, and the dispatcher pointed him toward a grimy drivers' lounge, which sported a soda machine, a cigarette machine, and a candy machine, all with handwritten OUT OF ORDER signs taped to their fronts. A couple of drivers were sitting on a beaten, fake leather couch, waiting for their shift to begin. They looked up as Robinson entered and identified himself.

An older man, bald, with a short ring of gray hair, nodded when he explained what he was searching for.

"That was me and the kid driving that route," the bus driver said.

"Th-Th-That's right," a considerably younger man, wearing a much fresher and cleaner blue uniform, stuttered in agreement.

"You recall that night?" Robinson asked.

"All the nights are pretty much the same. Up and down. Up and down. Late at night, mostly tired people. Drunk people. I don't know if I remember anything special. . . ."

"A young black man. Nervous. In a hurry . . ."

"No—"

"S-S-S-Sure, th-th-there was, remember? You hadda yell at the g-g-g-guy to s-s-s-siddown. . . ." the younger driver interrupted. He looked eagerly at the older man, who rolled his eyes back in frustration.

"I don't like to make trouble," the driver said in a halfhearted apology. "Ain't my business. I just drive."

"Tell me," Robinson demanded.

"Not much to say. Guy gets on. Slams some change in the box. Bus is nearly empty, but he stands there, looking out, acting nervous, just like you said, and telling me to get going, get going, put a move on it. Like he was in some big fucking hurry. I yelled for him to siddown and he told me to fuck myself, and I told him I'd rip his fucking head off and that kept up for a moment or two, you know, fuck me, fuck you, so a couple of stops up, I told him to either siddown or get off. He sat down. Not that big a deal, Detective. Happens all the time."

"Where did he get off?"

"Godfrey Road. Transfer to a city bus. Don't know where he was heading, but I can guess."

Walter Robinson nodded. "Recognize the guy again?"

"Maybe. Yeah, probably."

"S-S-Sure," said the younger driver.

"See him, call me. I'll be back in touch. May want you to look at some mug shots."

"I'll be here."

Robinson left the bus terminal. He drove a few blocks over to Collins Avenue, parked, and walked through to the boardwalk that the Army Corps of Engineers had constructed for the old folks to walk up and down the beach. He stood, leaning up against the wooden railing, staring out toward the waves. There was small surf running, just the mere insinuation of ocean power, rebuking the sand and rough coral stone beach. He let the hot salt air clear his lungs, and he talked to himself with some astonishment: You were right, goddammit. He rode the damn bus. And now, maybe, you've got a chance.

He inhaled long and hard and thought: Screw the statistics.

Walter Robinson spoke to the night sky and expanse of dark sea and the man he believed had killed Sophie Millstein. *You thought you could just come over here and rob and kill a little old lady. Well, you were goddamn wrong.*

*I'm going to find you.*

# EIGHT

## _THE WOMAN WHO_
## _━━━━━━TOLD A LIE_

THE young woman closed a shade, making the room
seem gray. There was a moment's delay while she fiddled with
the videotape machine, then an electronic interference bar scarred
the television picture. A second later Simon Winter saw Sophie
Millstein on the screen.

He leaned forward in his chair, listening carefully. The young
woman sat down next to him.

Sophie Millstein wore an expression that mingled a small
amount of anxiety with discomfort. Winter noted she was wearing one of her finer, go-to-services dresses and realized that she
had fixed her hair carefully. She wore white gloves on her hands
and she clutched a matching pocketbook. For an instant he wondered how he had failed to take notice of her appearance on a day
when she had left the Sunshine Arms dressed up, as if ready for a
wedding.

"Do I look okay?" she asked nervously.

A voice off camera replied: "You look fine."

"I was worried," Sophie Millstein said. "I've never been on
television, and I wanted to look nice. This dress . . ."

Her voice trailed off, its tone a question mark.

"You look just fine," repeated the off-camera answer. Simon

Winter recognized the voice of the young woman who sat quietly beside him.

"I don't know what I'm supposed to do," Sophie Millstein said.

"Just relax and don't worry about the camera," the young woman's voice reassured.

Sophie Millstein shifted about in her seat. "I'm not so sure this is a good idea," she said hesitantly.

"Just ignore the camera, Sophie. You'll get used to it in no time. Just about everyone is nervous at first."

"Really? Everyone?"

"Everyone."

"Well, that makes me feel better. But I don't know what it is I'm supposed to say."

"What do you want to say?"

"I don't really have much to say. Not at all."

"But you came here," the young woman said. Her voice was soft. "Something told you to come here and tell us something. What was that?"

Sophie Millstein hesitated again, and Simon Winter could see her eyes narrow with concentration.

"They should all know," she replied.

"Who should know?"

"All the people too young to remember."

"What should they know?" the young woman prompted off camera.

"What happened. The truth. Because it really happened."

Sophie Millstein's jaw clamped shut and she folded her arms across her chest.

After a brief quiet, the voice of the young woman, soothing, coaxing, asked: "Why don't you just tell me what happened to you? That's a good enough place to start."

Sophie Millstein opened her mouth once, then closed it tightly again. Winter could see her lower lip quivering ever so slightly. She remained like this for almost a minute, the videotape machine recording her silence faithfully.

Then, finally, Sophie Millstein gasped, as if she'd been holding her breath. A few words trickled out: "These are things I wanted to forget so I do not talk about. Not for many years, not even with Leo. I wish he were here now, because he would help me. . . ."

"But he's not here, and you've got to do it alone."

Sophie Millstein nodded. Tears forced their way into her eyes and she struggled with her composure. Again silence crept onto the tape, save for a rasping noise that the old woman made as she fought for air.

"Alone," she said finally. She looked across at the camera, and then Simon Winter saw his neighbor on the television screen seem to gather herself. She bit down on her quivering lip, straightened her shoulders, and looked out, directly at the camera, shedding discomfort and the terror tyranny of memory, and began speaking, a torrent of words and images bursting through, a maelstrom of recollection. Like a wave, it broke upon Simon Winter, and he gripped the edge of his chair to keep his own balance.

". . . We were three days on the train. Jammed down together, like animals, in our own filth and dirt. People died around us, one lady, I never knew her name, she died and for eight hours I could feel her weight pressed up against my back, and I couldn't do anything about it until the old man she was next to, he died too, and I could push her backwards so that the dead fell against the dead, and I remember how still she was, and white, like someone had carved her out of stone. I kept thinking afterwards that I should have found out her name. I wanted to know her name, so that I could tell someone. But I didn't. The air, I can still taste the air in that train. Every morning, still. I remember it. Maybe that's why I came down here to Florida, because the air is so clean, and I wouldn't have to remember it the way it was those three days. It was like compressed together evil, just thick and harsh, like a disease covering us. Hansi held me, that was my brother Hans, he was fourteen, two years younger than me, but he was strong, he was always so strong. I was short, but he was tall and he held me so I wouldn't try to help Mama or Papa, who was coughing and grew so weak, I thought he would die, but he kept waving to me and saying, I'm fine, I'm fine, don't worry about me. Everything will be all right, but of course it wasn't, though, I knew we would die when we got to the place, Auschwitz, but still, when they opened the door and the fresh air came in, I thought it would be all right to die, because just once I could breathe fresh air again, but even that wasn't to be, because even in the cold, the stench from the dying was so great, I couldn't breathe, and they were yelling *Raus! Raus!* and everyone had to pile out of the train, and we were clutching each other, trying to stay together but I couldn't hold Hansi anymore, because they made us get into lines, women on one side and men on the other, and I saw him holding my father and I didn't know where my mother was, and they kept yelling, forcing us in line, the dogs were barking and snarling and I didn't even see anyone try to run, we were all so weak and stumbling toward a table. The S.S. man just looked and asked a question or two and then pointed one way or the other, but of course, you know all about that. That's been told over and over, but it happened. It happened to me. He sat there, with his gray greatcoat and his hat, the one with the death's head insignia, I remember that. And he wore gloves, so that it was just this black leather hand pointing one way or the other, it was so quick. And I saw, just for a second as my line stepped forward, I saw Hansi and my father, and my father was coughing and Hansi was holding him, and the S.S. man pointed to the left for my father, and to the right for Hansi, but Hansi shook his head and helped my father over to the left and that was it, oh my God, he wouldn't leave him, so he went to his death. Hansi was so strong, he might have lived. He might have, that's what I always thought. He was wiry and strong, with muscles that grew even when we had nothing to eat for days. And he always smiled, did you know? He just lived so well, fourteen, and always happy and smiling, even when everything was awful and everything was all death and dying and he looked over toward me in that little instant, and I knew that he knew he should let Papa go to the left but he wouldn't, he held his arm and helped him be strong too. He was just a boy, but he knew. He smiled at me. Oh my God, he smiled at me, just like he was saying it's all right to die even though I haven't lived yet. Fourteen, but he was the strongest. So he went to help our father and so he died and I was alone forever. Oh Hansi, why didn't you go to the right?"

Tears were streaming down Sophie Millstein's cheeks, and Simon Winter thought: How many tears can you store up in fifty years?

On the tape, the young woman's voice asked: "Do you need to take a break?"

"Yes," Sophie Millstein said. Then she added: "No."

She stared at the camera.

"I lied," she said, suddenly forceful.

"What lie?" asked the young woman.

"When I reached the table and the S.S. man, he was a doctor! A doctor! How could a doctor do what he did? He asked me how old I was and I said sixteen and he was thinking and then he started to lift his hand, and I thought he might point to the left, and I said very fast, but I am an electrician. And he looked at me and I said my father, really, was an electrician, and I was his assistant, but that he taught me everything, and so the S.S. man would think I could be useful, and he pointed to the right."

"Did you know . . ."

"Nothing. Not really. I lied and I lived."

Sophie Millstein grew quiet. Then she added: "It always bothered me, did you know? I mean, of course, there was nothing wrong, but my mama and my papa—he was really a professor of linguistics at the university—they had always taught us that a lie was like a sin and that it was like a little dark spot on your soul that you could never quite clean away and that it was always, always, always better to tell the truth than to put that little mark there next to your heart. And I hated that, you see, that S.S. man, he made me lie to save myself. And everything else that happened to me, it all seemed like a part of that lie. And I hated them and I guess I hated me for that."

"If you'd told the truth . . ."

"I would have died."

"So, you became an electrician?"

For an instant Sophie Millstein paused, and Simon Winter saw her eyes narrow again with remembered hatred. She struggled with the words, but after a moment they leaked out.

"No . . ." she said slowly. "No. That's what I told Leo. That's what I told anyone who asked. But that was a lie too. They shaved my head. They shaved my entire body. And I became a whore."

She took a deep breath. Her words seemed to shiver with cold. "And that's how I lived. A whore."

Sophie Millstein reached down, and Winter saw her retrieve a lace handkerchief from her pocketbook at her feet. She dabbed her eyes and then looked at the young lady, off camera.

"I guess I was wrong," she said bitterly. "I have lots to say."

Sophie Millstein gazed toward the camera, her eyes still glistening with tears. Again she breathed slowly, deeply.

"It has been very hard for me to forgive myself," she said softly. "I feel all these years like I did something terrible and wrong. And I cannot just blow that feeling away into air like it was dust or fluff."

Again there was a silence on the tape, until the young woman's voice said:

"Sophie, you lived. That was what was important. Not how or why or what you had to do. You lived, and you shouldn't feel guilty."

"Yes. That is true. I have told myself that over and over all these years."

Sophie Millstein hesitated again. Tears now flowed freely down her cheeks, smudging the makeup she'd carefully applied.

"I guess all this time I thought it was wrong. Living when so many others died."

Again she paused.

"Can I have a little glass of something?" she asked with a small, delicate smile, like a child who has realized they've just read their first word all by themselves. "Perhaps a little iced tea?"

Sophie Millstein on the tape abruptly disappeared, replaced by gray bands of electronic interference followed by a blue title board with her name, the date, and a document number on it.

Esther Weiss rose and flicked off the television. Then she went to the window. The flat blinds being raised made a rattling sound. Light streamed into the room, and Simon Winter blinked sharply. He saw the young woman hesitate by the window, as if gathering herself.

She turned toward him. She was casually dressed, in jeans and a loose-fitting cotton shirt. Her mane of curly hair fell down to her shoulders and seemed to frame her face with intensity.

"Did you know how remarkable a woman Sophie was, Mr. Winter?"

Simon Winter felt a catch in his own throat and shook his head.

"An extraordinary woman. You cannot quantify bravery, toughness, dedication, will to live—all those things that are just words, Mr. Winter. Words that describe concepts that seem unbelievably distant and lost in society today. All the survivors had them to some degree, but Sophie, Sophie was a bit special even among special people, Mr. Winter. Did you know that about your neighbor, Mr. Winter?"

He shook his head again.

Weiss continued: "It's all oddly deceptive. She looked like just a little old lady. A little dizzy, perhaps. A little crazy, maybe."

She looked at Simon Winter.

"Everyone's typical Jewish grandmother. Chicken soup and kvetching about this or that. Right?"

Winter didn't answer.

"That's what you thought, right?"

He nodded slowly.

"Well," she said hesitantly, "you were damn wrong." The woman looked hard at him. "Just completely goddamn wrong."

The young woman rubbed what were the start of her own tears away from her eyes. Winter saw her take a deep breath.

"That was just the first, you know, getting started. Breaking the ice, so to speak. We had high hopes. But your neighbor was only able to make one additional tape before she was—"

She stopped abruptly.

"Damn," she said. "Murdered, goddammit."

Simon Winter remained silent.

"Unfair. What sort of world is this, Mr. Winter? Isn't there any justice at all?"

Winter didn't reply. He understood: What is there to say? She's right.

"Did she talk much about her time in Berlin, before her deportation?"

The young woman looked down at some notes on a page. When she looked up, Simon Winter saw her eyes glance toward his forearm. He realized she was looking for a tattoo.

"Why exactly? You're not a survivor, are you, Mr. Winter?"

"No," he said rapidly, thinking instantly that that was somehow an inaccurate response. "I was once a policeman."

"Why Sophie's story, now?"

"It was something she said. Right before her murder. About the man who turned her in."

"U-boats," Weiss said.

"I beg your pardon."

"U-boats. That was one of the nicknames the people who tried to hide out in the cities used. Because they were beneath the surface. It was a very difficult life. I will give you some books about what they tried to accomplish. Remarkable, really. Hiding in the midst of a police state dedicated to your very destruction. I think, in history, there are few people who were able to show the sort of creativity, resourcefulness, bravery, oh I don't know. These were extraordinary people, and so few survived the war to tell their stories. That's why we were all so excited when Sophie came to us and started making tapes. I don't really think we can understand today the sort of courage those people had without their firsthand testimonies. And the life? Starvation. Fear. Always fear. They could never stay more than a few days in any location. They had to move about, frequenting spots where they wouldn't stand out. When they could, they bribed people. Jewelry usually. If they had gold coins, so much the better. Sometimes they could even bribe the catchers and maybe gain a few days' extra suffering, before being caught and sent off to die."

"That's what I've learned."

"Who have you been speaking with?"

"Rabbi Chaim Rubinstein. A Mrs. Kroner and a Mr. Silver."

"I know these people. They were U-boats, like Sophie."

The young woman hesitated, then shook her head. "Jewish people employed by the Gestapo to hunt down other Jews. In a society that seemed to breed irony and betrayal in equal amounts, they were maybe the most . . . I don't know—what? Morally unique?"

She paused while Winter inhaled sharply. He saw her glance toward the window, her eyes tracking the shaft of light that speared the room.

"Do you suppose someone like that would go to a special ring in Hell, Mr. Winter?"

He did not answer that question, though he thought it a good one. Instead, he started to ask: "Did she describe—"

"It's an incredibly important subject, Mr. Winter. A sort of moral cannibalism. Betraying your own people to monsters in order to save your own life. Over the years, we have had several important scholars visiting the center to study the tapes."

Esther Weiss glanced at Simon Winter.

"She made one other tape. I'll get that."

The young woman went to a bookcase and started rummaging through shelves of tapes. She double-checked one against a master list, then turned to Winter.

"Here it is. You want me to get the shade?"

He shook his head. He felt somehow that the nightmares contained on all the tapes were safer in the bright daylight. She nodded and fed the tape into the video machine.

Sophie Millstein appeared on the television screen again. This time she was wearing a less formal dress, one of the many flower prints that Winter recognized. Two electronic interference bars marred the screen and every little motion Sophie Millstein made was jerked by the tape's speed as the young woman fast-forwarded to the point the conversation started.

"Right about here, I think . . ." Weiss said. She punched a button and Sophie Millstein's voice returned to the room.

The disembodied voice spoke first.

"Sophie, how was it that you happened to be caught?"

Sophie Millstein put her hand to her mouth, as if to prevent the words from tumbling out. Then she sat foward rigidly, like an eyewitness in court, and spoke:

"I remember it was the only time I saw Hansi scared, because he came home that day saying he might have been seen by someone. He wasn't sure, you know, everyone changed so much in those years. You could stare right at someone you'd known for years and not recognize them. The war did that. And starvation and Allied bombs all the time. But Hansi was upset. Still, the next day he went out to look for some work. We needed to eat and there was no choice and it was possible that Herr Guttman at the print shop would give him some bread for a day's work and bread was too important. So he went, and he didn't come back that night at all, until late, long after dark, slipping past the night curfew guards, which was something he never did, because if he'd been caught without papers it would be all over, and even if they believed his papers it might be all over anyway. He came home and I saw him speaking closely, frightened again, with Papa, who refused to let Mama or me hear what they were saying. But I saw Papa go to the coat that had all our money sewed into it, and he came back and gave Hansi a ring. A gold ring. Papa's wedding ring. Hansi took it and went back out, through the trapdoor, out of the basement. He returned a few minutes later and I remember him saying to Papa everything will be all right now, but maybe only for a few days, and so they talked about moving us. I didn't want to move. The basement was warm and as safe as anything when the bombing raids came over. Maybe that was why we didn't move as fast as we should have. They came two days later. Gestapo knocking at the door. They took us out. I remember poor Frau Wattner standing, watching, with two soldiers on either side of her. She looked so scared. She was saying, But I didn't know, I didn't know, I thought they were just *bombengeschadigte*! She turned to Papa and spat in his face! *Schweinejude*! she said, but we all knew she had to say that, still, the word hurt. We were put in the car by the Gestapo man and I looked back once and saw soldiers throw poor Frau Wattner up against the side of the house. Papa made me turn my head, but I heard the submachine gun, and when I looked back, I could not see her anymore. . . ."

On the tape Sophie Millstein was once again fighting tears. She held up her hand.

"I'm sorry, Esther," Sophie Millstein said. "Poor Frau Wattner. She brought us soup when we had none. I do not think I can speak of that day right now."

"Sophie," the young woman's voice coaxed from off camera. "These things are important."

Sophie Millstein nodded toward the camera.

"Hansi wouldn't say much. Not that night. After Mama and Papa were asleep, I crawled over to where he was lying underneath his greatcoat, we had no blankets, really. I asked him:

'Hansi, what is it? Who is it?' and at first he wouldn't answer, but I poked him hard and he held his hand up so that just a little light that came in from the only little window we had threw a shadow on the wall, and then I knew. . . ."

"Knew what?" the young woman's voice prompted.

"I knew he was out there. And I knew he would sell us to the Gestapo before too long. I knew that. I must have stiffened or gasped or something, because right away Hansi says, 'No, don't worry. I've paid him something and he will leave us alone. . . .' But I didn't believe that and I don't think Hansi did either."

"That man. The one he met . . ."

"The one who turned us in."

"Yes. How did—"

"From the academy, I think. Not a classmate of Hansi's, but perhaps someone a few years older. That must have been it, because my brother cursed, which he never did, and I remember him saying it would have been better never to have learned to read or write at all."

Sophie Millstein paused, then added coldly: "He knew. That night in all that dark. You know, I remember the bombing was going on, off at Templehof, again, like so many times, and we could hear it in the distance, growing closer, and usually that scared me, but not that night. That night I remember praying that perhaps one of the British bombers would get hit and drop its load short and have it all come down on us just quickly and painlessly and it could all be over."

She continued quietly: "Hansi knew, and I knew and I suppose Mama and Papa knew that we were all dead already. We were dead at the very moment that *he'd* first spotted Hansi. Dead each moment that he'd followed my brother around the city, every stop on the streetcar, every step on the sidewalk. Dead every second that he'd watched and waited for his opportunity. Dead when he'd trapped my brother in a corner in some alleyway and hissed at him 'Jew! I know you!' in some snake's voice. We were dead when Hansi pleaded with him. We were dead when he forced Hansi to take him to Frau Wattner's basement and dead when he demanded a bribe. He was killing us when Hansi handed him the ring and whatever money we had and heard him promise that great lie. No, we were all dead, even though he promised us life."

Sophie Millstein paused. She was breathing hard on the tape, her face flushed with rage.

"But you lived, Sophie," Esther Weiss interjected softly. Sophie Millstein's eyes narrowed and her voice rasped in reply:

"I lived? You think anyone who went through that lived? Ach, you don't know anything! We all died, right inside! Maybe the body went on. Maybe we could still breathe. Maybe we still woke up every morning and saw the light of day, but we were dead inside! Dead!"

"Sophie, that's not true," the young woman argued gently. "You lived. Others lived. There was a reason for that. It was important that you lived."

Sophie Millstein started to reply, then stopped. Her eyes filled once again with tears. "I'm sorry, Hansi," she said slowly. "I'm sorry, Mama and Papa. I'm sorry to everyone who died."

She took a deep breath and nodded.

"Esther, I have loved living, that's true. Maybe it wasn't a perfect life, maybe I shouldn't have done some things I did, or said some things I said, but I have and there's no going back, is there?"

"No, there isn't."

Sophie Millstein started to say something, then stopped. She seemed to think hard, then she whispered, "And to think . . . he was one of us." She shook her head. "I need to take a break," she said.

"Sophie, this is important. What about the man who turned you in? We need to know about him."

"I know, I'm sorry. Perhaps tomorrow. Or next week. But I need to think of happier things, Esther, because sometimes these memories just make my heart want to stop."

There was a momentary pause, then the young woman's voice replied: "That's fine, Sophie. We have plenty of time. All the time you need."

Then there was another blue slate, with a date and document number, before the screen went blank again.

Esther Weiss turned off the television and shook her head. "I was wrong," she said. "She didn't have time. Damn." She sighed and eyed Simon Winter. "So, there was just that. Her brother paid the catcher—maybe a former schoolmate, teacher, who knows? It wasn't like the majority of good Germans were hiding Jews—a bribe. But it didn't work. They got denounced anyway. Denounced and shipped off to die. Does that help you?"

"Perhaps." He was thinking hard, trying to measure what he'd heard. He summoned Sophie Millstein's words spoken in his apartment on the day of her death: *I only saw him that once, and for such a little time. . . .* Would you ever forget that face? he demanded of himself suddenly. Would you recognize that face, no matter how few seconds you saw it that day fifty years ago, no matter how the years had aged it? Would you ever forget?

He answered that question instantly: no.

Then he turned the equation around in his head. Would the owner of that face ever forget what he'd done?

No.

The young woman hesitated. Winter saw a frown pass her eyes before she added: "You know what's odd? That was what she wanted to talk about the night she was killed."

"What?"

"She left a phone message on the Holocaust Center's tape recorder. It was after hours and no one was here. She just said she was going to come in and she wanted to talk about her arrest."

"What exactly did she say?"

"Just that. It was very brief."

"Did you tell—"

"I called the police. They didn't seem very interested."

Winter nodded. "They believe she was killed by a narcotics addict, or someone similar. Someone who's done a bunch of robberies near Sophie's apartment," he explained.

"That's what they told me," she said. "But you seem troubled, Mr. Winter. You don't believe them?"

He paused. He was struck by the German words that had rolled from Sophie Millstein's tongue. I never realized, he thought. All those years, watching her coming and going, living right across from her in the Sunshine Arms, and I never knew. Some detective you were, he reproached himself.

"Of course I believe them," Winter said slowly.

"So, why are you here, Mr. Winter?" the young woman asked.

He thought how stupid he was. All those years as a policeman, day in and day out, living daily with all of Death's caresses, in every manner of murder. And Death had walked right into the Sunshine Arms and been right there when he'd reached for his pistol to take his own life, and for some evil reason had taken the wrong person. Not him, but his neighbor.

"I'm here," he said with a hard-edged tone, "because someone murdered a person close to me."

He glanced quickly toward the window, as if the bright sunlight streaming through could help remove the dampness of his heart. He guarded his words carefully, doling them out with a cold precision: "On the night she died, when she called here . . . did she use the phrase *Der Schattenmann*?"

Weiss shook her head. "No. I don't believe so. The Shadow Man? No, I would have remembered that."

Simon Winter gritted his teeth. "Does it mean anything to you?"

"I don't recall it. But . . ."

"He might have been the catcher."

"That would be reasonable. They all went under pseudonyms and nicknames. And she describes her brother's hand . . ."

"Did any survive the war?"

"Maybe one or two. One, a woman, was tried by the Russians, did some time, and now lives quietly in Germany."

"The others?"

"They disappeared into the camps. Or into the rubble. Who knows?"

That's right, Simon Winter thought. That's the question.

# NINE
## —THE HELPING HAND

**W**ALTER Robinson followed the G-75 bus as it accelerated across the Julia Tuttle Causeway, leaving the Beach as it headed toward the core of Miami. It was midday; he saw a belch of smoky exhaust absorbed by the spongelike heat as the bus churned up the three-lane highway.

Miami has a linear quality to it. The city stretches north and south along the coastline, clinging to Biscayne Bay with an urban tenacity, taking not only the image that it wants to show the world, but also a sort of internal bearing from the glistening, azure waters. In recent years it has begun to flex to the west toward the soggy expanse of the Everglades, growing housing developments and shopping malls like so many boils on an infected man's back. But these are the inevitable eruptions of shifting population trends. In attitude and essence, Miami remains a coastal city, oriented toward the ever-changing fields of blue-green ocean.

Walter Robinson, however, hated the water.

It was not that he didn't enjoy looking out over the ocean, a view he frequently sought out, especially when considering a case in hand. He had long since discovered that the sea's rhythms had a subtle, encouraging sense and that the monotonous sounds of the waves against the shore helped to filter out extraneous details and focus his thoughts, and so he appreciated the great expanses of ocean and bay as tools which aided him. His hatred, however, was a more political one.

He thought the water was something that belonged to the wealthy. There are dozens of docks and marinas and boat ramps in Miami, and none abut areas where blacks live in any numbers. He had become aware of this at a young age, when he would walk from the poverty of what is known as the Black Grove, through increasing affluence, down to the water, where he could watch the well-heeled and influential mount sailboats, speedboats, or large cabin cruisers and idle past the shore, heading out through the bay. In his solitude, watching, he was aware that his color made him different from virtually everyone heading toward the water. He had complained of this once to his mother, the elementary school teacher, and her response had been to insist that he learn to swim, if he was going to frequent the watery areas of Dade County. It was only as an adult that he'd realized that many of his schoolmates had never bothered to acquire this skill, so ingrown was the prejudice that the water belonged to others, not them.

So Walter Robinson had forced himself to become a powerful swimmer—fast, strong, and confident even when the ocean currents pulled and tugged with dangerous desires.

As he drove across the causeway, speeding to keep pace with the hurrying bus, he glanced at the bay, which shimmered on either side of him. He was always unsettled by the trip between the Beach and Liberty City; the bay seemed to mock the blight that rose up a half mile inland from the shoreline. Six blocks, perhaps nine, and any memory of the water dissipated in a rigid, unforgiving dusty heat. He kept close to the G-75 bus as it downshifted on an exit ramp, sending another cloud of dirty gray smoke into the air, and descended into the inner city.

The G-75, he knew, in unspoken truth, existed for a single purpose. It made the loop between a half-dozen stops in Liberty City and a similar number on Miami Beach so that the cleaning women, dishwashers, lawn men, and the occasional private nurse who lived in the city could get up early and ride through the heat to their difficult and low-paying jobs, without complaint or hope, and then make the return trip at night, swaying with noise and speed as the bus hurtled across the causeway.

He kept a street map on the seat beside him, and as the bus maneuvered down Twenty-second Avenue, he noted the location of every pawnshop and check-cashing store. There was a depressing frequency to these businesses, at least one per block.

The pawnshops, in particular, interested him.

Which one? he wondered to himself. Which one would open for you in the middle of the night? Which one did you slip right into, trying to shake off the last droplets of panic? Which one gave you the quick and easy, no-questions deal?

This was just an educated guess on his part. He knew that a sophisticated burglar would have a regular fencing operation that he would frequent. Some fringe person who could be trusted. A fence, as well, would be able to handle more expensive pieces of jewelry, and give a higher return.

But a professional fence would also have more sense than to deal with some strung-out crack-bedeviled low-life, Robinson thought. So, he guessed, his quarry didn't have a regular bank where he could take his stolen goods and make what in Liberty City passed for a regular deposit. He drove along, speaking to himself:

"No, my man. You were all strung out, weren't you? And you'd want to get rid of almost all this stuff real fast, so a pawnshop would be right. One that you knew keeps two sets of books. One that would simply fork over some tens and twenties and not ask any questions. Enough to keep you from getting rich, but not enough to keep you from getting high, right, my man?"

There were seven such shops along the G-75 route.

Walter Robinson parked and smiled to himself.

"You wouldn't want to walk far, would you? You'd just want to get rid of the stuff nice and quick and get some cash and forget about that big step you just took. You know what step I'm talking about, my man? The one where you went from punk and burglar to the big time. The step that's gonna put you on Death Row in Raiford Prison wondering what it is about life that's so sweet because it's gonna be taken away from you."

Robinson stepped out of the car and felt a blast of heat rise from the sidewalk, enveloping him. He locked the unmarked car and hummed a snatch of a song to himself.

He breathed in deeply and thought: No, my man, you don't know how close I am, but I'm close. Real close. And gonna be closer still, before you know I'm right there beside you.

He paused and let his eyes sweep into a low-slung housing development across the street from where he stood. Three small children were playing with a garish pink-colored plastic scooter bike on a dusty brown spot between cement walkways. Behind them were two two-story-high rectangular apartment buildings. Graffiti marred the fading white paint on the walls. Most of the doors and windows were open to the oppressive humidity; if there were air conditioners, they either didn't work or were too expensive to operate. Occasionally a loud voice, raised in some sudden anger, flung an expletive or two through the hot air over the heads of the children, who played on, oblivious to the sound. Robinson knew that as the day dwindled into nighttime, the same voices would be accompanied by the inevitable sound of liquor bottles smashing and an occasional, but hardly infrequent, gunshot.

He hesitated, and two of the playing children stopped and looked up toward him. They pointed, and he realized how he stood out, in his tan suit, button-down shirt and tie, polished shoes. The children stared at him, put their heads together momentarily, then returned to their game, ignoring his presence.

He shook his head and thought: Seven years old and already they make the cop. In ten years will some policeman come looking for them with his pistol drawn? He did not have to answer that question.

He looked around to see if he could spot someone keeping an eye on the children as they played, but saw no one. At least, when I was growing up, my mother watched me, he thought. The memory filled him with a sense of isolated sadness, and he turned away quickly, back to his task.

A breeze swirled some dust around his feet, but brought no relief to his temple, and he set off down the block toward the first of the pawnshops. He stood outside, pausing before pushing his way inside. As he reached out his hand for the door, he heard a car pull to the curb behind him, and he turned quickly.

It was a white City of Miami police cruiser. The sunlight hitting the car's hood almost blinded him. A window rolled down and he heard a familiar voice:

"So, it's the famous Beach detective, here to make trouble."

Walter Robinson shaded his eyes from the glare and quickly replied: "Well, only because you deadbeats and do-nothings let all your bad guys come make trouble in my town."

He heard laughter from the passenger seat, and as he stepped to the side of the cruiser, another voice said:

"Well, better there than here, that's for sure."

The cruiser's door swung open and a large black man, wearing the navy-blue uniform of the city police, with a sergeant's stripes on the shoulder, stepped out. There was a quick handshake and a "Hey, Walter, my man, how yah doin'?"

"Fine, Lionel, just fine."

The police sergeant was joined by a thin, considerably smaller Hispanic officer, who also shook hands. "Hey Walt, amigo, *cómo está*?"

"What's that foreign tongue you're talking, John?" Walter Robinson grinned and accentuated the man's name.

"It's Juan, not John, and don't you forget it, you big old black gringo. You're as bad as my partner. And anyway, it's gonna be the national language any day now, and we're gonna force you guys to speak it."

The three men laughed together.

"So big guy, you on a case?" the police sergeant asked. His name was Lionel Anderson, and Walter Robinson knew that on the street he was called *Lion-man* at least in part for his regal bearing, but also because of his no-compromise attitudes. He had been a classmate of Robinson's at the academy, as had Juan Rodriguez, the other sergeant at his side.

"Why else would I want to visit this particular locale?" Robinson replied.

"Maybe because you miss the ambiance, the sense of community spirit and attitudes?"

"I think it's the cooking, partner. The detective cannot get proper black cuisine out on the Beach. He's tired of chicken soup and matzoh balls. He needs a fix of collard greens and ham hocks."

"Well, perhaps," Lionel Anderson answered. "Sure taste a whole lot better than those fried banana things you're always wolfing down and forcing me to eat. Disgusting."

"Plantains are good for you. Help you learn a new language and understand a whole culture."

Robinson shook his head and said: "Hell, Juan, the Lion-man can't even understand the one he's got, and you want him to understand another? A new one?"

"Well, Walt, amigo, I admit you gotta point there. . . ."

The three men started laughing again.

"So," Anderson asked again, "whatcha doing over here in scenic Liberty City?"

"You know about that killing we had the other night?"

"Little old lady?"

"Right."

"We had a flyer. Stolen jewelry. Came out of your office."

"That's the case. I think maybe the perp rode the G-75 over and back."

"You think he took a bus to kill somebody?"

"I don't know he meant to kill anyone. He'd been having some luck over the past coupla weeks just doing B and E's."

"That weren't no routine breaking and entering the other night."

"No, you're right about that. But I figure he still had to get back, only this time all the hot stuff he's used to carrying is a mite hotter. Maybe like burning a hole in his pocket . . ."

". . . And so," Rodriguez said, "you think he just jumped off the bus and wanted to dump it quick and he'd take whatever he could, right?"

"You got it, Juan."

"Makes sense. I mean, none of it makes sense to any reasonable person. But in this world, sure. Makes sense."

"So," Robinson continued, "I'm looking for someplace that maybe hasn't been keeping regular hours, you know? Someplace maybe that's open in the middle of the night . . ."

Lionel Anderson and Juan Rodriguez looked at each other momentarily, then almost in unison they said: "The Helping Hand."

"What?"

"The Helping Hand pawnshop. Three blocks up . . ."

"Great name, huh?" Rodriguez said.

Anderson shook his head. "Maybe three, four times, guys on my shift have been complaining about the dude that runs the place. They say that place is open at the oddest times, day and night, and they ain't dumb, they know what that means. Anyway, the owner's name's Reginald Johnson. Got a gal working with him named Yolanda, says she's his niece down from Georgia, but I don't buy that and neither does nobody else around here. Ain't *nobody's* niece look like Yolanda. She's one of those girl-women. I mean, she's the entire package. Tits that go north. Butt that heads south. Long legs and something real special waiting at the top of them, you can bet. We're talking sweeter than your ordinary sugar, that's Yolanda. Anyway, word is, he's trying to expand his operation a bit. Got a couple of receiving stolen property busts, but they always fizzle, you know? Walks in, pays a bit of cash to some lawyer, gets it all continued to the next century, shifts it from court to court, finally pleads it out to misdemeanor possession of stolen goods, pays a fine and he's back in business thinking he's a whole lot smarter than the cops, the state attorney, and the rest of the world. I hear he's moved into a new house and filled it with new furniture, because Yolanda, she wants a real home. I was told he has his eye on a new Buick for Yolanda too. A nice red one. Now, Walter, you know I wish *I* had a niece do what she does. . . ."

The policeman laughed and his partner joined in, grinning, slapping a hand against his leg, nodding his head.

"Now, you just know he's gonna be looking to keep her happy, and *you know* that the way things are going, well, little old Yolanda, she may not be the brightest light around, but it ain't gonna be too hard for her to figure out who's who and what's what and she's gonna get a quick taste for the nicer things and the finer things."

"Ain't life sweet," Juan Rodriguez added.

"And you know, those things cost money. . . ." Lionel

Anderson rolled his eyes and opened his palms skyward, as if exhorting the heavens to rain down some cash.

"I think I get the picture."

Rodriguez smiled. "I would just *love* to see you screw up this nice little side business he's got going. And, if your perp came from here, why, the Helping Hand is sure where he'd run first and fastest. Only one problem . . ."

"What's that?"

"I think old Reginald has figured out that he can't be leaving that stolen shit around his store too long, because even us dumb old cops gonna come looking for it. I don't know where he connects, but I think he's dumping that stuff fast."

Lionel Anderson nodded. "You may be too late to find that stuff in the store. And you ain't gonna get no warrant on a hunch."

The big man smiled over at his partner.

"Still, it wouldn't do no harm to help this brother detective out and watch old Reg squirm a bit. Likely even he understands the difference between receiving stolen property and accessory to first-degree murder. Perhaps we can enlighten him further."

Walter Robinson let some of the amusement the two uniformed officers were sharing linger on his face, but inwardly he felt a narrowing, a harshness, and allowed himself the hope that he was riding the right path.

"Lead the way," he said quietly.

The Helping Hand was a narrow storefront, its windows set behind thick black bars. The door itself was reinforced with steel plates and several dead-bolt locks, giving the entrance to the pawnshop all the welcoming appearance of some particularly dark, medieval fortress. Walter Robinson saw that a series of mirrors prevented anyone arriving inside the Helping Hand from discovering any shadow in which to hide. A video camera mounted adjacent to the front door switched on as the door opened, a detail that Juan Rodriguez immediately pointed out.

"Hey, Reginald, my man," the wiry policeman called out in accented language. "This is very fancy shit. Very high-tech. I like it. I do. *Muy bueno.*"

"I got to protect my stuff," came a sullen voice from behind a counter.

Reginald Johnson was a short, thickset man, scowling, close-eyed, with bodybuilder's arms that pressed hard against the cloth of his sport shirt. He wore a holstered nine-millimeter pistol on his right hip to discourage any customers from debate, and Robinson suspected that a twelve-gauge was lying on a counter shelf just out of sight, within easy reach.

"Whatcha doing here?" Johnson asked. "You need a warrant to search the place."

"Why Reggie, we're just inspecting the merchandise. We like to see what the local merchants have to offer. Just our way of helping to promote good police and community relations," Juan Rodriguez said, his voice filled with mockery. "Like this show-case filled with guns, Reg. Now, I just know that you can produce the paper on each and every one of them, am I not right?"

Rodriguez drummed his fingers on a glass countertop.

"Sheeit," the pawnshop owner muttered.

"Reg, you want me to get the gun file from the safe?" This question floated from the darkened rear of the pawnshop.

"That sweet voice would be Yolanda," Lionel Anderson whispered to Robinson. "Hey! Sugar. Come on out here and say hello to my partner and me!"

"Yolanda!" Reginald Johnson admonished quickly, but not quickly enough.

"Is that Sergeant Lion-man?" she asked as she stepped beneath the fluorescent lights that illuminated the interior of the pawn-shop. Walter Robinson quickly realized that his old friend had not exaggerated Yolanda's considerable attributes. She had cocoa skin and a sweep of night-black hair that cascaded down across her shoulders. She wore a tight, white, vee-necked T-shirt that forced one's eyes directly into her cleavage, and she grinned at Lionel Anderson, whose attention was riveted on her barely con-tained breasts. "Why, Sergeant, how come we don't never see you no more?" she asked. "I've been missing you."

Anderson rolled his eyes back, looking up toward the ceiling for assistance in answering the question.

"Why, sweetness, if I knew you wanted to pass the time of day with this old cop, why don't you know you'd get the best police protection that this city has to offer? I mean, round-the-clock, twenty-four-hour police protection. . . ."

Yolanda laughed and shook her head. Walter Robinson wondered if she was fourteen or twenty-four. Either was a strong possibility.

"Yolanda! Go get those papers from the safe!" Reginald Johnson almost shouted.

The young woman turned to him, frowning. "I already asked you if'n that's what you wanted," she retorted.

"Go get them so we can clear these cops out of here."

"I'm going."

"Well, get a move on, gal."

"I said I was going." Yolanda turned toward Lionel Anderson. "I'll be right back, Sergeant Lion-man." Then she glanced over at Robinson. "I didn't know you and your little partner were gonna bring a handsome friend along on this visit," she added.

"I'm Walter Robinson. Miami Beach P.D.," he said.

"Miami Beach," Yolanda said wistfully, as if she were talking about some faraway, exotic location. "Reggie ain't never taken me over there to look at the waves. I bet it's right beautiful, ain't it, Mr. Detective?"

"It has its attractions," Robinson replied.

"See, Reggie, I told you so," Yolanda said, turning and pouting.

"Yolanda!" Johnson yelled again, without effect.

"Little partner! Little! Yolanda, you break my heart!" Juan Rodriguez interrupted, grinning. "I may not be some big old lunk like him, but you got no idea. You ever heard of Latin lovers, Yolanda? They're the best. *Muy perfecto!*"

"I never heard that." The young woman smiled at Rodriguez. "I'll bet you'd like to prove it too."

Rodriguez clasped both hands over his heart, as if smitten, and Yolanda laughed.

"Yolanda, go get those papers," Reginald Johnson muttered. He stomped across the store, grasped her by the arm, and steered her to the back office area, behind a wire-mesh gate and triple locks.

"I ain't done nothing wrong," the pawnshop owner insisted. "And you stop screwing around with Yolanda."

"Your niece," Anderson reminded him.

Johnson scowled again.

Walter Robinson started to move throughout the small store, inspecting the items in various display cases, a dizzying collection of weapons, cameras, toaster ovens, tape recorders, cutlery, a waffle iron, several guitars and saxophones, and occasional pots and pans. The accessories of life, the detective thought. He moved quickly over to a display case containing an assortment of jewelry and began examining each earring, necklace, and bracelet. He pulled out the flyer he'd prepared and began checking the descriptions of items stolen from Sophie Millstein's apartment against what he saw arrayed on the shelves in front of him.

Reginald Johnson approached Robinson, leaning over the countertop toward him, his voice low and iron. "I got paper on all this shit too, Detective. You ain't gonna find whatever it is you looking for."

"Is that right?" Robinson replied softly, very coldly.

"That's right."

"I'm told you keep pretty late hours."

"Sometimes in this neighborhood, people got a need to make a transaction at night. I got plenty of competition, or maybe you ain't noticed. Just trying to serve the clientele, Detective."

"I'll bet. How about Tuesday last?"

"What about Tuesday?"

"You open late?"

"Maybe. Probably."

"Anyone come in late? Maybe midnight."

"I don't know if I recall nobody."

"Try harder."

"I'm trying real hard, and I don't just recollect nobody."

"You lying to me?"

Johnson scowled. "You finished hassling me, or do I got to call my lawyer?"

The two men continued to stare at each other, before Walter Robinson said: "Fifteen to life, Reg. That's for starters."

"What you talking about fifteen years?"

"I'm talking accessory to first-degree murder, Reg. Maybe you want to think about that a bit before you try to recall last Tuesday and who may or may not have been in your store here late that night."

"Don't scare me. Don't know nothing about no murder. I think maybe I'm calling my attorney right now. Maybe he'll be looking to file a harassment suit."

Reginald Johnson seemed inordinately proud of the word *harassment*. He repeated it two or three times for Walter Robinson's benefit.

The detective glanced down into the shelf of jewelry again and wished he had pictures of the stolen items, rather than simple descriptions. Every piece looked more or less the same to him, and he thought this was the inevitable result of being single, and not paying much attention to the subtleties that attracted women's eyes. He tried not to let discouragement show in his face.

"I think maybe you'd better be showing up here with a warrant, you want to look closer," Johnson said confidently.

As he spoke, Yolanda emerged from the office area, buzzing herself through the locked steel grating, carrying a sheaf of papers.

"I got all that stuff for the guns, you want to see it," she said. She approached Reginald Johnson. The two uniformed sergeants came over to where the pawnshop owner was standing.

Yolanda spread the papers out on the counter. "We got it all," she said. "Ain't no illegal guns in there, Sergeant." Her voice seemed to combine pleasure and disappointment simultaneously. "Like that big old thirty-eight right there," she said, leaning over the countertop. "We got the license and registration right here."

None of the policemen looked at the weapon that had Yolanda's attention. Instead, each had occupied his eyes with a generous inspection of her breasts as she bent over the glass display.

"I do believe you on that one, honey," Lionel Anderson said quietly, appreciatively.

"Yolanda!" Johnson blurted out once again, still angry.

The young woman stood up, straightening coquettishly. She smiled at the police sergeant, then over at Walter Robinson.

Robinson, however, was no longer watching the young woman's cleavage; his eyes centered instead on the light brown skin of her throat. The fluorescent lights of the pawnshop made the single gold strand she wore flash brightly.

Robinson turned to Reginald Johnson. He leaned forward, narrowing his eyes, letting harsh, barely controlled fury slide into his voice, so that each word carried a promise of ferocity.

"Your niece sure has a pretty name," he said.

Johnson didn't reply.

Yolanda looked around suddenly, as if the detective's tone had frightened her.

"Why, thank you," she said hesitantly.

"A very pretty name," Robinson repeated.

The room grew quiet. Lionel Anderson and Juan Rodriguez moved to either side of him, and he heard both men unsnap the leather flaps that held their service weapons in their holsters. At the same moment, Robinson abruptly jackknifed his body across the countertop, seizing Johnson's arms and pulling them forward, throwing the burly pawnshop owner off balance. His chest slammed against the countertop with a thudding sound and he cried out "Hey!" in surprise.

Robinson grabbed Johnson's neck with one hand and forced the man's head down while he twisted his arm. He realized that Rodriguez had seized the pawnshop owner's free hand and was pinning it to the case.

"I want my attorney!" the man cried out. "What you be doing? I ain't done nothing! Let me be!"

"No, you ain't done nothing," Walter Robinson whispered.

He was breathing hard and he placed his face right down next to the pawnshop owner's.

"Yolanda's such a pretty name," he continued harshly, softly. "So, you tell me, you low-life scumbag motherfucker, why she's wearing a gold necklace with the name *Sophie* on it?"

Robinson lifted his eyes toward the young woman, who gasped and put her hand to her throat in sudden memory. She looked over at Lionel Anderson and protested, "But it was real pretty. . . ."

Reginald Johnson groaned, and Robinson heard Juan Rodriguez reach for his handcuffs, which made a wondrously satisfying, musical, jangling sound.

# TEN

## *THE WAY IT ALL WORKS*

Espy Martinez flashed her identification to the desk sergeant, who directed her toward the bank of elevators with a cryptic, "Third floor. They're expecting you. . . ." before turning back to a paperback novel resting on top of a stack of paperwork. The book sported a voluptuous, barely clothed woman wielding an antique pistol on the jacket, and instantly gathered the desk sergeant's total attention. She hurried past him, her shoes making a flat, eager sound against the polished linoleum floor.

The elevator rose silently through the center of the building. She stepped out as the doors rattled open, looking for Walter Robinson, but spotted instead a detective from the robbery division who had been her lead witness in a case several months back. He looked up from a notepad and smiled. "Hey, Espy! Moving up into the big time, huh?" She shrugged her reply, and he added: "The show's down there. Squeeze time."

It wasn't hard for her to guess what he meant by that, and she grinned in anticipation. She followed the detective's finger down a narrow corridor, beneath fluorescent lights, into the core of the police headquarters, giving her the impression that she was somehow being sealed away from the unforgiving heat and sunlight outside. The air-conditioning ducts poured icy air into the small space, and she shivered involuntarily. She realized her footsteps had disappeared into an industrial gray carpet; all she could hear was the rasp of her own breathing. For a moment she felt completely alone, and she realized this was precisely the sensation that suspects were supposed to have as well.

Midway down the hallway there were a pair of doors facing across from each other. A small plastic sign on each said: INTERROGATION 1 and INTERROGATION 2. There were windows in the corridor, so that a person could stand in the hallway and stare in at the subjects in each room. Espy Martinez realized this was one-way glass; that she could see in, but the people inside could not see out. She noticed a small intercom system next to the window.

She hesitated and saw Walter Robinson sitting in one room, across from a young, strikingly attractive black woman, who had obviously been crying. She turned and saw a stocky black man sitting at a table in the opposite room. He was drumming his fingers against the plastic surface, glaring at a pair of uniformed City of Miami policemen, who studiously ignored him. She watched the man light a cigarette, angrily tossing the spent match into an ashtray filled with discarded butts. The man swiveled about in his seat impatiently, a movement that caused both policemen to raise their eyes momentarily and stare pointedly at him until he settled back into his chair. Then they went back to ignoring him. She saw his mouth form an obscenity, which she suspected he spat into the stale room air. It had no effect on the policemen.

She turned and entered the room where Robinson sat.

As she came through the door, he quickly rose. "Ah, Miss Martinez, glad you could make it."

"Detective," she replied, with a false formality.

Walter Robinson, smiling, but not particularly pleasantly, turned to the young black woman. "Yolanda, take a long look at this woman here."

The young woman raised her reddened eyes toward Espy Martinez.

"You see the nice suit, Yolanda? Take a look at those shoes, Yolanda. Check out the heels. Pretty sharp, huh? See the briefcase? That's real leather. Nothing cheap. You see all that, Yolanda?"

"I see," Yolanda replied sullenly.

"You can tell right away that she ain't a cop, right, Yolanda? You can see that, can't you?"

"She don't look like no police."

"That's right, Yolanda. This is Assistant State Attorney Esperanza Martinez. Miss Martinez, Yolanda Wilson."

Espy Martinez nodded at the young woman, whose eyes reflected nothing but fear.

"Yolanda," Robinson continued, in a low voice that contained equal parts threat and seduction, "you try to make a real good impression. You try to make the best impression you can, because Miss Martinez, well, Yolanda, you know what she does for a living? You know what she does each and every day? Every hour that the sun is up, Yolanda? You know what she does?"

"No," the young woman replied, looking toward Espy Martinez then back at the detective. She dabbed at her eyes with a ragged piece of tissue paper.

"She puts people like you in jail," Robinson said harshly. He rose and gestured to Espy Martinez. "Think about that, Yolanda."

The young woman looked as if she'd been slapped. "I don't want to go to no jail, Mr. Robinson."

"I know that, Yolanda. But you got to help me keep you out. You got to tell me what you know."

"I'm trying. I told you everything."

"No, Yolanda, I don't think so. And I haven't learned what I need to learn. A name, Yolanda. I want the name."

"I don't know," the young woman pleaded. Her voice rose into a whine. "I don't know. Reggie, he never told me no names."

"Smart girl like you? Yolanda, I just don't believe you."

The young woman dropped her head into her hands, shaking back and forth. Her shoulders heaved. Robinson let a momentary silence slide around her, deepening Yolanda's fear, then she said:

"I didn't know about no murder, Detective. Please, you got to believe me. I didn't know there was no harm involved. Where's Sergeant Lion-man? He'll tell you. Please."

"Sergeant Lion-man can't help you, Yolanda. This woman can. You think about that. We'll be back."

He led Espy Martinez back into the corridor, slamming the door hard on Yolanda's helpless sniffling.

"This is the part I like," Robinson said, although Martinez had the impression that he actually liked all parts of the job.

"What is it that you found—" she started to ask, but Robinson anticipated her question and produced a small plastic bag containing a gold necklace. He handed it to Espy Martinez, who saw the name Sophie and the pair of small diamonds that adorned the *S*.

"That's what Yolanda was wearing."

"You sure . . ."

"You think it belonged to some other Sophie?"

"No. But . . ."

"Well, we'll get a positive from forensics later. Maybe the son or the neighbors can ID it. But it was hers. Trust me."

"Okay, Walter. What's the procedure?"

Walter Robinson smiled. "Well, you've already met Little Miss Tears and Contrition. The problem is, she's telling the truth. She really doesn't know all that much, although she might know the name. I'm not sure yet. Yolanda's smarter than you might think. Some of those tears might come from the proverbial crocodile. But, hey, when she got a long look at that briefcase . . . well, we'll see. Cops are one thing. A real live prosecutor, well, that's bound to be a novel experience for her, and I'd bet she's thinking hard right now. On the other hand, over there, behind door number two . . ." Robinson was grinning as he spoke, and Espy Martinez was forced to smile at the game-show host persona the detective mocked. ". . . is Mr. Hardcase I Want My Lawyer. Now, I know he's got the information we want. The procedure is simple. Play one against the other."

"If he's asked for his lawyer, then we're required—"

Robinson made a face. "Espy, come on. Sure he's asked for his lawyer. He was shouting about his lawyer as soon as I walked into his pawnshop. I just need to make sure he understands the, uh, ramifications of his reluctance. Give him a chance to see the light. The opportunity to do the right thing. He ain't even been asked any real tough questions yet."

"Well . . ."

"Espy, this is the way it all works. You watch."

"Walter, I'm not sure I get it."

"It'll be pretty clear pretty quick. And I'll bet you're a real fast study."

"We'll see about that. What is it you want me to do?"

Walter Robinson grinned. "I want you to scare the hell out of him."

Before Espy Martinez had a chance to reply that she wasn't sure she could scare anyone, Robinson tapped on the glass window to the interrogation room. The two police officers inside immediately rose, and the pawnshop owner called out, "Hey, where you going?" as they exited, slamming the door shut behind them. Robinson made quick introductions in the hallway.

"Espy Martinez, this is Juan Rodriguez and Lionel Anderson."

"Sergeant Lion-man?"

"In the flesh." The sergeant's huge paw enveloped her own hand, pumping it up and down. "Aren't you the one who put those kids away? The home invasions?"

"My claim to fame," Martinez replied.

"That was a nice piece of work," Juan Rodriguez interjected. "Those kids, they were gonna kill somebody for sure."

"Not now," she said.

Both sergeants grinned. "For sure," Rodriguez said. "At least not until they get out."

Lionel Anderson turned to Walter Robinson. "Next step?"

"Look, guys," Robinson whispered swiftly. "You go in and make Yolanda feel a whole lot better about her chances as long as she cooperates with us. Make her think that just everything's gonna be okay, as long as she keeps her mouth moving. No lies. Got it?"

"Gonna be a pleasure, Walt, old buddy."

"If there's one thing Lionel here knows," Juan Rodriguez said to Espy Martinez, "it's how to make young women feel better about their delicate situations. . . ." He punched his partner on the arm as he spoke, and he drew out the word *feel*, adding a profusion of *e*'s to its center.

"I do have some expertise, ma'am," Sergeant Anderson said, putting a finger to his forehead in mock salute.

Then the two uniformed sergeants headed into the first interrogation room. Robinson smiled at Martinez. "That wasn't a rough assignment," he said. "Okay, ready to put the fear of God and the criminal justice system into Mr. Reginald I'm A Tough Guy Johnson? Let's go."

Robinson didn't wait for an answer, but pushed into the room. Martinez jumped to stay close.

Reginald Johnson looked up and scowled. "You call my lawyer?"

"What's that number again, Reggie?" Walter Robinson asked.

The pawnshop owner merely grunted a response. "Who she?" he asked.

"Why, Reggie, I'm surprised. You don't recognize her?"

"Never seen her before."

"You certain?"

"Sure, I'm certain. Who she?"

Robinson smiled once, then he leaned forward, pushing his face close to the pawnshop owner's, hovering over him like a parent about to strike a child. "Why, Reggie," Robinson hissed, "I'm sure you've seen her in your nightmares, 'cause she's the biggest trouble your sorry ass has ever seen. She's the person who's gonna see you do hard time, Reggie. Right up in Raiford Prison. Twenty-four-hour lockup, and I'm just sure there ain't gonna be nobody up there as sweet as your Yolanda. In fact, you'll be lucky if somebody doesn't turn you into *their* Yolanda. You catch my drift, Reggie?"

The words seemed to force the stocky man back hard in his chair. He stole a quick glance at Espy Martinez.

"Your worst dream, Reggie," Walter Robinson said.

"I ain't done nothing. Don't know about no murder."

"Is that right?"

"You think I ask all the folks who come through my doors where they got their shit? No way. All I do is figure out the price and write the ticket. Don't need to go about asking no questions."

"Maybe not, but you know who brought that necklace in. The one Yolanda thought was so fine that she just had to put it 'round her neck."

Johnson didn't reply for a moment. "I can't be telling no police about my business. Wouldn't have no business," he finally answered, rocking back in his chair, crossing his arms over his chest as if this statement were his final say on the entire matter.

"Oh yes, you can," Robinson argued. " 'Cause your business is now my business, and that's a problem."

Johnson scowled and grew silent. Espy Martinez sat in a chair at the end of the table, watching the detective as he moved about, walking behind the suspect, leaning over him wordlessly, then stepping back, and finally pulling a chair up close to him. She watched Robinson as she would an accomplished actor on a stage. Every movement he made, every motion, every tone assigned to every word, was calculated to achieve an effect. She watched as he unsettled the pawnshop owner, skillfully undressing him of every arrogance and obstinacy. She took a deep breath, fascinated, wondering when she was supposed to interject herself into the performance and doubting whether she would have any of the same skills.

Walter Robinson continued to stare at Reginald Johnson, narrowing his eyes, not wavering, until the pawnshop owner turned abruptly away, snarling an obscenity.

"Sheeeit. Don't know 'bout no murder," he added. But there was a slight waver in his voice.

The detective let the room fill again with silence. He did not move his eyes away from the suspect. After a moment he slowly exhaled, his breath hissing into the stale room air.

"Maybe I was wrong. . . ." Robinson said quietly. "Maybe I was wrong about you, Reggie."

Johnson turned back, a look of surprise hitting his face at the sudden change in the detective's attitude.

"Maybe I was wrong. What do you think, Reggie? Was I wrong?"

"Yeah," he replied eagerly. "You was wrong."

Without taking his eyes off the pawnshop owner, Walter Robinson asked: "What do you think, Miss Martinez? You think I was wrong about Reggie here?"

Espy Martinez was uncertain for an instant as to how to reply, but finally, in as flat and cold a voice as she could manage, she said: "You're never wrong, Detective."

"No, maybe this time I was wrong about old Reggie here."

"I don't think so, Detective," Martinez said.

"Am I wrong, Reggie?" he asked again.

"Yeah. Shit, yeah. You're wrong."

Robinson continued to let his gaze bore in hard at the pawnshop owner. He let false hope gather momentum in the little room.

"All this time, I was thinking Reggie here, all he did was take a little bit of stolen goods from the wrong man. And you know, Miss Martinez . . ." He frowned at Reginald Johnson. "You know, maybe I'm wrong about that. Maybe there weren't no other person, showing up at the Helping Hand late Tuesday last, all eager and anxious and breathing hard and sweating a bit too much and ready to make a deal, any deal, right Reg? No, maybe there weren't no other man at all. Maybe I was all wrong about that Reggie . . ."

He hesitated one instant, just letting the words burrow into the pawnshop owner's confusion, before continuing.

". . . No, Reggie. Maybe there weren't no other man at all. Maybe keeping that Yolanda in those fine clothes and driving that fine car and buying all that fine furniture for that fine new house, well, maybe you figured you better work a little harder. Maybe you figured you had to put a little bit more cash in the old register. So maybe, Reggie, you didn't need no other man at all. No, sir. No, you just took that old G-75 bus right on out to Miami Beach, and you just started doing all those break-ins. Did pretty good at it, right, Reggie? Until that old woman Tuesday last, she wakes up and then you got a problem, huh, Reg? A real problem. So you killed her, right, Reggie? That how it happened?"

Robinson suddenly jabbed a finger into the pawnshop owner's face. "You killed her, you sonofabitch!"

Reginald Johnson looked wildly at the detective, recoiling in fear. "I didn't kill nobody! I told you! Don't know nothing about no murder!"

Robinson suddenly reached across the table and grabbed Johnson's hands. He forced them onto the table surface with a resounding slap, turning the palms up.

"You're strong, Reg. Got nice big hands. Didn't have no problem at all choking that little old lady, did you? Did you!"

"Don't know nothing about no murder, no old lady!"

He tried to pull his hands back, but the detective held them on the table, pulling Johnson forward, off balance, staring again, harsher.

In the silence that grew in that instant, Espy Martinez felt a heat pour through her body. The words seemed to come from someone else, not her, but she heard them reverberate in the small room.

"Receiving stolen goods, two to five. That's gonna be easy time, medium security. Then comes burglary, five to ten. That's getting a bit more serious, but, time off for good behavior, maybe only do three years. But then you jump up to assault. Now you're in real trouble, Reggie. Jesus, the state attorney, she just *hates* it when old folks get assaulted. So that'll bring you ten to fifteen. And maybe the judge's gonna think hard about retaining jurisdiction on the case, cut that parole board right out of the situation. So no good behavior on that one . . ."

Espy Martinez paused, gathering her breath. She saw the pawnshop owner struggling at the far end of the table. It was as if all the words and numbers added up to so many knots around his chest. She continued, lower, harsher, oddly aware that in some clear, unfamiliar spot within her, she was distinctly enjoying herself.

". . . But then you really hit the big time, Reggie. Accessory to first-degree murder, fifteen to life. But nobody gets the fifteen, Reggie. Especially when the victim is a little old lady. Everybody gets life, up in Raiford. Not a nice place. Not a nice place at all . . ."

She looked coldly at him.

"And then we're right to the end of the line: first-degree murder. Well, you know what that buys in this state, Reggie. Two thousand two hundred volts of electricity."

She made a gun shape with her hand and added: "Zap. You're history."

Johnson, hands still held on the tabletop by the detective, tried to swivel in his chair toward Martinez.

"What you talking about! Death penalty! I told you I ain't done no murder!"

Espy Martinez leaned forward. "I got enough to make a case, Reggie. More than enough. Doesn't make any difference, though, how much evidence I have. . . ."

"What you mean?" the pawnshop owner asked desperately.

"Little old lady. Never hurt no one. What do you think, Reggie? What do you think a bunch of nice white middle-class Miamians are gonna say when they see you come walking into that courtroom? All black and angry and tough. You think they're gonna care whether we got *any* evidence at all? No way. Not after I get up and tell all those white folks that it was you strangled the life out of her. That it was your fingers wrapped around her throat, choking her until she was dead! All they're gonna think about is that it could have been their mother, or their aunt Mabel. You think after they hear that, they're gonna give a damn if we have *any* evidence? They're just gonna want to see your sorry ass disappear. So, what do you think that nice white jury's gonna say?"

"I didn't!"

"Guilty. Guilty as charged."

She hesitated, watching the words slap the pawnshop owner like punches.

"And the judge? Reggie, what do you think that white middle-class judge's gonna do? Somebody who needs all those people to vote for him come next election day?"

"I'm telling you, I didn't do nothing!"

"All those white folks, Reggie. What do you think?"

Again silence gripped the room.

Espy Martinez took a deep breath and pointed at Reginald Johnson. "Zap," she said again. "Goodbye, Reggie."

Walter Robinson finally let go of the pawnshop owner's arms.

Martinez rose. She looked down at Reginald Johnson with as haughty a glance as she could manage.

"Detective, you keep this piece of shit company. I think I'll go talk some more to Yolanda. She and I, well, we get along a whole lot better, and if I'm gonna make somebody a nice deal, the kind of deal where they get to go on home at night and pick up their life again, well, I'm thinking maybe I'd rather it be that pretty young woman. And I just know that Sergeant Lion-man'd rather have me cut her some slack, rather than this piece of shit. . . ."

"You can't give Yolanda no deal! She don't know nothing!"

"You'd be surprised what that gal has picked up, Reggie. Why, she's just filled with all sorts of information."

"She don't know. . . ."

"But she'll be the one to walk." She said this flatly, nastily.

Walter Robinson smiled and nodded. He was having trouble keeping himself from bursting into applause. Reginald Johnson seemed to calculate quickly in a panic, then he blurted:

"I didn't know where the shit came from! Man calls me up, middle of the night, wants me to meet him at the store, make a deal, well, I didn't know! Didn't ask no questions! Just went on down, met him outside, he was waiting, like. That's the truth! Didn't know about no murder."

"Who, Reggie?" Walter Robinson asked.

"I tell you who, you got to promise—"

"Who! Goddamn it! I'm not promising you anything, you sack of shit! Who?" Robinson screamed into the pawnbroker's face.

Reginald Johnson twisted in the seat a final time, like a man trapped beneath a wave, trying to find the surface. Then he slumped forward and said:

"Man's name is Leroy Jefferson."

"He a junkie?"

"Man likes a pipe, I'm told."

"He a regular customer of yours?"

"He been in pretty regular last month or so."

"He got a street name?"

"Yeah. They calls him Hightops because he always wearing those fancy basketball shoes."

"Where's Hightops live?"

"King Apartments. Number thirteen, I think."

"Unlucky number," Walter Robinson said, rising from the table, leaving the pawnshop owner with his head in his hands.

# ELEVEN
## *A MAN OF*
## *PRECISION*

At very nearly the same moment that Walter Robinson and Espy Martinez emerged from the interrogation room with the name of the man they believed had killed Sophie Millstein, Simon Winter was sitting down in a stiff-backed chair across the desk from a young homicide detective named Richards, who seemed unable to decide between acting politely toward the older man or impatient with his questions.

"Thank you for seeing me on such short notice, Detective," Winter began.

"It's a closed case, Mr. Winter. I had to get the file back from records."

"I appreciate your taking the time."

"Yeah, well, no big deal, but I don't exactly get your interest in this guy's death."

Winter decided to lie. "Well, Stein was related to me—a distant relative—through marriage. And you know how hard it is for people who haven't seen someone in years to accept the fact of his death, much less a suicide. So because I was down here, I got assigned the task of checking it out—even though it's been months. You know how some people are. Kvetching, disbelieving. Never letting things just go, and finally getting around to asking someone to go ask some questions . . ."

"Uh-huh."

"Families. Sometimes they can be—"

"A major pain. Sure. I got you."

"There you go," Winter said with a flagrant shrug.

This falsehood seemed to placate any of Richards's inconvenient anger at having his day interrupted by a curious old man.

"Yeah. I guess. Well, anyway, closed case, Mr. Winter. Pretty much cut and dried. One shot. Left a note. Not much for us to do, except tidy up and cart out the body. No big mystery."

"You were there at the scene?"

"Yeah. My case. Just a matter of collecting the documents and filing a report. I don't really remember it all too much."

"Who found the body?"

"Cleaning lady, I think I remember. Maybe twenty-four hours postmortem. It's in my summary."

The young man shoved a brown accordion file across the desk toward Simon Winter. "Have at it. It wasn't anything special or out of the ordinary. You gonna be able to handle the photographs, Mr. Winter? They aren't too pleasant."

"Ahh, I believe so. Thank you, Detective."

"Well, you take a look. Then I'll answer any questions, if I can. Deaths like these, they all seem to pretty much get lumped together, understand? It's hard to remember specifics. You want coffee?"

"No thanks."

"Well, I'll be back in a bit."

He stood up and left Winter holding the file. For a moment the older man hesitated, just letting his fingers creep across the rough brown paper, like a blind man reading Braille. He thought of all the case files he'd stuffed with photographs, reports, summaries, and evidence in all his years, and he smiled, delighted to have one in his hands again. He lifted it, measuring its weight. Not much, he thought. Then, with an eagerness that he knew was completely inappropriate, but which he was incapable of denying, he unsnapped the rubberized cord holding it together and looked inside.

He went to the crime scene photos first. There were only a half-dozen eight-by-ten glossy color pictures, perhaps a tenth of what

there would have been in a homicide scene. The two most promi-
nent pictures showed an elderly man slumped backward in a
brown leather desk chair, his arms thrown out to the sides, almost
as if in astonishment. Blood had dripped down between his eyes,
from a gunshot wound in his forehead, staining the collar of his
sport shirt. There was a clear splatter pattern on the wall behind
Herman Stein, marred by flecks of brain and bone. Stein's eyes
were open in death, beneath a scarlet and gunpowder-blackened
entry wound. His mouth was slightly open, as if in wonderment.
He had been nearly bald, with just a few tufts of white hair around
his ears. The blood streaking his face made him seem like a gar-
goyle. Simon Winter studied the pictures carefully.

Tell me something, he said inwardly.

He flipped to another picture. This showed a large .38 caliber
pistol dropped to the floor beneath Stein's outflung hand. This
was followed by a close-up of Stein's face. Then there was a photograph of an electric typewriter next to the desk. In the platen of
the machine was the suicide note. Another close-up picture
showed that Rabbi Rubinstein's memory was accurate.

Simon Winter read: *"I am tired of life and miss my beloved
Hanna and am going to join her now."*

He put the photographs aside and turned to the detective's
summaries. There was a brief description of the scene, and a list
of neighbors who had related the facts of Mr. Stein's most recent
depression. There was a telephone number for Stein's next of kin,
a son with the unusual name of G. Washington Stein, and an address at a large New England university. He flipped through the
autopsy protocol, which described a most obvious death. There is
little medical surprise in what happens when a .38 caliber soft-
nosed bullet is fired from a point-blank range into a person's
forehead. Blood toxicology was negative, save for traces of
ibuprofen—arthritis, Simon Winter thought immediately. Winter
saw a short notation on an additional form, mentioning the rabbi's
visit to Detective Richards, and he saw a copy of Stein's letter.
There was no mention of its contents in any of the detective's
conclusions, which were simple: suicide due to mental depression
and age.

They would have written the same about me, he thought.

Then he flipped through the file another time, trying to find something. Other than the mention in his own letter, there was nothing linking Herman Stein to Der Schattenmann.

Simon Winter frowned, just as Detective Richards returned holding a cup of coffee.

"Not much, huh?" said the younger man.

"No, not much."

"Case like this," Richards continued, "we don't really go hunting about for a whole lot. This was pretty much a textbook suicide. A man with no known enemies—even his neighbors said that he was always friendly and polite. History of depression since his wife died a half-dozen years ago. I found some mood-elevating drugs in the bathroom cabinet. That's in the report. . . ."

The detective sighed, then continued.

"And he left a note. A note and a single gunshot wound to the head. Doesn't take a rocket scientist—"

"The gun, did it belong to Stein?"

"Uh, no. Or, at least, no record. No registration. Just another illegal weapon. Must be millions of them in Dade County. I wrote down the serial number. . . ."

Simon Winter copied that figure. "Any ballistics reports? Fingerprints?"

"What for?"

"Did the cleaning woman ever say she'd seen the weapon before? Or somebody else, you know, to put it in his possession?"

The young detective flipped quickly through the reports.

"Nothing here. But that wouldn't be so unusual. Most folks don't want the cleaning woman to know where they keep their gun. It'll get stolen."

"True enough," Simon Winter said. Then he asked: "The position of the deceased, it didn't bother you some?"

"How so?"

"Well, you're gonna shoot yourself, I guess usually you'd put the gun up like this . . ."

He made his hand into a pistol and held it to the side of his head.

"Or like this . . ."

Again he demonstrated by putting his index finger into his mouth.

"Sure," Richards replied. "That's what I'd expect. Never wanted to kill myself, so I never gave it much thought."

"But holding a large handgun up against your own forehead, like Stein did, that's sort of unusual. I mean, you've got to hold it out there, and then pull the trigger, what, with your thumb maybe, to get enough strength."

"Yeah. I can see that. What's your point?"

"It's just unusual."

"Well, suicide is suicide. I mean, he coulda jumped. Lived way up on the tenth floor of that condo. Or swum out into the ocean. It's only a block away. Or walked in front of a bus. We've had all of those. So, yeah, maybe holding that big old thirty-eight like that wasn't how you or I might have done it, but hey, different strokes."

Richards looked over at Simon Winter closely. "You got some expertise in this sort of thing, Mr. Winter?"

"Used to be a cop. City of Miami. Retired years ago."

"Hey, my old man was a city cop. Took one in the leg, though, back in the late Sixties. Had to retire too."

Winter thought for an instant, and then recalled a heavyset man with a florid face.

"I remember. Bank robbery, right? He chased the guy for six blocks, bleeding all the way. Finally got him."

"Hey, that's right." The young detective brightened. "Damn. You got some memory."

"How's your dad now?"

"Still runs a fishing boat down in Islamorada. Lotsa cold beer and gals who like to get an altogether tan. Has it pretty good."

"I'm glad to hear that."

"Hey. Mr. Winter, you want me to copy all this stuff for you? Maybe then you'll think of something else."

"That would be great. But one other quick question . . ."

"Sure. Fire away."

"The gun. You found it right beneath his hand, right?"

"Yeah. Right there. One bullet gone. Five more in the cylinder."

"But wouldn't the force of the shot, and his hands flinging backward . . ."

Simon Winter demonstrated slowly, throwing his hands out wide and leaning back in his seat.

". . . Well, wouldn't you expect the gun to be a bit farther away?"

The young detective smiled. "You're still pretty sharp, Mr. Winter. Yeah, I might . . . if it were some little twenty-two or twenty-five. But that old thirty-eight musta weighed a ton. Big as a brick. It wasn't gonna travel far."

Simon Winter nodded. "Place was all locked up when the cleaning woman came?"

"Yup. Like I said. She let herself in with a passkey. No mystery there."

Simon Winter nodded. "I'd still like those copies."

"No problem. You just keep them to yourself. They're official police documents. Understand?"

"Hey, the rules haven't changed that much since I sat behind a desk like yours."

Detective Richards laughed and walked off to a copying machine while Winter sat waiting, thinking of the last moments of Herman Stein. It's all absolutely clear-cut and correct, he concluded—and all totally screwed up and impossible. Both at the same time.

It took him several efforts to penetrate the telephone switching system at the University of Massachusetts; each time he'd dialed professor G. Washington Stein's direct extension, he slid inexorably into telephone limbo. It was not until he managed to get the secretary in the English Literature Department that he was able to get connected. He hated making this sort of phone call; had hated making them when he'd been a detective. But he took some relief from the thought that months had passed since Herman Stein's death, and perhaps some of the rawness of that single gunshot wound had scabbed over.

"Professor Stein?"

"Yes. No extensions. Final papers are due Wednesday. Who is this, please?"

"Professor, my name is Simon Winter. . . ."

"You're not a student?"

"No. I'm an investigator. I'm calling from Miami."

"An investigator? And what are you investigating?"

Winter paused, trying to think of a concise answer to that question. He couldn't think of one.

"Professor, I apologize for coming to you on a difficult subject, but just prior to his death, your father wrote a letter to my"—he hesitated, trying to think of a word to describe the three old and frightened people in the rabbi's apartment—"my clients. . . ."

"My father wrote a letter? To whom?"

"A rabbi he didn't know. Another man who'd lived in Berlin during the war until being caught up and shipped to a concentration camp."

"I see. A letter to a man he didn't know? What was in it?"

"He said he'd recognized a man he had not seen since—"

"The war."

"That's right. This man—"

"The Shadow Man," the professor interrupted coldly.

Winter's heart jumped. "That is correct."

Professor Stein seemed to be gathering his breath, and for an instant the telephone line was silent. Then he continued, dryly:

"My father often saw Der Schattenmann, Mr. Winter. He saw him in his dreams, and then they turned to nightmares and he would awaken shouting, yelling, sweating, and it would take my mother hours to calm him. He saw him in lines at the bank and movie theater crowds and rolling a grocery cart down the aisles of the supermarket. He saw Der Schattenmann in the cars that pulled past us on the freeway and waiting at the local bus stop. Once I took him to a baseball game at Fenway Park, and he saw Der Schattenmann in the rest room. Another time he spotted him in the crowd at a New York Knicks game we were watching on television. The Shadow Man was everywhere, Mr. Winter. Everywhere in my father's imagination."

Simon Winter slumped down in his chair. He was sitting in his own living room, centered on his worn sofa, a pad of paper and several sharpened pencils in front of him on the table, and he suddenly felt as if he was ridiculous.

"So," Winter started hesitantly, "if just prior to his death—"

"He told someone he'd seen Der Schattenmann? This would be only slightly unusual, Mr. Winter."

"Slightly?"

"Yes. The only thing out of the ordinary, is that almost always—I can't think of a different occasion that I know of—he would call me, or my brother or sister, with the news of the sighting. And it would be one of us who would go over the circumstances and the memories and slowly, but certainly, talk him out of what he thought he saw. I cannot recall him ever contacting a stranger."

"You don't think he ever truly saw—"

Again the professor interrupted. "No. But I spoke with him a day before his death, and he didn't mention anything to me. He was upset. More nervous, more anxious, more depressed than I'd ever heard him before. But he kept speaking about our mother, not Der Schattenmann. I think he might have mentioned him, if he'd seen him."

"So you could calm him and talk him out of what he thought he saw?"

"Correct."

"Did he seem scared?"

The professor paused, then replied: "Perhaps you could add fear into the mix of all the things he was feeling. I remember I was worried, and I called my siblings, and we decided one of us should go down to Miami and visit him, but, of course, by the time we got it all worked out, it was too late."

Again the professor hesitated, before adding: "Do I sound cold, Mr. Winter? Unfeeling?"

"No," Winter lied.

"It's an odd thing, Mr. Winter. To hate someone you love for doing something to themselves. You feel so many things."

"I'm sorry to bring it up like this."

"No, it's all right. In a funny way, it is easier to talk with a stranger than someone you know. Did you ever meet my father, Mr. Winter?"

"No."

"He was an unusual man."

"How so?"

"He felt debts. He was constantly trying to repay debts."

"Money?"

"No. Debts of the soul, Mr. Winter." The professor laughed, as if recalling something amusing. "I'll give you an example, Mr. Winter. My full name is George Washington Woodburn Stein. Not your run of the mill, ordinary name, huh?"

"No."

"I shall tell you the story of how I got my name, and that will help you understand my father a little bit. He was caught, along with my aunt, uncle, and grandparents, in 1942. They were underground in Berlin. . . ."

"Der Schattenmann?"

"Yes. He recognized my uncle, or so my father said. Spotted him in a bunker during an air raid."

"And?"

"What do you think, Mr. Winter? The Gestapo came. Took them away. They all died in the camps."

"I'm sorry."

"My father, however, he managed to survive. He was seventeen by the time the war was closing down. Of course, all hell was breaking loose near the end. The S.S. guards marched them all from camp to camp as the front kept changing. I suppose, in their own way, these were as terrible as anything else that had taken place. To have survived so far, through so much, only to be driven into exhaustion with Allied troops only miles away. My father said so many were dying then, just dropping by the side of the road, almost as if the mere hope of survival could kill you."

"He lived."

"Yes. But only barely. He said he collapsed in a barracks. It was night and they had marched dozens of useless, absurd miles. Marching to die. They hadn't eaten in days. Typhus, the flu, pneumonia—you name it—was killing them, one right after the other. They could hear artillery in the distance, and he once told me that the sound was like hundreds of people knocking on the great doors of Heaven. He expected to die. When he awoke in the morning, he said he was surprised to see sunlight, and he knew it would be the last time he would see the day, so he crawled from his bed—not a bed, really, a slab of wood in one of the barracks—out the door, knowing that an S.S. guard would shoot him before he got too far, but that it would be worth it, just to feel the sunlight on his face one last time. But the guards had fled during the night. The camp was quiet, save for the sounds of astonishment and death. My father crawled out into the assembly yard. *Arbeit Macht Frei.* That was the slogan. He said he decided he would wait there for his own death. Seventeen, Mr. Winter. Seventeen, and waiting in the sunlight to die.''

The professor took a deep breath over the phone.

"I loved my father," he said. "But you know, sometimes it seemed as if from the age of seventeen on, he was always waiting to die."

The professor hesitated, recalling another memory, then added: "When he moved to Miami Beach, that's what he said. He still wanted to die in the sun. It seemed the right place for him."

"But your name?" Simon Winter asked.

"He said he fell asleep as the sun rose over him. And after a while he heard an angel speaking above his head. He always said he was so surprised, because the angel spoke in English. My father knew English, because he had grown up in . . . well, that's another story. But he knew the language, and he said he heard the angel say: 'But here's one that's alive . . .' and he opened his eyes expecting to see Heaven, but instead he looked up into the face of Sergeant George Washington Woodburn. A very black face, Mr. Winter. A black angel. Sergeant Woodburn was with the Eighty-eighth Tank Battalion. You know what they nicknamed themselves? 'Eleanor Roosevelt's niggers,' but that's another story too. And so, Herman Stein, my father, he reaches up and touches this Sergeant Woodburn on the cheek and asks, 'Have I died?' and Sergeant Woodburn, he says, 'No, son, and you ain't.' My father always thought this was so funny, later. The sergeant spoke with as thick an Alabama accent as you can imagine, and it had been probably five or six years since my father had heard a word of English, and that was always refined, British, you know very, very upper crusty sort, but he said he could recall every word that sergeant said. So Sergeant Woodburn, he reaches down and picks up my father and carries him right through the camp, shouting

'Medic! Medic!' and my father always said all he could remember was these strong arms holding him—he only weighed sixty pounds—and this great black man crying for a doctor and saying, 'You ain't dyin' boy. No sir. You ain't gonna die. . . .' "

The professor's voice seemed thick with emotion.

"So Sergeant Woodburn carries my father to an aid center and a doctor, all the time saying over and over: 'You ain't dying, no sir.' And when he awakens again, he's in a hospital, and that is how he lives. And that is how I came to be named for Sergeant George Washington Woodburn. When I was growing up, every couple of years my father and mother would pack us all in the family car and we would drive down to Jefferson City, Alabama, to visit the Woodburns. He became fire chief. Raised six sons; the youngest is a graduate student right here at the university. We'd have these reunions and my father and Chief Woodburn would always tell the same story. And they'd joke, and laugh, and the chief would try to pick my father up in his arms like he did that day, but he couldn't anymore, and everyone would laugh. He passed away himself just a little over a year ago. We all went to his funeral. Jefferson City, Alabama. It was very hot and my father cried for hours. We all did."

The professor took another deep breath. Simon Winter could hear tears gathering in his voice.

"My father, you see, Mr. Winter, he understood debts."

Winter did not know exactly what to say. He was fortunate, however, because the professor did not seem to be finished.

"I'm rambling," he said. "I apologize."

"No, not at all. Was your father in academics, like you?"

George Washington Woodburn Stein laughed quickly, as if relieved to be heading in a different direction. "Oh, no, not at all! He was a jeweler. The family, in Berlin, had been antique jewel merchants. That was why he'd learned English as a young child. And French as well. They traveled extensively. Very cosmopolitan. They were amongst those Jews in Germany that simply couldn't perceive the extent of the evil about to be delivered to them. The family tree went back centuries. My grandfather must have thought he was more German than the people who finally shipped him to his death."

"A jeweler?"

"Correct. A man of incredible precision, when he was working on stones. My father had a delicacy, a gift. He was an artist of the exact, Mr. Winter. He loved jewels, because they lasted forever, he said. Like a play by Shakespeare—that's my field—or a painting by Rembrandt, or a Mozart piano concerto. Immortal, he would say. The stones are of the earth, and they can live an eternity. Stones were alive, to him. They had personalities and character. He would speak to the settings, as he crafted them. He had hands like a surgeon's—that's what my sister became. Eyes like a sharpshooter. Even at the end of his life, his vision was extraordinary—"

The professor hesitated, a catch in his voice tripping his last words.

"Something is wrong?" Simon Winter asked.

"Well, yes and no."

"Something is bothering you?"

"Yes. Mr. Winter, I don't know if—"

He stopped.

Winter probed gently: "What is it, Professor Stein?"

The voice on the other end of the telephone was hesitant. "I don't know you, Mr. Winter. I cannot see your face. I am reluctant to speak of doubts with a stranger." The professor's language was oddly stilted, increasingly formal.

"I am an old man too," Winter said abruptly. "Like your father. I am an old man who was once a detective, and I have been asked by some other old people to find out if this man, this Shadow Man, is actually here on Miami Beach. They are frightened, and I don't yet have an answer to their fear, Professor. They did not know whether to believe your father when he told them he'd seen Der Schattenmann. They do not want to believe he is here. But then, there was another sighting. And another death. And that is why I called you."

"Another?"

"Yes. Only this was a murder."

"Someone was killed? But how?"

"A break-in. Apparently a narcotics addict."

"So, not anyone like the Shadow Man?"

"That's the belief."

"And the connection to my father's death?"

"Only this: Both your father and this other person believed they spotted the Shadow Man shortly before their deaths."

The professor hesitated. Surprise lingered in his voice. "That is remarkable." He paused again, then added: "You know, that's the sort of thing my father would have enjoyed, Mr. Winter."

"Enjoyed?"

"Yes. He was a tremendous fan of mystery writers. I don't know exactly how he acquired this taste, but he did. Sir Arthur Conan Doyle and Agatha Christie and P. D. James. He was particularly fond of Harry Kemelman's series about the rabbi who investigated crimes. Do you know those?"

"No, I'm afraid not."

"They're actually quite intriguing. He forced me to read some once, right about the time I received my doctorate. Said I was in imminent danger of becoming dull. Too many learned, academic texts. Too much studying. I remember him shoving an armful of paperback novels at me and telling me that they were filled with quandaries and McGuffins and red herrings. I have to admit they are very clever."

The professor returned to silence. Finally, he said: "Ask your questions, Mr. Winter. Then I will explain what is bothering me."

Simon Winter took a deep breath. "The gun. He committed suicide with a thirty-eight caliber. . . ."

"My father abhorred weapons, Mr. Winter. I was surprised to learn he had one. He was a gentle man. But it was Miami, and it is a violent place, so I suspected he simply hadn't told anyone."

"The position he killed himself . . ."

"Yes. A gunshot right above the eyes. That upset me, Mr. Winter. My father loved his eyes. They were the avenue to his art. I never thought he would do anything to damage them."

"I see. . . ."

"And another thing. The way the Miami Beach police described how he held the pistol . . ."

"Yes?"

"Well, it would have been hard for him. His hands, you see. All those years working with fine jewelry. All those precise carvings.

All those delicate touches. His hands had grown arthritic. Pulling a trigger, especially with his thumb, would have been extremely painful."

"You said this to the police?"

"Of course. But they pointed out that he'd been depressed and lonely and people in a suicidal frame of mind overcome physical limitations. That, I imagine, is true."

The two men waited, as if expecting the other to fill in the silence on the phone line.

"What else?" Winter finally asked.

"It was probably nothing, but it truly disturbed me."

"What?"

"The police didn't attach any importance to it, but you know, families look at these things differently. . . ."

"What is it, Professor?"

"The suicide note."

"What about it?"

"Well, it was written in my father's style. Direct. To the point. I told you, precise. It was exactly what he would have written if he were about to kill himself. He had long ago made his peace with his children. We knew he loved us. He knew we loved him. There wasn't anything to add to that, unless he was going to go on and on, and that wasn't his style, Mr. Winter. No, he was direct. Direct and concise."

"I see."

"No," the professor said abruptly, "you don't see. The note. The goddamn note . . ." Bitterness scored the professor's voice. Still, he maintained a certain pedantic approach. "What is a suicide note, Mr. Winter? A message. A final statement. Last words. There may only be a few words involved, but they are crucial, are they not?"

"Of course."

"So, you accept the postulate that he was trying to say something. That this was his last message to me, and my brother and sister and his grandchildren, whom he loved. And through all his sadness and loneliness, despite all our efforts to include him, still this was his final statement on this earth."

"Yes."

"Then tell me why," the professor asked slowly, his own voice deep with renewed despair and confusion, "tell me why after all those years of marriage, he would not place the final *h* on my mother's name?"

"I'm sorry?"

"Hannah, with an *h*, Mr. Winter. Not Hanna. My beloved Hannah . . . but misspelled. Misspelled by a man of exactness and precision. So, you tell me, Mr. Winter. What message is in that omission? Does it say something to you?"

It did. But Simon Winter did not reply to the professor's anguished questions.

# TWELVE
## *IN A PERFECT*
### *WORLD*

**T**HE plan was simple: Sergeant Lion-man was to be the uniform. He would knock once, announce, then step aside while a detective borrowed from the Beach robbery division took out the dead bolts with a swing or two of a sledgehammer. The detective was a part-time bodybuilder nicknamed the Lumberjack and accustomed to being called in on arrests that needed the quick destruction of a locked door. Then, when the door was open, Walter Robinson would lead the arrest team into number 13.

In a perfect world, Espy Martinez thought, the suspect will be groggy with drugs or sleep, then disoriented by noise and fear. He should be meek, passive, and willing to surrender without a struggle.

She sat in the dim rear seat of an unmarked police car, staring out across the nighttime black-and-gray-tinted universe of the decrepit housing project. She had never been to anyplace like the King Apartments, especially not in the hours after midnight. Streetlights carved pathetic slices of the night away, as if by holding out a tiny portion of the darkness, they could delay the decay that constantly chewed at the edges of the low-slung, three-story buildings. Despite the hour, she could still hear an occasional shouted obscenity and a child's haphazard cries. A moment after they had arrived, she thought she'd heard a stray gunshot coming from someplace beyond the fringe of the streetlights, whining past, like a lost evil thought. She could just barely make out a graffiti message spray-painted on one tan wall of the apartments: 22 SHARKS RULES. She assumed this was the street gang that extorted money from businesses and controlled the drug trade on Twenty-second Avenue.

In a perfect world, she thought again.

Then she shivered, despite the festering heat.

Walter Robinson turned, right at that moment, and saw her look up at him expectantly. "You sure you want to be here?" he asked.

She nodded. "It's my job."

"Your job is to put this Leroy Jefferson away. Your job is in a courtroom, starting tomorrow morning when we arraign the bastard for Sophie's murder, wearing a sharp blue pin-striped suit and carrying that big old leather briefcase and saying 'Your Honor this and Your Honor that and the State requests no bail be set. . . .' You don't have to be here," he said.

She shook her head. "No. I do. I want to be here."

Robinson smiled gently and waved his hand in the direction of the King Apartments. "Espy, why in this entire godforsaken world would anyone want to be here, if they didn't have to?"

He grinned at her and she smiled back.

"Ahh," she said, "your point is well taken." Then she thrust the smile aside and added quietly, "I just need to see things through. All the way through. From start to finish. Beginning to end. It's my nature."

"Well, if you insist . . ."

"I insist."

". . . Then you wait here until we have the cuffs around him. You come up and watch me giving him his rights. Maybe we can avoid the usual police brutality charges from the public defender's office if you witness the arrest."

Again she nodded. Walter Robinson looked at her closely and wondered what it was that she was trying to prove. It was certainly not to impress him, he thought. She had already managed that. But he realized there was some other agenda working within Espy Martinez, and he suspected it would not be too long before he discovered what it was. He continued to watch as she turned her head just slightly, her eyes sweeping across the open courtyard of the King Apartments. For an instant he allowed himself to fix on her profile, the curve of her hair as it swept down next to her cheek, and the girlish way she pushed it back. Then he turned in his own seat and removed his pistol. He checked the clip on the nine-millimeter, then double-checked to see if he had his spare.

"All right," he said.

"Which one is it?" she asked.

He glanced up at the King Apartments. "Last one on the left, near the stairwell. Second floor."

She followed his eyes. There was an exterior set of stairs at either end of the flat, rectangular building. An open-air corridor ran the length of each of the three stories. She thought it was a singularly ugly set of buildings, and wondered how it had ever acquired its distinguished name. The politics of neglect, she thought. Martinez turned away just as Robinson returned his pistol to his shoulder harness. For an instant she tried to imagine what it was like for him or for Sergeant Lion-man or for any other black officer to come in the middle of the night to the King Apartments searching for another black man with a warrant for the first-degree murder of a white person. She wanted to ask Walter Robinson about this, but could not. Not at that moment. So instead, she spoke words that seemed to jump out of some forgotten part within her:

"Hey, Walter," she whispered as he was getting out of the cruiser, "you be careful."

He laughed his response. "Careful is my natural state of being."

The Lumberjack and another detective stepped out of another unmarked car and approached Robinson. Across the street, he saw the two City of Miami sergeants giving instructions to several uniformed officers. They were the backup. After a moment, the two sergeants hurried across the street.

Juan Rodriguez spoke first. "Lion-man's all set, Walter. A couple of guys around back. The rest, right behind you. Let's do this real quick. In and out. Grab the slime-bucket before his neighbors raise hell. Then we can take our time with the search of his place. *Comprende?*"

"Sounds good. Who's going around the back?"

"I think the young guys."

"Come on, Juan, rookies?"

"Hey, they gotta learn. They're okay. Real fire-eaters. Been on the street almost a year. Both of them. And anyway, there's only one little bathroom window on the back end. The perp's gonna have to have wings to get out that way. Walter, buddy, the King Apartments are just like some jail. Hell, most of the places even got bars on the windows. Only difference is, they're trying to keep folks out instead of locking them in. But the effect is pretty much the same. All we got to do is take out the cell door on number thirteen and sweep up what's inside. Like the song says: no place to run, no place to hide."

"You're making it sound real simple. I like that," Robinson said. "All right. Everybody ready? Lion-man, you wearing your vest?"

"Yeah, I put the damn thing on. It's goddamn hot and uncomfortable and it makes me look fat, and I don't like that."

"Rather have your vanity or a sucking chest wound, Lion-man?" Rodriguez asked sarcastically.

Espy Martinez cut in quickly. "Ahh, but Sergeant, many women like a big man. If you know what I mean . . ."

The other policemen all grinned as Lionel Anderson tipped his hat toward Martinez, trying to conceal a slight embarrassment at the double entendre.

"Yes ma'am, of course they do. But size where it counts."

Espy Martinez leaned over and punched the sergeant in the chest. "Just wear the vest," she said.

"For you, of course."

"Maybe for that Miss Yolanda too."

"Ahh, I had not considered that issue, Miss Martinez."

"Everybody wear their vest," Martinez said to the assembled men. Heads nodded. "Except me," she continued, "because I'm staying here where it's safe."

The men laughed, as if thankful to have whatever tension that had gathered eviscerated by Martinez's lightheartedness. She wished she could tell them all that the joke and the grin and everything else in the nonchalant way she stood in the center of the group was a lie, but she did not. Instead she turned to Walter Robinson. He nodded at her. He knows, she thought.

Robinson held up his hand to get everyone's attention. "No screwups," he said. "Everybody take another look at this guy Jefferson's mug shot."

He passed these around.

Lionel Anderson looked at the picture hard. "You know, I think I remember this guy. What's his street name?"

"Hightops."

"Gotta be the same guy. Played a little ball for Carol City High maybe ten years ago. Strong to the hoop, but no outside touch."

"He's got a different kinda outside touch now," Robinson said. "Assault, burglary, weapons violations, misdemeanor possession, felony possession reduced. I mean, we're talking a book-length sheet. The all-American bad guy. Probably armed. I mean, definitely armed. Let's just snatch him quick. Any questions?"

There were none. He hadn't expected any. This was well within the policeman's routine: A person who had been wrong for years had finally stepped up and killed someone. The only thing surprising about the arrest was that the suspect hadn't murdered before. Of course, Robinson thought sardonically, I haven't seen his juvenile record. He shrugged inwardly.

"Everybody set? Let's do it."

He handed the arrest warrant to Lionel Anderson, and the policemen headed off into the King Apartments. Espy Martinez felt a sudden unsettled feeling. She reached down into her pocketbook and took hold of her small semiautomatic pistol. She chambered a round, then exhaled slowly, holding the weapon tightly, bracing it up against her side, waiting for something to happen so that she would not have to stand for long in the encapsulating night that she hated so intensely.

Leroy Jefferson, a young man who did not expect to ever grow old, sat quietly in his underwear at a scarred and stained, shaky wooden kitchen table inside number 13, imagining how his life would improve if he could ever get enough of a stake together to start dealing drugs, rather than simply consuming them. It was a fantasy of the mundane; he pictured himself in newer clothes, driving a large car. He was partial to the color red, and he wondered idly whether his suit or his vehicle should be that shade, only, upon reflection, to decide that perhaps both would not be excessive.

He reached out and toyed with the glass pipe on the table. Leroy Jefferson had long, bony hands. Athlete's hands: the fingers were curved in a predatory fashion, like talons; the veins stood out on the backs, as if pushed up by sinew, muscle, and strength. An artist would probably have thought them beautiful, in a rough-hewn, violent sort of way.

He ran one cracked fingernail down the edge of the pipe.

His girlfriend slept in an adjacent room; he could hear a light snore, almost a wheeze, as she turned over, tangled up naked in a single sweat-damp sheet. They had not been together long, and he did not expect that they would stay together much longer. They had fallen together more out of affection for the drug than for each other. Their coupling was an occasional act of mutual convenience.

Beneath his finger, friction made the glass pipe feel hot, but then, he realized, the whole world was hot. His girlfriend shifted position again noisily, and he wondered how anyone could sleep with the temperature in the small apartment creeping steadily up through the thickest part of the night.

What was it? he asked himself. Seventy-five? Eighty? Ninety fucking degrees? You couldn't even breathe the air; it was almost like it tasted of bitter wet heat. He wanted a beer from the small refrigerator, but knew there was none. There wasn't even a soda, or a tray of ice. The tap water was brackish and lukewarm. He thought of standing under the shower but had trouble unfolding his long legs from beneath the table and taking a step in that direction. He blamed his lethargy on the heat as well. He stared angrily across at the living room jalousie window, cranked open to let what little breeze there was meandering about Liberty City enter the apartment.

Cold air, he thought to himself. That's what he wanted more than anything. Just nice cold air that would slip over his body like a light shirt. He lifted one of his hands to the back of his neck and swept away some of the sweat that had gathered there. It glistened in his palm. In Miami, he thought, rich people never sweat—unless they want to.

This thought infuriated him, because he knew it was true.

He continued to eye the open window, as if he could force it to provide some relief, almost as if he expected to see the wind as it slid between the glass plates. His frustration made him alert, so that when it was sound that penetrated the window rather than cool air, it only took him a second to realize what was happening.

One set of footsteps, moving unsteadily and haphazardly on the stairwell, that would be a neighbor, stumbling home drunk.

Two sets of footsteps, moving slowly, deliberately, that would be a drug dealer and his muscle, looking to collect on an overdue debt.

But the rat-a-tat-tat of several pairs of heavy shoes moving fast on the stairs could only be one thing; Leroy Jefferson rose sharply, dashing the pipe onto the floor, knocking over his chair, and crossing the room in one large stride. His girlfriend snorted once and opened her eyes in surprise as he pushed her aside, reaching for the pistol he kept beneath the mattress. He half whispered, half shouted the word "Police" just as a fist thundered against the door to apartment number 13, and the same word was shouted out by Sergeant Lion-man. The policeman and the murder suspect had almost spoken in unison.

The girlfriend grabbed the sheet, pulling it toward her breasts, and screamed: "Leroy, no!"

But Leroy Jefferson ignored her. Spinning in a half crouch by the mattress and raising his pistol, he fired two shots from the bedroom, across the living room and into the front door just as it buckled sharply from a sledgehammer blow, the two pistol reports bracketing the crash of iron against the wooden door frame.

As soon as he had knocked and announced, Sergeant Lion-man had sprung aside, giving the Lumberjack room to swing the sledgehammer. The burly detective howled like an injured animal when, just as he delivered his first blow to the door frame, the second of Leroy Jefferson's shots deflected off the metal plate of the dead-bolt lock and slashed into the bulging bicep of his left arm. Skin, blood, and sinew exploded in a vibrant scarlet mass. He twisted around, the hammer falling with a thud to the corridor floor, slamming backward into a metal grate railing. The Lumberjack continued to wail, his head back, his legs jerking spasmodically, like a runner helplessly trying to accelerate in deep sand. His screams were bursts of unworldly noise that rose through the sudden cacophony of shouts from the other policemen as they dove for cover or threw themselves against the apartment complex cinder-block walls.

The two rookies sent to the rear of the apartment heard the shots, heard the Lumberjack's tortured screams, and sprinted, guns drawn, for the front of the building, where they were immediately sure they were needed.

Sergeant Lion-man, cursing as he saw the detective squirming and quivering with pain, reached down and seized the sledgehammer. He swung back, like a dead pull hitter centering on a lazy fastball, and crashed the hammer into the door frame. The sound of wood splintering, giving way, mingled with another shot from within the apartment. This shot also penetrated the wooden door and creased the air above Sergeant Lion-man's head, and he roared a second vibrant flood of expletives as he smashed the sledgehammer into the frame again.

Walter Robinson grabbed the Lumberjack and pulled him away from the potential line of fire. Behind him, he could hear Juan Rodriguez swearing in Spanish, a torrent of *mierda*s mixed liberally with a Hail Mary and then shouting for Lion-man to keep back. He could hear another member of the arrest team calling in a 10–45, officer down, on his portable radio. Lion-man bellowed again, furious, possessed, and lifted the hammer for a final blow that would separate the door from the frame. Robinson heard, amidst all the jumbled clatter of screams, footsteps, curses, the sound of glass breaking, a tone that he could not quite decipher in the split second that it took for Sergeant Lion-man to deliver his last assault on the door.

As the door frame cracked and splintered and then suddenly gaped wide, thanks to a resounding kick by Sergeant Lion-man, Robinson rose and burst forward.

He tumbled through the opening, followed immediately by Rodriguez and two other policemen. They were all shouting "Police! Freeze!" and swinging their weapons right and left, two hands on the grips, as they had all been taught. The first thing they saw was Leroy Jefferson's girlfriend, standing naked in the center of the room, shrieking. She threw a kitchen water tumbler in their direction; it exploded in shards on the wall behind them, and one of the City of Miami officers ducked and fired his weapon at her. He missed. The bullet smashed into the drywall behind her, no more than six inches from her ear, sending a plume of white dust into the air. Juan Rodriguez had the presence of mind to reach out and seize the officer's hand, pushing it down so that he would not fire again, screaming incoherent anger in two different languages as he did so.

Walter Robinson peered about. There was so much confused noise that it obscured his vision. It was almost, he thought, as if he could feel the abrupt absence of his suspect. He turned toward the naked girlfriend, who was standing rigidly, eyes open, making no effort to cover herself, as if astonished to be shot at and still be alive.

"Where is he?" Robinson screamed.

She stared blankly at him.

"Where is he?" Robinson shouted again. This time the girlfriend's head jerked to the side, and he followed the brief look she tossed toward the bathroom.

"Damn," he said beneath his breath. He vaulted across the room, like a high jumper approaching the bar, and pushed himself against the wall next to the closed bathroom door. He gingerly reached out and tried the knob. Locked. He took a single deep breath, and stepped back, before delivering a massive kick at the flimsy door.

It buckled and sprang open.

He leapt into the tiny bathroom, instantly spotting the broken-out window. He threw aside a chair that had been used to smash the glass. He jumped into the tub, almost slipping on the smooth surface, and reached for the windowsill. He steadied himself and looked out into the night precisely at the spot where the two rookie officers were supposed to be. But he saw only the vague, ghostly shape of Leroy Jefferson, two stories down, rising unsteadily from the backyard dust, illuminated by weak gray light, gun in hand.

He yelled: "Freeze!"

Jefferson turned, looked up at the window, and then wheeled and ran.

"Goddamn it!" Robinson shouted. "The bastard jumped."

And in that moment he realized there was no one outside the apartment, except Espy Martinez.

"Jesus!" he said. "Espy! Watch out!" he screamed helplessly through the shattered window. Then he pivoted and ran desperately for the front door.

Alone at the edge of the darkness, Espy Martinez started forward, then stopped. She just barely made out Walter Robinson's shouted warning, coming, as it did, out of the night and the noise, but it merely underscored the confusion that she already felt.

Watch out for what?

She had seen the assault on the apartment from her vantage point at the assembled police vehicles; it had played out like some distant theater performed in a strange language, elusive in its meaning. The gunshots, the shouts and yells, the deep booming sound of the sledgehammer against the door—she knew that something had gone wrong, but was incapable in her position of deciphering precisely what that was.

Again she started forward. She thought it important to do something—to move, to act. She could feel insistence racing through her body, making a din within her, smashing up against all the abrupt sensations of doubt and fear that wanted to throw chains around her limbs. As these warring emotions struggled for control, she saw a shadowy figure bounding fast toward her.

Leroy Jefferson sprinted barefoot across the rough dirt and patches of cement that formed the entranceway to the King Apartments. He had no real idea where he was heading, possessed solely by the idea of escape. Slices of broken glass tore at the soles of his feet, but he ignored them.

He had a sudden flashing memory of being on the court, ahead of everyone, the ball in his hands, rising alone toward the basket. The shouts from the policemen behind him faded away, mingling with distant remembered cheers from a jam-packed gymnasium. The air around him seemed to rush past his ears, like a tropical storm flexing its muscles; he was surprised to realize that for the first time in what seemed like months, he felt cool.

The figure that loomed up in front of him seemed an apparition.

He could see it was a woman; see she was crouched over and that she held something in her hands; see that the something was a weapon. He saw, too, that the woman's mouth was open, and he understood she was screaming something at him, but all these somethings only forced him to move faster. He swerved, but saw her weapon track him. He tried to dodge, to switch direction, but his momentum carried him headlong forward, and he realized, in the same moment, that he had lifted his own pistol and was tugging at the trigger. There were three shots left in the cylinder, and he fired them all. The booming sound of the pistol crashed through the heat.

Espy Martinez saw Jefferson's gun, saw too that it seemed aimed directly at her, and yelled "Freeze!" for what she thought was the millionth time, and had the sudden idea that the word was completely ridiculous, because it had no effect on the tall, wiry figure that was descending upon her.

She hesitated, and in that moment he fired.

She thought instantly: I'm dead.

And without really recognizing what she was doing, she started pulling hard at the trigger of her own weapon. She did not know if she closed her eyes or not, or if she lifted her hand to shield herself or not, or if she ducked or sidestepped, or whether, in truth, she remained rigid, locked into her crouch, fully expecting a small projectile to pick her up and toss her abruptly into death's eager embrace.

The three bullets from Jefferson's gun buzzed about her. One grabbed at her purse, severing the leather strap, ripping it from her arm. The second tugged like a bored child at the sleeve of her light jacket and passed by harmlessly. The third, howling in what she later supposed was frustration, smashed into the window of the police cruiser behind her, exploding the glass.

Sweat dripped down her face, stinging her eyes, and she was filled with astonishment: No—I'm alive.

She realized that she was still pulling the trigger of her weapon, only the clip had long been emptied. She was unaware that she had fired. There should have been noise. She should have felt the gun bucking in her hand. A faint smell of cordite rose about her, like an unwanted perfume. She had to force herself to stop her finger twitching against the trigger. She looked down at her body, as if taking a quick inventory, astounded that she wasn't bleeding somewhere. In that instant, she abruptly wanted to laugh, and she lifted her eyes. Only then was she able to focus on Leroy Jefferson.

He writhed on the ground, perhaps twenty feet in front of where she stood, kicking up spurts of dirt as he twisted in pain. He clutched at his leg, and she could see blood welling between his fingers. He tried to rise once, bent over, still grasping his smashed kneecap, and he stumbled forward a few feet before falling back, like a thoroughbred with a broken foreleg, trained by instinct to finish a stakes race but unable to comprehend why it cannot run.

She stood, watching him, also unable to move, in that moment equally crippled. She listened to his screams of pain, blood streaking the dusty sidewalk, empty as the clip in her pistol.

Time has a curious elasticity; she was unsure whether she stood looking at the wounded suspect for minutes or seconds before Walter Robinson streaked across the open courtyard and threw himself onto the thrashing man. Sergeant Lion-man was only a few steps behind him, as were the other officers. The gunshots—those fired at her and those she had fired—still rang in her ears, deafening her. She only slowly became aware of the crescendo of sirens that were scoring the night; the bursts of red and blue strobe lights from other police vehicles and ambulances; the squealing of tires.

She watched as Walter Robinson pummeled Leroy Jefferson, finally twisting the suspect's arms back and tightening handcuffs around his wrists savagely. She looked away as Robinson rose and aimed a kick at the shackled man. Her eyes met Sergeant Lion-man's. He was standing in front of her, and it took her an extra moment to realize that he was shouting at her.

"Are you all right? Are you hit? Are you okay?"

She shook her head. "No, I'm fine," she replied matter-of-factly.

Anderson threw a huge arm around her shoulders and gently pushed her back a half-dozen feet. He steered her onto the seat of the police cruiser with the shot-out window, sweeping shattered glass away with one hand as he pushed her down.

"Sit here," he said. "I'm gonna get the paramedic."

"No," she repeated. "I'm fine."

She watched as Leroy Jefferson was flipped over onto his back like a beast about to be branded. Two emergency medical technicians wearing blue jumpsuits were tending to his leg. Another, a young blond-haired man, hovered in front of her.

"I'm fine," she said a third time, before he had a chance to ask the obvious question. She looked up and saw Walter Robinson behind the man. His face was rigid with a succession of pale angers and fears. She smiled at him.

"He missed," she said.

"Jesus, Espy, I—"

"I got him, though. Is he going to die?"

"Not unless they leave me alone with him. The bastard . . ."

"He was running and he missed. I wonder—"

"Don't think about it. You're okay." He bent down beside her. "Jesus," he said. He wanted very much to put his arm around her, the way the big sergeant had, but he held back. She seemed very small, sitting half in, half out of the patrol car.

And then, to his surprise, she looked at him and laughed out loud. After a second he joined her, hesitant at first, but then giving way. Sergeant Lion-man and Sergeant Rodriguez came up. They started laughing as well, as tension fled from within all of them. It was like the greatest practical joke in the world: to be alive when you should be dead.

After a moment their laughter tapered off, and Espy Martinez let out a deep sigh.

"I'm gonna drive you home," Walter Robinson said.

"Yes," she replied. She could feel adrenaline fading from her and a massive exhaustion setting in. She saw the paramedics lifting Leroy Jefferson onto a stretcher, moving him to the open door of an ambulance. She saw another ambulance moving off, its siren cutting through the lights.

"There goes the Lumberjack. Poor bastard ain't gonna be lifting weights no more," Anderson said. Sergeant Lion-man glanced over at the stretcher crew. "Hey, hold it!" he called out. "Walter, buddy, you do the honors, huh. Right here. And Miss Martinez, you come witness him getting his rights right now, please. Then maybe we can all get the hell out of here before we have a riot."

Espy Martinez looked up and saw that a crowd had started to gather on the edge of the lights, milling about.

Walter Robinson nodded, and stepped to the side of the stretcher. "Leroy Jefferson," he said, in an even, angry tone of restrained fury, "you're under arrest. You have the right to remain silent. You have the right to an attorney—"

"I know all that shit," Jefferson interrupted between pain-clenched teeth. "What you think I did?"

Robinson stared down with fury that was restrained by only the barest strands of self-control.

"You had to kill her, huh, Leroy? Couldn't just take her stuff. Maybe even knock her out. You could have managed that no problem, right? Big guy like you. She was just a little old lady and you had to go kill her. . . ."

"What you talking about?"

"You didn't even know her name, did you, Leroy?"

"Who you talking about? What little old lady?"

"Her name was Sophie Millstein, Leroy. Just a little old lady, living alone on Miami Beach. Trying to live out her years nice and quiet and peaceful. No harm to nobody. And you had to kill her, you sonofabitch. And now you're going away, you motherfucker."

Leroy Jefferson looked both confused and pained.

Then, abruptly, his lips curled back, half snarl, half laugh, and he said: "You more of a fool than I thought. I didn't kill any old lady."

"Sure you didn't," Robinson said, icy sarcasm in his voice.

But Leroy Jefferson shook his head. "All this," he said. "All this and it ain't me done it. Damn." He appeared genuinely confused and saddened.

"All this for the wrong me," he added.

He dropped his head back onto the stretcher as the paramedics thrust it up into the back of the ambulance none too gently, leaving Walter Robinson standing outside as the doors were slammed closed.

"No, nobody ever does anything," he said quietly, almost to himself, but Espy Martinez overheard him. He turned toward her. "Sure he didn't do it," he said. "We're going. Now."

Martinez nodded. She felt completely exhausted. She thought that if it were not for an odd sensation of something not unlike fear, but not precisely fear, that remained echoing within her alongside the suspect's words of denial, she could fall asleep right there.

# THIRTEEN
## SODDIT

HE watched the shadows on the whitewashed wall of the hospital corridor; the glow from the fluorescent lights at the nurses' station caught the profile of anyone who walked past, sending a sudden, dark, vaguely human shape skittering across the flat in front of him. At one point he lifted his own hand, to see if he could add to the gray ghostlike forms, but the light angle was wrong.

Walter Robinson shifted in his seat, trying to find a comfortable position, knowing that none was available. He glanced at a clock and saw that the night had almost fled, and he supposed it wouldn't be long before the shadows skulked away, as the day's light penetrated the hospital hallways.

He was exhausted, but anger like adrenaline kept him alert.

He tried to remain fixated on the man occupying the recovery room, thinking it would be simplest to blame Leroy Jefferson for everything that had gone wrong that night. But inwardly Jefferson shared space in his rage with himself. Walter Robinson played over the sequence of events, trying to discern precisely where it had all gone sour, where he had made the mistake that resulted in the shooting. The procedure had been textbook. The setup had been perfect. But getting a cop shot and wounded on what should have been a routine, if tricky, arrest stoked his frustration. The

180

preliminary word on the Lumberjack was not good; extensive muscle and bone tissue damage. A career that had evaporated in a single moment. He had spent a few minutes with the policeman's wife, but his hackneyed words of apology had been ignored. He'd briefed the Beach police brass, and they made a statement to the press. He had wasted time hanging at the back of the room as two dozen reporters and cameramen asked questions, then he crept away to the hallway where he currently sat. He did not know what awaited Leroy Jefferson; in that moment, he wished Espy Martinez had blown the suspect's head off. It would have made for some troublesome paperwork, but probably would have been considerably more satisfying for all involved.

He let this bloodthirsty thought linger within him. Even with everything that had gone wrong, he recognized he should have felt some satisfaction. After all, he'd cleared the case: Jefferson was charged with the first-degree murder of Sophie Millstein. In the Beach homicide offices there was a large chalkboard with active cases listed on it. Sophie Millstein's murder would come off the board. He'd done his job.

Robinson let a whispered expletive slide through his lips.

He leaned his head back against the wall, closing his eyes for a moment, expecting to see the bedlam at the King Apartments played out again, like on a screen behind his eyes, but saw instead himself, holding Espy Martinez by the elbow, walking her slowly up the sidewalk to her duplex with all the stiff-edged formality of some eighteenth-century courtier. On the long drive across town, she had fluctuated between a babbling, nonstop excitement, words coupled with obscenities tumbling from her mouth, and moments of dark-ridged silence. One second she had blurted: "Jesus fucking Christ, I can't believe it, I shot the fucking bastard, didn't I? Right in the fucking leg, Jesus. I mean, it's all so fucking unreal. The motherfucker fired and I fired and I got him. Just fucking well got him, didn't I?"

And when he'd replied, "That's right. You did," she lapsed into an electric quiet, as if the interior of the car was vibrating, but there was no sound. He tried to search within himself for some other words to say to her, but was unable to find any, so remained silent. Once, she gasped, and he'd turned to make sure she was all right, only to see her shake her head and stare out at the glow of the city lights as they swept past.

At her house he'd stood on the doorstep, asking her, "Are you all right? Are you sure you're all right? Should I call someone? You gonna be okay alone?" listening to her reply that she was fine, and all the time wanting to step inside the apartment with her, and being unable to. Like a goddamn teenager on a first date, he berated himself. Maybe the worst first date in the history of the world.

Again he muttered an expletive and opened his eyes. He clenched a fist and raised it in front of his face.

"You going to hit me, or are you saving that for my client?"

Walter Robinson followed the sound of the voice and looked up at the man speaking. He was a lanky, curly-headed man with a ready grin at the corners of his mouth that contradicted an intensity in his eyes. He wore jeans and running shoes without socks and a white knit sport shirt that had a stain on it, and Robinson knew he'd hurried from his bed to get to the hospital. But the attorney also had a loose-limbed insouciance in the way he leaned up against the hallway wall across from the detective, placing himself where there had only been shadows a few moments before.

"Hello, Tommy," Robinson said slowly. "What are you doing here?" He knew the answer to this question, but asked it anyway.

Thomas Alter was about the same age as Walter Robinson. The detective figured they probably would have been friends if he were not a senior assistant in the county Public Defender's Office, which made him and all the local homicide detectives natural adversaries. One rarely becomes overly fond of people whose job it is to rip and rend one's work in the protected cloister of the criminal courtroom. Respect, certainly. Often a sort of grudging acknowledgment that they were all part of the same machinelike process. But a genuine affection was impossible.

"I'm here to make certain that our Mr. Jefferson receives proper medical treatment, which doesn't include giving you a statement until he's had time to speak with his attorney, which, for better or for worse, happens to be yours truly."

"He's not *our* Mr. Jefferson. . . ."

"All right. *My* Mr. Jefferson . . ."

"Come on, Tommy. He needs to be arraigned, make a statement of indigency before you get him. In the meantime, if he wants to talk to me . . ."

"Yes, ordinarily, yes, Walt. Correct. But not this time. Jefferson was in court just under a week ago on a lousy possession charge, which the State intends to drop because I eviscerated the search warrant. But they haven't got around to doing it officially, so, Walt, old buddy, I am still attorney of record. There you have it. You cannot speak to him without me or someone from my office present at all times. Got it?"

"If he wants to—"

"At all times. You read him his rights, and I'm telling you he isn't waiving any of them."

Thomas Alter continued to smile, but his voice had lost any lightness.

Robinson shrugged, trying to hide the irritation that ricocheted about within him.

"At all times," Alter repeated. "Got that, Walt?"

"Yes."

"That means around the clock. Twenty-four hours. Seven days a week."

"Don't you trust me, Tommy?"

"No."

"Good. Because I don't trust you either."

Alter smiled wanly. "Well, then I suppose we're even."

"Nope. The one thing we'll never be is even, because I wouldn't be here trying to protect a scumbag like Jefferson."

"Right. I guess not. Too moral for that, huh?" Alter's voice had a mocking sarcasm attached to it. "So how you doing, otherwise? Rough night, I hear . . ."

"I would say so."

"Too bad about the guy who got shot. Friend of yours?"

"No. Not really."

Alter nodded. "Is Espy okay?"

Robinson hesitated, then replied, "Sure. Maybe a little shaky, but she's fine."

"Good. She's not like some of the sonsofbitches in that office.

She's reasonable. Tough but reasonable. And pretty too. Glad she didn't buy it out there in the jungle. Sounds like a close call. Wouldn't go near the King Apartments, personally. Especially after dark. What was she doing out there anyway?"

Robinson didn't reply.

The young public defender looked over at the detective. He smiled. "Go to bed, Walter. You look tired. This mess will still be waiting for you later. In fact, it's gonna be around for a while."

Robinson rose. He looked across at Alter, who continued to lean back against the wall. The lawyer glanced down the hallway toward a pair of uniformed officers who sat outside the recovery room. The two cops were watching the detective.

"Tell 'em, Walt."

"Fuck you, Tommy."

Alter grinned again, but his eyes were hard. "No," he said quietly, "fuck you, Walter."

He raised his voice and called out loudly: "Get this. No one talks to Jefferson except authorized medical personnel and representatives from the Dade County Public Defender's Office! And when you finish your shift, you make sure your replacements know. You got that?"

The words echoed in the corridor, and the two cops stared blankly toward Walter Robinson, who reluctantly nodded.

"Well, thanks, Walt," Alter said briskly. "But I think I'll still tape an order to his door." The lawyer removed a letter with the seal of the P.D.'s office on it. "Same letter being delivered to the arraignment judge and to Espy Martinez and her fucking boss Lasser, this A.M.," he added.

"You covering all the bases, Tommy?"

Alter glared at Robinson. "You think it would be the first time we represented some poor fuck who got the mistaken impression that a homicide detective was his last, greatest, and only true friend in the entire fucking world, and promptly ran his mouth and his ass right onto Death Row? You think it would be the first time some homicide detective that maybe didn't have the strongest case in the world walked into court and got up on the stand and swore to tell the whole fucking truth and said, 'Yes sir, Your Honor, the defendant orally waived every fucking constitutional right and then confessed to that murder to me. Privately, yes sir, no problem . . .'? Well, you know what, Walter?"

"What's that, Tommy?"

"It ain't happening this time."

Robinson felt drained. He wanted fresh air, hoping for a steady breeze that perhaps might carry him like a sailor adrift, home, to his own bed. He abruptly felt like a man at the end of an all-night poker game, who looks down and sees his stake has dwindled and the cards in front of him are nothing but a useless bluff.

Still, he couldn't resist adding an angry statement: "You know, Tommy, this is a bad dude. He's a junkie and a psychopath and a bad-ass. He's gonna go down. Don't you already have a couple of clients on the Row? How many, Tommy? Two? Three?"

"Just one," Alter whispered bitterly.

"Really, Tommy? I could have sworn you used to have more. . . ."

"Yeah. I did."

"Oh, right. I remember. I guess we'd just have to say that one of those clients just fell prey to natural attrition, huh, Tommy? Doesn't that sound like a nice and safe and reasonable way to describe someone being strapped into an electric chair?"

"Fuck you, Walter."

"He was a cop-killer, right, Tommy?"

"That's right."

"Not much sympathy in the legal system for cop-killers, huh? That was a tough closing for that jury, wasn't it? Trying to make twelve people feel downright nice and cozy with some bastard that stuck a gun in an undercover cop's mouth after making him strip naked and told him he had enough time for one prayer, right? One prayer before dying, wasn't that what the bastard said? But then he pulled the trigger before the cop even got half the Our Father out. . . . Wasn't that the case, Tommy?"

"You know it."

"Well, my guess is you've already started working on your closing for Jefferson's jury, huh, Tommy? You got something special in mind that maybe explains the really good reason why that rat bastard had to strangle a little old lady? And I'd say our

Mr. Jefferson is right lucky that all he did tonight was ruin a cop's arm and his career. But it doesn't make a difference, does it?"

"What do you mean?"

"Because he's going to the same place."

"Death Row? Don't count on it, Detective."

"No. I meant Hell."

"Don't count on it," Thomas Alter repeated coldly. Now even the corners of his mouth had lost the crinkle of familiarity, replaced with a hard-edged coolness that Walter Robinson recognized from a dozen cross-examinations. He felt out of control, like a car skidding on a rain-slick highway. He knew Alter was a formidable opponent and angering him was a mistake. But he continued, letting all the night's exhaustions and frustrations guide his responses.

"No, Tommy. Bet the house. That's where he's headed."

"Maybe so. But not on this piece of shit case."

"Really? I got motive, I got opportunity, I got an after-the-fact accomplice and I got an eyewitness at the scene, and I got fifty says you are just totally fucking wrong, Counselor."

Robinson tried to hold his tongue, but could not. Exhaustion and frustration pummeled him, forcing him to blurt out information that he knew he should have kept to himself.

"Really?" The attorney imitated Robinson's voice. "And you're covered, Detective."

"Well, we'll see, won't we."

"That's right, Walter. We'll see."

The two men glared at each other. Alter spoke first.

"You know they saved his leg. But that's it. Just saved it. He'll maybe walk about a bit, but that leg ain't never gonna work no more like it used to. . . ." The lawyer slipped into a familiar street talk, as if to diminish the seriousness of what he was saying.

"Breaks my fucking heart," Robinson replied.

"Yes. Well, I wouldn't expect a man who's going to spend the rest of his life in pain and limping about to cooperate a whole helluva lot with the folks that did that to him."

"We don't need his cooperation. All we need is for him to take his rightful spot on Death Row."

Alter smiled again. "You couldn't be more mistaken, Walter." He spoke with the overblown confidence of a snake-oil salesman.

Robinson shook his head and turned his back, thought it was almost morning, and if he were fortunate, the sun would just be rising over the edge of the Beach as he drove over the causeway to his apartment, filling the air around him with blades of clear light, slicing away all the stale anger of the night past, allowing him to think freely about Espy Martinez.

For two days she had been the toast of the State Attorney's Office. Toughness in a courtroom was one thing; toughness in the real world gained a completely different level of respect. The other assistants had busied themselves with a search through a variety of nicknames—Deadeye, Quickdraw, Make My Day Martinez—trying to find one that might stick.

Even Abraham Lasser had made one of his rare pilgrimages from his own office through the warren of desks and cubicles to applaud Espy Martinez on her success, which was an odd thing, when she thought about it; her boss, her coworkers, all congratulating her for not being shot and killed. Lasser had stuck his wiry-haired head around the corner of her door and sung out in a creaky voice: "Ahh, the young Annie Oakley, I presume?" And then, after shaking her hand and clapping her on the back, lifting her arm up like some fighter in a championship ring, he whispered to her that she should make certain that she nailed Leroy Jefferson to the maximum, a penalty he did not have to spell out for all listening. Then, later that day, he had circulated a memo throughout the office, praising Espy Martinez for her quick thinking—though she did wonder idly what she had managed to think quickly about—and reminding all the other assistants that they too were sworn law enforcement officers and should arm themselves appropriately, at appropriate moments, so they could take appropriate action, under appropriate circumstances, after using appropriate judgment, as she had. He did not define what he meant by *appropriate*.

Espy Martinez enjoyed the attention, let it distract her from what she was doing. When Walter Robinson called her, she felt a rush of excitement, as if he was the key part of what had taken place.

"So, Espy, how're things?"

"Well, the guys in the office next to me persist in whistling the tune to *High Noon* every time I walk past. Other than that, things are okay."

He laughed. He could hear a vibrancy in her voice.

"We need to get together, start wrapping the case tight."

"I know," she said. "I haven't been concentrating."

"Have you spoken with Tommy Alter?"

"Not yet. Well, actually, just once. Jefferson was arraigned in absentia. The hospital won't release him to the jail for another week or so."

"I took his fingerprints this morning. Alter was there, but wouldn't say anything. He just watched. Jefferson looked like he was in pain, which isn't so bad. Leg's still in traction, but it goes into a cast tomorrow. The doctor said he's looking at maybe two, three more operations down the line. I told the doctor it would be a waste of time. Real loud voice, so that Jefferson and Alter could hear me."

"That's cold," she said, laughing.

"Hey, what do they say? All's fair in love and war, and this sure ain't one of those things. . . ."

"What's next?"

"Well, I'm taking the prints to be checked. We should be able to put him right in the apartment. I took his mug shot and made a photo lineup and showed it to my bus drivers and they put Jefferson on the right bus at the right time. I'm gonna take the same photo lineup over to Mr. Kadosh tomorrow morning. Because the bastard's in the hospital, a real lineup's out. Then we have the pawnshop owner to testify to the stolen goods. I filed a truckload of charges on poor old Reginald and young Yolanda too. Most of them were bullshit, but enough to keep the two of them toeing the line. Lion-man will be all over their action anyway, to make sure. The search of the King Apartments didn't turn up anything from Sophie's place. He must have dumped it all at the Helping Hand. But still, all in all, it seems pretty tight to me."

Espy Martinez nodded, but changed her tone: "Alter seemed confident. I noticed that."

"Same to me."

"Why?"

"I don't know. I can't see a reason, except that he's an arrogant sonofabitch who always acts confident as hell right up to the moment he realizes he's got no defense. Then he'll come whining and begging for a plea bargain. Should be in a couple of weeks. Give him his moment or two."

"No plea. That came down from the boss."

"Good. He'll want it, you know. That's what the defense strategy will be: Find some little weakness that he can exploit into some worry, so that instead of taking a risk with a jury, we'll settle for the mandatory twenty-five."

"I don't think the State will agree to that."

"That's what he'll be shooting for. Anything that keeps Jefferson off Death Row will be a victory for him."

"I wish we had a confession."

"Yeah. Make things perfect, wouldn't it? And I would have got one out of the bastard if Alter hadn't shown up."

"Juries like a confession in a murder case. Makes them feel certain they're doing the right thing. Especially when they have to vote on the death penalty."

"I know that. But we've got just about everything else."

"Can we go over it all one more time? Maybe we can see a problem ahead of time if we talk it out? I'd rather be lying in wait for Alter when he comes walking through the door, hat in hand. Makes it easier to say no."

Robinson grabbed at this opportunity. "Why don't we make it dinner, or something? I'll bring the case file, we can eat something, go over it slowly. . . ."

Espy Martinez hesitated. Her skin flushed red and she felt hot. "Walter, I don't know about mixing work and . . ."

She didn't finish, but he jumped into the silence.

"Hey, don't worry about it. A real date would be going to a movie or a play or a concert or a game or something. You know, where I show up at your place wearing a tie and carrying flowers and a box of candy and I open the car door for you. A real date requires nervousness and polite small talk and manners. This is something different. I kinda feel I owe you something for the other night. I mean, you weren't supposed to end up shooting someone. I feel downright guilty about that."

Martinez smiled, then replied: "It wasn't your fault."

"Well, it sure didn't happen the way I had it all worked out in my head."

"Hey," she joked, "do you think I mind if all of a sudden everyone around here thinks I'm dangerous?"

"Dangerous and notorious?"

"That's right. Two-fisted and pistol-packing. A woman to be reckoned with."

The two of them laughed.

"All right," she said. "Tomorrow night."

"I'll pick you up at your office?"

"No, at my house. You remember how to get there?"

He did.


They did not, of course, end up talking about the case, except in a perfunctory fashion at the start of the evening, almost as if it was something necessary that they had to get out of the way. He took her to an open-air restaurant that overlooked Biscayne Bay, the sort of place where the waiter behaves pretentiously and then serves mediocre food that is obscured by heavy sauces and a spectacular view. As they sat, he could see the blues of the water deepen, traveling from far out in the ocean toward the shore, first a pale, sky color, to a more solid azure, and then finally into the deep navy, almost indistinguishable from black, that heralded the summertime night. City lights blinked on and seemed to score the water surface, as if painted on the rippling waves by an Impressionist.

She sat across from him and knew it had all the easy romance of the tropics. She could feel a light breeze blowing through the folds of the loose-fitting dress she wore, touching her skin in hidden places with the familiarity of an old lover. She leaned her head back, then ran a hand through the sweep of her hair. She looked over at Walter Robinson, thought him terrifically handsome, and thought too that were her parents to see her sitting across from him, they would not speak to her for days, unless they were persuaded this meeting was all business. So, in deference to this image and to at least create the illusion of work, she asked:

"Jefferson?"

Robinson smiled. "Right. A working dinner. I would say things are looking dark for Leroy Jefferson, which might be a pun, but we'll leave race out of this."

She nodded. "How so?"

"Well, just before I left the office tonight, I got a call from Harry Harrison—I mean, how does someone get a name like that, anyway?—over in the fingerprints section. Guess whose prints showed up on Sophie Millstein's bureau drawer?"

"Our man Jefferson?"

"None other."

"Well, that's that, isn't it?"

"Yes. Pretty much so. Harry said he still has to check the prints on the jewelry box, the sliding glass door, and the body print they took from Sophie's throat, but thought we'd like to know what he'd come up with so far."

"Goodbye, Mr. Jefferson."

"And Kadosh gave us a pretty good identification from the photo lineup."

"What's pretty good?"

"He picked out Jefferson's mug shot and said he couldn't be certain unless he saw the man in person, but he was pretty sure he was the man. The key thing with the old guy is keeping him away from his wife. He's sort of used to having her tell him everything he thinks, and she has an opinion on everything."

"Everything?"

"Trust me. Everything."

"So?"

"So, I can't see the problem. If there is one."

"Where does that leave us?"

Walter Robinson grinned. "Actually, right here. Glass of wine?"

Espy Martinez nodded. She watched him pour her glass, then she slowly drank some, letting the cool, fruity taste descend through her. She looked out over the bay and thought for an instant that what she was thinking was like plunging into the waves after sunset.

"Tell me, Walter. Who are you?"

He smiled. "Who am I? I'm a police detective that's almost got his law degree and—"

She held up her hand. "No. Not what are you. Who are you?"

Robinson thought he heard an earnestness in her voice, and abruptly realized that she was asking more of him than he'd expected. He felt a momentary reluctance, but then, before he had a chance to check himself, started to speak slowly, quietly, almost as if part of a conspiracy.

"I swim," he said, lifting a hand toward the bay. "I swim alone, when no one is watching, far from shore. In deep water. One mile, at least. Two, sometimes."

He stopped there. He did not describe what he liked to do, which was to drive out to the tip of Key Biscayne to the state park at Cape Florida late in the afternoon, when all the beet-red tourists and the beered-up teenagers had already packed their picnic lunches and were trying to beat the shadows home. He would slide into the water and, taking powerful overhand strokes, push himself against the waves out past the red and white marker buoys, past any boundaries, to where he could feel the conflicting tug of tidal currents pulling at his arms and legs. There he would turn, treading water, and stare back at the key, down toward the rows of condos, or off past the ancient abandoned brick lighthouse, where the ocean joins the bay. He would let the waters rock him, as if they were trying to insist they were safe, when he knew they were not. After a few moments he would take a deep breath and once again battle the rips and flows, dodging the occasional man-o'-war with its lethal sting, ignoring all thoughts of sharks, teasing exhaustion and the inevitable death it would bring, until he was able to touch sand beneath his toes, and he would drag himself back onto the beach, safe again, breathing harshly.

"Why do you swim?" she asked quietly.

"Because when I was growing up in the Grove, none of the black kids ever learned how to swim. There were no pools and the beach was three bus transfers away. We lived in the most watery county in the entire nation—did you know that?—but we never learned how to swim. I remember, every year or so, there was always a story in the paper about some black kid drowning in a canal, where he was fishing or gigging frogs or just playing around. Slipped and fell into four feet of water and panicked and struggled and cried out, but no one was ever there and so they drowned. The white kids never drowned. You see, they had pools behind their homes and were taught. Breaststroke. Australian crawl. Sidestroke and butterfly. All that happened to them was they got wet and maybe they got yelled at when they got home and tracked water into the house."

He put his glass of wine down.

"I sound angry. I don't want to sound angry."

She shook her head. She realized she had been told something important, almost like a clue hidden on a page of a mystery novel and that later she would see why it was important.

"No," she said. "It makes it easier for me."

"Easier for what?"

She didn't reply. What she thought was: understanding what's going to happen.

"So, Espy, now I have a question for you," Robinson said after a moment's quiet.

"Go ahead. Shoot." She laughed slightly. "Maybe that's a bad choice of words for me."

"Tell me why you're alone."

"What do you mean?"

He made a small gesture with his hand, as if to say: You're young, you're beautiful, educated, and intelligent—and should be surrounded with suitors. Which she took as a compliment of sorts.

"Because I've never found anyone who—"

She stopped, uncertain how to proceed. For a second she hoped Walter Robinson would step into the silence with some other question, then realized he wouldn't, and so she continued, a small hesitation in her voice. "I suppose because of my brother." She took a deep breath. "My poor dead brother. My poor dead dumb brother."

"I didn't know, I'm sorry," he started.

"No. It's okay. It's been almost twelve years. Labor Day weekend. He was to start law school the next week. . . ."

"Car accident?"

"No. Nothing that innocent. He was coming back from a snorkeling trip in the Keys with a couple of college friends. It was getting late, and they stopped at a convenience store to get something to eat. You know, stupid stuff: chips and beers and Ring-Dings and Slim Jims and all that crap that twenty-two-year-old males consume with such passion. Anyway, there they are, it's a little half bodega, half 7-Eleven, just off South Dixie Highway, way down below Kendall, and they've got all this junk and my brother is teasing the little old Cuban lady who's running the store. You know, asking her if she's got a daughter, and if not, is she single, good-natured stuff, and they're both laughing and speaking in Spanish, and he's kidding his friends, because they're Anglos and can't understand what he and the little old lady are talking about, when a guy comes in through the front door wearing a stocking mask and waving a forty-four-caliber Magnum. He screams at everyone to grab the floor and somebody open the register. And everybody just freezes, then they do what he says, but he's impatient, you know, because he's wired on PCP, I guess, or maybe he's just mean, or maybe he doesn't like Latinos, I don't know, but when the old woman hesitates, he just reaches out and pistol-whips her, right across the face. One minute she is joking and flirting with my brother, my poor dumb brother, and the next she is bleeding, her nose busted, her jaw broken. And my brother gets up, just to his knees, and shouts at the guy to stop it, leave her alone, and the guy takes one little look at my brother and laughs just once like he's not sure who's crazier, my brother or himself, and then shoots him, right in the chest. One shot. Boom! The old woman screams and starts praying, and my brother's friends are hugging the floor, figuring they're next. And they would have been, because the bad guy turns to them and points the Magnum and pulls the trigger. Once. Twice. Then he spins and points it at the old woman, and pulls the trigger a third time. Nothing. Click. Click. Click. They're too shocked and scared to realize the bastard only had one bullet in the gun. The bad guy laughs and then

he heads out the door with the cash from the register and a bag
of Doritos. . . ."

She took another deep breath. "One bullet and a bag of
Doritos."

"I'm sorry—" Robinson started, but she held up her hand.

"My poor dumb brother who should have kept his mouth shut
but that wasn't the kind of guy he was, doesn't even make it to
South Miami Hospital."

"It's okay," Robinson started, unsure whether he wanted her to
continue.

"No," Martinez said quietly. "I should get all this out. I was fifteen, home in bed, asleep. I heard my parents crying, and then
they went to the hospital. They left me behind. Alone. I sat up all
night in the dark waiting for them to come back. I never did see
my brother again, except at the funeral, and then he didn't really
look like himself, you know. I mean, he wasn't grinning and
teasing me like he always did. It was three days before I was to
celebrate my *quince*. Do you know what that is?"

"Well, sort of. It's a party Latin girls get when they turn
fifteen. . . ."

"Well, yeah, it's a party. But it's more than that. I don't suppose it's quite as big a deal as a bar mitzvah for a Jewish kid, because that's all religion, but it comes close. It's this celebration
that announces that now you are a woman. There's tradition and
the sense that now you belong to something. It's filled with fancy,
frilly dresses and giggling and slow music and chaperones, you
know, parents watching all these children behaving like adults. In
the Cuban community, it is an important event. You plan it for
months. At fifteen, it's the only thing you think about for days and
days. But mine turned into my brother's funeral."

"It must have been difficult," Robinson said, then thought that
sounded stupid because it was so obvious. So instead, he reached
across the table and touched Espy Martinez's hand. She immediately grabbed his and held it tightly.

"In my house, you see, my dead brother dominated everything.
He was supposed to become a lawyer. Take over my father's
business. Become important. Influential. Raise a family and

become something. And they never said it, but when he died, that all fell to me. But something else did too."

"What's that?"

"Revenge."

"How do you mean?"

"In Cuban society, hell, for almost all Latins, a death like that is a debt. My father and mother, they were made old by his murder. It fell to me."

"But what could you do?"

"Well, I couldn't just take a gun and shoot someone. I had to find some other way to pay."

"The killer?"

"Never caught. At least, not officially. A guy fitting his description got busted coming out of a Dairy Mart with the register contents up in Palm Beach County two weeks later, but my brother's friends and the old woman couldn't pick him out of a lineup. The M.O. was the same. Wore the same mask, shouted the same words. Laughed the same way. Fit the pattern. But they couldn't prosecute him for my brother's murder."

"What happened?"

"He got fifteen then, but did five. He's back in again. I keep tabs on him. I get the prison people to keep running informants through his cell, see if he'll talk, maybe accidentally. Just maybe say what happened to that forty-four Magnum that disappeared. Maybe shoot his mouth off about getting away with murder. I keep my brother's case file in a drawer in my desk. Keep it updated, you know. Addresses. Statements. Whatever it will take, so that if I can ever link him concretely, the case is ready to go."

She took a deep breath.

"No statute of limitations on first-degree murder. No statute of limitations on revenge."

She looked at him.

"Obsessive, I suppose. But it's in the blood."

Again she paused, and he tried to think of something to say. But as he stumbled over his own words, she continued:

"So, I guess, he's why I went to law school. Instead of my poor brother. And he's why I became a prosecutor, so that one day I could get up in front of a jury and point at the bastard and say he's the one that killed him. Killed the little old lady who owned the place too, in reality. She had a weak heart and six months later passed away."

"I'm sorry," Robinson said. "I didn't know." He realized this was about the stupidest, most trite thing he could say, but couldn't stop himself.

Espy Martinez touched her free hand to her forehead. "No," she said, "it's all right. So there you have it. I'm sorry. We were having fun and then I launched into all this and now you look like someone caught swearing in church."

She reached out and took a long drink from her wineglass.

"I'd like to make a joke and get us laughing again," she said.

Walter Robinson thought for a moment, wondered why he felt something was missing, and then realized what it was. Before he could stop himself, he asked the question. "The suspect in your brother's shooting . . . he was black, right?"

Martinez didn't answer right away. Then she nodded. Robinson sighed and started to lean back, thinking to himself: There it is; there it ends. He began to get angry, not with Espy Martinez, or with himself or with anything other than the entire world, when she shot her hand out and grabbed his again, holding him fiercely, as she would if she were dangling on some precipice.

"No," she said slowly. "He was him and you are you."

He leaned back toward her, feeling a rush of excitement.

She smiled. "My name," she said. "Do you know what it means?"

"Espy?"

"No, silly. Esperanza."

He grinned. "It's not like I don't know any Spanish at all. It means *hope*."

She was about to reply, when the waiter arrived with their dinners. He hovered by the table, balancing the plates of food, unable to set them down over their arms, stretched across the table. He coughed and said, "Excuse me," and both Espy Martinez and Walter Robinson looked up at him and then laughed.

They ate in a rush, skipped dessert, ignored the offer of coffee. It was as if the simple confessions that they had made to each other had released them from the usual posturing, circling, feints and fakes of connection. She was quiet as he drove her across the city, to her front door. There, he stopped the car and turned off the engine. She remained in her seat, looking toward the side of the duplex occupied by her parents. She assumed they were watching.

Robinson started to say something, but she wasn't listening.

Instead, she turned to him and whispered with an intensity that surprised herself: "Take me someplace else, Walter. Anyplace. Anyplace at all. Your place. A hotel. A park. The beach, I don't care. Just someplace different."

He paused, looking at her. And in that moment they thrust themselves together, embracing, lips meeting electrically, and she pulled him to her, thinking that she was yanking all the loneliness and troubles in her entire life off balance and askew, and hoping that somehow the weight of him pressed against her would stabilize the windstorm of emotions soaring within her.

He took her back to his own apartment. He closed the door behind them, and they grasped at each other on the floor of his living room with the slippery urgency of a pair of lawbreakers worried about discovery. They tugged at each other's clothing with a frantic need that transformed itself into a quick coupling, almost as if they had no time to get to know each other's body. Espy Martinez simply pulled Walter Robinson down on top of her, trying to envelop him; for his part, he felt like a balloon blown to within a micrometer of explosion. That her skin had a particular softness, the curve of her small breasts, the shape of her sex, the taste of the sweat that gathered on her neck—all this was information and knowledge that he was only obliquely aware of as he pushed down toward her with demands that seemed ancient and impossible and were welcomed by her with thrusts of her own.

When he finished, he rolled to the side, breathing hard. He lay back with his forearm across his eyes. After a second he heard her say: "So, Walter, do you have, like, a bedroom? A bathroom? Kitchen?"

He opened his eyes to see her beside him, lifted up on one elbow, leaning over him, grinning.

"Well, actually, yes, Espy, I do. All the usual and expected conveniences of modern life. A refrigerator. Cable television. Air-conditioning. Wall-to-wall carpeting . . ."

"Yes," she said, laughing, and letting her hair brush over his chest. "I found the wall-to-wall carpet. It was right beneath me."

As she spoke, she lowered her lips to his chest, then laid her cheek on his breast, listening to the rapid-fire beats of his heart.

"Enthusiasm," he said.

"So, Walter," she said quietly. "Who are you?"

He did not answer this time. Instead, he gathered her face in his hands and kissed her slowly. Then he pulled her to her feet and then reached down and lifted her up in his arms.

"Bedroom," he said.

"Romantic," she replied, still laughing. "Just don't bump my head."

This second time, they paced themselves, letting fingers, lips explore each other. "There's time," Walter Robinson said. "There's all the time in the world."

Afterward he slept. But Espy Martinez felt an odd restlessness. She was both exhausted and depleted, but at the same moment filled with the satisfaction of the smitten. For a short time she watched the detective sleep, studying the relaxed angles of his face, caught by a shaft of moonlight that slid through the window. She held her hand up against his cheek, to see the way the wan light illuminated her pale skin and made his dark flesh glisten. She had the thought that she'd stepped past some sort of fence, then berated herself, thinking that she was allowing herself to muse in racial clichés, and that if she expected to have another night beside Walter Robinson, she should try to shed these thoughts as she had pulled off her clothing: rapidly.

She slid from the bed and quietly maneuvered into the living room. It was a small apartment, in an undistinguished condominium. There was a nice view, looking back toward the bay and the city. She found his desk in one corner, placed so that he could see through the windows toward Miami. There was a picture of an elderly black woman framed in one corner. On the wall were diplomas from the police academy and from Florida International University. There was another picture of a much younger Walter

Robinson, dusty, a streak of blood on one cheek, dressed in a football uniform, holding a ball aloft. She recognized the colors of Miami High. She turned and saw on his desk a casual mingling of law texts, research, and police department reports. She saw his notes on Sophie Millstein's killing.

She continued to move stealthily, naked, through the moonlight.

She whispered again: "Who are you, Walter Robinson?" As if she could find some paper, some document, that might explain him to her. She went to the kitchen and smiled when she inspected the bachelor's array of cold beers and cold cuts that occupied the shelves of his refrigerator. She went back into the living room and noticed for the first time a watercolor on one wall. She approached it and saw that the artist had drawn an expanse of ocean, lit by shafts of sunlight, but that in the distance dark thunderheads had formed, giving the entire painting a sensation of threat. It was difficult in the semidarkness to make out the artist's signature, and she leaned toward it, peering closely, until she saw that it was only two initials: W. R. They were stuck deep in a corner, hidden right at the point where the colors changed from light to dark.

She smiled and wondered where he kept his easel and paints.

Then she returned to the bedroom and slid beneath a sheet next to him. She breathed in deeply, inhaling all the smells of their lovemaking, and closed her eyes, hoping but not really believing that there would be other nights like the one dwindling into morning around her.

He hesitated before touching her, then took a single finger and brushed back the sweep of hair from her forehead. He gently pushed at her shoulder and said, "Espy, we're gonna be late. It's morning."

She did not open her eyes, but replied: "How late?"

"It's eight-thirty already. Late."

She kept her eyes closed. "Are you in a hurry, Walter?"

"No," he said. He smiled. "Some mornings, you just got to take your time about things."

She reached out with both arms, like a poor actress mimicking a blind person, feeling the air, until she found his arms and shoulders and she drew him down toward her.

"Do we have time?"

"Probably not," he said, tugging the sheet away from her, pushing himself toward her.

Afterward they showered and dressed rapidly. He made some coffee, which he handed to her. She took a single swallow and grimaced.

"Jesus, Walter. That's terrible! Is it instant?"

"Uh, yeah. I'm not much of a cook."

"Well, we'll have to stop and get some real café Cubano on the way to the Justice Building."

"Do you want me to take you home, get your car?"

"Nope," she replied. "Just take me to the office."

He hesitated, then gestured with his arm, sweeping it about the apartment. It was a lost motion, speaking more of words that were difficult to speak than of anything else. "Okay," he said. "But when can we, I mean, I want to . . ." and then he stopped.

She laughed. "Get together again?"

"Correct."

"I don't know, Walter. Where are we going to go with this?"

"I'd like to go further," he answered.

"So would I."

They smiled at each other, as if some sort of agreement had been struck.

"Tomorrow, then," he said. "I have to work a late shift tonight."

"Okay," she replied.

They joked and laughed most of the way to her office. They stopped for coffee and a sweet roll, which seemed hilarious. A cormorant flew low across the bow of his car as they crossed the causeway, which seemed comical. The midmorning traffic had a rollicking, amusing quality to it. When they pulled to the front of the Justice Building, they were both close to giggling.

She stepped from the car and leaned back. "Will you call?" she asked.

"Of course. This afternoon. Don't want to forget about Mr.

Jefferson. Those other fingerprint examinations should be finished by now. I'll call you with Harry Harrison's report."

"Brought together by Leroy Jefferson. If he only knew."

Walter Robinson laughed loudly. "I wonder what he'd say."

For a moment they looked at each other, each feeling the same, that they were standing at the starting line to something. And it was into that silence that they heard her name being called.

"Espy!"

She turned and Robinson craned across the seat to see who was shouting. High on the steps to the massive courthouse building they could both see the lanky form of Thomas Alter. He waved, and then bounded down the steps toward them.

"Hey, Walt, lucky to catch you here too."

"Hello, Tommy. Get any killers off today?"

"Glad to see you too. Not yet. But you never know. It's still early."

He smiled, with just a touch of Cheshire cat grin.

"So, Espy? You guys got your case together? You gonna put the screws to Leroy Jefferson?"

"Tommy, you know the office's policy on discussions. They have to be formal, with a stenographer. But I can tell you off the record that selling any plea is going to be tough, especially to Lasser. He doesn't like it when little old ladies get strangled. Ruins his whole day. So, I'd say no chance. No chance at all."

"Really? No chance?"

"You heard me."

He didn't seem fazed by this news. "Well, I don't suppose, then, you'd like to see this. . . ." Alter reached into his briefcase and pulled out a sheaf of papers.

"What's that?" Robinson asked. He had stepped from the car and walked around to the sidewalk, standing next to Martinez.

"Lie detector test," Alter said abruptly.

"And?"

"Well, guess what?"

"Don't give us that coy crap, Tommy. What are you saying?"

"I'm saying that on this particular test my client demonstrated no signs of deception. None whatsoever. And you know what question we asked him?"

"What?"

"The question was nice and simple: 'Did you kill Sophie Millstein in her apartment?' And guess what? He said no, and the machine says he's telling the truth."

"Bullshit!" Robinson exploded. "People can con those. . . ."

"Well," Alter replied slowly, "that's what I thought you'd say. So I used the same guy that her office and your office uses. Vogt Investigations. How long have you guys kept old Bruce and his magical machine on a retainer?"

"Bullshit! I don't care what he passed, he still—"

"You haven't been to your office yet, have you, old buddy?"

"No."

"Been busy, huh?" Alter grinned at Espy Martinez.

She burst out, furious. "This is all crap, Tommy, and you know it. A lie detector test doesn't mean a thing! It's not evidence. It's not anything. So cut the crap. . . ."

"Interesting report came into the Beach homicide office this morning," Alter continued, ignoring the anger flushing the faces of the prosecutor and the detective. "I mean, the sort of thing that just makes you wonder if there could be anything stranger in this odd world. . . ."

"Tommy, cut this shit, before I punch you out."

"What are you saying, Tommy? What report?"

The defense attorney grinned again. "It is fun to see you two self-righteous avengers of society looking so discomfited. Perhaps you'll indulge me for a moment while I appreciate this little show."

"What report?"

"Fingerfuckingprint report, you conceited bastard."

"How do you—"

"We've got some friends in your office."

"What are you saying, Tommy?" Martinez demanded, her voice shrill.

"What I'm saying, Espy, is that somebody else killed Sophie. That's what I'm saying."

"Bullshit!" Robinson interjected. He reached toward the defense attorney, then managed to pull his hands back at the last second.

"Soddit," Martinez spat out. "Soddit. C'mon, Tommy, you can do better. The old 'some other dude did it' defense. You think I'm so young I've never seen that bullshit before? How about something more original. Something more creative. Not the old Soddit defense . . ."

Alter wheeled toward her, pushing his face down angrily, abruptly shedding all the teasing jocularity he'd employed. "Oh, you think it's boring? You think it's unoriginal?"

"That's right!"

"Well, guess what, boys and girls," he said, his voice low, conspiratorial, and filled with sarcasm. "It also happens to be true."

Alter turned to Walter Robinson.

"The fucking body print. Right from her neck. Right from the fingers that went around old Sophie's throat. That nice little partial thumbprint that your guys lifted from her skin. Guess what? It belongs to somebody. But not to Leroy Jefferson."

He stepped back.

"So, chew on that, kids. And take a nice look at this lie detector report. And when you're ready to ask real nice and politely for our help in finding Sophie's real killer, well, you just know where I'll be waiting."

He paused, then added: "And Walter, old buddy, you bring the fifty you owe me, huh?"

Thomas Alter dropped the lie detector report to the cement sidewalk, where a light breeze riffled the pages as he turned and strode purposefully away.

# FOURTEEN
## THE MISSING H

**S**IMON Winter thought: *He*'s here. Somewhere right in front of me. Maybe he's strolling down the wooden boardwalk, or eating an ice-cream cone purchased from the vendor on the corner. Perhaps he's in that group waiting in line for a table at the News Café. He could be that man reading the *Herald* on that bench near the bus stop. He could be anyone. But he's here and he's killed at least once, and maybe twice. I don't know how yet. But he has. And he managed to make one killing look like an old man's suicide, and I think he made another killing look like a junkie's frantic handiwork, and I think if he needs to, he will kill again, because he's not having any trouble with murder.

None at all.

Winter took a deep breath and spoke out loud, muttering: 'How do I find you, Shadow Man?"

A teenage couple was walking past, a few feet away. They each wore mirrored sunglasses that glinted in the sun, and they turned when they heard his voice. Then they spoke to each other in Spanish, laughed, and wandered off.

They made him angry. Just another old person talking to himself. That's what they thought. He started to watch two young women on roller skates dip and swerve amidst the late afternoon crowds on Ocean Drive. The sidewalks were filled with the

curious and the trendy, moving between the restaurants and outdoor cafés that dominate the Art Deco section of South Beach. It
is a place of fast cars and neon signs; loud music, bass-heavy
salsa or screeching guitar-driven metal, competing against the occasional squeal of tires and blaring horns. No one talks, everyone
shouts. Miami, and by extension Miami Beach, honors the immediate, Simon Winter thought. If it's new and noisy and colorful,
it's instantly accepted as part of the city's preferred image.

The women on roller skates wore identical tight black Lycra
shorts and fluorescent pink halter tops. One had dark hair, the
other blond. They moved with a sinuous grace, legs pumping to
pick up speed, then relaxing, gliding ahead effortlessly. The
crowds parted to let them pass, then closed ranks like some educated but disorganized army.

He sat on a bench across the street, his back to the pallid blue
waters that curled effortlessly against a wide expanse of chalky
sand. He realized that the street clamor that filled the air obscured
the rhythmic music of the ocean surf rolling in against the shore.
He could smell the salt air mingling freely with the aromas from a
dozen different menus being prepared in as many kitchens. He
wondered for a moment why anyone would think that man's
sounds or smells were preferable to nature's. He looked down the
beach.

How do I find him? he demanded of himself.

From where he waited, he could see the small bandstand at
Lummus Park, and as he watched, he saw a half-dozen elderly
men and women moving slowly away from the beach; the end-of-
the-day retreat. They carried aluminum lawn chairs and folded
parasols. The bandstand is a popular place, often crowded, although the gatherings there seem to grow slightly smaller with
each passing month. It is an odd place, a cement slab that radiates
blistering summer heat, next to an old, low-slung and faded,
institutional-green-painted storage building. A microphone and
small amplifier are placed outside every day by city workers.
Then, one after the other, the old retirees still living on the Beach
rise to entertain each other with songs. A sign on the wall limits
each singer to three efforts. The songs flow forth nonstop through
the wavy hot air, a variety of Eastern European languages cou-

pling with an occasional effort in English and a frequent reliance
on Yiddish. It has a touch of the absurd about it; more often than
not the old people seem mildly ridiculous, crooning away, mixing
verses, dropping phrases, humming the forgotten parts. The
singers gesture and pose, arms wide, in imitation of lounge acts
everywhere. Only rarely do notes fit music, do tunes correspond
with words. The old voices have a raspiness or a tremulousness
that cracks and frays the songs. Some chant, some keen, others
ooze lugubriously. But the singers continue, regardless of the flat-
ness of the voices, because it is memories that they are evoking.
Often the singers are overwhelmed by the noise and raucous
sounds that emerge from pumped-up jukeboxes and muscular
stereo systems across Ocean Drive. But the old people sing on,
oblivious to the competition. And when finished, receive the
same enthusiastic applause and generous praise from their fellow
singers, regardless of whether a word could be heard or not.

Simon Winter shook his head and stood up. He walked slowly
down the street, passing the elderly people with their lawn chairs
as they headed one direction, following the two young women on
roller skates, who briefly flashed between a pair of shiny red
sports cars and then disappeared ahead of him into the dusky remains of the day's light.

His eyes tracked a Miami Beach patrol car that maneuvered
slowly through the throng of traffic. He was abruptly reminded of
a time he'd been fishing in shallow waters in the upper Keys, fly-
casting for bonefish, and had spotted the solitary profile of an osprey circling lazily in the air, riding the currents of wind and
thermal blasts of heat. He had quickly recognized that the bird
was not really hunting. There was no energy in its search. But it
was opportunistic; when it spotted a bar jack cruising too close to
the surface, it lifted its wings and plummeted, talons outstretched,
splashing into the light chop with a resounding explosion, then instantly rising back into the hot air, a rivulet of silvery water
streaming from its white wings. It had as little luck fishing that
day as he had. Still, as the hours passed and no fish showed, it
seemed happy just to curl in great graceful circles in the air, like a
part of the sky itself.

It's been a long time since I've been on the water with a fishing rod in hand, hunting, he reminded himself. Ten years perhaps. He tried to remember why it was that he'd quit, but could not recall a reason. It seemed to him that somehow he'd stopped doing all the things that used to make him who he was, and that maybe if he started doing them once again, he wouldn't be so eager to blow his own brains out.

His feet slapped against the dusty sidewalk. He let the osprey fade back into his memory, and turned his thoughts to the man who left the final letter off his wife's name.

*I know who killed you, Herman Stein.*

*You were smarter than he thought, weren't you? Even though you were terrified, and you knew you were going to die, you were still clever enough to leave a message behind. The missing H. It took a long time for someone to figure out what you were trying to say, but I know now.*

Simon Winter concentrated on Herman Stein's death, trying to form a portrait of the events in his mind. It was a simple, effective technique, one refined over years of standing above dead bodies. Create a mental moving picture of what happened and then you'll see a way to find the man who did it.

All right, first question: *Access*—how did he get into the apartment?

*Front door. Did you open it for him? No, you wouldn't do that. You were elderly and upset and frightened. You wouldn't open the door without checking the peephole first. So how? The hallway. Were you regular and routine, like so many old people? You were a man of precision, Herman Stein, did you go out to the deli on the corner every morning for breakfast and return at the same time after eating the same bagel with cream cheese, cereal, and coffee, just like a clock chiming the time? Yes, that would be you. And stalking you would have been easy, even knowing that you were scared and perhaps thinking of taking precautions. And so, all he would have to do is to wait for you to go out, and then take up a position in that hallway, trap you on your return. Is there a stairwell? A fire escape? A closet?* Winter knew without going to the dead man's apartment that there was some space that a person could wait in without being seen.

He breathed out slowly. Some of the terror that Herman Stein had felt slid into his own veins.

You knew he was out there, and you knew it wouldn't do any good this time to call your sons or daughter, would it? It was always the same. When you spoke of Der Schattenmann, they persuaded you otherwise. Like the little boy who cried wolf, you knew they would not believe you, even though this time was somehow different, and you were scared right to your core, weren't you? So you wrote the rabbi a letter and put it in the mail.

Because you were all alone and facing death.

So how did you know about the rabbi?

Winter made a mental note of this question. Find an answer, he thought, because if Herman Stein can find out about the rabbi, so can he.

So there you were. He trapped you in the hallway and forced you into the apartment. Then he sat you down in the desk chair. Did he make you type your own death letter? I think so, because that was where you had the idea to leave off the H. Did it give you a moment's satisfaction? Did it strengthen you just a tiny bit, help you to turn toward the gun as he pushed it at your forehead?

Simon Winter thought: Herman Stein, I take my hat off to you. You were a brave man, and no one knows it except me.

The old detective paused. He had reached the entrance to the Sunshine Arms.

Did he talk to you, Herman Stein?

What did he say?

Winter could see the old man sitting stiffly in his desk chair, eyes open wide, seconds before dying. He could see the fear, he could feel the same rush of dizzying anguish that Herman Stein must have felt. To have come so far, only to finally arrive face-to-face with a nightmare.

He stood on the sidewalk. The day's heat still radiated up through the wavy air, but he remained oblivious to the sensation. Instead, in his mind's eye, he started to place the faces of killers he had known onto the vaporous shape across from Herman Stein. He ransacked his memory, right through the long catalogue of crimes. A psychotic who'd used a butcher knife on his wife and children; a contract killer who'd preferred a small caliber pistol shoved up against the base of the skull; a gang enforcer who liked to use a baseball bat, starting with the legs, then moving methodically upward, allowing his frenzy to grow. He mixed into this gallery a few serial killers, a pair of punk teenagers who'd killed for thrills, several rapists who'd discovered a greater, more noxious excitement. One after the other he fit these characters onto the form, only to discard them onto the dust heap of his memory.

He lifted his hand to his forehead and wiped away the thin line of sweat that had gathered just below the rim of his old baseball cap.

You're not there, are you, Shadow Man? You're not going to fit into any cop's memory, are you?

Simon Winter glanced over toward Sophie Millstein's empty apartment as he trudged toward his own. Tell me something. Anything, he demanded silently. But the apartment stood blankly, a shaft of final daylight illuminating one wall. He opened his door and stepped inside, letting the cool air flow over him like a clear thought. He congratulated himself for leaving the air conditioner running, worrying only momentarily about the bill from the electric company that would inevitably reflect his wastrel ways. As he stepped into the living room, he saw that there was a message on the telephone answering machine. He wanted something to drink, suddenly parched. He thought he remembered some canned lemonade in the refrigerator, and he took a step in that direction, then stopped, turning toward the machine.

He punched the playback button and after a moment of hissing, electronic noises, heard the rabbi's voice. It sounded distant, tinny. But the anxiety contained in each word was still crystal: "Mr. Winter? Please call me as soon as you can . . ."

There was a momentary hesitation, before the rabbi added:

"It's Irving Silver. He's disappeared."

There was another pause, and then:

"I was wrong. Oh, my God. We should have let him get a gun. . . ." And with that the machine clicked off.

# FIFTEEN
## THE LOST MAN

I$_N$ their faces he could see anger and fear vying for control.

Simon Winter gave a small wave and hurried toward Frieda Kroner and Rabbi Rubinstein. They were standing outside the long porch of the Columbus, an old residential hotel a block from the ocean. The flat white walls of the building seemed to glow against the lustrous night black, like the graying embers of a near-dead fire. In the midday, he knew, the porch would have been crowded with the elderly residents of the hotel, patiently taking the sun, but now it was empty, save for two dozen scattered lawn chairs and the two people anxiously waiting for him.

The rabbi was nervously rubbing his free hand across his forehead, as if trying to scratch out a thought. The other hand was clutching a black-bound copy of the Old Testament close to his chest. He saw that Winter had spotted this, and so he said, instead of an introduction: "In times like these, Detective, the Word of God brings comfort."

Winter nodded. "And what does He say?"

"He says to trust in His wisdom."

That's what He always says, Simon Winter thought.

Frieda Kroner pointed toward the front entrance to the hotel.

"There is where Irving isn't," she said. "He is gone." She hesitated, then added: "The Shadow Man got him."

"How can you be certain?" Winter asked. She did not reply, nor did the rabbi. Instead, she turned and charged up the stairs, her momentum seeming to sweep the others along in her wake. Winter paused as the three of them entered the lobby. On one wall was a fading mural depicting the hotel's namesake arriving at the New World. It had that 1930s stylized feel to it, an immense fiction; all the gestures were heroic, all the figures, natives and Spaniards alike, had a calm and reverential air to them, as if they innately understood the moment in history that they were depicting. There was no hint of strife or blood or terror or any of the things that were to soon follow. In front of the mural there was an old black leather sofa. In the center of it a thin, gray-haired man sat, reading a newspaper in Yiddish. He looked up at them as they entered, then turned back to the paper studiously. But Simon Winter noticed he had placed his eyeglasses on the seat beside him, so that in truth he was listening and watching them. Curiosity, the detective thought, occasionally seems to be the province of either very young or very old age.

"This way," Frieda Kroner said. She grasped his elbow and steered him toward the corner of the lobby, where a man sat at a small desk adorned with an antiquated plug-in-style telephone switchboard. He was younger than they were, and Hispanic. He shrugged as they approached.

"Mrs. Kroner," he said in heavily accented English. "What can I say? I have no word from Mr. Silver. Not in the slightest."

"Did the police speak with you?"

"Yes. *Sí*. Of course. Right after you called them. They ask me if Mr. Silver is unusual to not be here, and I say yes, and they ask if I notice anything unusual or funny, but this I do not notice, and so they give me a number and I am supposed to call them if I should know anything, but that is it."

"Stupid," she muttered. "Der Schattenmann is killing us and the police are wondering if there is something unusual. Damn!" She shook her head vigorously. "I want you to let my friends and I into Mr. Silver's apartment."

"Mrs. Kroner, I—"

"Immediately."

"But this is—"

"José," she said, drawing herself upright, her face riven with demand, "right now." She swung her hand toward the rabbi. "This man is a rabbi. You cannot keep him waiting."

She said this with such authority that the clerk immediately rose, nodding his head toward Rabbi Rubinstein. "But only for a minute, Mrs. Kroner, please."

The inside of Irving Silver's tiny apartment was immaculate. A few books arranged by height on a shelf, magazines on a coffee table placed carefully, like a display, so that their titles could be easily read. On a bureau top were the expected photographs of distant relatives. Simon Winter slid a hand across the surface. Behind him the rabbi and Mrs. Kroner waited expectantly, as if they were anticipating some pronouncement. He moved quickly through the small space; it was only a single bedroom apartment, smaller even than Sophie Millstein's or his own. The bed was made with hospital corners. He stopped by a cheap linoleum kitchen table and saw that there were two place settings arranged on top. Irving Silver had been expecting company. There was no indication of a struggle, no signs of a break-in. No evidence that Irving Silver had been taken someplace against his will. In short, what Simon Winter saw was the apartment of a man who might have stepped out to purchase some missing item at the corner store, and who could come walking back through the door at any second.

He turned toward the others.

"You see," Frieda Kroner said, pointing at the place settings. Then her finger started to waver in the air and he saw her jaw start to quiver around the next words that cracked from between her lips: "Irving is dead."

The rabbi turned and threw an arm around Frieda Kroner as her shoulders heaved with yet another sob. But he turned his eyes toward Winter and he nodded.

Behind them, in the hallway, José the desk clerk shuffled about impatiently. "Please, Mrs. Kroner, is not necessarily possible true," he said. "I must lock up, please."

Back in the lobby, Winter saw that the man reading in front of the mural had disappeared. Frieda Kroner continued to cry as the rabbi steered her toward the exit. But when they reached the sidewalk, she abruptly straightened up, shaking loose from Rabbi Rubinstein's arm. She looked wildly toward the two men, then stepped aside, turned to the empty street, and in a loud, furious voice, shouted in her native German: "You will not win this time!"

The words echoed emptily down the street.

Simon Winter tried to comfort her. "Mrs. Kroner, I don't see anything to suggest—"

She spun about angrily. "You are a detective and you cannot see?"

The rabbi clapped his hands together in frustration. "This is how it was. This is how it is!"

"We should have known better," Frieda Kroner said bitterly. "Us of all people. If you wait. If you do nothing. If you sit around. Then they will come for you. . . ." She hesitated, then shook her head. "No. Not *they*. *He* will come for you. This time, it is only a he. But it is the same, Detective. If you do nothing . . ."

"Then you will die," Rabbi Rubinstein said coldly. "Nothing has changed. He will find us and we will die."

"Like he found poor Sophie and Mr. Stein and now Irving."

The man's name seemed to snag on her lips.

She stood in the wan light from the entrance to the residential hotel, staring intently at the streams of darkness that melded onto the cityscape.

"Irving is gone," she said. "The Shadow Man got him."

"I told you," Rabbi Rubinstein said quietly. "I told you. He means to kill us all."

Frieda Kroner sighed deeply, nodding her head. She trapped a half gasp, half sob near the back of her throat, and Simon Winter saw her eyes were tinged with red. "Irving, you must be thinking, Mr. Winter, is not such a pleasant man, but you are mistaken. There is much kindness within him and good company, especially for an old lonely widow like myself. And now he is gone. I did not think it would happen like this."

For a moment she seemed to totter on the edge of grief. Then she growled a guttural, angry sound, like some sort of wounded, dangerous beast.

"This is the way it always was," she added harshly. "One moment they were right there, at your side, and then, the next, they were gone. Disappeared. Vanished as if a hole had opened up in the bottom of the world and swallowed them up."

"This is true, Detective," the rabbi added. "Soon there will be none of us left and no one will remember the Shadow Man."

"Back up," he said. "Let's start at the beginning. What makes you so sure Mr. Silver has disappeared. What do you mean, gone?"

Frieda Kroner answered sharply. "Gone means dead. That was how it always was."

"How?"

Rabbi Rubinstein held up his hand, a small, conciliatory motion. "Frieda, tell Mr. Winter. Then he will understand."

She glared for a moment at the rabbi, then replied:

"Irving is a man of habits. If it is Monday, then he goes to the fish store, the fruit stand, and finally the supermarket. Then he takes his purchases home and he puts them away. Then he goes to the library to read the out-of-town papers, and then he takes a short walk on the boardwalk, and finally he comes home and telephones me and perhaps we go to see a movie because on Monday it is not so crowded as the weekend. If this is Wednesday, then Irving attends the bridge club in the afternoon, after stopping by my place to pick me up, and sometimes staying late. On Thursday, he has a discussion group at the library. On Friday there are services in the evening. These are the things that make up Irving's life now, just as they do mine, and the rabbi's as well. It is not so different for many of the survivors, Mr. Winter. We practice order and regimen. It is as if the Nazis somehow installed a clock in each of us, and we must fill it with precision. So, when I arrive at Irving's home and he is not there to attend the bingo at the civic center, as we do on every Tuesday, then I know that Irving is in trouble. And there are only three sorts of trouble out there for people like us, Mr. Winter."

"What are those, Mrs. Kroner?"

"There is disease. Disease and age, Mr. Winter. Sometimes

they seem like the same thing. Perhaps Irving has had a stroke or an accident . . ."

"But we called the hospitals, and they have no record of him," Rabbi Rubinstein interjected.

"And there is violence. Perhaps some one of these young people who are taking over the Beach with all their noise and fast cars has mugged him in some alleyway . . ."

"But this the police do not report." Again the rabbi stepped in.

"And then, of course, there is Der Schattenmann."

"You spoke with the police?"

"Yes. Of course. Right away," the rabbi said. "They told us that they cannot file a missing persons report for twenty-four hours, but they were kind enough to check the accidents and crimes for us. And even then, they said there was nothing much they could do."

"Not until they find a body. Or some evidence of a crime having been committed," Frieda Kroner added bitterly. "An old person on Miami Beach who is not home when he should be is not maybe the crime of the century, Detective. They do not treat this like the Lindbergh kidnapping. They are polite. But that is all. Just polite."

She hissed, to herself: "The Shadow Man lives amongst us, and they are polite!"

Simon Winter nodded. He knew this. Absent a kidnapping note, a bloodstained crime scene, or some other overt and unmistakable sign, the police would limit their inquiry to a teletype message to the other local forces and a be-on-the-lookout-for, with perhaps a distribution of a picture at the daily roll calls.

"Tell me, could there be some other explanation for his disappearance?"

"Like what?"

"Fear. Perhaps he went to visit relatives. . . ."

"Without telling us?"

This didn't seem likely.

"Has he ever experienced forgetfulness? An episode of blackouts?"

The rabbi shook his head angrily. "We are not senile! None of us, thank God, suffer from dementia! If Irving has disappeared, there can be but one explanation!"

Simon Winter thought hard. All the old people on the Beach were creatures of habit, some in the extreme, like Irving Silver. Like Sophie Millstein. Like Herman Stein. They had all built lives around moments of certainty, as if the inflexible demands of this appointment, this schedule, this meeting, this meal, this medication, all precluded the spontaneity of death from entering their lives.

And, he thought, who is more vulnerable than someone of rigid habit?

Winter shook his head. "But even if this were the Shadow Man, well, Sophie was attacked in her apartment. Herman Stein died in his apartment. His pattern seems clear—"

Now it was the rabbi's turn to interrupt with an exasperated shake of the head. "You still do not understand, Mr. Winter! Does a shadow have form? Does a shadow have substance? Is it not something that shifts and changes with every motion of the sun or the moon or the earth? That was why he was so frightening, Mr. Winter. Back then, back in Berlin . . . If we'd known he liked to ride the trams, well, then we would have avoided the trams. If we knew which streets he walked, or which subway he frequented . . . If we knew which park he took the air in . . . But none of these things were known. Every moment was different. And why would he be different today? If he kills Sophie and poor Mr. Stein in their apartments, then the Shadow Man will shift form and find some other location, and that is where Irving lies now. I know it!"

These final words cracked and splintered in the stale humid air on the street. For a moment the old rabbi was quiet, then he added fiercely: "He would have fought. Fought hard and long. He would have bitten and scratched and used everything he had. Irving was tough. He was a hard man. He took his daily walks. He lifted things and swam in the ocean on warm days. There was still muscle there, and he would have fought hard, like a tiger, because Irving loved life."

"There were no signs of a fight."

"I could see that. It means the Shadow Man stole him from the street."

"That would be difficult. Most of the time this place is crowded. Look at the porch. Ordinarily there would be dozens of people watching the street. . . ."

"This would be difficult for most criminals, yes, Detective, you are correct," the rabbi said patiently. "But you must remember: This is what he did, over and over, for all those war years. Quietly and unobtrusively he ended your life. Tell me, Mr. Winter, have you not felt your hand slip while it holds a razor, and when you look up into the mirror, see that you have sliced yourself? That there is blood running down your chin? But did you feel the pain of the cut? No, I think not. And that is the sort of man he is."

Frieda Kroner nodded her head in agreement, then snarled and whispered in a low, angry grunt: "We must find him. We must find him today or tomorrow or this week or next, but we must find him. Otherwise, he will find us. We must fight back."

"Even against a shadow," the rabbi added.

Simon Winter nodded. He thought to himself: *This man is something different.* He felt his imagination start to grind away, mechanical, factoring.

"What was it you said, Mrs. Kroner? Last time? He is one of you?"

"That is correct. He must be a survivor as well."

"Then that is where I will start. And you two also. He will be out there, in a synagogue, at the Holocaust Memorial, at a condo association meeting, as he was with Mr. Stein. There must be names, lists of names. Of organizations and congregations. That is where we will start."

"Yes, yes, I see," the rabbi said. "I can contact other rabbis."

"Good. Eliminate anyone under the age of sixty. . . ."

"He will be older than that. Why not make it sixty-five? Or sixty-eight?"

"Yes. But we are all old, and we all know some people wear their years differently. Some look younger, some older. I think to perform two—maybe three—killings, the Shadow Man will have the strength and appearance of a younger man. Let's keep that in mind."

The rabbi nodded. "Like the man on trial in Israel. He was in the papers again today." Simon Winter's mind's eye quickly formed a picture of a man accused of being a former death camp guard. He had been on the television nightly and in the daily papers. He was a hulking man, thick through the middle, with wide shoulders and arms like wooden pilings. He was balding, and had a roughness about him that was unsettling. Flanked by a pair of armed policemen, the man always wore a prisoner's jumpsuit, but not the attitude or appearance of a prisoner.

"You have seen this man, this Ivan the Terrible?" Rabbi Rubinstein asked, and Winter nodded in reply. "You can see, can you not, Detective, that this is a man who was never broken? Never crushed? Never beaten down and starved? With us, it is not exactly the same, is it?"

"I don't follow."

"It is not that we survivors are less . . . I am not sure how to put it, but let me suggest this, Detective: A true survivor wears a mark just as surely as I wear this tattoo."

He held up his forearm and pulled back the dark shirtsleeve he was wearing.

"See how it has faded with time? But it is still there, is it not? And we are no different inside. There is a mark there. As the years pass, it becomes less. But it is still there and will never totally disappear. You can see it in the slope of the shoulders, or maybe behind the eyes. This I believe is true for all of us."

"What are you saying?"

"This man, Der Schattenmann, he will say one thing. But he will not have the truth within him. And, if we look hard enough, we will be able to see that."

"This is correct," Frieda Kroner added decisively. There was a momentary pause, and then she continued, with a secretary's efficiency. "I know all of Irving's memberships. The bridge club and the discussion groups . . . I can get those lists."

"Excellent. And addresses. And descriptions, if you can get them. Remember detail. Any little thing could tell us what we need to know."

"What do you mean, *detail*?" she asked.

"He was a Berliner once. Would he speak with an accent, like you do, Mrs. Kroner? That is just a possibility. He may not."

"Yes. Yes. This makes sense. I can see that, but in the meantime, how do we protect ourselves?"

"Change your routine. If you have been going to the supermarket at three P.M. every Wednesday afternoon for the past ten years, then change. Go at eight A.M. Start taking different routes. If you want to go to the boardwalk for a stroll, fine, just turn and head two blocks in the wrong direction before doubling back. If you are going out, call your destination first. Let them know you are traveling. If you always ride the bus, take a cab. Find someone to accompany you. Move in groups. Travel erratically. Zigzag. Stop in front of plate-glass windows and spend a few seconds watching the people behind you. Turn suddenly and examine the street you've just walked down. Be alert."

"This is wise," said the rabbi.

"He may try to come at you as something familiar, a deliveryman or a postman. Trust no one. Even if you have been going to the same deli and eating the same corned beef at lunch for the last ten years, now you must change. And no longer trust the counterman, even if he's the same face you've seen every day since you moved to the Beach. Think: Nothing is safe. Everything could hide a shadow."

Frieda Kroner narrowed her eyes in appreciation.

"This will keep us alive?" she asked.

"It might. There are no guarantees. A gun is no guarantee. Or a pit bull."

"Or the police," she said bitterly.

"That is correct. The police solve crimes that have happened. Rarely do they manage to prevent something from taking place."

The rabbi interrupted suddenly. "We could go away. Just leave town perhaps?"

"Forever?"

"No. This is my home now."

"Then I think it wiser to defend it."

"Yes. If we had thought that way fifty years ago, sixty years ago perhaps . . . No, let us not think of those things. Let us think about staying alive now. Today. Tonight. Tomorrow."

Winter hesitated before continuing, watching the rabbi's face as it drifted momentarily back in time, seeing the remembrance of evil mark each line and furrow around his eyes, across his forehead, at the corners of his mouth.

"There is one other thing," Winter added slowly. He saw the rabbi's eyes swing slowly back across the landscape of decades and arrive at the present, recovering an unsettled nervousness.

"What is this one other thing, Mr. Winter?"

Winter replied quietly. "Let's all assume that he knows who you are. And where you live. Let's assume right now that he is confident because he doesn't believe anyone is searching for him. Let's assume he could be planning his next attack right now."

Frieda Kroner gasped. The rabbi stepped back abruptly. "Do you think it so, Mr. Winter?" he asked with a stroke of panic painted on his words.

"I do not know, but I believe you must consider the worst."

"But how?" Frieda Kroner demanded.

"Perhaps Mr. Silver told him."

"No. This I do not believe. No matter what the pain. No."

Winter nodded. "Perhaps you're right. But there is one other thing that I just remembered."

"What is that?"

The memory made him feel helpless, impotent and stupid. He wondered for an instant whether Irving Silver might be standing in front of him had he recalled this simple fact a few days earlier. He abruptly pictured himself, standing next to the young black detective amidst the heat and raised voices of the crime scene technicians as they processed Sophie Millstein's apartment. He saw in his mind's eye his own finger pointing toward the telephone stand, and he recalled his words to the young detective.

"Sophie's address book was missing the night of her murder."

"What?"

"Her telephone address book. It wasn't in its customary location. It was gone."

"You think Der Schattenmann . . ."

"If he saw it, he might have grabbed it. And you both were in it, because I saw her open it to get your telephone numbers."

"But we do not know—" the rabbi began, then stopped abruptly. He rocked back and forth on his heels, a faint grin just starting in the corners of his lips. "This is like a chess game, is it not, Detective?"

"In a way, yes."

"He has made moves. He has controlled the board. It is as if we have been unable to see his pieces go from square to square. But now, perhaps, it is our turn. There are three of us and we have some tricks left, do we not?"

"I think we do," Winter said.

"I am not scared," the rabbi said suddenly to Frieda Kroner. "No matter what happens, I cannot be scared. I do not think that Irving was either, when he came for him. And I do not think you will be anymore. Have we not seen the worst that this earth can manufacture? Is there some greater terror than Auschwitz?"

Oddly, then, Frieda Kroner smiled as well. "We lived through that. . . ."

"We can face up to this."

Simon Winter saw the old man reach out, seize the old woman's hand, and give it a small, reassuring shake. He thought he should say something, but could not think of words. After a moment Frieda Kroner turned to him. She did not speak, but he knew that they were all beginning to get ready for whatever the next move was.

Esther Weiss leaned back in her desk chair inside her small office at the Holocaust Center. She did not seem surprised to see him.

"You have more questions, Mr. Winter?"

"Yes," he replied.

"This is to be expected. When one cracks the lid on Pandora's box, many questions slide out. What is it you need to know?"

"Is there a registry or a list of Holocaust survivors, you know, a directory of sorts, that you have here?"

The young woman raised her eyebrows momentarily, then shook her head. "A list of survivors?"

"Correct."

"Like the membership of a club or a social group?"

He paused, but then said, "Yes, though I realize that sounds odd."

"That would be anathema, Mr. Winter."

"I'm sorry . . . I don't see—"

She interrupted him swiftly. "Mr. Winter, these people became Holocaust victims *because* they were put on lists. Registers. Directories. Allotments. There are all sorts of innocent words that take on horrific meanings when you connect them to the roundups and transports. No, Mr. Winter. There are no more lists, thank God."

"But here, at the Holocaust Center, and the other memorials . . ."

"We guard the names of the people who have spoken with us, who continue to speak with us, very carefully. Privacy is an important issue for these people, Mr. Winter. It is hard to understand how these people can be both unique and special and terribly ordinary, all at the same time. Many have lived simple, unexceptional lives, save for those years swept up in the camps. Consequently, these memories—even though they share them—have a privacy to them that we protect. They do the same at the center in Washington, and the one in Los Angeles. Yale University keeps their collection of videotaped recollections under lock and key. They have more than two thousand."

"How many Holocaust survivors are there here on the Beach?"

"On the Beach? This is hard to say. A few years back it was estimated that there were fifteen thousand survivors living in South Florida. From Boca Raton and Fort Lauderdale all the way down to South Beach. But they are growing old. The number dwindles monthly. That is why their recollections are so crucial."

She eyed him with some apprehension.

"We have no list, Mr. Winter. These people come to us."

He thought hard for a moment, then tried a different tack. "Suppose I were to backtrack. Try Immigration and Naturalization. Would they have records, you know, from the Forties or early Fifties . . . ?" His query dwindled as Esther Weiss shook her head.

"I doubt it. Certainly they have records of people entering the U.S. and how it was managed. But an overall compilation? For Holocaust survivors? No. And there were so many different routes here, not just to the U.S., but within the nation after they arrived. From the Lower East Side to Skokie, Illinois, or Detroit or Los Angeles and finally to Miami Beach. These are not official travels, Mr. Winter. They are recorded only in the memories of the people who made the trek."

"But surely there must—"

"Surely what? In Israel they have been attempting to simply document the names of the people *killed* in the Holocaust. The number is at three million, slightly less than half. No, Mr. Winter, lists don't exist. Only disarray and memories of nightmare."

She paused, examining the consternation in his face.

"There is a question, but you won't ask it. You know something, but you won't say it. You want me to help you, but you won't say why."

Simon Winter shifted about in his seat. He was dismayed. He berated himself inwardly for thinking the Holocaust would be like some great Department of Motor Vehicles, with names, addresses, telephone numbers, and current photographs. He looked over at Esther Weiss, who was staring at him with anticipation. It was not within his ordinary approach to matters to relinquish information. He stayed quiet for an instant, until the young woman shuffled some papers on the desk in front of her.

"When I came in before . . ." he started slowly.

"After Sophie Millstein's death," she continued for him. He nodded.

". . . You recall I was interested in a man Sophie knew only as Der Schattenmann."

"Of course. The catcher. You were speaking with the other Berliners. I remember."

"I am afraid that this man, the Shadow Man, is living here on Miami Beach."

Esther Weiss opened her mouth as if to say something, then stopped. She seemed to take a deep breath before continuing. "Here?"

The question seemed as suddenly pale as her skin.

"I believe so."

Hesitancy slipped into the young woman's words. "But that would be . . ." She shook her head. ". . . incredible. Horrible. I can't believe . . ."

"I think he has killed, Miss Weiss. I think he is stalking survivors. I think he stalked Sophie. And another man, a Herman Stein . . ."

"I knew Mr. Stein."

"And possibly another. Irving Silver."

She shook her head.

"No. Irving Silver was in here. Two weeks ago. Talking to the camera, recording his memories."

She reached toward the phone, as if to put something in her hands.

"He is missing."

"Have you spoken with the police?"

"I haven't. Others have."

"What do they say?"

He shrugged. "Unless there is evidence of a crime . . ."

"But the Shadow Man? Here? Someone should . . ."

"What, Miss Weiss? Someone should investigate? Certainly. The police? The Justice Department? The damn Supreme Court?"

"Yes, yes. They have special investigations at the Justice Department. They have found Nazis. . . ."

"Is this man a war criminal, Miss Weiss? It would be easier if he was."

She stopped. "Of course he is," she said briskly.

"Are you certain?"

"He collaborated. He helped. Without him . . ." She looked at Simon Winter sharply. "Surely that must constitute a war crime."

"I wonder."

Esther Weiss exhaled slowly. "I think I see your point. And where would the evidence be? The proof?"

"I suspect the proof is mostly dead."

She nodded. "I see," she said. She leaned back, rubbing her hand across her forehead. For a moment she turned toward the window, then she swiveled back around, facing him.

"What is going on here, Mr. Winter? Please tell me what is going on?"

But that was a question he wasn't yet prepared to answer.

* * *

Simon Winter left the Holocaust Center with the promise of assistance and the names of some two dozen scholars who had specialized in studying the survivors. Mostly they were academicians and sociologists, with university listings. Some were associated with legitimate and well-known Jewish organizations. A few were independent, authors working on various accounts of the Holocaust. The problem was, as Simon Winter looked at the list, his hand by the telephone in his apartment, they could tell him much about the past, while he was trying to probe the present and divine the future. He stared at his list and checked off the three that lived in South Florida.

A secretary at the European Studies Department at the University of Miami took his name and number, but sounded extremely skeptical that any professor would return the call of a retired detective purposely vague about the nature of his inquiry. The second man was a writer, living in Plantation, working on a book about the collaboration of the Vichy government in shipping out thousands of French Jews to die in Germany.

"I can tell you about the south of France," the man told Winter regretfully, "but Berlin, no."

The man hesitated, then added, "Of course, like everyone who studies the Holocaust, I can tell you about death. Deaths by the hundreds, thousands, murder as commonplace as the sun rising in the morning or setting at night. Murder as a train schedule, regular and routine. Is that what you're interested in, Mr. Winter?"

Simon Winter hung up, understanding that he needed something different, something unique, some observation or some connection, something that would pitch him out of the darkness of all the memories into the specifics of finding the Shadow Man. He thought: There must be some conjunction between the past and present that I can grasp. Something physical. Something palpable.

He could see none. He slammed a fist against the table.

Impatience filled him.

Taking a deep breath, he dialed the third number. He almost slammed the receiver down when the mechanical sound of an operator informed him that the number had been changed. He noted the new listing, and then called that. He almost hung up on the fifth unanswered ring, only to hear a gruff "Hello?" on the seventh.

"Is this Mr. Rosen? L. Rosen?"

There was a hesitation, then a reply. "Louis Rosen. Who is this? If you're selling subscriptions or insurance or seeking a donation, forget it." The man spoke sharply.

"No," Winter said. He quickly introduced himself and explained, "I got your number from the Holocaust Center."

Again the speaker paused. "Those numbers are supposed to be confidential."

"I believe they are, but these are unusual circumstances."

"Unusual? What could be so unusual that they would break a promise of confidentiality?" The man's voice didn't soften, but gathered an edge of curiosity.

"I have reason to believe that a man who operated in Berlin as a catcher is living in South Florida."

Rosen hesitated. A silence clung to the line before he answered in a steady, cold, but compelling tone.

"That is intriguing. A catcher? Only a few survived. Same as the Kapos in the camps. If you could find this man, it would be truly interesting. There are so many questions."

"What sort of questions?"

"All questions that begin with the great Why, Mr. Winter."

"What do you suppose the answer to that might be, Mr. Rosen?"

"I would be speculating. My area of study is Poland. The Warsaw Ghetto."

"You had family?"

"Of course. And I too."

"I see."

"But that is a different story, is it not, Mr. Winter?"

"Yes. But could you speculate what sort of personality I am looking for?"

Rosen seemed to be gathering his thoughts before he replied. "That is a fascinating question, Mr. Winter. What sort of personality? Do you truly think you want to open that particular door, Mr. Winter?"

"I need to know. I need something to grasp hold of."

"This, of course, is the great How at the bottom of all questions about the Holocaust," Rosen continued, his voice sinking a bit deeper. "It stands only a step closer to the surface than the great Why."

"I'm only beginning to understand," Winter said.

"No one ever really understands," Rosen said coldly. "No one who was not there. The numbers were so immense. The cruelty so common. The evil so complete."

Simon Winter was silent. He could sense the man on the other end thinking.

"And so you want to know about a catcher? Not a fanatic. Not a Nazi. Closer to what the papers like to think of as a criminal psychopath. Remorseless. Relentless. Do you not think they would first excuse themselves by arguing they did what they did in order to save themselves and their own families?"

"That would be reasonable."

"But it is of course untrue. Most didn't save anyone, including themselves. Only the truly clever ones, I suppose. And they would be a special breed, would they not? To survive? High odds."

"Yes."

"So, right away, you know you are dealing with a systemology of lies, are you not, Mr. Winter? A person who cannot be self-delusional, because only someone who saw clearly what was happening could take the necessary steps to remain alive. But someone comfortable with distortions. Someone who embraces deception. But that would not be all, would it?"

"I'm listening."

"There would have to be something beyond simple expediency, would there not? A ferocity. A steel will to live. The catcher would be someone who would never find anyone's life to be even remotely as important as their own. So, perhaps, you will be looking also for a man of some ego. A man who thinks he has done great things. This will not be a stupid man. Not like some dull-witted, hulking camp guard. Not even the accountant's mentality of some S.S. bureaucrat that made certain the transport trains ran on schedule. For a catcher to survive required true genius. Creativity. Do you not see that?"

"Yes. But how would I find this person? Here, among all the survivors?"

Rosen paused again, then laughed briefly.

"Oh, this would be impossible, Mr. Winter. Like a needle in the proverbial haystack. Among thousands, one is not precisely who he says he is. But still, he would be expert. He would know everything that all the survivors know. He would have all their own terrors memorized, because he participated in them. He would have access to all the same nightmares, but not wake up in the middle of the night shouting the name of some long-lost relative who went to the gas. You see, Mr. Winter, he would be completely intact, completely authentic. Yet intrinsically wrong. And somewhere within him a hatred so virulent . . . It would be fascinating. Fascinating."

"I must find him."

"It is a him? Some of the catchers were women. You have a name?"

"Only a nom de guerre. Der Schattenmann."

The name didn't seem to register.

"And you believe he is here?"

"Yes."

Rosen's voice maintained an evenness as he spoke. "And you want desperately to find him? Why would that be?"

"I believe he has killed."

"Ah, now that is interesting. Killed whom?"

"Someone who might have recognized him."

"This makes perfectly reasonable sense. And your involvement?"

"The victim was my neighbor."

"Ahh, this too makes sense. Revenge?"

"I want to stop him."

Rosen again grew silent on the other end of the line, and Winter thought for a second or two that he should say something, but did not, and into that space the man finally spoke quietly, deliberately, saying: "I do not think you will be able to."

"Why is that?" Winter asked.

"Because he must be an expert in death. All kinds of death."

"So am I."

"So is Time, Mr. Winter. And Time has a better chance than you."

Simon Winter rose from his table and walked to the window. Late afternoon sunlight filled the courtyard of the Sunshine Arms. The trumpeting cherub seemed inanely pleased, basking in the end-of-day heat, before the oppressive night humidity settled on the city. For the first time since Sophie Millstein had knocked at his door, Simon Winter felt a sense of defeat. All he'd heard, from every voice, was the same thing: death and impossibility. He lifted a hand to his forehead and rubbed hard, turning the skin red with frustration. This will kill me, he thought. I will die from impotent futility. This thought made him smile ruefully to himself when he recognized that that was precisely what he had been preparing to do when Sophie Millstein knocked on his door.

He decided that he would take a walk to see if movement could spur loose some idea for a productive avenue of inquiry, and so he turned and grabbed his battered Dolphins baseball hat and had his hand on the doorknob when behind him the telephone rang. He paused, wondering whether he should let the machine take it, then decided this was wrong, and bounded across the room, sweeping the receiver off the hook just as the machine went into its recorded message.

"No, I'm here, hang on," he said over his own metallic taped voice.

"Mr. Winter?" It was Frieda Kroner.

"Yes, Mrs. Kroner, what is it?"

"Irving," she said. Her words were iron-hard. "The lifeguard station at South Point. The very last one before the jetty. We will meet you there."

He saw a trio of police cars parked on a sandy strip next to the entrance to the beach. Off to the side was a small park, with a meandering exercise course wandering through it. The park had a half-dozen picnic areas and a set of swings and seesaws; it was a popular place on weekends; many of the immigrant families that clung to the tip of South Beach in narrow, low-slung apartments, used the spot for parties. It was a favorite park for the homeless as well, because it wasn't well patrolled at night, and a favorite too for fashion photographers shooting magazine layouts, because the park abutted Government Cut, the wide channel used by the cruise ships to head out into the open ocean. It sometimes had little moments of theater, where some man whose hopes and clothes were in tatters watched hungrily as chicken and plantains were grilled and children played, a few feet away from where a model wearing thousands of dollars worth of evening wear and jewels pranced and preened for a cameraman.

From the long jetty one could see for miles out to sea, or look back toward the clear skyline of the city. Across the Cut was Fisher Island, a condominium complex serviced by its own ferry, populated by the wealthy, the very wealthy, and the obscenely rich. The jetty was also popular with fishermen, although the beach itself received less attention than the other spots at South Point. By virtue of being at the tip of Miami Beach, it gathered the roughest water and the most dangerous riptides. Some surfers liked it. The tourists were usually warned to move a mile or so up the expanse of sand. There was a boardwalk that led out to the jetty. Once he was on that, he quickly spotted the solitary life-guard station at the end of the beach.

He saw a half-dozen blue-uniformed police officers milling about the faded green wood of the lifeguard stand. At the same time, he spotted Frieda Kroner and Rabbi Rubinstein standing apart, perhaps twenty feet away, watching the policemen, who seemed unsure what to do. A single crime scene technician, in a jacket and tie despite the heat, was bent over the sand, but he could not see what the man was examining. There was another man in a suit, leaning over, but his back was to Winter, who couldn't make out what the man was searching for.

He hurried forward, his basketball shoes making a clopping sound on the wooden boardwalk, like a horse trotting on pavement.

The rabbi turned as he approached, but Frieda Kroner kept watching the policemen.

"Mr. Winter," the rabbi said slowly, "thank you for coming."

"What is it?"

"They called us. Frieda, actually."

"Did they find Mr. Silver?"

"No," Frieda Kroner said, not taking her eyes off the policemen. "They found his clothes."

"What?"

The rabbi shook his head. "The policeman called her. Apparently some kid, a teenager, tried to use a credit card at a shopping center, and the clerk selling the video games didn't think this child, whose name turned out to be Ramón or José or Eduardo, looked much like an Irving, and so she summoned a policeman. And the teenager says this, and then says that, and lies this way and that, but soon enough gets around to telling the truth when someone gets a bit tough with him, and he says he finds this wallet with the credit card. They do not believe him, but he insists, and so the police bring him down here and he shows them."

"What?"

"Irving's clothes. Right on the beach, as if he left them there."

"And the wallet?"

"It was on top."

Simon Winter nodded.

"This is where he killed him," Frieda Kroner said quietly.

The old detective took a deep breath, thinking, *I don't think so*, and stepped away from the rabbi and Mrs. Kroner and started to pace across the sand. With each step he grew increasingly angry, raging away within himself, once again feeling the same incompetence and stupidity. And within each step of anger, another voice within him tried to calm him, tried to force him to stay alert, because, he thought, perhaps there is something here to learn, and he knew that frustration, perhaps better than anything else, could serve to blind him to knowledge.

Two of the uniformed officers peeled away from the group and stepped in front of him.

"This area is closed, old-timer," one of them said with the arrogance of youth.

"Who's in charge?" Winter demanded sharply.

"Detective's in charge. Who wants to know?" the patrolman replied with an edge.

Winter wanted to reach out and shove the younger man aside,

but hesitated, and in that second heard a voice that seemed to be familiar:

"I am, Mr. Winter."

He looked past the young patrolman's shoulder and saw Walter Robinson slowly rising from the blond sand beach. Robinson gestured at the patrolman. "Let him come over."

Simon Winter stepped across the sand. Walter Robinson did not offer his hand, but said instead: "I thought you would be here. If not, I would have found you."

"Why is that?" Winter asked.

The young detective didn't reply, except to ask a question. "You knew Mr. Silver?"

"Yes."

"And Sophie Millstein as well."

"That is obvious, Detective."

Robinson grasped Winter by the elbow and led him to where a crime scene technician was taking a few pictures.

The technician looked up at Robinson. "Come on, Walt. Let me bag this shit and let's get back to real work."

Walter Robinson shook his head.

"All right, Mr. Winter," he said quietly. "You were a detective once. What do you see?"

The technician overheard this question and interrupted with his own answer: "Walter, come on. How obvious can things be? Old man wants to end it all, comes on down here at night, no one around, folds up his clothing nice and neat and heads into the surf. Body will turn up in a couple of days up the beach a few miles or wherever the currents wanna dump it. Should be calling the Coast Guard to keep an eye out."

Robinson glared at the technician. "That's what you see," he said coldly. "I'm interested in what this gentleman sees."

Winter was studying the beach carefully. He saw Irving Silver's clothes, folded just as the technician said, prepared like a man afraid of making a mess in death.

"The wallet was right on top?"

"Yes," Robinson said.

"Anything on the beach?"

"Not that we can find."

"No note?"

"No."

"Have you examined the clothing?"

"Just in its current position."

Winter knelt down beside the clothes. "May I?" he asked.

Robinson squatted beside him. He held up a plastic evidence bag. "Go ahead," he said.

There was a straw porkpie hat. Simon Winter picked it up and turned it over. He saw the initials I. S. scratched into the dark-stained sweatband. He pointed at these to Robinson, then dropped the hat into an evidence bag. Then he picked up a floral-print polyester shirt. The flowers were greens and blues and vinelike, entwined in design, making the pattern a maze of variegated shapes and colors. He started to pass the fabric beneath his eyes slowly, feeling it between two fingers, until he reached the collar, and there he stopped. He could feel his heart suddenly accelerate, and for a moment he felt dizzy.

"There," he said quietly, almost a whisper.

Robinson leaned over and touched the fabric where Winter was pointing. He picked up the shirt and held it up into the fading light, squinting as he examined the texture.

The young detective nodded, letting out a long hiss of breath. "Perhaps," he said. "I think you're maybe right."

Winter stood up and looked out to sea. Each wave seemed to reach up and catch a piece of the fast-dropping night, then thrust the darkness up onto the shoreline.

"It's blood," Winter said. "Irving Silver's blood."

"There's not much," Robinson acknowledged slowly. "It could be nothing more than a shaving cut." Then he turned to the technician. "Collect all this stuff carefully." He waved at the uniformed officers. "I want this whole area taped off. It might be a homicide scene."

Simon Winter remained silent for a moment, watching the ocean, feeling the onshore breeze start to dwindle, making space for the oppressive summer night.

"He's not there," he said softly.

"Who isn't there?" Walter Robinson asked.

"Irving Silver." Winter raised a hand and stretched it toward the ocean. "That is what it is supposed to seem like. That he's out there drowned and disappeared. Swallowed up. But he isn't."

"Where is he, then?" the young detective asked.

"Somewhere else. Somewhere distant and lost. Out in the Everglades maybe."

"A body one place. Clothing here?"

"Correct."

Walter Robinson whistled softly and stared out at the ocean as well. "That would be clever. It would really screw us up." He hesitated, then added: "I think you may be right."

Winter turned then, and looked at the young detective. "You said you were going to find me. Why?"

"Because," Walter Robinson replied slowly, "I have lately become interested in history."

# SIXTEEN

## A LEGAL GAME OF CHICKEN

THERE was a pay telephone across from the nurse's station inside the locked ward at Jackson Memorial Hospital, and Espy Martinez paused there. She quickly dialed the number of the Miami Beach Homicide Unit. For the third time that afternoon she was forced to leave a message for Walter Robinson. She hung up the receiver with an irritated snap to her wrist, banging it down. Then she took a deep breath and eyed the corridor that led to Leroy Jefferson's room.

She wondered for an instant whether she was closer to the truth or about to lose sight of it completely. Then she paced down the hallway, listening to the smacking sound her heels made against the polished linoleum floor. Someone was crying in one of the rooms she passed, but she could not see who it was. The sound of sobbing, however, seemed to keep cadence with her quick-march down the corridor.

The prison guard on duty at the wire-mesh gate was an older man. She recognized him from a half-dozen courtrooms. He had a brushy, crew-cut, gray shock of hair and thick forearms adorned with intricate tattoos. He gave her a little wave and a crooked smile as she approached.

"Hi, Mike," she said. "This must be easier than hauling guys back and forth between the jail and the Justice Building."

"Well," he said, "all I got to do here is make sure I don't catch something, and sit around reading the paper."

"Any good news?"

"Never is."

"Feeling okay?"

"Sure am."

"Then sounds to me like you've got easy duty."

"You got that right, Miss Martinez."

"Is Alter here?"

"Just a couple of minutes ago. Went in with the doctor."

She started to sign in on a log sheet attached to a clipboard when the guard whispered, "I think poor Leroy's having a bit of trouble with the pain today, you know, Counselor? He's been on that buzzer to the nurse's station all morning. I think maybe you shooting up his leg and him not being allowed no crack pipe, well, maybe it's made him a tad *tense*, if you catch my drift, Miss Martinez."

"Uh-huh," she said, nodding.

The guard grinned. "I mean, he might be just a little bit rocky today. You might squeeze him a little bit, if you get the chance, know what I mean?"

Espy Martinez managed to smile, despite the feeling that it was going to be herself that was squeezed, not Leroy Jefferson. She put her index finger to her temple, making a small salute. Prison guards, she thought, know everything and have a remarkable ability to sense the direction of any wind that blows through the justice system.

As she pushed her way into the hospital room, she heard the sound of retching, and a long, complaining, "Sheeit." She summoned a wry, mocking, inquisitive look and stepped into the room. She immediately looked at Leroy Jefferson, his leg still immobilized in traction, struggling to sit up in bed. As he turned to face her, she saw a thin line of perspiration gathered at his forehead. He wiped the back of his hand across his lips.

"Not feeling too good, huh, Mr. Jefferson?"

The accused man scowled, then he bent over and spat into a bedside wastebasket.

"Bitch that shot me," he said beneath his breath.

"He's okay," Thomas Alter said quickly, rising from a steel folding chair. "Isn't that right, Doctor?"

A young white-jacketed physician was standing beside Jefferson. He nodded. "The discomfort is normal."

"Normal, shit," Jefferson said. "I want another shot."

The doctor glanced at his watch, then down at his chart, and shook his head. "Nope. Not for at least ninety minutes. Maybe two hours." He said this coldly, without feeling. As he spoke, Martinez saw a wave of hurt and nausea wash over Jefferson's face. He started to bend toward the side of the bed and the wastebasket, then managed to stop, pushing himself back hard, as if tired. "Ain't got nothin' left in me," he whispered. An intravenous tube running from a stanchion down into his arm rattled. Martinez looked away for a moment, absorbing the stark surroundings in the small room. White walls. A gray steel grate over a dirt-streaked window, so that even the day's sunshine seemed smudged as it crept into the room. A single, utilitarian bed, and bedside table. A paper cup and a cheap plastic jug for water. As bleak as the jail cell that awaited him barely a block away.

Alter looked irritatedly at the young physician, who replaced the chart at the bottom of the bed. "I think he could use something," the attorney said.

The doctor looked up. "You're the lawyer, right?"

"Correct."

"Well, stick to the fucking law, then," he said quietly. The doctor looked over at Espy Martinez. "My brother-in-law's a cop," he said. He jerked a thumb toward Leroy Jefferson. "He's okay. His leg hurts like hell, and he's in withdrawal. So he's feeling mighty sick, and every time he makes a move for that wastebasket, it must feel like someone's sticking a knife in that knee and twisting it around. But it isn't anything that will kill him. It just isn't making him happy. Making him happy isn't exactly my job. Keeping him alive was." The doctor slid past her and out the door.

Leroy Jefferson's hands were clenched tight, into balls. "I ain't never gonna walk right again 'cause of you," he said.

She shook her head. "Breaks my heart," she replied. "I told you to freeze. And instead you tried to shoot me. Screw you."

Leroy Jefferson scowled again, and started to speak, but was cut off by Thomas Alter.

"That's not the purpose of this meeting," the public defender said.

"That's right," Martinez said. "The purpose of this meeting is to determine whether or not I think this defendant has the capacity somewhere within him to tell the truth, which, right now, I seriously doubt."

Alter waved his arm dramatically, like some overwrought actor on a dinner theater stage. "Then get out. Take him to trial. Do what you want, but you won't get his help, and it sure looks to me like you're going to need it."

Espy Martinez managed to grip hold of herself, and spoke quietly. "Look, the lie detector test is persuasive, but not conclusive. . . ."

"You gonna put an innocent man in jail?" Leroy Jefferson demanded. She ignored him.

"What about the fingerprint?" Alter asked. "How're you going to get around that?"

She didn't answer this, but instead said, "So maybe it wasn't his hands around Sophie's throat. But there's clear-cut evidence he was in Sophie's room, and that he stole items. So, perhaps he had an accomplice. Perhaps there were two of them there that night. That still makes him guilty of felony murder." She looked over at Jefferson. "Penalty for felony murder in this state, in case you weren't aware, is the chair."

"Shit," Jefferson said. "Didn't kill nobody and didn't have nobody with me."

Alter glared at his client and said, "Just shut up and let me and the prosecutor talk. What are you saying?"

"I'm saying that before I go any further, I want to know what you mean by help. Give me some proffer of your client's evidence."

"Not without a guarantee."

"What sort of guarantee?"

"That he gets a deal. No prison time."

"Forget it."

"Then go screw yourself. Find that old woman's killer without him."

"That's what we'll do."

"Sure you will. Good luck. You got any idea who left that partial on her throat?"

"I'm not answering that sort of question."

"I didn't think you did," Alter said, smiling, relaxing. He turned to Leroy Jefferson. "You just keep your mouth shut, Leroy. Dealing with the State is just the same as waiting for that shot of painkiller. It hurts. You feel sick. But eventually they come to you. And then everything is all right."

Jefferson seemed gray and pale. He nodded. "I saw him," he said.

"Saw who?" Martinez asked quickly.

"I said keep your mouth shut!" Alter shouted.

Leroy Jefferson leaned back on a pillow. A single rivulet of perspiration ran down his cheek, but he grinned at Espy Martinez.

"Gonna need me," he said. "Ain't gonna find no killer, 'less I show you who. I saw him good. I saw him kill that old lady."

Martinez clenched her own teeth together. "You know I've filed enough charges against you to keep you up in Raiford Prison for a thousand years. Ten thousand years. Forever. Until you shrivel up and rot away. And that's where you're gonna be."

Jefferson just shook his head and repeated: "Gonna need old Leroy. You go ask that detective, he tell you."

Martinez looked over at Alter.

The public defender shrugged. "What can I say, Espy? He's telling you the way it is."

"Really? Why is it that I don't find it easy to believe Mr. Jefferson? Maybe because he's a strung-out, lying—"

"You're going to have to believe him, Espy, because he was the one that was there."

"Yeah, him and one of his junkie buddies. The only deal I'll cut will be to life in prison. He gets to save his sorry ass by testifying against whatever low-life friend of his killed Sophie Millstein."

"Weren't no friend, I tol' you," Jefferson said, smugness penetrating through the pain. "Were a white guy. An old white guy."

Thomas Alter smiled again. "I think we've helped Miss Martinez out quite enough already."

"You're saying that . . ."

"He was there. He saw the killing. He ran away. What more do you need to know, Espy? There's your precious proffer."

"You mean this low-life witnessed a murder then robbed the victim before the neighbors got there? Is that what you're saying?"

She was unable to conceal the astonishment in her voice.

"You figure it out," Alter replied with a shrug. "Life sure is strange."

They were all silent for a moment.

"Nice seeing you, Prosecutor," Thomas Alter said. "You get back to me, okay? We're not going anywhere. And now you know the score."

Espy Martinez stared hard at Thomas Alter, letting her eyes burrow into his, until he finally let his self-satisfied grin slide from his lips.

"You think I'd cut this piece of garbage a deal after he almost killed a cop and almost killed me? You think he's gonna walk on those charges?"

Alter sat quietly, infuriatingly, in his chair, as if assessing both what she'd said and how angry she was.

"I don't think anything, Espy. All I think is that Mr. Jefferson knows something that you're gonna want to know, and the price of that knowledge is steep. But then again, the cost of enlightenment is always high. See? I can be a philosopher."

"That's right. The price is right up there. You see? I'm a fucking philosopher too," Leroy Jefferson cackled, although the last words were twisted with a sudden twinge of pain that made the corner of his lip twitch.

"Better not price yourself right out of the market, Tommy," Martinez said briskly.

"Please shut the door on your way out," the public defender replied.

As usual, the summons to Abe Lasser's office was written in red ink to underscore the urgency of the request. All of Lasser's summonses were urgent, she thought, whether they really were or not. She quickly flipped through her messages, looking for one from Walter Robinson, but there was none. For a second she managed enough distance to wonder whether she was anxious to hear from her lover or from the detective working the case. She didn't know the answer to this question but suspected that each desire hummed like a tuning fork within her, each a different tone, but equally insistent.

Lasser was standing by his window when she entered his office, staring out over the city.

"You know, during the riots, I was standing right up here, right at this window, and I could see all the way to the tire store, the big discount one on Twenty-first Avenue. I had some binoculars and I even saw the guys set the place on fire. They were running right around the side and then they stopped and they piled up some debris and I saw them toss some gasoline on it. Like some sort of demented troop of evil urban Boy Scouts." He pointed and laughed, although not at anything particularly funny. "It was four blocks away, and it seemed like something I was watching on television."

He turned from the window.

"Damnedest thing," he continued. "These little antlike figures way down there, scurrying about, torching that big old warehouse. Thing burned for almost two days. And here I was, chief felony prosecutor for the county, witnessing the whole rotten thing from my window and not able to do a damn thing about it."

She nodded, thinking: There's going to be a point somewhere.

"Like watching an accident happen, but worse, because this wasn't an accident, it was a crime. Much worse. Deliberate, destructive. No act of God. An act of man."

He stepped away from the window.

"Acts of God, we leave to higher authorities, Espy. But acts of man, those are precisely why we're here. They're our job." He smiled. "I sound like a philosopher," he said.

"Tommy Alter said the same thing to me, barely an hour ago."

Lasser grinned. "Really? Stands to reason, I guess."

He moved behind his desk. He had removed his suit coat, and she saw that his white dress shirt was tapered to his waist, obviously tailored. She kept quiet while Lasser picked up the copy of the lie detector report.

"I hate these fucking things," he said. He dropped it to the desktop as if it were infectious. The pages flapped momentarily. "So, Espy, do you feel like you're standing at a window about to watch a crime take place and unable to do anything about it? If this scumbag Leroy Jefferson walks, it will be a crime. As sure as I'm standing here now, it will be just like an arson. It will be like putting a match to some flammable bit of material. Sure, he may smolder and smoke for some time. A week. A month. Maybe six months. But then he will go and do precisely what this damn report says he didn't do: kill some harmless little old lady. You understand that, Espy?"

"Yes sir."

"You've met Mr. Jefferson. What is the prognosis for him becoming a contributing member of society?"

These last words were spoken with unbridled sarcasm.

"The prognosis is dim, sir."

Abe Lasser burst out laughing. "Dim. Yes, I'd say. More like nonexistent."

He sat down suddenly and immediately rocked back in his chair. "Maybe, Espy, we'll get lucky. Perhaps fucking Leroy Jefferson will kill some other scumbag instead of some tax-paying, God-fearing, innocent member of our community, though I doubt it, because the slimeball seems to like robbing little old ladies, and I would suspect that he will return to that profession just as quickly as he can."

He hesitated, then added, "Even if he is limping along thanks to your twenty-five-caliber arrest. So, tell me, Espy, do you feel lucky? Is there some little Hispanic leprechaun guiding the Martinez family fortunes, set to deliver some good luck in your direction? Or perhaps a fairy godmother that will sing bibbity-bobbity-boo, wave her magic wand, and send Leroy Jefferson off to kill one of his own ilk, instead of someone's beloved grandmother?"

"I don't think so, sir."

Lasser spun about in his chair. "Ahh, such a pity."

He stopped and bent toward the desk, poking at the lie detector test. "Got to admit, fucking Tommy Alter knows what he's doing. Gets our own man to run the fucking test. A nice touch. I've got to remember that, you know, so the day that Tommy comes in here, hat in hand, we get a little payback. Just between us philosophers." He swiveled about, leaning back, placing his hands behind his head.

"So what're you going to do, Espy?" Lasser asked abruptly.

"I'm sorry, what am I—"

"Right. What are you going to do? Your case. Your decision. I'm merely here to, uh, assist you."

Espy Martinez felt her skin flush. "I thought . . ."

"You thought I'd make the call?"

"Yes."

He shook his head. "No. Your case. Your call. I only present certain guidelines. Like this: Jefferson is charged with two counts of attempted murder for shooting at you and at that detective. Seems to me that those transactions have nothing to do with Sophie Millstein's murder."

"Yes."

"But on the other hand, an actual murder, especially a heinous one, such as Sophie Millstein's, well, that case takes significant precedence over a shootout, even one as dramatic as Mr. Jefferson's."

"I see."

"Do you, Espy?"

She could feel a solitary anger winding up within her, and she did not think she could control it from spilling forth. "I see that it is my butt on the line."

Lasser nodded. "Inelegantly put, but accurate."

She breathed in harshly. It seemed as if the office was suddenly hot. "If Jefferson provides us with Sophie's killer . . ."

"Then you're a hero, with the headlines to prove it."

"But if it is all bullshit and I cut him a deal and then he goes out and kills someone . . ."

"Then the news stories won't be quite so laudatory, will they?"

"No. They won't."

Lasser continued to rock in the chair. "It would be better if

Walter Robinson could make a case without Jefferson. Any chance of that?"

"I don't know. It's like starting from scratch. I don't even think he's got a lead. We were all set to start putting Jefferson in the electric chair, when it all went to Hell with that report."

"Nasty little device, the polygraph machine. Makes everything gray and fuzzy. Not clear-cut and pristine."

"So, I'm not sure what Walter can come up with."

"Trail is cold already. Have you ever seen the statistics on solving homicides? Every day that passes without an arrest . . ."

The chief prosecutor held up his hand, then, as he spoke, he started to curve it downward, like measuring the fall off a cliff. "Maybe that partial thumbprint the killer left behind?"

"I believe he's already run it through the computer with negative results. I think he did that first."

"So Sophie's killer isn't a criminal who's been fingerprinted recently. That's a bad sign."

"Apparently not."

Lasser continued, "Tough sledding, then. Of course, the converse is true for Tommy Alter and Leroy Jefferson. If Robinson can somehow, magically, get headed in the right direction, well, then the value of some murderous junkie's testimony diminishes rapidly, doesn't it?"

"Yes."

"I'd like to see that," Lasser said, tilting backward, as if daydreaming, his eyes for a moment sweeping the ceiling. "Like to see old complacent Tommy Alter's face when we tell him we don't need Mr. Leroy Jefferson. That would give me pleasure."

"Jefferson claims to be an eyewitness to the killing."

"He does? Ah well, would that all the witnesses in the world were saints, virgins, or Boy Scouts. That makes it sticky, doesn't it?"

"How so?"

"Well, that would be a difficult explanation to make to the Millstein family and to some whore scribbler over at the *Miami Herald* who finds out about all this and who calls us up on the phone one day with a uniquely nasty set of questions—you know, having to admit that the State rejected an *eyewitness's* testimony because he was, shall we say, unsavory? I don't think that particular explanation would look good in print."

"No sir. Me neither."

"They will find out, Espy. You know that, don't you? The *Herald* will find out. The bastards always do." He cleared his throat. "A tricky situation, Espy. Tricky." Lasser glanced down at a file on his desk. He picked it up and thumbed through it almost haphazardly, as if distracted. "You'll let me know what you decide to do, won't you?"

She kept her anger in check. "Yes sir. As soon as I make a decision."

"Don't hesitate."

"No sir."

"And, Espy, keep one thing in mind as you work your way through the mine field. One priority . . ."

"What is that, sir?"

"We find, we prosecute, we convict, Sophie Millstein's killer. I made that promise. To a fuck***ing*** rabbi, of all people. What could I have been thinking? Bad lesson there, Espy. If you're going to promise something that may be well-nigh impossible, better make that promise to someone who doesn't count for much either in this life and especially not in the next. So, unfortunate as it seems, I mean to keep that promise." He looked up from the papers on his desk quickly and jabbed a finger at her. "You're going to keep it for me."

Espy Martinez nodded, but felt only slippery black ice within.

Lasser laughed, but the sound only slightly diminished the tension in the room.

"Lighten up, Espy," he said, although she realized there was nothing to lighten up about. "This is what makes criminal law so intriguing." He smiled. "It has a certain existential quality to it. Life gambles, I like to call them. It is sometimes like we're caught up in a game of high-speed chicken, souped-up situations racing headlong right at each other, wondering who's going to flinch first, played out in suits and ties, in wood-trimmed courtrooms, with rules and judges and all the trappings of civilization, but where we're really talking about something almost primitive, something ancient, aren't we?"

"What would that be?" she asked bitterly. She felt utterly alone.

"That would be justice," Lasser replied offhandedly.

# SEVENTEEN
## NOT SOMETHING FROM THE WORLD
## HE KNEW

About an hour after beginning to listen to the two old people tell him a story so hard to imagine that even the jaded homicide detective within him rebelled, Walter Robinson held up his hand, bringing a halt to their conversation. He realized he needed a moment to think, a moment to absorb what he'd heard, and so he suggested that he bring them all coffee, or a soft drink.

Frieda Kroner scowled. "We drink coffee while *he* plans!" she said angrily. Rabbi Rubinstein added quickly, "I think we should continue."

Robinson glanced over at Simon Winter, who had said little since they'd all returned to the Beach homicide offices. But the old detective shook his head. Robinson stared hard at the older man, who realized in that second that he was being asked for help, and so, quickly, changed his mind. "Maybe a soda," Winter said.

The rabbi and Frieda Kroner swiveled in their seats at the sound of his voice. Frieda Kroner frowned and started to say something, but the rabbi diplomatically shushed her before the words tumbled out. "Perhaps coffee. With sugar and milk," he said, and the old woman at his side reluctantly nodded. "Two sugars," she muttered. "To put sweetness back in my life."

"All right." Walter Robinson nodded. "Just take five. I'll be right back."

He left them all sitting in one of the interview rooms, walking swiftly out into the corridor. For a moment he felt an immense exhaustion sweep over him, and he leaned back against a wall, closing his eyes. He wanted to blank his imagination, but could not. For a long, spinning second, he found himself wondering what it must have been like, packed tightly into a cattle car, the press of people choking away his breath. Work Makes Free, he thought suddenly. He opened his eyes and wheezed like a man at the end of a long run.

From down the corridor he heard the sound of a young woman crying. He welcomed the distraction. It was a long, steady sound of someone slowly sliding down grief's slope, not urgent, but desperate. He knew the case; a twenty-one-year-old mother of three small children, the oldest being five, had left them unattended in her small apartment while she went to the corner store for diapers and groceries. She was Nicaraguan, and had only been in the country for a few months—which is to say, just long enough for her husband to disappear, and not long enough to find any friends who might help her out with baby-sitting—and the rattrap that she lived in was a place that would never show up on any of the Chamber of Commerce's idyllic photographs of bikinied, suntanned, happy-go-lucky Miami Beach. At the young woman's apartment, there were no screens on the windows and the air-conditioning was out, so they were left wide open to the day's heat. While she was gone, the three-year-old had climbed out of the crib she'd placed him in, and managed to get up to the windowsill, trying to catch some stray breath of fresh air, or maybe just interested and curious in the street noises because that is the way children are. Perched high, he had lost his balance and tumbled out, headfirst from the third story of the apartment building, landing on the cement of the sidewalk just as his mother approached the building, so that she had had one horrible vision of her child whirling through the air, before landing with an unholy crunch almost at her feet.

She had screamed then, but since arriving at the homicide offices, had retreated into a wordlessness interrupted only by an occasional cry for Santa Maria, Madre del Dios, and tightly clutching her rosary beads.

Walter Robinson let out a long, slow sigh. The young woman doesn't understand, he thought. She barely understands this death, and she doesn't understand this country, and she probably wouldn't understand much anyway because she is poor and uneducated and alone, and surely she doesn't understand why the *policía* have taken her two other children away and are getting ready to charge her with criminal negligence. After all, she was going to the store to buy them milk with the few remaining dollars she had because she loves them.

He shook himself off the wall and let the young immigrant woman's cries drift into the background realm of noise that is more or less commonplace in police stations, even modern ones with recessed lighting and industrial carpeting on the floors. It was sad, but sadness was the norm, and he knew that no one in uniform or carrying a badge ever allowed these sadnesses to accumulate within them, although he recognized that each one probably made some little scratch somewhere on the psyche. He started to walk down the corridor briskly, standing aside when another interview room door opened and two detectives emerged, struggling with a handcuffed teenager.

"Come on, tough guy," one detective said, but the teenager, his face pockmarked with acne, framed by ringlets of long stringy hair, sporting a tattoo extolling the virtues of a heavy-metal rock band high on the considerable muscle of his arm, instead of following orders, slammed back into the detectives. The three of them abruptly tangled up, teetered for a moment as they all lost balance, and then fell to the floor.

As Robinson stepped quickly toward them, the three men struggled briefly. The teenager's legs flailed out as he tried to kick at the detectives. They, in turn, rolled over on top of the suspect in a practiced fashion, immediately gaining the advantage. He stopped a few feet back from the fighting men. It reminded him, in an odd way, of contentious brothers, where the older ones sit on the youngest until he stops fighting back.

"Need help?" Robinson asked, almost offhandedly.

"Ahh, no thanks, Walt, buddy," one of the detectives replied as he calmly reached down and grabbed a handful of long, stringy black hair, then slammed the teenager's face hard against the floor.

"Fucking asshole cop!" the kid yelled.

The policeman slammed him again.

"Motherfucker!"

The second detective maneuvered around, placed one knee square in the teenager's back, and twisted his arms savagely.

"Got that right, at least," he said between clenched teeth, irritated more than angry.

"You sure you don't need a hand?" Robinson asked again.

"Not for this punk cocksucker," the detective replied.

"Fuck you!" the kid yelled. But his desire to continue struggling was fast diminishing, as his face was bashed into the floor. "Fuck you both!" the kid managed between slams.

"What's the deal?" Robinson asked.

"Fucking punk kid got burned in a drug deal. Fuck, some drug deal. Fifty bucks worth of rock. Goes home, gets a nine-millimeter out of his daddy's bedside table, and goes and finds the kid who burned him. Shoots him right on the street, right in the head, right in front of Miami Beach High, just as school's getting out. Sort of an unusual extracurricular activity, huh? Made a real pretty show. I mean, kinda like *Miami Vice* usta be, except no flashy clothes and trendy haircuts and no fast cars and no speedboats. But real live blood all over the fucking place. Over fifty fucking bucks, you dumb punk." The detective had slammed the kid's head down with each word of the final sentence, keeping time with the sentiment.

"And you don't look like Don Johnson," Walter Robinson said.

The detective, a young man, smiled and shrugged. "But hey, I'm trying."

The teenager went limp. The two detectives pulled him to his feet, and the kid snarled. "Fuck you, cop," he said again. He leaned his head back as a bright stream of blood ran down over his lips and chin. "You broke my fucking nose!" he whined. "Motherfuckers!"

"No, we didn't," the younger detective answered calmly. "The floor did."

"Fuck you," the kid repeated as the older detective laughed at the younger's disingenuous statement.

"Can't you come up with something original, asshole?" the older of the detectives complained sarcastically. "I mean, punk, don't you figure we've had enough people telling us to go fuck ourselves like almost every minute or at the very least every hour, on the hour, every fucking day, like so much that it don't mean a helluva lot to us anymore? I mean, it just doesn't cut it, insult-wise. Like sticks and stones can break my bones, you know, that sort of thing. So, how about something clever. Show off that intelligence of yours. Be original, punk. Say something that will really piss us off. Give us that satisfaction, at least."

"Fuck you," the surprised teenager replied.

The older detective turned to Walter Robinson. "Makes you wonder about the younger generation, doesn't it, Walt?" He grinned. "Too much television. Kills the mind. Too much loud music. Dulls the senses. Right, punk?"

"Fuck you," the kid repeated sluggishly.

"See what I mean?" the detective said. He gave the teenager's arms another jerk and twist.

"Owww!" the kid yelled. "Fuck you. I'm gonna do juvie time anyway, asshole."

"For first fucking degree murder? No way, punk," the detective said. He started to half shove, half pull the suspect down the corridor, toward the elevator that would transport them to the lockup, where the teenager would stew for a few hours, while the inevitable stack of paperwork was completed.

The second detective paused next to Robinson and dusted the residue from the small struggle off his suit. As he swept his hands across the fabric, he whispered, "Fucking kid is probably right. The kid he shot is in a coma but probably will pull through, although he ain't gonna have a real excellent life from now on, and we'll have to lower the charges to attempted homicide and assault with a deadly. What a world, huh, Walt? Shoot somebody over a measly fifty bucks worth of rock and end up with some judge saying 'Naughty, naughty, please don't do it again ...' Ah, well, we'll give it a shot. Try to persuade them to treat him like an adult. Except he's just barely sixteen. Shit. Sixteen going on twenty-six." Then, without waiting for a response, he hurried after his partner and the suspect.

Walter Robinson watched the trio move out of his sight, and thought: *This I understand.* In his world, a baby left alone and falling from a windowsill, a teenager who attempts murder and expects to get away with it—these were the events of every day. There was nothing shocking, nothing unique, nothing even remotely exceptional about these crimes. They just happened. Tomorrow there would be other crimes, just like them. The detective's eyes fastened on the door to the interview room, where the two old survivors and an ancient policeman waited for him to return with soda and coffee so they could continue telling a tale of a hatred and evil so virulent that he was having trouble imagining it. He realized that there was not one word of what they had told him that he could grasp hold of with any familiarity. All he knew was that he'd been plunged into a system of murder that even unsettled him, and he wondered for a moment whether or not there wasn't a Shadow Man that lurked on the edges of everyone's history, somewhere.

He asked himself suddenly: How do you find a criminal who is not a criminal like any other?

Good question, he thought. He did not know that Simon Winter had posed the identical question of himself days earlier.

How do you find this man?

Find his mistake. He's made one somewhere.

How do you find his mistake?

Figure him out. Understand the Shadow Man, and you'll see where he made an error.

Understand? What sort of man hates the way he does?

This question made Walter Robinson breathe out sharply. He did not know the answer, but suspected the old people waiting in the room could show him.

He shook his head. You're thinking too much, he told himself. He tried to shrug it all off. He hurried toward his own desk. He knew there was a telephone call he very much wanted to make.

\* \* \*

Espy Martinez grabbed the telephone receiver before the first ring had been completed. "Yes?"

"Espy . . ."

"Walter, Jesus, I've been trying to reach you. . . ."

"I know. I'm sorry. I was at a crime scene, and now I've got these people in an interview room."

He stopped there, and both of them were silent for a moment.

"I wanted to talk to you," he said. "I just wanted to talk."

She laughed, relief in her voice. "That would be nice, you know. Just to talk about you and me. Us. Or maybe the weather . . ."

"It's goddamn hot. . . ."

"Or how about sports? Are the Dolphins going to win the pennant?"

He grinned. "Good idea, but wrong sport."

"Okay, how about the future?"

"Our future? Or Leroy Jefferson's?"

"Good question. Leroy fucking Jefferson."

Walter Robinson smiled. "You're beginning to sound like a cop. Maybe we should just call him Leroy F. Jefferson. Or F. Leroy Jefferson, if you want to make it sound classier."

She shook her head. "It's inevitable, I guess. Business first. I went to see Alter and his delightful client. What a sweet guy, Mr. Jefferson. Outgoing. Pleasant. Gives one a real sense of optimism about the world we live in."

"That bad, huh?"

"Well guess what? You know what he is? Leroy fucking Jefferson, the *eyewitness*."

"He saw the murder? He was there?"

"Yeah. And then like the good citizen he aspires to be, he immediately robbed poor Sophie Millstein. Her body wasn't even cold."

"Jesus Christ what a—"

"No kidding. The problem is, the killer was—"

"An old white guy," Robinson blurted.

"How did you—"

"I think," Robinson said slowly, "that you better come over here and listen to the people I've got in the interview room."

"How did—I'm not sure I get it. But I'll be right over."

"There was an old-timer at the scene that night. Sophie's neighbor. He told me that she was scared. Scared of someone she knew fifty years ago. Fifty years and in another world. And I just goddamn ignored him then, instead of paying attention. So, after we got the lie detector report, I came back here and went over my notes and saw his name and, well, it's pretty far out, but maybe, just maybe, she had reason to be scared. Damn it!"

"What?"

"It's not the first damn rule of being a homicide detective, but it damn well ought to be."

"What's that?"

"Listen to everyone, and don't discard anything just because it doesn't seem to fit right away, because maybe it will before everything is over."

Martinez felt a surge of excitement. "Do you think maybe you have a lead? Something good? I'd love to tell Alter and Jefferson to get lost."

"Don't get your hopes up, Espy. What we've got are some scared old people and maybe a killer like none I've ever heard of. Like nobody's ever heard of."

He stopped there, hesitating, his mind churning. Then he added, "But if Leroy fucking Jefferson saw him, damn, that's something. That's something we can use."

Espy Martinez rose at her desk. "All right, I'm on my way."

"Great. Hurry. These old folks might start getting worn-out."

"And afterward . . ."

Walter Robinson smiled, and the tone of his voice lifted slightly. "Well, afterward, we can go discuss the case, or whatever you want. Although, I seem to recall that the last time we discussed the case, things were, well, pretty damn convivial. But if you want to talk about the weather, well, hell, let's see where that leads us."

Martinez flushed and grinned. She hung up the telephone, stuffed some papers in her briefcase, and hurried from her office. It was late, and there were only a few prosecutors and secretaries left about. She bounded down the stalled escalators in the Justice Building, passing empty, darkened courtrooms, waving at the guard by the front doors, who hardly looked up from his copy of *Penthouse*, so intent was he on the breasts and genitals exposed on the glossy pages that he looked for all the world like a student cramming for an exam. Outside, the night air was thick with heat, lustrous with city lights that delivered glowing illumination. Her eagerness overcame her usual unsettled fear; she rushed for her car with determination and desire, feeling as if she was heading toward, if not solutions, at least the beginnings of some answers to a wide variety of questions.

Simon Winter kept his mouth shut and watched as the rabbi and Frieda Kroner patiently repeated their story for the young woman from the prosecutor's office. He noticed a glance or two, shared between Espy Martinez and Walter Robinson, and suspected there was more there than professional friendship, but he did not really concern himself with this, other than to note inwardly that Espy Martinez seemed every bit as beautiful as his landlord's daughter, and this made him slightly envious. As for himself, he contributed as little as possible.

When Herman Stein's death came up, both the old survivors turned to him, and he realized he was supposed to say something, so he did: "Stein was murdered."

Walter Robinson shook his head just slightly. "A closed-door suicide."

"He misspelled his wife's name."

"But surely he was tense, depressed, anxious. . . ." Espy Martinez interrupted.

Winter looked at her, searching her face with his eyes, examining the curve in her brows, the shape of her eyes, looking for signs of something other than youth and inexperience. "Yes, he was those things."

"And you don't think that could have caused him to make a mistake?"

"Not in a million years. Not that mistake."

Martinez shot a quick glance over at Robinson. But he had leaned back in his chair, lowering his chin to his chest in thought, but still staring right at Simon Winter.

"Walter?" she asked. "What do you think?"

"I think people make mistakes all the time," he said slowly. "But I don't think the mistake on that note was made by Herman Stein, unless he meant to."

Frieda Kroner immediately slapped her hand hard on the wooden surface of the table in the interview room. It made a sound like a pistol shot. "Ach! I told you so! So, you believe, do you, Mr. Young Detective? So now you are beginning to see?"

"I'm still here," Robinson replied quietly. "I'm still listening." But inwardly, Walter Robinson was churning, filled with an abrupt, torrential surge of anxiety. For a moment he tried to concentrate on the two old people, masking the surge of suspicion within him, but this was difficult as his imagination began to fill with an unsettling, eerie dread. He worked hard to stifle this concern, thrusting it aside for the moment, knowing that he would revisit it before long.

"I know what you're thinking," Winter said quietly. "It has just occurred to me as well."

Robinson turned to the ancient detective and measured the look on his face. There was no doubt in his mind that Winter was correct. He had been struck by the same horrific thought at the same moment. Robinson nodded to the elder man, like forging a link or grasping each other's hand and shaking, as if an agreement had just been struck between the two of them.

"What are you saying?" Espy Martinez asked.

"I'll explain later," Robinson replied. "Please." He gestured toward the rabbi and Frieda Kroner. "Please continue."

But the rabbi held up his hand. "There is something? Something different?" He quickly looked over at Winter. "Something has just taken place, and I want to know what it is."

For a moment everyone in the room was silent.

From somewhere else in the police headquarters came the noise of shouting, momentarily overcoming the soundproofing, but it receded quickly. The rabbi folded his arms across his chest, awaiting an answer to his question. Frieda Kroner saw him do this and once again she slapped the wooden tabletop.

"Mr. Winter, Detective Robinson, what is it?" she demanded. "I may be old, but I am not like a child to be told little lies and have things hidden from me because of who I am. So please, if this is something to do with poor Sophie or Mr. Stein and now my dear Irving, please, you are to tell me now!"

"Frieda is absolutely right," Rabbi Rubinstein said sharply. "You have seen something. Perhaps a little light on the Shadow? I hope. . . ."

Simon Winter shook his head. "No. Nothing this fortunate." He looked over at Walter Robinson and then at Espy Martinez, who had a look of confusion on her face.

"Walter, what the hell's going on?" she asked. "Did I miss something?"

Robinson shrugged and smiled, but not at anything even the slightest bit amusing. "It was simply a detective's thing. A click, you know. An observation. A worry. Mr. Winter and I . . ."

". . . saw the same thing at the same time," Winter said, completing his sentence.

"And what was it that you saw?" Rabbi Rubinstein questioned.

The old detective and the young detective shared a quick glance. Then Winter turned to the rabbi and Mrs. Kroner. "I apologize. I should have seen this from the start. I am not as sharp as I once was. I'm sorry."

The rabbi made a quick, impatient gesture. "Mr. Winter, what is it?"

"Herman Stein dies in a locked room. Sophie dies, and the police immediately go searching for the junkie that killed her. Irving Silver disappears into the ocean, or so it appears. And we think you two will be next. But it occurs to Detective Robinson all of a sudden—and this, Mrs. Kroner, is what makes him shift about in his seat and maybe feel a little sweat on the back of his neck and a little twinge in the bottom of his stomach—it occurs to him that maybe, just maybe, Herman Stein wasn't the first. Am I right, Detective?"

Walter Robinson slowly nodded in agreement. "You're doing fine," he said softly.

Espy Martinez inadvertently lifted her hand to her mouth, covering it in surprise, unaware that she had made this motion like a hundred Hollywood actresses.

Frieda Kroner's face seemed to collapse.

Rabbi Rubinstein slid back in his chair, as if pushing himself back from the table, away from what Simon Winter was saying.

"You see," Winter continued, "what the detective thought was this: Why is this man starting to murder now? And the obvious answer is: He isn't."

Winter looked around at the others, finally resting on the two other old people. "Do you think perhaps that you are the last remaining Berliners that know of the Shadow Man? Or could there be others, that you do not know about? Do you think maybe there were once twenty? A hundred and twenty? A thousand and twenty? How many survived the basement? The train transport? Then survived the camps? Then found their way through the maze to the world here? How many people may have caught a glimpse of him, in an alley, at Gestapo headquarters, on a tram or in a shelter when the bombs were falling? Do you not think that he has spent every waking moment since the last bullet was shot and the last fire of the war doused, thinking of all those faces, frightened that this one or that one will be the person who rises up and exposes him? And what would that make him do?"

The others remained quiet, unwilling to put words to this question.

Simon Winter turned to Walter Robinson. "Does that pretty much sum up what you thought?"

He nodded. "Pretty much. Except it could be worse."

"Worse?" Espy Martinez asked. "How?"

"Accept for a moment that this Shadow Man exists and that he's killed maybe three times successfully. How many others? Over how many years? In how many places? Did he retire to Miami Beach last year? Or twenty-five years ago? Where has he been and how many people have lost their lives? We know nothing, except who he was once, fifty years ago, in Berlin, in the middle of a war, and even then, we have no name, no identification, no fingerprints or identifying marks. We have only these people's recollections. Recollections based on terror and a momentary glimpse of someone when they were little more than children themselves. How do you connect the present to the past?"

Espy Martinez took a deep breath. "I know how," she said quietly.

The others all swiveled and looked at her.

"Mr. Leroy fucking Jefferson," she said.

It took several moments for Frieda Kroner to respond: "This is an unusual name for a person to have. . . ."

And Espy Martinez realized that she had automatically attached the obscenity to the suspect's name without considering the more delicate ears of the older people, who did not use the word *fuck* with the same constancy as virtually everyone connected to the criminal justice system. She immediately apologized.

"I'm sorry, Mrs. Kroner. Leroy Jefferson is the man Detective Robinson originally charged with Sophie Millstein's murder. Apparently he was at her apartment—or just outside it—and witnessed this Shadow Man enter and commit the crime."

"So," the rabbi said slowly, "this man can tell us what the Shadow Man looks like today. He can describe him?"

"Yes. I believe so."

"Identikit," Winter said. "A police artist could work with him and come up with something current. That would be a start. Can he provide other information? A license plate maybe?"

"I don't know," Martinez replied. "Not yet. The price of Mr. Jefferson's cooperation is high."

"How high?" Robinson interrupted.

"He wants to walk."

"Shit!" the detective muttered.

"Walk?" Frieda Kroner asked. "He is crippled?"

"What he wants is to be released from pending charges. Freed."

"Ahh, I see. And this is a problem?"

Espy Martinez nodded. "He shot and wounded a policeman."

"He must be an awful man to do such a thing," she said.

"Indeed," Martinez replied.

Simon Winter was thinking quickly. "If we had a good picture, you know, something reasonably close . . ."

Martinez turned to him. "Yes? With that picture what?"

"Well, first off, it would go a long ways toward helping the rabbi and Mrs. Kroner. It would help them to be prepared. They wouldn't be sitting around waiting to recognize some man they only saw for seconds fifty years ago. They would know what the man stalking them looks like. That would be an immense advantage. Help level the playing field."

"This is true," Mrs. Kroner said. "We would not be so vulnerable."

"But more, it gives me an idea or two."

"I think I know what you're thinking," Walter Robinson said slowly. "You're thinking that there is one thing in the entire world that this man is frightened of, and makes him act quickly, and one thing only: losing his anonymity. Correct?"

Simon Winter nodded and smiled. "We seem to think alike."

"And," Robinson continued, "if we can threaten that anonymity, then perhaps we can do something else."

"What would that be?" Rabbi Rubinstein asked quickly.

Simon Winter answered coldly for the both of them. "Set a trap."

# EIGHTEEN
## PLAYING THE HAND
### THAT'S DEALT

THE Lumberjack lived in a modest three-bed, two-bath house on a quiet cul-de-sac in North Miami, a suburban neighborhood where every other house had a powerboat on a trailer parked by the side, and where the residents lived from barbecue to barbecue, weekend to weekend. It was clean, kept up, a place where policemen and firemen and city workers spent their money in sturdy, stolid pursuit of upward mobility in single-story, cinder-block homes with small, in-ground pools in the rear. The rooftops were flat white or red tile. Lawns were mowed, hedges trimmed. The late-model four-wheel-drive trucks that towed all the powerboats to the water some three or four miles away were all polished brightly, glistening in the midday sun.

An occasional dog barked as Walter Robinson rolled slowly down the street, looking for the Lumberjack's address. He assumed that the dogs were barking at his skin; no blacks in this neighborhood, he thought. Just the mixing of white and Hispanic that has a certain inevitability in Dade County. The middle-class blacks in the same economic sphere as the Lumberjack tended to bunch together in their own neighborhoods, where there weren't quite as many shade trees, or books for the elementary school library, where there were a few more brown spots on the lawns, and bank loans were a little harder to come by. These neighborhoods were always a little closer to Liberty City or Overtown, a little closer to the edges of poverty. He had an odd thought as he pulled in front of the Lumberjack's house. He remembered all the early explorers who set out for the New World overcoming their fear that the world was flat and that they would sail off the rim into oblivion. This was the sort of historical information that his mother, the dutiful teacher, would speak of over dinner, when she wasn't patiently but insistently correcting his table manners. They were wrong, he thought. The world is round. But it is the people in it who manufacture the edges, making it frighteningly easy to sail off the brink, where there are still monsters waiting eagerly to swallow you up.

Heat like an angry complaint greeted him as he stepped from his car. The walkway to the Lumberjack's house glowed, filmy air hovering just above the cement. He saw a wooden swing set around one side of the house, and in front there was a small collection of bicycles and tricycles abandoned by the garage door. Across the street a middle-aged woman, wearing cutoff jeans and a Mickey Mouse T-shirt, was cutting the lawn. She stopped, shutting off the mower, as he stepped from the car. He could feel her eyes tracking him as he approached the house.

He rang the bell and waited, hearing a set of harried footsteps after a moment or two. The door swung open and a young woman stared out. She wore baggy long shorts and a bathing suit top and had her dark hair pinned back sharply. A baby clutching a bottle was draped on her hip.

"Yes?"

"I'm Detective Robinson. Can I see your husband?"

She hesitated, without smiling. "He's still in some pain," she said.

"I need to see him," Robinson repeated.

"He needs to rest," she whispered.

Before he could reply, a voice bellowed from within the house: "Honey, who is it?"

The Lumberjack's wife seemed to want to close the door, but instead she swung it open, calling out at the same time, "It's Detective Robinson, here to see you." She jerked her head toward the rear of the house, and Robinson stepped in. He saw immediately that, for a house with small children, it was extremely neat. There were trimmed plants in an étagère, no toys underfoot. In the entranceway there was a large crucifix hanging over a blessing. He passed the expected wall decorations: framed photographs of babies and parents, a selection of posters advertising forgettable art shows.

One thing surprised him as he entered the living room. On the wall above the matching sofa and love-seat set was a large, brightly colored painting, realism in the primitive Haitian school, obviously painted by someone with little education and great talent. It was a marketplace scene, great splashes of vibrant color interrupted by the resonant blacks of the faces of the country people populating the market. It was striking, fascinating in a way, because it pulled him momentarily into that small world, as if allowing him to sense a little bit of the story of each character on the canvas. He stared at it, astonished to see it in the Lumberjack's home. He had seen many of these paintings, usually hanging in the trendier art galleries in the rich sections of South Miami and Coral Gables. They had an odd attraction for the wealthy; a combination of something native and something articulate; the better examples of art from the impoverished Caribbean country were destined for the walls of the million-dollar homes overlooking Biscayne Bay.

"Kinda different, huh?" the Lumberjack said quietly. He had entered the room from a side door.

Walter Robinson turned away. "It's a nice piece," he said.

"Wouldn't have expected it here, huh?"

"No," Robinson said slowly.

"My wife was an art student a couple of centuries ago, like before kids and mortgages and all that, and she picked it up on a trip down there. Never could understand why anyone would want to go to Haiti on vacation, you know? Just a lot of people getting poorer every second of the day. That's why they're forever trying to come over here."

"Coast Guard cutter stopped another boatload just off Key Biscayne the other day," Robinson said.

"Well, there you have it," the Lumberjack replied. "Anyway, the wife hauls that sucker around, everywhere she went, always saying someday it'd be worth something. You know what? Sucker would go for ten, maybe fifteen grand now. Best investment we ever made, even if it is kinda strange hanging there. I got to insure it. Hell, I'd rather have a new Aquasport twenty-footer. But hey, you get used to everything after a while."

"I suppose so."

"Well, what do I know? Kinda ironic, though, isn't it?"

"Why's that?"

"Well, hell, some poor sucker painted that thing and maybe got a few bucks for it, maybe enough for a meal or a new chicken or a tank of gas or something. But that's it. And his painting, well, it makes it all the way here to the States, nice and easy. He'd probably be willing to die to get here, just like so many of those poor suckers. And you know the damn painting's worth more than he ever will be. Now, that's irony, huh?"

"Yes. It is."

"Hell, you can bet those paintings don't got to come across the ocean in some handmade, falling-apart boat that's more likely to sink fifty miles from shore than it is to land on Miami Beach, huh?"

The Lumberjack turned and settled gingerly into an easy chair.

"You an art lover, Walter?"

"It's an interest of mine."

"Never did much for me. But hey, what do I know? The wife usta take me to shows and such. I learned to keep my mouth shut. Just stand around, nod, drink the imported fizzy water, and eat the hors d'oeuvres. Agree with everybody. Easier that way, especially when you don't know shit."

His arm was still encased in a cast that rose up to his neck. The cast forced the arm out ninety degrees from his body, so that the Lumberjack looked like a particularly gangly bird, hopping about with a broken wing.

He grimaced as he shifted position.

"Sucker still hurts," he said.

"What's the word?"

"No more fucking surgery, thank goodness. Four months trussed up like a fucking puppet, then maybe six, eight months rehab. Then, maybe, just maybe, back on the job. But it's dicey, you know? No one really knows what the fucking arm will do until we try to do it."

"How're you doing?"

"Wife going crazy with me around. Kids getting a bit tired of it too. I mean, I'm like a fucking kid myself. Can't drive anywheres. Can't do much of anything. Watching a lot of television. What the hell do people see in those soaps anyway?"

Walter Robinson didn't answer, and the Lumberjack smiled. "Going a little crazy myself," he added.

The Lumberjack leaned back, then squirmed around.

"Can't fucking get comfortable," he said. After a few seconds spent shifting position, he looked across the room and one eyebrow arched up. "So, Walter, you didn't drive all the way out here just to see how I was doing, did you? I mean, that would have been okay, if you did, but hey, we weren't big buddies or anything, so I'm thinking there has to be some other reason, right?"

Robinson nodded his head, just as the Lumberjack's wife came into the room. "Baby's napping," she said. "Thank the Lord. Don't make a sound for an hour or so." She looked over at Robinson, as if she were expecting him to start singing or dancing.

"There's a problem with the case against Leroy Jefferson. I just wanted you to hear it from me instead of someone else."

"Problem?" asked the wife.

"What sort of fucking problem?" the Lumberjack asked, his voice cramping into a demanding guttural sound.

"Jefferson has been cleared as a suspect in that old woman's murder. But he can provide substantial information in that case, and in perhaps two other homicides. Very substantial information."

"What are you saying?"

"I'm saying he's about to get a deal."

"Fuck! What sort of deal? I'll tell you the deal that motherfucker ought to get! I'd like to take my revolver and shove it right up his ass and pull the trigger. That's the deal I'd give the bastard."

"You're going to wake up the baby," the wife said softly. The Lumberjack stared over at her. He opened his mouth, but stopped before words came out. He turned back to Walter Robinson. His eyes had narrowed.

"Tell me what you're saying?" he demanded again.

"I'm saying he may walk in return for cooperation."

The Lumberjack slammed back in the seat, and Robinson knew the motion must have sent rivets of pain through his arm. The policeman snarled, and a sound like a mean dog slowly slid between his teeth.

"He's going to shoot me and get away with it?"

"We're trying to squeeze him. Going to dangle lessers in front of him, see if he'll do some time—" Robinson stopped abruptly as he saw a dark glare form on the Lumberjack's face. "But you know the deal. You know the priorities. You know the way this works."

"Yes. Fuck, though, I never thought it'd be me getting screwed." The Lumberjack hissed breath out slowly. "I don't think I like it. Not one little fucking bit. And I don't think it'd go down real sweet with the rest of the fucking department. I mean, cops are generally unhappy when other cops get shot, right, Walter? I don't think the rest of the department's gonna be too pleased when the shooter takes a hike, courtesy of the fucking state attorney."

"He's gonna clear a homicide. He's gonna help us take a real bad guy off the street."

"Yeah, and put another one out there," the Lumberjack replied.

Walter Robinson was uncomfortable answering this. It was fundamentally true.

"I'm sorry," he said. "I just thought you'd want to hear it from me."

"Yeah, well, thanks a whole fucking lot." The Lumberjack turned away momentarily, then swiveled his head quickly, staring hard at Robinson. "This your deal, Walter? This your idea?"

Robinson paused before replying. He thought abruptly of the rabbi and Frieda Kroner, and then had a sudden, chilling vision of the Shadow Man himself, stalking them. Then, just as swiftly, he thought of Espy Martinez, and he knew he didn't want the Lumberjack's anger and resentment poured out all over her, so he gritted his teeth and answered: "Yeah. Sure. It's my deal."

"Gonna clear some cases, huh? Maybe make your fucking star rise a bit, right? Gonna get one of those department commendations, maybe a promotion, huh? Lead the pack in homicide with cleared cases. Maybe get the fucking newspapers to write you up. The new, black star on the Beach, right?"

Robinson tried to ignore the racial comment. "No. Maybe going to keep someone from killing again. That's the deal."

"Sure," the Lumberjack said sarcastically. "Sure. And you don't give a damn that it gets you ahead."

"You're wrong."

"Sure I am," the policeman said. "Took me nine years in uniform to get my gold shield, then I get stuck in robbery and car theft for another three years. How's that for affirmative action? How long did it take you, Walter? And you went straight to fucking homicide. Big-time move, Walter. No time in the trenches for you, huh? And now I may never work again, thanks a lot."

Both men were silent. The Lumberjack seemed to be chewing something. "You do what you've got to do," he said. "That's the territory. I understand. Do what you have to."

Walter Robinson rose. "Okay," he said. "Thanks."

"And I'll do what I have to do," the Lumberjack replied.

Robinson stopped. "What do you mean by that?"

"Nothing. Not a single fucking thing. Now get out."

"What did you mean?"

"I told you. Not a fucking thing. Door's that way."

He wanted to say something else, but couldn't. He stepped out of the living room and reached the front door. As he swung it open, the Lumberjack's wife came up behind him.

"Detective?" she said quietly.

He turned. "Yes."

"It was your arrest he agreed to help out on. Your plan. And you almost got him killed. He may be disabled forever thanks to you. And now you're going to let the slimeball who did it go free? I hope you rot in Hell, Detective." She said the word *Detective*, but he suspected within the anger that flared in her eyes, the Lumberjack's wife had an altogether different word in mind. He wondered why she didn't use it.

"Get out of my house," she said. He thought he heard a rolling *n* sound stopped at the end of her sentence, as if she were battling to avoid the racial epithet. But then, he thought abruptly, maybe he was wrong. Maybe she was only furious and she didn't have the slightest intention of calling him a name. Maybe she never noticed that she lived in a world that was both as segregated and frightened of blacks as any pre–Civil War plantation. Maybe, but he doubted it. He thought that this was the nature of Miami; it is a place where people think *nigger* but won't say it out loud. He was instantly overcome by the need to get out, get away, get back to his job. He simply nodded, stepping out of the cool central air-conditioning, into the unrelenting midday, summer heat, feeling as if he'd somehow tracked dirt into the spotless home. As she slammed the door behind him, he heard the clamor of the baby awakening with tears.

Espy Martinez hated the sound of glee that Tommy Alter was unable to conceal in his voice.

"Knew you'd come to reason, Espy," he said.

"No, Tommy, that's incorrect. It's expediency. Not reason."

The two of them were sitting in a corner of the cafeteria at the Justice Building. Untouched coffee steamed from cups in front of them. A few other prosecutors and public defenders occupied other tables, rarely mingling, and when they did come together, generally it was either to trade insults, challenges, or rivet together an arrangement, just as Martinez and Alter were doing. These other attorneys would glance over at the two of them occasionally, but through tacit understanding of the process, no one sat at the closest tables, creating a buffer zone about them.

"Well, whatever you want to call it. What's the offer?"

"He's got to do some time, Tommy. He can't shoot a police officer and walk away from it."

"Why not? Police arrive to arrest him for something he didn't do. They're the ones smashing down his door, waving their weapons. He's lucky he didn't get shot then. He's lucky *you* didn't kill him for something he didn't do. Seems to me you guys ought to be apologizing to him."

"He witnessed a murder and then robbed the victim. Somehow, I don't think apologies would be completely appropriate."

"Well, no time, that's our position. He'll take probationary time, if you want. Plead to some lessers. Burglary. Assault. But he isn't going upstate. Not after helping you folks find a killer. Maybe even stopping someone before they kill again."

Espy Martinez inhaled sharply. "What are you saying, Tommy? Kill again? What has he said to you? Do you know something?"

"Did I touch a nerve there, Espy? No, I can't say I know anything for certain. Just speculating, you know. Figure that there had to be a reason that old woman got killed, and maybe that same reason will apply to someone else. Just a guess."

Martinez hesitated and Alter smiled.

"You're going to get what you want, Espy. A real, live witness. It may not be the best deal in the world, but it isn't the worst deal that's ever been made in this building."

"He assists completely. Full statement. Description. Works with the artist. Does just anything that Walter Robinson asks him to do, and then he's available for a trial and he testifies truthfully when called. Got that? Any failure to appear, any reluctance, any false or misleading statement, any unexplained absence, any goddamn slip of the tongue, and he goes away. A long trip for a long time, got it, Tommy?"

"That's acceptable. Shall we shake on it?"

"I don't want to shake your hand, Tommy."

He laughed. "Somehow, I didn't think so. Relax, Espy. He'll help you bring your man in, and then think what a fucking hero you're gonna be. Just keep that in mind when we go to the judge. I'll make sure it's on his docket for the morning. They can bring Jefferson over early. He's just graduated to a wheelchair."

Espy Martinez nodded. "I want to do this during his regular calendar call—as quietly as possible. Just a quick plea colloquy and then out he goes with the detective."

Alter smiled and rose. "Sure. Makes sense to me."

"We have to maintain the integrity of the investigation."

"What a nice, important-sounding phrase that is. Sure you do."

"Tommy, don't get me angrier than I already am."

"Now, why would I want to do that?" he asked. He didn't wait for an answer. Instead he turned away and started across the cafeteria. Martinez saw him make a fist and punch the air in satisfaction. She tried to keep in mind the two old people on the Beach, trying to persuade herself that what she was doing verged on the medicinal; it would keep them alive.

There was one lanky teenager who appeared to have a little more quickness and a little more lift, and when the ball was in his hands, he seemed to move effortlessly toward the basket. From his seat on a bench, just inside the chain-link fence, Simon Winter watched as the teenager dominated the game, sliding remorselessly past bigger players.

He thought: I was like that once.

And then, smiling, he tried to envision what he would have done to stop the teenager. This was technical thinking, the language of precision placed within the fluid context of the basketball court, and he realized that indulging in these fantasies was like fulfilling a child's need for candy; not altogether necessary for life, but something that delivers a momentary pleasure. He studied the teenager carefully. The young man was tall, nearly six-four, but that would still have given Simon Winter a slight height advantage. First rule, he told himself, deny him the ball. Beat him to that spot at the top of the key where he likes to receive the pass, then don't let him turn and square up to the basket. Make him get the ball on the wing, where he has a little less room to maneuver. Force him onto his left hand—he seems to be less confident in that direction—and when he pulls up for the jump shot, he doesn't seem to rise as swiftly. Take away the baseline, so he can't bring it around to his right. Insist he settle for that drop-step, fadeaway jumper, Winter concluded. He will make some, but most will rim out. Keep your feet moving and make him work hard for everything he gets and eventually he will slow down and start searching for a pass, and when that happens, you know you will have done your job.

Winter nodded and smiled. Playing the game in his head always resulted in the same thing: victory.

On the court before him, Winter saw the teenager knife between two defenders and deposit the ball with a gentle, soft touch. He thought to himself: The young man knows how to play. A smashing, backboard-rattling dunk may be impressive, but the real players recognize and admire the move that gets one there, not the result.

"Is this your game, Mr. Winter?"

Simon Winter pivoted in his seat at the sound of the voice. "It was once, Detective."

Walter Robinson slid onto the bench next to him. "Not me," he said. "I wouldn't play the game. It was always what everyone expected: You're black, athletic—surely you must play basketball. Instead, I played a little high school football. I was a tight end on a real good team. Won the city championship."

"That must have been nice."

"Probably the best day you could ever have. Seventeen, going on eighteen, walking off the field bloody, dazed, and exhausted, but the winners. Nothing like it, ever again. Has a sort of purity to it."

"Were you good, Detective?"

"Not bad. Not bad at all. But not nearly big enough to play the position in college. Tight end is an odd job, Mr. Winter. Most of the time you're fighting it out on the line, smashing linebackers, defensive ends, another drone defending the glory boys at running back and quarterback. But every so often, kinda like a reward for all that hard work, you're cut loose downfield, and you explode out into the secondary, finally on your own, and the ball is zipping your way. There's always this great moment, defenders surrounding you, ball heading toward your hands, that you realize it's up to you. If you drop it, it's back to the salt mines. Back to being the worker bee. But catch that ball and you're free to do what you want, make of it what you can. Those were the moments I liked."

"There is poetry in sport," Winter said, smiling.

"And metaphor as well," Robinson added.

"How did you find me here?"

"The Kadoshes. They told me you liked to come down here to the park after dark and watch the basketball games."

"I didn't think they were that observant."

Robinson grinned and Winter shrugged, adding, "Of course. You're right. Lesson one: The neighbors always know more than they let on. There you have it. So, that explains how you found me. Now the question is why?"

"Because Leroy Jefferson goes to court tomorrow morning and by noon will be sitting next to a police artist, giving us a description and a statement, and once we have that, then we must take the next step."

"Baiting the trap."

"Exactly."

"I think we must be very cautious," Simon Winter said.

"Yes. Why?"

"Because, Detective, we are in an extremely vulnerable position."

Walter Robinson nodded. "Go on," he said.

"We must find this man. We must find him this time. We have this one chance and we can't screw it up."

"Keep going," the detective said.

Simon Winter paused, watching the players pivot and weave on the court in front of him. The sodium vapor lights gave their skin a yellowish tone, almost as if the sweat and muscles were sickly and the struggle they made over the ball was against some odd disease.

"If we do not identify and stop the Shadow Man, if we merely spook him, he'll disappear. He can go anywhere. Be anything. If he slips past us, there is no telling where he will go. You see, we know nothing of his roots, of his history, not since the end of the war. So we know nothing of his resources. How do you pursue someone without substance? Do you think he'll leave behind a trail that we could follow? I doubt it. Not if he's reached this point after so many years. So I think we should assume that this man Leroy Jefferson is going to provide us with our one and best hope. We must get him this time."

"You've been thinking about this?"

Winter nodded, then looked over at Robinson.

"As have you. In fact, I bet that's why you came tonight to see me."

Robinson extended his feet and stretched backward, relaxing. "You had quite a reputation in the City of Miami department."

"You pulled my service record?"

"Of course. Wanted to know who I was dealing with."

"That's all crap, you know. Solved this case. Made this arrest. Received this commendation. Doesn't tell you about who I am."

"No, that's true. So, who are you, Mr. Winter?"

Simon Winter paused. Then he pointed out at the game. "See the kid with the ball?"

Walter Robinson nodded. "The kid draining the twenty-footers?"

"Yes. That one."

"Uh-huh. What about him?"

"He wouldn't score like that on me."

Robinson started to laugh, then stopped, and instead he watched the teenager play, saw the quickness in his first step, saw the burst of speed as he made a crossover dribble.

"Outmuscle him?" he asked after a moment.

"No. Just start taking things away, one by one. And then, when he doesn't expect it, force him into the double-team. Catch him unawares. He'll turn the ball over."

Robinson breathed out slowly. "Difficult."

"But the only way."

"You're right. That's how you think we should do it?"

"Yes. The trap must have a fine line. Invisible defense. The Shadow Man must think something is available to him. Success. But really he is doing what we want. Where we are waiting. That's how it must work."

The two men were silent.

"The two old people, Rabbi Rubinstein and Frieda Kroner . . ."

"Don't worry about them. When the time comes, they will do what they have to."

"I've put a squad car in front of each of their apartments twenty-four hours."

"No. You have to take those away. We can't make him warier than he already is."

"But what if—"

"They understand the risk. They're the bait, and they understand."

"I don't like that."

"How else would you do it?"

Walter Robinson paused. "I still don't like it much," he said finally.

Winter smiled. "You see, that's the advantage I have over you, Detective. I don't work for anyone. No City of Miami Beach paycheck for me. I don't have to worry about anything except succeeding. I don't have to worry about what it will look like in the papers or to my superiors or anything. When I said we could set a trap, that's what I meant. And a trap requires bait. It has to be fresh and attractive and it always runs the risk of being eaten, doesn't it? That maybe the springs on the trap won't slam shut at precisely the correct moment, and maybe the quarry will race away after robbing the trap of bait. So, my recommendation to you, Detective, is that you play this very close to the vest. That your friend, Miss Martinez, and you keep this to yourselves. Then if it all goes wrong, you can blame it on me."

"I wouldn't do that."

"Sure you would. And it would be okay. I'm just a crazy old ex-cop, and it wouldn't bother me in the slightest. Hell, probably make my life more exciting."

"I still wouldn't do it."

"Why not? I'm old, Detective Robinson. And you know what? Nothing frightens me anymore. Got that? Nothing. Except maybe not catching this sonofabitch."

Simon Winter smiled and applauded a nice shot on the court in front of them. "I don't think I want this guy to outlive me."

"I think you've got some good years left."

The old man laughed out loud. "Well, at least they are years, even if I wouldn't leap to characterize them as *good*."

"All right. I'll pull the squad cars. What then?"

Winter's voice gained a certain coldness with his response: "Then we force him to make a move."

"How did you imagine that going down?"

"Well, ordinarily, with a picture of a suspect, you'd be likely to flood the place with it. Get it on the television news and make the *Herald* run it on their front page. Post that picture everywhere, right? Hope maybe someone will make a call."

"That's the standard drill."

"Won't work with this guy, will it?"

"No," Robinson said. "Not from what I'm beginning to see. All that would do is make him take off."

"Of course, if we scared him off, that might save Frieda Kroner and Rabbi Rubinstein. Scare him off and they might live out their lives in peace."

"Always looking over their shoulder, expecting him back."

"But alive."

"True enough. But alive."

Both men were quiet for a moment. The air around them was filled with the sounds of the game, voices raised, the slap of bodies coming together, the chain of the net rattling as the ball slipped through.

"So, we don't do what is standard," Robinson said. "What do we do?"

Winter smiled. "I had an idea," he said carefully. "You see, *he* won't know that we have his picture, and he won't know that we're waiting for him. So what we do is very subtle. We *suggest* something. We do just enough to make him move rapidly, maybe before he is quite ready."

"I follow. What sort of suggestion?"

"At services one evening, perhaps the local rabbis make references to, oh, say, the shadow that has fallen over the community. At the Holocaust Center, we post a sign requesting anyone with any knowledge of wartime Berlin to contact Rabbi Rubinstein. Maybe have that same announcement made at a few of the condo association meetings. Just enough so that the right words and sensations creep back to him and he thinks he must make a move. But not so much that he decides to flee."

Walter Robinson nodded his head. "This seems tricky," he said quietly.

"Have you ever been on the flats off Key Biscayne, fishing for bonefish, Detective? It's a great sport. The fish are very skittish in shallow water, attuned to every sound and motion, anticipating threats. But they are hungry, and the flats are where they find the shrimp and small crabs they consider delicacies, so that is why they are there. The water is gray-blue, a hundred colors, changing with every breath of air, and the fish appear as the slightest small alteration in the color scheme. One writer once called them ghosts. You stare at the water for hours, and then, suddenly, you'll see that little motion, that minuscule departure in tone, that indicates a fish. Then you cast, and if you lay the fly just gently, a foot or so in front of that indistinct shape, you will hook a bone-fish, which is something sportsmen all over the world look forward to."

"I've heard that," Walter Robinson replied.

"You should learn to fish, Detective," Simon Winter said. "It will help you understand, as it did for me."

Robinson grinned in spite of an unsettled nervousness inside. "When this is over, will you teach me?"

"It would be my pleasure."

Robinson hesitated, before asking: "This is like fishing?"

The older man smiled. "Precisely."

# NINETEEN
## *THE CHERUB'S*
## *WARNING*

**T**HE game had ended and Walter Robinson insisted that Simon Winter accompany him back to the Sunshine Arms. They rode through the nighttime world of downtown Miami Beach in the detective's unmarked cruiser. Winter kept glancing at the small computer unit attached to the center of the dashboard and finally said, with a small, wry grin:

"That damn thing really makes me feel old."

He looked up, his eyes gathering in the street life they rolled past. The older detective sighed slowly.

"What?"

"You know, look at this. See what's happening?"

Robinson let his eyes rest on a tangle of white limousines and gleaming, dark luxury cars double-parked midway down the block outside a nightclub. The club had a large, two-story purple and red neon palm tree flashing above its front door. There was a crowd of people on the sidewalk, mostly young, white or Hispanic, upwardly mobile, early twenties. They were just out of college, newly minted with an MBA or a law degree, and searching for a little diversion on their way to their first big score. They mingled with the older but trying-to-appear-young types. There was a smattering of a category that seemed unique to Miami, the drug-culture hangers-on; young men in particular, who affected the airs of a *narcotrafficista*: gaudy shirt open to the waist, gold chain around the neck, fine linen suit, as if this successfully concealed the realities of their lives as clerks and accountants. It was like a masquerade, where everyone portrayed some exotic, wealthy, heartless Colombian hit man, which, of course, helped to hide the few but legitimate killers that were mixed amidst the crowd, in the same outfits. The women, for the most part, seemed to favor high, spiked heels and hair flounced into manes. They dressed in spangles and silks, peacocks as colorful as the sign that blinked above them. As Simon Winter and Walter Robinson slid past, the bass-heavy sound of rock and roll with a Latin accent shook the car.

"What do you see, old-timer?" Robinson used the word to poke fun at Winter, who recognized this immediately, and so replied in a fake-crotchety-old voice filled with wheezing and accented with pseudoirritation.

"What I see is change, young fella. On one side of the street, the Broadway Delicatessen. Used to serve the best chicken soup on the Beach. Probably still does. Next to it, there's a grocery, where the old folks like me get fresh fruits and meats that haven't been collecting frostburn for a month. The sort of place where they know your name and if you're perhaps a little short of cash one week, will wait until the social security checks come in for you to pay."

Simon Winter paused, then resumed, in his normal tone of voice: "A year from now, maybe two, they won't be there, will they? You see, that nightclub is hot, and that means competition, and the space across the street suddenly has value, because—and you know this, Detective—a new dollar always seems to be worth more in our society than an old one."

Robinson nodded. He let his eyes trail into the crowd outside the nightclub. He saw a bouncer muscling a rowdy client, a man dressed in a white suit that cost considerably more than a detective's weekly paycheck. He saw that Winter had seen the same scuffle.

"Too much cocaine. The problem with cocaine is it makes you do incredibly stupid things and makes you think you're incredibly smart to do them."

Winter laughed. They continued driving, leaving the crowded sidewalk in the rearview mirror. Simon Winter gestured for Robinson to turn.

"Wrong direction," the younger man said as he turned the wheel, obligingly.

"I just wanted to see something," Winter said. In a moment they turned again, so that they were traveling adjacent to the beach, and beyond, to the ocean. "Always liked this," Winter said slowly. "Older I get, the more I like it."

"What's that?" Robinson was trying to drive and to stare past the older man, out at the great expanse of black sea.

"No matter how many hotels and nightclubs and condos we put up, the sea is always there. Can't do anything about it. Can't fill it in. Can't pave it over. That's what I like. Do you like the ocean, Detective?"

"When I was young, growing up, no, I hated it. But now I've changed."

"Good."

Robinson nodded, and turned the car again. Within a few minutes he had located the Sunshine Arms and pulled to a stop by the entranceway. Winter put his hand on the door handle, then hesitated.

"Do you think about the men you pursue, Detective?"

"Sometimes. But more often, they're an object rather than a personality. They're the culmination of a set of facts, or a series of observations. They're more like conclusions than people."

"For me, the bad guys would get under the skin, you know? They would stop being a case file number, and become something very different. And then, there were always a couple that became special."

"They stay with you?"

"Forever."

"I don't know if I've ever had one like that."

"How many open cases do you have?"

"Lost count, Mr. Winter. They seem to pile up rapidly. And my clearance rate is ahead of all the other detectives in the bureau."

Simon Winter shook his head. "In my time, every homicide was something at least a little special."

"Not anymore."

"What do you think of the Shadow Man?"

"I don't know yet. It's hard to get a feel for him. I'll say this, though. He's got me a bit more antsy than any other case I've ever worked. You know how it is: Usually you have a pretty damn good idea precisely what you're looking for, even if you don't have a name and a face to find. You know what sort of person it is. Character traits, psychology—whatever—it fits into the normal scheme of things. No surprises. This guy seems a little different."

He paused, then corrected himself. "No, a lot different."

"Why are we hunting him, Walter?"

This was the first time Simon Winter used Robinson's first name, which the younger detective noted.

"Because we think he's killed one, two, maybe three or more times."

"Serial killer?"

"Well, not exactly. He sure as hell doesn't fit any FBI profile I've ever seen. But multiple homicides. Isn't that a good enough reason?"

"It's a good reason, but the wrong one."

"Want to run that by me again?"

"It's the wrong reason. You're here because this is your job. To serve and protect. I'm here because he's killed my neighbor, and that makes me feel a debt, and because he may kill these other people, whom I cannot even consider friends, but whom I've made some promises to. But those aren't really good reasons, any more than yours are. I don't think you or I, or your pretty friend in the State Attorney's Office, will ever grasp the best reason. The rabbi, he knows, and so does Frieda Kroner. You see, we can comprehend one dead body, or two or even twenty and say: There's a criminal that needs to be stopped. But they see the Shadow Man and they see hundreds, thousands, millions all going to their death. They see their brothers and mothers and fathers and uncles, aunts, nieces, nephews, neighbors, friends, acquaintances, and everyone else. You think those deaths will ever be anything but numbers to us? But they're not numbers to those people, are they?"

Simon Winter opened the door and stepped to the sidewalk. He leaned back toward Walter Robinson.

"Shouldn't let old men muse on these things. Just muddies the waters, huh?"

Robinson nodded slowly. "I think," he said carefully, "that you and I should catch this man, and then consider what he's done." Again he paused, then added: "Everything he's done."

"Yes," Simon Winter said. "We should catch him."

He straightened up and closed the door. He gave the detective a small wave as the cruiser pulled away. He watched the taillights disappear into the darkness down the street, blinking once and then turning aside, leaving him alone on the sidewalk. There was a richness to the air, as if the tropical night somehow was concocted with a small portion of molasses or maple syrup. He thought this a deceptive thing; the warmth made one ignore the dangers after the sun had set. He suddenly started talking inwardly with his anonymous quarry: Did you do your best worst work after dark? Is that when you became truly dangerous? People are more vulnerable in the nighttime; is that when you came for them? A night like this one?

He thought to himself: yes.

Simon Winter listened to the distant street noises blending with the inevitable sounds from the apartments on his block, television sets, music, voices raised in an anonymous argument. No children crying, he realized. Not in this part of the city. We are all old here, he said to himself, and the noises we make are old noises.

Winter took a step toward his apartment, then stopped and stared over at the empty fountain and the dancing cherub in the center.

"So," he said out loud, "what tune do you have for me this evening? Something lively, I suppose? Something to cheer me up?"

The cherub continued to play soundlessly.

"Well then," Winter asked abruptly, "what have you seen tonight? Anything different? Anything unusual?"

He stared at the statue, meeting the cherub's dead eyes, as if waiting for a reply. He stayed like this for a few seconds, then swung about abruptly, surveying the entire courtyard. The murdered Sophie's apartment remained dark, and above her, only the blue-gray glow of the television illuminated the Kadoshes. As he watched, a single light in old Finkel's apartment switched off. He pivoted, fixing on the windows of his own place. The darkness within seemed liquid, shifting like the ocean he'd gone out of his way to see only a few minutes earlier. Slowly, he moved his gaze around the courtyard, turning a full circle as he examined the shadows and shapes, inspecting each corner, probing each angle.

There is nothing here, he told himself.

Have you gone crazy?

You are alone and tired, and you should get to bed.

He took a step forward, then stopped.

A night like this one, he repeated to himself.

For a moment he breathed in hard.

But he doesn't know me, Simon Winter insisted. He doesn't know I'm out here, and he doesn't know I'm looking for him. He thinks his enemies are old, frail survivors, with fragile recollections and shaky memories that may have endured through the decades. Those are his targets. Not you. He doesn't know about you.

Or does he?

He realized, in that moment, that he'd unconsciously raised his right hand to his left breast, as if he was wearing the shoulder holster with his old revolver, as he had for so many years.

There is nothing here, and you are alone, he insisted, and you are being foolish. Then he corrected himself: Being cautious is never foolish. You may embarrass yourself by trusting your instincts, but that is all you will do, and the alternative is far worse.

He took several steps forward, hating instantly the sound that his shoes made on the sidewalk. Like a drumroll, he complained. Move quietly. He gingerly stepped onto the grass strip next to the walkway, muffling the sound as he approached the building.

He paused outside the front door, his hand a few inches away from the door handle. Slowly, he pulled his fingers back.

If you open that door, he will hear it, he told himself. He will know the sound, and he will gather himself and be ready.

He will be expecting you to arrive home like any tired old man, hurrying to bed and a few hours of fitful sleep. He will expect you to jerk the front door open, fumble about impatiently in the vestibule until you find the key to your apartment, and then barrel ahead, right in.

Simon Winter retreated from the doorway, sliding into a shadow of his own.

He leaned against the side of the building and listened, but could only hear the normal night sounds that he expected. He searched through these noises, trying to find something out of the ordinary, which would tell him something other than the fear that he felt easing through his body like some infectious disease.

All right, he thought. Where would he be?

In the vestibule? No. The light is on and he doesn't know the habits of the other tenants. There's no place to hide there, not like Herman Stein's building.

Then inside?

Yes. Inside.

How?

That's obvious: the patio door. Just like Sophie's. Same shabby lock that will break at the mere insinuation of a screwdriver.

Once inside, where?

Simon Winter searched the memory of his own small apartment like a general poring over a map. Not the kitchen; the streetlight reflects off the white linoleum, making it bright. Not the bathroom either; not enough room to maneuver in that small space. The living room, then, or the bedroom? One or the other. He continued to think hard, then told himself: not the bedroom. He would expect me to flick on the lights as I enter, and other than the narrow, small closet jammed with clothes and boxes and otherwise useless junk, the lights would destroy any hiding place. So it has to be the living room. Maximum surprise.

Winter began snaking his way around the side of the building, heading carefully, noiselessly, to the back. He heard a small dog yapping from another apartment, down the block. As he moved around the corner, he picked up some speed. He can't hear me now, Winter told himself. He slid up against the back fence, dodging the wan light coming from the neighboring apartment complex, homing in on the small tile patio in the rear of his apartment. Something rattled about in a garbage can, near the back alley. A cat, he thought. Or a rat.

As he moved he carried on an imaginary conversation with his quarry: What will you be carrying? A gun? Perhaps. Something small and efficient. Twenty-two or .25 caliber, an assassin's weapon. But you still wouldn't like the noise it would make, would you? Draw attention rapidly, no matter how silent you thought it was. That's always a problem in Miami and on the Beach. People know the sound a gun makes. No one says: 'What was that?' or 'Was that a car backfiring?' Not in South Florida. They know gunshots. So maybe you'd carry the gun just for show. Just for the threat. But you wouldn't want to use it, would you? You'd rather use your hands, like you did with Sophie. That's what you like, isn't it? To be close when they die, isn't that right? You like the sounds of life departing, the smells of death. You like that feeling that comes over you when you steal that final breath, don't you? It wasn't the same thing when you watched them packed shoulder to shoulder, tears to tears in a cattle car, that mustn't have been nearly as satisfying, but you were younger then, and probably only beginning to understand the marriage you'd made with murder. Back then, you were still experimenting with what you liked, weren't you?

He stopped.

But I'm too big, he thought. If you've come hunting for me, then you know that I'm not small, like a child, like Sophie was, or wizened, nervous, and filled with fear, like Herman Stein and Irving Silver. No, I'm not somebody you quite know, am I? And this has made you wary, and so you will move quickly and efficiently when you have the opportunity, won't you? You will want to know why I'm hunting you, you will have a dozen, a hundred questions, but given the choice between information and just removing the threat, you will take the easier course, right?

A knife.

Simon Winter nodded to himself.

He is probably a knife man. That would be quiet enough for him. He would not like the blood, not like the struggle, because he would know that every second we're together and he's searching with that blade for my heart, he could be leaving some bit of incriminating evidence behind. But he would accept this worry, just to remove the threat he feels.

Winter felt his pulse accelerate, then slow, as he grew cold within himself.

So, it will be a knife. Delivered without hesitation.

He continued to move closer to the patio.

But you won't expect this, will you? You won't expect me to come in the same way you did. You'll be waiting in the living room, near the front door. It swings to the right, so there's a large dead spot to the left, which remains dark, blocked off from the vestibule light by the solid wood door as it opens. You will have seen that spot, won't you? You will have seen that right from the first minute you were inside, and that's where you'll be, because you will think that I will step inside, right into your path unawares, not seeing you until I shut the door right on my own death and not seeing the knife until it bites through my solar plexus, thrusting upward just as you were taught once, weren't you? That's what you think will happen, that's what they showed you, didn't they? All those men in black uniforms so many years ago. Make a single thrust and make it work. Draw the victim in on top of you, pulling him off balance, so that his own weight against the blade kills him.

He was only a few feet from the sliding glass door, and he crouched down.

The gun is in the drawer of the bedside table. Did he go in there and search for it? You damn old fool, he berated himself. Leaving the weapon precisely where any two-bit crook or break-in artist would look first. But did he do that? Or is he simply waiting for you now?

Simon Winter realized that was a chance he'd take.

The patio door would crash back, making a racket, but he could cross the kitchen space in a single stride, heading directly for his weapon. At least this small element of surprise would be his, he thought. Then he corrected himself: *unless* he was watching, and he saw your hesitation in the courtyard.

What then?

He didn't want to think of this. He reached out slowly and just touched the sliding door. A residual part of him thought: This is all crazy—you are alone. But the door moved. He pulled on it as quietly as he could, and it slid an inch, just past the lock, which rattled slightly as the door traveled on its runners. He realized in a second that the lock had been broken, and then he rose and threw the door back, slamming it hard. In the same motion, he vaulted through the kitchen, heading for the bedside table and the gun he hoped was there.

From the living room, a darkness to his left, there was an explosion of sound, a smashing noise of alarm that he ignored as he soared toward his weapon. He reached out through the blackness of the apartment for the bedside table. His hand found the knob and he jerked it open, hearing the gun within the drawer thud against the wooden frame. He thought himself fumbling, hurrying, wrapping his hand around the familiar shape. He slipped as he spun around, facing the nighttime that had chased him into the room, sliding down to a sitting position on the floor. He brought the gun up to his eyes, two hands on the weapon, into a shooting position, his ears listening for the hurried sounds of attack.

There were none.

His breathing filled the room, a cacophony of tension.

In his haste he had knocked the reading lamp to the floor, sending the shade skittering across the room. He found the lamp with his foot, then slowly he reached over and switched it on.

The room flooded with light.

Like a sailor raising a beacon against a storm, he lifted the lamp up as he slowly climbed to his feet. He could see his own shadow streaking away from him, toward the living room. He set the lamp down, and stepped forward gingerly, searching for the wall switches as he moved. He could see a thin shaft of light coming from the living room. He continued foward, keeping the wall at his back, the pistol raised in firing position, hammer cocked. He moved slowly and deliberately around the corner, ready to formulate the command to freeze, halt, whatever, his own training coming back after lying dormant for so long. But he quickly saw that he wouldn't need the word.

Simon Winter breathed out slowly, staring at the sliver of light from the apartment vestibule. The front door was cracked open about six inches.

He moved forward, ready to pursue the man across the night, then stopped himself, recognizing he would already be gone.

He let air whistle between his teeth.

So, he spoke inwardly, you were waiting right where I thought.

He shook his head. But I didn't think you'd be that smart. Or be able to move that quickly. You heard the noise behind you, and instead of letting it cripple you with surprise, you acted instantly, and you saved yourself.

This impressed the old detective. Not many people can function with an animal's cunning or instinctive sense of preservation, knowing to flee at the first sound that is unexpected. People are generally more clumsy and hesitant.

But not the Shadow Man.

So, he thought, now you are already away, racing ahead. And you are more than a little concerned, aren't you, because now you know I'm not like Sophie or the others. I'm a little closer to you, aren't I? And that probably will keep you awake tonight, but it will also make you more careful the next time. And it will make you decide that maybe the next victim should be someone a little easier, correct? But you will be worried too, perhaps for the first time in how many years? Truly worried, because you will know that I know something about you, and that frightens you more than anything, doesn't it? But you will reassure yourself, because you know that you're still hidden, that I do not know your name or your face. Your anonymity is intact, and that will help you finally fall asleep, feeling your safety is secure. What you don't know is that soon I'm going to take that away from you too.

Simon Winter nodded, almost congratulatory. I'm beginning to know you, he said to himself. But the sensation of satisfaction was short-lived, because he realized now that the Shadow Man knew just as much about him as well.

There were several messages waiting for Walter Robinson when he returned to his desk in the homicide offices. He flipped through these rapidly. A few had to do with other open cases he had. There was one from a Mark Galin at the *Miami Herald*, but he didn't know the reporter, although he had a vague recollection of reading his byline. It was late, however, and he knew the only message he would return was from Espy Martinez.

She sounded groggy when she picked up the telephone.

"Espy? It's Walter. Were you asleep?"

"No," she lied. "Well, maybe a little. Where are you?"

"In my office. I'm sorry. I shouldn't have awakened you."

"It's okay." She was stretched out in her bed, like a cat awakening from a perch on a sun-strewn shelf. "I tried to reach you earlier. Where were you?"

"Out getting to know our Mr. Winter. An interesting guy."

"Sharp?"

"As sharp as they come. You should see his service record. Nothing but commendations and awards. I think we've got something worked out. What about you?"

"Jefferson gets his deal tomorrow morning. As short and sweet as I can make it. Zip, zip, zip, so I don't have to spend too much time watching Tommy Alter pat himself on the back for finally finding someone to represent who's more important alive than wasting away on Death Row. Then, as soon as the plea is finished, you get him. Will you meet me there?"

Robinson hesitated. "Uh, yes. Sure."

She sat up in the bed. "What is it?"

He smiled. "I guess my adrenaline is pumping away. You know, you get so used to working late at night that you forget other people aren't quite so midnight-oriented. Maybe in my next life I should come back as a vampire. Or a werewolf, howling at the moon. Something who skulks around after dark. So, forget it. I'll meet you there in the morning."

"Wasn't there a horror movie about—"

"Yeah. It was called *Blacula*. Dracula with an Afro. It set race relations back maybe a hundred years. Not one of Hollywood's finest. I saw it when I was a kid. All the kids in my neighborhood thought it was pretty funny. So, anyway, go to sleep. I'll see you at the hearing."

"No," Espy Martinez said softly. "You were going to say something. What was it?"

Walter Robinson hesitated once more, then shrugged. He told himself that tumbling off a cliff was easier if you just jumped.

"Well," he said slowly, "I know it's late, but I was sort of hoping I could drive you. In the morning, that is."

He stopped, embarrassed. Then he quickly added: "Oh, look, forget it. We can get together tomorrow. Or this weekend. I can hold my libido in check until then. It's late. Go back to sleep."

Espy Martinez had sat up in her bed and, holding the telephone in one hand, was searching around the bed for a hairbrush with the other.

"You can't come here," she said. She pictured her parents asleep or, more likely, trying to listen through the thin walls that separated the two duplexes. "Don't ask why, because it's complicated and all wrapped up not in who we are, but who we might seem to be."

"You lost me," Robinson replied.

"No," she continued. "I'll come to your place."

He hesitated, caught between practicality and desire. "Maybe you shouldn't. You'll need to be fresh in the morning. On top of things."

She laughed. "There's a good dirty pun in that last statement."

He grinned. "You know what I meant. Or at least what I thought I meant."

"Walter," she said slowly as she began sliding the brush through her hair, "I need to say something."

"Go ahead."

"We play by so many rules and regulations. That's what our jobs are: enforcing the rules. Policeman and prosecutor. And in my family, there were always expectations, which are precisely the same thing as rules. The dutiful daughter filling in for the murdered son . . ." She took a deep breath and continued: "So, maybe in a little way, you, who you are, and me, being myself, well, we're a little outside all the accepteds and normals. And so, if I want to come over there and be with you, I think that's a good thing, maybe because it's not right and reasonable. What's reasonable is getting a good night's sleep. Well, maybe I don't want what's reasonable. Not all the time. Not tonight. Maybe what I want is something far different."

She stopped. "Jesus." She whistled slowly. "What a speech. I should save all that for the judge. Did I make any sense at all?"

He wanted to say: *more than I could ever have hoped for.* But instead he answered: "I'll be waiting for you. Please hurry."

And so, she did.

# TWENTY
## THE FREED MAN

Espy Martinez left Walter Robinson asleep in his bed. He had tossed and turned throughout the night, once calling out a name that she did not recognize before falling back into a deep, solid sleep. She slid gingerly from his side, dressing quietly in the thin morning light, then carrying her shoes until she reached the hallway outside his apartment. Leaving him like some cat burglar who'd robbed his night of passion, gave her a sense of accomplishment, made her feel unpredictable and perhaps a little mysterious, and she enjoyed this.

But by the time she reached the Justice Building downtown, she'd let these sensations slip away from her, replacing them with the tough edge that she suspected she'd need in that morning's hearing. She parked her car and then paced swiftly through the lot, letting her heels click determinedly against the macadam, her stride purposeful and directed, giving her the appearance of someone who not only knew where she was going, but someone who wouldn't tolerate any departures from her preestablished route. She nodded at other attorneys and court personnel heading into the building, still moving quickly; if not precisely eager to confront the morning's task, at least prepared inwardly to accept it and move on.

The escalator deposited her in the center of the fourth floor, in the midst of a jam of people waiting outside the entranceways to the eight courtrooms located there. Occasionally a bailiff would emerge through one of the sally-port doors and call out a name in an exasperated voice. Clutches of people circled around various lawyers: defendants and their families with eager, worried expressions, cops in uniform, cops in plainclothes biding time, drinking coffee from plastic cups, waiting their turns. The hallway was a sea of people, all gathered for different cases, filled with fear, doubt, disgust, anger, a cacophony of emotions. She could hear laughter and sobs, often coming from competing groups. The lawyers in her office likened calendar calls to cattle roundups, complete with similar deep lowing noises. She could hear at least a half-dozen different languages being spoken loudly: Spanish, Haitian-French, Jamaican patois, tourist German, and many English variations, ranging from the deep-South drawl to New Yorkese. She pushed through the crowd of people until she found the right courtroom, then hesitated briefly before heading inside. As she paused, she heard a voice say:

"There she is, there she is! I told you, I told you, we should go get seats. . . ."

She turned and saw an elderly woman standing between two white-haired men. The men wore the basic Miami retiree outfit: Bermuda shorts, checked shirts, and porkpie hats. The woman had on a flower-print dress and a cardigan sweater with stripes. One of the men brandished a cane.

Buzzards, she thought instantly. She smiled in their direction. All courthouses attract a percentage of older people, who perch inside the courtrooms, following the various cases with the determination of soap-opera addicts. They come to know the jail and court personnel, have opinions on the cases, review the performance of prosecutors and defense attorneys, critique the jurors' decisions, cheer when bad guys are sentenced. Mostly, they were harmless, fixtures with an occasionally astute observation or two. More often than not, they fell asleep during the longer hearings, and sometimes their snoring had to be interrupted by a quick shake on the shoulder by an irate bailiff. Some had been hanging around the courthouse for years, long enough to see some defendants several times. Like their nickname, they arrived early, roosted on the sidelines, then disappeared at night. Espy Martinez had always tried to be friendly to them, call them by their first names when she knew them, which made her popular amidst a group seemingly oblivious to the brutish comments made by most of the younger, less experienced lawyers.

"Hi, Espy," the woman said. "All the excitement's for you, dear."

"What?" she asked stupidly.

"Why, your case was in the paper this morning," the woman continued. "Right on page one of the Local section. That's what's brought out the crowd."

"I've got it here," said one of the men. He put down his cane and began searching through a tattered newspaper. "See?"

He thrust the newspaper at her, and her eyes fell on the story, played across the middle of the page: ACCUSED MAN CLEARED IN KILLING; PLEA SEEN IN COP-SHOOTING CASE.

"Shit!" The expletive burst from her lips.

"Is there a problem, dear?" the old woman asked.

She shook her head, but this was a lie. "Can I keep this?" she asked.

The old man nodded his head, touching his index finger to his cap rim.

"We've got to get in," the other old man said. "Otherwise all the good seats will be taken."

"Is it true, dear?" the old woman asked. "The story says he's going to help you on another case, that's why he's getting a deal. Is it right? I hate it when these awful men get deals. I wish you'd just put them in jail, Espy dear. Even if he is going to help, I still wish you'd make him go to prison, because I think he's not a very nice man, is he? Not this man, no. A bad man. Are you sure you've got to do this?"

Espy Martinez didn't reply. Instead she scanned the story. There were few details, other than the essential one that Leroy Jefferson was cleared of killing Sophie Millstein and was expected in court that morning. The story didn't directly link his cooperation to the investigation of her death, but that inference was obvious. There was a predictable statement from Abe Lasser about preferring witnesses to be holy men, but sometimes being forced to take what was available. She recognized his comment for what Lasser termed *midnight quotes*—which were colorfully phrased truisms that sated some *Herald* reporter who called late at night, long after office hours.

She grimaced. It wasn't a long story, but it was more than enough to draw attention to something she'd wanted handled quietly.

"Damn," she said again. "Damn your eyes, Tommy Alter. Couldn't keep your mouth shut." She looked at the three old people. "Have you seen the *Herald* reporter? Or any television crews . . . ?"

They all nodded in unison.

"Already inside," the old woman said.

"Come on." The old man tugged at her sleeve. "We won't get seats. It's packed in there and I want to get a seat."

The trio of buzzards hopped across the corridor, leaving her standing outside, clutching the paper. She squeezed it tightly, hoping to force some of the fury she felt out through her fingers, hoping to maintain her composure. Then she turned abruptly and followed the old people into the courtroom.

A single television camera lurked in one corner. The cameraman spun and tracked her like a determined sniper as she pushed her way down the center aisle. It was a dark place, a sort of hybrid between the old churchlike style of some courtrooms, with wooden pews and deep, brown oaken benches and railings, and the ultramodern, offset lighting, theater style that was becoming increasingly prevalent. The effect was of a high-ceilinged room with a limpid off-white light that was neither auditorium nor living room. It was as if the courtroom had been designed to make everyone sitting in it uncomfortable, forced to strain to see properly in the dim light and lean forward to catch the words spoken amidst the poor acoustics. In Florida, she understood, it just went to show that on any public construction project, it makes much more sense to hand your inevitable bribe money to actually competent workmen and not waste it paying off the vast number of inept contractors, regardless of how many city councilmen they might happen to be related to.

She saw Tommy Alter sitting behind a defense table with two

other public defenders. She stepped up behind him. "You sonofa-bitch," she whispered. "This wasn't supposed to be a goddamn carnival."

He spun around to face her. "Well, good morning to you too, Espy."

"You promised me," she said bitterly. "This was going to stay quiet until we'd finished with Jefferson. I've half a mind to walk on the whole deal. Reinstate the charges, you bastard. Let your precious client spend some more time waiting in jail. How about that? Maybe let him do six months in county lockup while I screw around with the case? Would he like that?"

Alter eyed her narrowly. "As usual, you leap to a conclusion and it's incorrect."

"What's incorrect?"

"I didn't call the fucking *Herald*, Espy. And when they called me, I wouldn't talk to them."

"Then who would? Who knew?"

Tommy Alter smiled slowly. "Well, I've got one guess. It's your guy, Espy."

"Walter? Don't be crazy, he wouldn't—"

"No," Alter interrupted. "Not Walter Robinson. How about your friend and mine, the Lumberjack? He's the one quoted in the paper saying he's none too happy about all this. Think maybe he made that call? Think maybe he doesn't care what he screws up, as long as he gets his precious opinion heard?"

She stopped, still clutching the newspaper in her hand.

Alter's smile slid into a grin. "Good guess, huh?"

She straightened up, nodding. "All right," she said. "We'll do it. But no comments to the press afterward. Got that, Tommy? You've been doing such a fine job keeping your tongue from flying about uncontrollably. Let's try to keep it up, okay?"

Alter lost grip of his grin and flushed. He started to reply angrily, but stopped himself. "Let's just get it on the record," he said after a moment.

Behind her the bailiff was singing out, "All rise," and without replying, she stepped over to the prosecution table. She watched as the judge, a small, wiry man with a bald, monkish pate and an upper lip that seemed surgically fixed into a sarcastic leer, swept

into the courtroom like some emperor in a hurry. After seating
himself, the judge peered out at the cameraman, one eyebrow
shooting up, then took in the filled courtroom. The raised eyebrow degenerated into an irritated scowl. He motioned to his
bailiff, whispered something to the man, and then waved at Alter
and Martinez to approach, with much the same motion one might
use with a poorly trained puppy who'd made a mess on an Orien-
tal carpet.

They dutifully gathered at the front of the bench.

"All right," the judge said. "I've got a heavy calendar today
and I want to get through it quickly because I'm in trial this afternoon. You two are the main show. Let's do your Mr. Jefferson
first. This is a plea, I gather?"

Martinez nodded. "Yes, Your Honor. A plea contingent upon
cooperation with investigators. It was supposed to be quiet. . . ."

"I understand, Miss Martinez. You'd prefer not to let slide too
many details of your ongoing investigation into the waiting note-
books of our local champions of the First Amendment. Correct?"

"Correct."

"All right, then, if this is satisfactory with you, Mr. Alter, we'll
limit the plea colloquy simply to what needs to be on the record. I
will give my standard 'If you do not cooperate, I will send you to
Raiford or Hell' speech, and then I can get on with business and
you can take the circus out into the hallway, so that you can successfully lie to, mislead, or deceive the press out of my presence."

"That's fine, Your Honor," Alter said.

"I will postpone any sentencing on the plea until I receive
memos from the two of you detailing the cooperation Mr. Jefferson provides. That's the sword you hold over his neck, Miss Martinez. But likewise, I understand that in return for his cooperation,
Mr. Jefferson receives a makeable cash bond and then one of
those lovely get-out-of-jail-free cards, correct, Mr. Alter?"

"That's the arrangement."

The judge expelled a burst of air. "I hope he's worth it, Miss
Martinez."

The judge rocked back in his high-backed leather chair as the
bailiff intoned, "The State versus Leroy Jefferson." Espy Martinez turned to take her place at the prosecution's table and saw

Jefferson being wheeled into the courtroom through a side door by a corrections officer. Jefferson frowned at her, but greeted Tommy Alter with a soul-shake.

"We're here on a plea?" the judge asked loudly.

"Correct, Your Honor," she replied. "Because Mr. Jefferson has agreed to provide substantial cooperation on several unrelated cases, and because our office has developed information indicating he was not responsible for the homicide he was initially charged with, a plea agreement has been worked out."

"Is that your understanding, Mr. Alter?"

"Yes, Your Honor."

"All right, Miss Martinez. Please read the charges."

She did this swiftly, racing through the assault, robbery, resisting arrest with violence, and a few other, incidental charges designed to pad out the length of the plea, but which would not change the actual nature of the agreement. The idea was to have him say *guilty* enough times that the actual meaning of the arrangement was obscured. She watched as the court stenographer's fingers flew above her recording machine. She finished and the judge gestured at Leroy Jefferson. Alter maneuvered the wheelchair to the center of the courtroom.

"All right, Mr. Jefferson. For the record, please state your name and address."

"Leroy Jefferson. King Apartments. Number thirteen."

"How long have you lived there?"

"Couple of years."

"Mr. Jefferson, are you currently on any narcotic substance?"

"Just what they give me for the pain in my leg."

"How much education do you have?"

"I went to high school."

"How far?"

"I got my diploma."

"Really? Do you suffer from any mental impairment or illness that would prevent you from comprehending the arrangement your attorney has entered into with the State?"

"What?"

"You sick, Mr. Jefferson? Are you crazy? Do you understand the plea?"

"I done pleas before, Your Honor. I know what they are."

"Good. You understand that by failing to live up to your part of the agreement, that I can rescind the plea and sentence you to over one hundred years in prison? I want you to have no doubt at all, that's what I will do."

"I'm gonna help them, best I can."

"Good. But you understand that in order to obtain the benefit of this agreement, you must help them to their satisfaction."

"They'll be satisfied. I promise that."

"Good. Now you're pleading guilty, because you are guilty, correct, Mr. Jefferson?"

"Yes. 'Cept I didn't do what they said I did when they came for me. Had nothing to do with that killing . . ."

"I understand."

"I ought to sue them for shooting me."

"Talk to your lawyer, Mr. Jefferson. But personally, I think you're lucky to be standing here today."

"Ain't standing, Your Honor."

The judge smiled, caught in a sarcasm he appreciated. "True enough. All right, Mr. Jefferson. As the clerk reads the charges, you say the word *guilty*. Miss Martinez, I assume you have plans for Mr. Jefferson?"

"Yes, Your Honor."

"Well, you can pick him up at your convenience at the jail. Madam clerk, start reading. And you, Mr. Jefferson, one thing . . ."

"What's that, Your Honor."

"Don't let me see you again. Don't screw up. You've got an opportunity here, don't mess it up. Because the alternative is a very long time in a very unpleasant place, and I will send you there just as quickly as you can curse out my name. Do you understand that, Mr. Jefferson?"

He nodded.

"Good. Then let's hear some guiltys."

The clerk began reading and Leroy Jefferson began answering. Espy Martinez took a quick glance back over her shoulder at the packed courtroom. Her eyes fell on the trio of old people, and she saw that they were surrounded by a dozen other retirees, all staring at her or Leroy Jefferson, hanging on every word. She swept her gaze about, lingering on other defendants, witnesses, policemen, and attorneys occupying every seat or leaning against every inch of free wall space, all waiting for her case to finish so they could get on with their own. She thought the justice system was like the sea; her own small wave had curled up and crashed against the sand, and now it was dissolving, racing back toward the ocean, while another wavelet was gathering to make its own assault on the shore. She heard the last guilty, turned back, and saw Jefferson being pushed out of the courtroom, and she gathered her papers, stuffing them into a briefcase, aware that the camera was tracking her again, feeling oddly as if it was not the only eyes following her path. She ignored this sensation.

Walter Robinson and Espy Martinez sat in the front seat of his unmarked cruiser, while Leroy Jefferson and Tommy Alter occupied the back. The midday sun filled the interior, glistening off the white hood. The air conditioner labored to overcome the heat. The bay stretched out on either side of them, reflecting shafts of sunlight. Robinson took a quick glance in the rearview mirror and saw that Jefferson was uncomfortably squirming in his seat—there was little room to stretch out his leg, which was still heavily wrapped in bandages. His wheelchair had been jammed into the trunk.

Robinson knew there was a large pothole in the right-hand lane of the Julia Tuttle Causeway, so he steered directly for it. The worn shock absorbers on the car thumped as he dumped the right tire into the pothole. Leroy Jefferson grimaced.

"Hey, Leroy," Robinson said cheerfully. "What number bus runs over the causeway to Liberty City?"

"That's the G-75," Jefferson answered.

"That's right. That's the one you rode that night, right? After you saw Sophie Millstein get waxed, right, Leroy? Rode it right back to Liberty City. All that hot stuff in your hands. What were you thinking, Leroy? What'd you think about what you saw?"

"Don't answer that," Tommy Alter said quickly.

"He's gonna have to answer. That's the deal."

Alter hesitated. "Okay," he said slowly. "Go ahead."

"Didn't think nothing," Jefferson replied.

"Not good enough, Counselor. I think you're going to have to inform your client that he's to be forthcoming. Expansive. Descriptive. A veritable poet, a wordsmith, when it comes to Sophie Millstein's murder and everything he saw that night. You tell him that, Tommy. Don't want to have to turn right around and head back to the judge's chambers."

"He'll tell you what you want to know. When we get there."

Espy Martinez said nothing, but watched Walter Robinson's face. The detective nodded.

"Okay. I can wait a few minutes. So, how's it feel to be free, Leroy? You got some plans for tonight? Little celebration, maybe? Got some friends gonna come over, have a little party?"

"Ain't got no friends. Ain't got no party."

"Oh come on, Leroy. Not too many folks are slick enough to talk their way out of shooting a policeman. You're gonna be an important man on your block. People likely will look up to you. I'm sure there'll be some sort of celebration."

Robinson's cynicism filled the car. Jefferson merely shrugged.

"Come on, Leroy. Not even a little one? Maybe invite over your friends from the Helping Hand?"

"I told you, they ain't my friends."

"Well, then how about an-all-by-yourself party, what do you think?"

"What you mean?"

"I mean, I know you've got some little stash hidden so good we couldn't find it when we tossed your apartment. Under a false board maybe or behind a loose cinder block. It's somewhere in that apartment, ain't it, Leroy? Just waiting for you, right? Nice and patient and ready, just like some really good and faithful friend, right? I mean, who needs other folks when you've got that pipe, right? That's why you were so eager to get out, huh? Gonna fire up that pipe, get yourself high again. That'll get rid of the pain, no shit."

"You crazy."

"Maybe. Maybe. You keep that in mind, Leroy. Maybe I'm a little crazy."

Walter Robinson abruptly slammed the steering wheel to the

right, jerking the car onto the rough shoulder next to the highway, sending a rooster tail of dirt and dust up behind them, instantly making all four passengers bounce wildly about, crying out, as the car fishtailed. He accelerated on the gravel and coral shoulder. The stony road made the car sway and heave, kicking up bullets of rock. Martinez clamped her mouth shut and held on as Robinson swerved between two cars, back onto the pavement. Behind them a driver leaned on his horn in frightened irritation.

"Come on, Walter, what are you trying to prove?" Alter demanded. "Just drive the car."

Robinson didn't reply. Something about Leroy Jefferson simply angered him; perhaps it was the sensation that the suspect was getting away with something, perhaps it was the self-satisfied, frustrating way Jefferson grinned at him. Robinson had one extreme thought: I know where that smile comes from. It was simple: Jefferson was ready to kill Sophie Millstein. All those break-ins that they knew he did, but couldn't prove. He was ready to start escalating the violence. Making the jump from robbery to armed robbery and then to murder. He would have done her for sure. But he didn't have to, because someone else was there, beating him to it, and he thought this was all some great cosmic joke. Funniest thing he'd ever seen. Walter Robinson breathed out slowly, gritted his teeth, and tossed the car around the off-ramp, the engine racing as he headed toward Miami Beach police headquarters.

They sat in one of the ubiquitous interrogation rooms, starting slowly, pausing over details, lingering over each component of the night Sophie Millstein died. Walter Robinson's thinking was simple. He wanted to get Jefferson's memory working hard, and, at the same time, he wanted to both relax and exhaust the man. Even with Tommy Alter's presence loosely guarding the words that his client spoke, Robinson thought he might be able to slide in some question, extract an answer that might inadvertently tie Leroy Jefferson to all the unsolved break-ins that preceded Sophie Millstein's murder. Or at least something that he might be able to develop later into a piece of evidence that would support an indictment. It would be nice, he thought, to arrive at Jefferson's house some fresh morning with a brand-new warrant for some crimes that were not part of the arrangement. Consequently, Robinson adopted a tedious, painstaking style, designed to bore everyone in the room. He asked about the weather, he asked about the bus rides. He made Jefferson describe the clothing he was wearing, and made Jefferson recall where he purchased his sneakers and why he bought that brand and how he was nicknamed Hightops and how he first got introduced to crack cocaine, and every other question he could think of that only occasionally bordered on the relevant.

He drew this out for several hours, letting the Identikit technician sit in a corner, waiting for his turn. The technician was a veteran, and well aware of what was going on. He kept his mouth closed. Occasionally Tommy Alter would impatiently interrupt, as the day dwindled around them, marked only by the single wall clock high on the wall of the interrogation room. Eventually the public defender rose, said he was going to get a cup of coffee and a newspaper to read, and asked if anyone else needed anything.

"I want something to eat," Jefferson said.

Walter Robinson pulled out his wallet and said, "Tommy, why don't you get your client a sandwich and a soda from the deli across the street. Maybe better get everyone a sandwich. Miss Martinez, maybe you can go along and give him a hand."

Espy Martinez started to object, but then recognized that Robinson probably had a reason for asking her to escort Alter, and the reason probably was to delay his return as much as possible, so she nodded.

"You're going to stick to the same material?" Alter asked.

"Yeah. Just going through it all slowly."

"Okay. We'll be back in a few minutes. Leroy, don't answer any question you're not comfortable with."

"No problem."

Alter exited, trailed by Espy Martinez. After a second or so of quiet, Walter Robinson started asking more cogent questions.

"Tell me, Leroy, did you always ride the bus when you did a break-in?"

Jefferson was slumped back in his seat, slightly distracted, toying with a pack of cigarettes, obviously feeling pretty confident and slightly bored. He shrugged. "Didn't have no car."

"Same bus every time?"

"It took me where I wanted to go."

"Weren't you scared some bus driver might remember you?"

"Nah. They change drivers around so much. And I went on different nights. And I was always careful, you know, to come out when the evening shift was driving and leave when the next shift took over."

"That was smart."

"I ain't stupid like some junkies."

"Why the same neighborhood each time?"

"Old people. Old buildings. Old locks. Weren't nobody gonna have a gun, come surprise me. I never carried my gun myself."

Walter Robinson nodded. "Sure. Makes sense. So, tell me how come you picked Sophie's place?"

"Oh, man, it was easy. I'd noticed it on another trip. Got that alley down the back. Not much light. Those patio doors, all you got to do is jam them up and off their runners and makes no difference what sort of lock they got. You're in."

"So, tell me about that night."

"It weren't too late, you know. Maybe midnight. I was right in the back, hiding next to the garbage cans. It was nice and quiet. No lights on, except upstairs, and they was watching the television real loud, which was gonna cover up any noise I made."

"Did you know she was inside?"

Jefferson shook his head. "Weren't no lights or sounds or nothing. I thought the place was empty for sure."

Robinson nodded again. Sure, he said to himself. Sure you thought it was empty. Like hell. But he didn't say this out loud. He merely made a mental check note next to the lie and continued.

"So you were out back. How long were you there?"

"Maybe half hour. Maybe a little more. I took my time about these things. Lot of guys, you know, they just smash their way right in. Me, I was more careful. Didn't want to get busted."

"And what happened?"

"Man, dude scared the shit outta me. I was just starting to get ready, you know, sneak across, do my thing, when I saw this little movement off to my side. I froze. Didn't make a move. I was already ducked down, you know, being careful. He must have been there watching, maybe ten feet away. I don't know how long he'd been there, man, the dude was so quiet, didn't even hear his breathing. I thought he musta seen me for sure, but I guess not because maybe he was watching that apartment so close and like he didn't expect anyone to be doing the same thing. Where I was, it was like a little black hole, no light in there at all, and I was hidden pretty good."

"So, you didn't see him arrive?"

"No, man. Man moved like a spook. Maybe like some damn ghost, he be so quiet. I don't know how long he was hanging there. Coulda been a couple of minutes, coulda been an hour. At least as long as me."

"Tell me what you saw."

"Dude slides across the patio, right up to the old lady's place. Man was slick, I'll tell you. Didn't make a sound. Not like some old guy bumbling and fumbling, you know. Dude had done this thing before, the way he moved. Damn, he had that sliding door open so quick, just like it wasn't even locked. Made one little noise, when he broke the lock, you know, then he was inside."

"What did you do?"

"Well, man, first thing I thought was to run, you know? Try someplace else, because I figured this old guy was gonna clean that apartment out. He was a pro, you could tell, and there weren't gonna be nothing left for me. But I was curious too, you know? Sort of wanted to see what was gonna go down."

"Sure. Makes sense."

"I mean, like it was almost like I thought I might learn something." Leroy Jefferson laughed briefly. "Man, I learned something all right."

"So, what did you do?"

"Moved right across the yard there, right up to the door. Couldn't see shit, so I stepped inside, real quiet. Into the kitchen there."

"Because you wanted to learn something?"

"That's right."

Robinson thought to himself: Not because you thought you might be able to pop the old man after he'd done all the work for you. You were gonna take him off, right then. Good thing you didn't try it, because the Shadow Man would have killed you so fast, you wouldn't even have known you were dying. But he said: "Go ahead. What happened then?"

"I heard them. Sound was coming from the bedroom. Weren't a lot of noise, but man, I knew what was happening. Old dude was killing her. It weren't like no fight, weren't even like much of a struggle. Just real quick, like the dude still knew what he was doing. I heard her make a sound like a little scream maybe, but not real loud and that was it for her. And I heard a cat too, you know that meowing noise they make. I heard that too. I slide down into the corner, trying to stay where it's hidden, you know? I think, shit man, he's killing somebody, let's get the fuck outta here, but before I can run, I see the dude again. Only a couple of feet away, man, he was moving fast, but just as quiet as before and he's out the door and gone."

"What did you do?"

"Well, I real quick stuck my head in, saw the old lady all tangled up in her sheets. Weren't much light in there, just streetlights, you know, coming through the window, but enough to see that jewelry box, so I grabbed a few things."

"You were in a hurry?"

"Sure. Jesus, man, just wanted to get outta there. But, like, this old dude had given me an easy score, and after all, that was why I was there in the first place, so shit, I wanted to, what you say, take advantage of the opportunity. But I musta made too much noise with the drawers and things, because I heard a door open upstairs, and then footsteps, and knocking on the front door. Figured I better get moving then, grabbed a few more things, anything, you know, anything that would fit in the pillowcase and might be worth something, and got outta there. Shouldn't have been so damn greedy, you know? If I'da left right then, when I heard the knocking, nobody'd have seen me. But man, when you're looking to make some money, sometimes you don't think right."

"The necklace?"

"Yeah. I saw it as I was leaving. Saw those diamonds. Man,

even in the dark they were glowing. Figured I could get something for them, so I grabbed it quick from her neck."

Walter Robinson thought: postmortem scratch explained. "And what happened next?"

"Fucking old-timer sees me running. Gets a good look too. Starts shouting for the cops. That's it, you know the rest."

"Let's go back to the man you saw commit the crime. . . ."

"Man was cold. Gave me the shakes. Don't want to see him again. Goes in, strangles an old lady, no reason I could see. Don't even steal nothing. Man was cold."

Walter Robinson paused. Jefferson had shifted about in his seat, sitting up, arms on the table in front of him, a nervous electric tension in his voice as he described the killing. Jefferson's easygoing, confident manner had changed, and he sensed some frightened urgency on the man's face.

"When I thought about it, later, you know, after I got my money from Reggie and was getting some smoke down, it kinda freaked me, you know. I mean, dude was just a killer, that's all."

Walter Robinson realized that in the generously psychopathic world that Leroy Jefferson occupied, a murder without some obvious profit connected to it was unsettling. There were probably dozens of killings that Leroy Johnson wouldn't have thought twice about. But this one made him anxious.

"Don't want to run into that dude on a dark night," Jefferson joked, leaning back in his seat. "You better be thinking the same, Detective. Man was a stone-cold killer."

"Did you ever hear him say anything?"

"No. Just quiet. Cool. Moved so easy."

"Okay, but you'd know him if you saw him again?"

"Sure. I got a real good look at him. Hell, better than the old-timer got looking at me, when I was running. This dude didn't move real fast, you see? Deliberate-like. Took his time to do things right. So I got a real good look at him. Both outside, and when he went right by me in the apartment. Good thing he didn't see me. Guess he weren't expecting no black man on his tail."

Walter Robinson nodded again. He still has a black man on his tail, and he doesn't know it. The detective gestured over at the

Identikit technician, who stretched like a dog awakened from a place next to a fire, and then approached with his valise.

"All yours, now," Robinson said.

"Okay, Mr. Jefferson," the technician said. "We're going to go real slow. You just form a mental picture of the man you saw. And I'm gonna show you a bunch of different facial shapes. And pretty soon, we're gonna have a picture of this guy."

Jefferson made a small gesture with his hand. "Sounds fine to me."

The technician produced a series of overlays on clear plastic sheets of paper. "Let's start with the chin," he said. "I'll show you these forms, and you concentrate on what you remember, and stop me when I get the right one."

"Hey, Detective," Jefferson said. "You bust this guy, you gonna be looking for the death penalty, same as you were with me?"

"Absolutely."

Leroy Jefferson nodded his head, wrinkling his chin as he thought hard. He turned his eyes to the plastic overlays.

"Didn't ever think I'd be helping the cops put the juice to no one," he said. "But the dude was a killer. No doubt about it." He pointed at one of the shapes displayed on the table in front of him. "Let's start with that one," he said.

Walter Robinson shifted in his seat and watched as the painstaking process of giving a face to the Shadow Man began.

Tommy Alter gave up after a few more hours, leaving after extracting a promise from Walter Robinson that Jefferson would be given a ride back to his home and that the ride would be direct and smooth. The Identikit technician was thorough and refused to be hurried, a man who enjoyed his work in the same way that an artist does as shapes take form on the canvas.

It was late when Espy Martinez and Walter Robinson stole a moment alone in the corridor outside the interrogation room.

"I'm exhausted," she said.

"Why don't you go home?"

She smiled. "Home for me is two things: boring or frustrating. Boring because I live alone and there's nothing there that makes me feel like who I really want to be; frustrating because no sooner will I close the door before the phone will ring and it will be my parents calling from their half of the duplex. My mother will want to know what I'm doing and who I'm doing it with and a dozen other questions I don't want to answer."

She shook her head. "Too tired to really sort these things out, Walter. But being with you is, I don't know, an adventure. Something way outside all the things I've ever done. I always did what was expected of me. And this isn't and I like that. I like it a lot." She reached out and just touched her fingers against his hand. "Is that wrong?"

"I don't know," he replied. "I'm not sure what I think, if I think anything at all."

"It did come out wrong," she said. "I'm sorry. Can't we talk at some other time, when we're not so tired?"

"Yes," he said. "That would be wise."

"I want to make this work," she said.

"Me too."

She paused. "I don't want to go home tonight."

He nodded. He was troubled, but desire overcame whatever doubts he had. He recognized this, thought himself slightly weak, and then thought that was stupid because thinking too much about any relationship was likely to doom it, and there was a great deal that remained to happen with Espy Martinez that he wanted to happen. So, instead, he reached into his pocket and pulled out his key chain. He worked the apartment key off the ring and handed it to her.

"I have the chauffeur duty with our man Leroy. You go back to my place and wait up for me, okay?"

"Would you like me to go with you?"

"No." He smiled. "It will give me the opportunity to needle the creep without feeling guilty that I might be violating the spirit of his agreement with the State of Florida."

"Okay," she said. "Just don't make him so pissed that he decides to run away."

"Isn't running anywheres, thanks to that little twenty-five caliber you tote around in your handbag."

"It's still there," she said. She hesitated. "And tomorrow?"

"Tomorrow we start on Simon Winter's plan. We'll go see him and the other old folks with our picture."

As he said this, the door to the interrogation room opened and the technician emerged. He was holding a white sheet of paper in his hand, staring down at it with an appraiser's eye. He saw the two of them look up at him and he said: "Jefferson wasn't too good with the eyes. I think that's because he never got a full-face look at this man. According to his story, mostly it was profiles, maybe three-quarters front. Never did look the man in the eyes, which is probably a good thing for him. Other than that, I think this came out okay. What do you think?"

Walter Robinson took the drawing and held it in front of him so that they both could look at it. What they saw was a picture of a tall, big-chested elderly man who wore his years with the firmness of a person considerably younger. His chin was sturdy, like a boxer's, with skin that remained tight. He had high-set cheekbones and a wide brow, giving the portrait the appearance of a man looking far into the distance. His hair was white, closely cropped like a soldier's, but thick.

"This is good," he said quietly.

"Hell, Walter, you could do the same." The technician was aware of Robinson's hobby.

"So, that's the Shadow Man," Espy Martinez said.

"I don't think the eyes are right," the technician repeated. "I just couldn't get them."

The eyes in the drawing were dull, vacant.

"No," the detective said. "These could be anyone's eyes. Not a killer's."

Eyes like razors, he thought. Walter Robinson held the picture in his hands and wondered what the rabbi and Frieda Kroner would say when they saw it.

The King Apartments looked very much the same as they did the night Walter Robinson arrived there to arrest Leroy Jefferson. He pulled his vehicle to the curb, crunching over some broken glass. There were midnight noises throughout the distance, all accompanied by the faraway sound of a fire engine with its deep-

throated horn sounding urgently as it pushed through the inner-
city night.

"Home sweet home," Robinson said.

Jefferson nodded. "Ain't much, is it?"

"Can't say it is."

"Maybe I'll get someplace new now. This place got a lot of bad
luck connected to it."

"What sort of bad luck, Leroy?"

"It's bad luck to get busted," he replied, grinning. "Even if you
do find a way out."

Robinson exited the car, retrieved the wheelchair from the
trunk, and opened the rear door so that Jefferson could swing
himself out, into the seat. This the man did, with an agility that
made Robinson believe the pain in his leg had diminished some.
Either that or he was eager to find what he knew was waiting
for him.

"You want me to help you upstairs?" he asked.

Jefferson shook his head, still grinning. "Ain't too interested in
having my neighbors know I been helping the police. They don't
consider this a necessarily good thing, you know."

"Not part of the local idea of civic duty, huh?"

"You got that right."

"How're you going to get up the stairs?"

"Maybe somebody's fixed the elevator. If not, I'll figure it out.
Ain't your business anyways."

Jefferson gave the wheels a push and rolled a few feet away, up
onto the walkway. Then he spun the chair about and looked back
at the detective.

"I did what you asked, right?"

"Yes. So far, so good."

"I told you I'd keep my part of the bargain."

"Just keep keeping it."

"You ain't got enough trust in human nature, Detective." Jefferson laughed. "Can't even tell when somebody's helping you
out. Wouldn't have no case against that old dude, 'cept for me."

"You just keep cooperating, Leroy. Don't move. Don't go anywhere. And don't get into any trouble. Got that?"

"Sure."

Jefferson laughed. The sound echoed down the street. He rolled the wheelchair back a foot or two, then added: "You know, you ain't so far from all this, Detective. Put on that suit, act like the man, but truth is, could be you right here and me right there."

Walter Robinson shook his head. "Nope. You're wrong."

But he didn't know whether this was true or not. He did know, however, that Espy Martinez was waiting for him, and he thought that more than anything else, at that moment right then, he wanted to get out of Liberty City, wanted to leave the King Apartments and return to the other world he lived in.

Leroy Jefferson laughed again, mocking the detective. He could feel a surge of exhilaration within him, and for the first time, as he measured the distance between himself and the detective, truly thought that he'd managed to beat the system.

"It feels real good to be free," he said. "Be seeing you." He spun the chair again and eagerly started rolling toward the apartment building. He did not look back as Robinson scowled, irritated but accepting, and climbed into the cruiser, quickly slamming the car into gear and accelerating through the coffee-black night.

To his surprise, the elevator was operating.

Leroy Jefferson thought this was a good sign, as the dull steel doors jerked to a close. There was a momentary pause, then a grinding sound before the elevator rose. The interior light dimmed once as it reached the second floor, and the doors seemed oddly reluctant to open, but eventually they did, and he pushed himself out onto the landing, thinking that everything around him was working quite as well as it ever had.

He maneuvered down the landing toward his apartment, breathing raspily with the exertion required to push the wheelchair. He could feel sticky sweat beneath his arms, dripping down his forehead across his cheeks and finally dropping from his chin to his chest. It was an irritating sweat, caused by hard work and humid, still, summer air, not the genuine sweat of athletic motion. He gritted his teeth and thought: Ain't never gonna be running up no court on a fast break again, and he inwardly cursed Espy Martinez and her unlucky shot, which had left him in such awkward pain. He slapped at the wheelchair and reminded himself that the doctors had estimated he'd be out of it within a month or so, which he wanted, because until he had his motion back, he didn't see much of an opportunity to create any income.

He knew he'd be all right for a while. He smiled to himself. Fucking detective was right. He kept a private stash behind a loose tile in the bathroom, two hundred dollars and a similar amount of rock cocaine in a plastic bag, thrust down between the plumbing pipes where it couldn't be seen even if you found the right tile. You had to snake your arm way down and know what you were looking for. He thought: maybe take a little taste, sell the rest. Gonna be okay just as soon as I get back on my feet, even with a limp. Things gonna work out. They always do.

He lifted a hand and wiped the sweat from his forehead, concentrating on the stash.

Just a little taste, he repeated to himself.

He paused outside the door to his apartment. The tattered remains of yellow police tape hung limply from the cracked and splintered door frame. The door itself had been replaced, but ineffectively. He reached out and pushed at it, and it swung open. Unlocked.

"Goddamn junkies, probably stole everything," he said out loud.

He shifted about in the seat of the wheelchair and bellowed back over his shoulder: "You fucking people. Got no respect for other folks' shit!"

There was no one outside to hear his complaint, but from a distant room he heard one voice yell, "Fuck you!" and from the opposite end of the corridor another shouted, "Shut the fuck up!"

He waited for a moment, to see if there were any other responses, but silence gripped the neighborhood. He couldn't see anyone on the street, or on any of the landings. He felt alone, which did not bother him, because he was not eager to share what he had waiting for him inside behind that false tile.

He remembered what Walter Robinson had said: home sweet home.

He pushed the door wide and rolled himself inside.

The apartment was hot, still, as if a month's oppressive days were collected within the walls. He slammed the door back shut behind him and reached out for the wall light switch.

His hand did not reach the wall. It was interrupted by an iron grip clamping down on his forearm.

In the same instant he heard an ice voice: "No, I don't think we need any light quite yet, Mr. Jefferson."

Fear like a runaway engine accelerated through him. "Who are you?" he choked.

The voice had moved around behind him and made a small laugh before answering. "But you know, don't you, Mr. Jefferson?"

The man seemed to pause, then he asked:

"You tell me: Who am I?"

At the same time as these words slid about in the darkness of the apartment, Jefferson was suddenly jerked backward, as the man released his arm and shifted his grip, throwing a muscled forearm across Jefferson's forehead, tugging his head back, exposing his neck. He gasped, reaching up involuntarily as he felt a knife icicle at his exposed throat.

"No, Mr. Jefferson, put your hands down. Don't make me kill you before we've had a chance to talk."

His own hands, fingers straining toward the blade, stopped in midair. Slowly he dropped them to the wheels at his side. His mind was moving quickly now, roaring past all the fear, trying to think of something to do. He opened his mouth to call for help, but then stopped, shutting it with a snap. Ain't no one gonna come, no matter what you say, he reminded himself. And maybe the dude'll cut your throat before you get the second word out. He remembered the choking cry that was all that Sophie Millstein managed before death. It made him shudder; he could sense fear loosening his control over his bowels, but he fought this, breathing hard and fast, controlling the quiver that found his hands, the twitch that discovered his eyelids. Talk your way out, he told himself. Keep talking. Make a deal.

"That's better," the voice said. "Now slowly bring your hands behind the chair, wrists together."

"You don't gotta do that, man. I'm gonna tell you whatever you need to know."

"Excellent, Mr. Jefferson. That is very reassuring. Now move your hands back slowly. Think of it this way: Any knot I tie, I can always untie. Alexander the Great proved that. Do you know who Alexander is, Mr. Jefferson? No? I didn't think so. But you do know this, don't you: It's always wiser to indulge a man who holds a knife at your throat."

The flat voice seemed patient, cold, with only a slight urgency at its fringe. But the knife blade bit against his skin, its demands obvious. The pressure increased just slightly, enough to draw a small line of blood. Jefferson pushed his hands behind him, as asked. He felt the knife slide around his throat, to his ear, to the nape of his neck, before easing away. He had a momentary urge to jump right then, to fight back, but just as swiftly the urge departed. He told himself: Stay cool. You can't run and you can't fight. There was a ripping sound and he felt his hands being bound with duct tape.

When his arms were immobilized, Jefferson felt the chair being wheeled into the center of the room. He waited, breathing like a runner trying to catch the leaders in a race.

"Who are you, man? What you want? What you got to tie me up for? I ain't going nowheres."

"That's correct, Mr. Jefferson."

"Who are you, man? What's the deal?"

"No, Mr. Jefferson. That's my question for you: *Who am I?*"

"Man, I got no idea. Some crazy white dude, that's who you are."

The voice laughed again. "Not a good start, Mr. Jefferson. Why would you lie to me?"

The man leaned down and poked with the knife blade at the bandages on Jefferson's ruined knee, sending a rainbow of hurt through his body.

"Jesus, man! What you doing? I don't know shit!"

"Who am I, Mr. Jefferson?"

He poked again at the leg, and Leroy Jefferson gritted his teeth.

"Who am I, Mr. Jefferson?"

"I don't know. I ain't never seen you before."

"I hate lies. Once again, who am I, Mr. Jefferson?"

"I don't know, I don't know, Jesus, why you doing this?" Leroy Jefferson's reply was high-pitched with anxiety.

The visitor sighed. Jefferson felt the knife on his leg, tightened his stomach muscles against the expected pain, but instead the voice simply continued.

"I saw you today, Mr. Jefferson. In the courtroom, pleading guilty to all those phony charges. I had had such high hopes for you, Mr. Jefferson, when I read of your arrest. Imagine my surprise this morning when I saw in the paper that you'd been cleared of Mrs. Millstein's murder—and that you were going to help the police in their inquiries. Of course, the story didn't say what inquiries those might be, but I thought it better to err on the side of safety. So I hurried right over to the courtroom and took my seat right with the rest of the curious and the concerned in the back, and waited for you to come out. You appeared preoccupied, Mr. Jefferson. All eager to get on with your business and not attentive to your surroundings. That's a bad habit for anyone of a criminal persuasion, don't you think? Always smarter to take stock of who's who and what's what, even in a crowded courtroom. Should have taken the time to go over each and every one of the faces that were packed inside. But you didn't do that, did you, Mr. Jefferson? Instead you conveniently provided me with your address. So, I came on over and decided to wait for you here, Mr. Jefferson. Because I had some questions and I have some doubts and I hate uncertainty. You're a professional criminal, Mr. Jefferson. Don't you think that is always the smartest approach: assume the worst. Assume there's a problem. And if there isn't, well, then you're pleasantly surprised. Isn't that right, Mr. Jefferson?"

"Man, I don't know what the hell you're talking about—"

The last words he spoke were swallowed by a sharp pain as the knife blade probed the bandages again, searching for skin and muscle. He breathed out harshly:

"Goddamn it, that hurts, man, I don't know what, you're crazy, just leave me alone. . . ."

"Who am I, Mr. Jefferson?"

Leroy Jefferson didn't answer. Tears of pain cluttered his face, running down his cheeks. Very little that the man said to him was clear. All he could taste was an acid dryness in his mouth.

"You a killer," Leroy Jefferson said.

The man hesitated, and Jefferson heard him inhale deeply.

"That's a start," said the man. "Here is a simple question: Who is Simon Winter?"

Leroy Jefferson was confused. He licked the sweat from his lips. "I don't know that name."

Pain like a rocket soared through him and he gasped out in the darkness, a scream rising within him, racing toward his lips, only to stop, gurgling in his throat when he heard the man say: "Stay quiet!"

His leg was aflame. The knife had scraped through the wrappings, twisting at flesh. Leroy Jefferson tried to bend forward, twisting against the confinements of the duct tape and the wheelchair. "Jesus," he said. "Don't do that, man. Please don't do that."

"Who am I, Mr. Jefferson?"

"Please, please, whatever, just don't do that again. . . ."

"That was only a start, Mr. Jefferson. I'll try again. Who is Simon Winter and what does he know about me?"

Leroy Jefferson let words burst through his lips, a torrent of fear, almost as if he could already sense the burning in his leg as the knife ripped at tendons and nerves.

"Man, I don't know! I never heard that name before!"

For a moment the man was silent and Leroy Jefferson searched through the darkness for the knife. He felt the man shifting next to him, reaching at the damaged leg, and he quickly added: "That's the truth, man. I got no idea, don't hurt me again!"

"All right," the voice said after a pause. "I did not think you necessarily knew the answer to that question." There was another silence before the voice continued: "Mr. Jefferson, you must have the patience of a spider. Spin your web and wait for your prey to deliver itself to you."

The voice hesitated, then continued: "Isn't that right, Mr. Jefferson?"

He answered quickly. "Sure. Yes. What you say."

A small, bitter laugh creased the darkness. "Who am I, Mr. Jefferson?"

"Please, I don't know. I don't wanta know, and even if I did know, I wouldn't tell nobody."

"Do you think I'm a criminal, like you, Mr. Jefferson?"

"No, yes, man, I don't know. . . ."

"You think I'm some parasite that kills and robs to support a disgusting drug habit? You think I'm like you?"

"No, no, that's not what I meant."

"Then, who am I, Mr. Jefferson?"

Leroy Jefferson sobbed his response, a plaintive plea mingled with the aching pain that came in waves from his ravaged leg. "I don't know, I don't know. . . ."

He heard the man start to move about the apartment, circling him, and he swiveled his head, trying to follow the shape as it traveled through the shadows in the living room. After a moment the voice asked, in a steady, mildly curious voice:

"Tell me, if you were to die tonight, right here, right in the next two seconds, Mr. Jefferson, would the world even hesitate for a second to note your passing?"

"Man, please, I'll tell you what you want, but I don't know what you're saying. You talking crazy talk. I don't understand. I just don't understand."

"I have been a part of great things, Mr. Jefferson. Some of the greatest moments this world has ever seen. Unforgettable events. Incredible times."

The voice emptied the room of everything except fear. Leroy Jefferson could see the man's outline as he moved past the diffuse, weak light tossed haphazardly into the room through the living room window by a streetlight lurking somewhere distant.

"Who am I, Mr. Jefferson?"

He shook his head in the darkness. "Oh, please don't ask me that! Man, I don't know who you are!"

The voice again slid a small, coarse laugh into the still air around him. It seemed to come from several spots at once, and Leroy Jefferson pivoted his head about, trying to find where the man stood in the ink-dark spots of the room. Again he wanted to cry out, but he knew it would be useless. He shivered deeply, and waited for the voice to ask another question. He felt confused, afraid. He barely understood what the man was asking. The language was beyond his experience. But then, so was the pain in his leg, which throbbed and gnawed at him, keeping pace with his heartbeats and the fear that ricocheted about within him.

"All right," the man said. He continued moving from side to side, sometimes pausing behind the wheelchair. Leroy Jefferson pivoted nervously. "Let's talk about your deal with the State of Florida. What sort of deal is it, Mr. Jefferson?"

"I got to tell them what I know about some crimes."

"Good. That's helpful. What crimes, Mr. Jefferson?"

"Break-ins. Robberies. Bunch of them on Miami Beach."

"Good. Keep going."

"Man, that's it! Whole pile of little shit crimes, some robberies, like I said. Maybe rat on some coke dealers too, that's what they want from me."

The voice moved around behind him. "No, that doesn't make much sense, Mr. Jefferson."

"I'm telling you the truth. . . ."

The man laughed. "You insult me, Mr. Jefferson. You insult the truth."

He suddenly felt the pressure of the knife against his cheek and he wanted to scream. The man must have anticipated this, because he whispered into Jefferson's ear: "Don't shout. Don't yell. Don't do something that might make me want to end this."

He bit back terror and nodded.

There was a second's delay before the man spoke. "How strong are you, Mr. Jefferson? Remember, don't shout out. You remember that, don't you?"

Jefferson nodded.

"Good," the man said. Then he slowly drew the tip of the knife across Leroy Jefferson's cheek, cutting a deep furrow in the skin.

Jefferson clenched down on his lip to avoid screaming. Salty blood ran into the corner of his mouth.

"Don't lie to me, Mr. Jefferson. I truly despise being lied to."

The voice was never raised. It stayed a low, cold tone.

Jefferson thought he should say something, but he was preoccupied with the knife blade, which tickled at his other cheek.

"One should always use their anger constructively, Mr. Jefferson."

The knife tip dug into his skin again, and was drawn slowly across the cheek, parting the flesh. Pain redoubled, and for an instant he thought he might pass out.

The man sighed, and moved to the side of the wheelchair. For just an instant his profile was caught in a wayward shaft of weak light. His white hair glistened, almost as if it were electric.

"There is a great difference between being old and being experienced, Mr. Jefferson." The man bent down over him. "Now consider what has happened. I've been quite patient with you. I'm not asking for something you cannot provide. All I demand is a little bit of honest information."

"I'm trying, please, I'm trying. . . ."

"I don't think you're trying quite hard enough, Mr. Jefferson."

"I will. I promise."

"Who knows about Der Schattenmann, Mr. Jefferson?"

"Man, please, I don't know that name."

"Who is searching for him? Is it the police, Mr. Jefferson? Or that attractive young prosecutor? The old people, I know about. But who else? How is it that you are involved in all this? Did you see me that night, Mr. Jefferson? I want to know and I want to know now. These are not unreasonable questions, Mr. Jefferson, but still, you persist in evasion. Because of that, you've forced me to deliver to you a pair of scars, one in either cheek. The wounds will heal, Mr. Jefferson, but the scars will remain to remind you of the evils of obstinacy. And you've forced me to probe about in your damaged knee. Do you not think I could ruin it completely, Mr. Jefferson? Perhaps I could just start to work the knife blade into all those healing sutures. What do you suppose that might feel like?"

"Please don't, man, I'm trying to help. . . ."

"Are you, Mr. Jefferson? I'm not impressed. Mr. Silver didn't lie, when I spoke with him under similar circumstances, although I would not characterize his behavior as completely forthcoming. But he had friends he wanted to protect, and so his reluctance was understandable. As was his death. And Mr. Stein, well, that was a meeting doomed from the start, right from the second he saw me, same as Mrs. Millstein. These were people that I knew, Mr. Jefferson. People I have known for decades. Since I was even younger than you. And they died, Mr. Jefferson, just as they always died. Quietly and obediently."

"I don't know what you're saying, man. Please leave me alone."

"I asked them the same question, Mr. Jefferson. They knew the answer."

"I'm sorry, please. I'm sorry. . . ."

"Who am I, Mr. Jefferson?"

Again he sobbed, his voice shut down from pain and fear. He did not reply.

After a moment he heard from behind him:

"I have more questions. You see, Mr. Jefferson, I know that the State of Florida wouldn't cut you a deal after you shot a policeman unless there was someone really special that they were hunting for. Someone who really mattered, mattered enough for them to do something I'm sure they found extremely unpleasant and distasteful. And that was letting you go. Nasty bit of work, that. Letting a junkie who almost murdered a policeman walk free. Must stick in the throat of every policeman and prosecutor in town. So, somehow I just don't think that you're helping them out on a bunch of insignificant crimes. No, there's someone out there much more important, isn't there?"

"Please, man . . ."

"Much more important, correct?"

"Yes, man, whatever you say!"

"That someone, of course, is me. It has always been me, but they never knew it."

The man in the darkness seemed to take a deep breath.

"So, now, Mr. Jefferson, I want the truth. Do you know no one has ever managed to refuse me, in all these years of asking questions. No one asked—no one!—has ever not answered. A remarkable record, that, don't you think? It was always so easy. People are so vulnerable. They want to live, and when you can take that away from them, it gives you all the power you need. You know something, Mr. Jefferson? They always told me. Back then, late at night. There were sirens in the distance from the air raids, and the streets were bombed out. A city of death. It wasn't all that different from your own neighborhood, Mr. Jefferson, which is a curious and interesting thing, don't you think? We've come so far, and yet, not really, have we? Anyway, Mr. Jefferson, they always told me what I wanted to know. *Where was the money? The jewelry? And where were their relatives? Their neighbors? Their friends? Where were the others hiding?* They always told me something that I needed to know, and they were smart people, Mr. Jefferson. Smarter than you. Educated. Resourceful. But I caught them, just as I've caught you. And then they told me what I wanted, and so will you."

Leroy Jefferson heard his own raspy breathing fill the room.

"Consider your situation for a second. . . ." the voice continued. It seemed to come from everywhere at once, and he felt wildly disoriented, adrift, as if he were not in his own apartment, in the part of the city he claimed as his own, where he'd grown up and spent almost all his waking hours, but was someplace else, drowning someplace far from shore. "You're already crippled, and now I've disfigured you with scars. What remains?" He pressed the blade up against Leroy Jefferson's lips. ". . . Or maybe you'd prefer to be blind, Mr. Jefferson? I could take your eyes. I've done that before. Are you willing to go through the rest of your life as a blind, dumb cripple? What sort of life would that be, Mr. Jefferson? Especially for someone of, shall we say, your economic and social background? I can deliver that, you know. . . ."

Leroy Jefferson saw the knife blade hovering in front of his face, reflecting the small light in the room.

". . . Or maybe something else, something important . . ."

The man abruptly dropped the knife down, pressing the flat of the blade hard against Leroy Jefferson's crotch.

"Isn't it remarkable how many different ways there are to hurt a man? Physically. Mentally. Emotionally . . ." The knife pressed down sickeningly, and Leroy Jefferson thought he might vomit.

". . . And some injuries accomplish all three. Right, Mr. Jefferson?"

Leroy Jefferson wouldn't allow himself to answer this question. Fear like a mist obscured his thoughts. He felt himself ensnared in some net that threatened to choke him no matter how he twisted or squirmed. He tried to force himself to think clearly, but it was difficult, with the man's even, cold voice echoing in his ears and the knife blade dancing around his body. Leroy Jefferson felt trapped within a whirlpool of pain and terror; he knew little, except that if he told this man the truth, if he told him that he had seen him before and seen him kill Sophie Millstein and that he had told these things to Walter Robinson and Espy Martinez and had provided them with his picture and had agreed to testify against him at a trial, then the man would surely kill him. And then he would probably kill the detective and the prosecutor and anyone else that threatened him. He knew this with a clarity that defied all the hurt that surged throughout his body, knew it because he recognized if it were he standing over some similar witness with a blade of his own, anger and fear and the threat of arrest might force him to do much the same, and this gave him a certainty that was as unwelcome in the small, hot room, as was the visitor himself.

He felt tears welling up in his eyes, dropping down, mingling with the blood on his cheeks.

"So, Mr. Jefferson, who am I?"

The question rang in his ear, urgent, terrifying. He took a sharp, deep breath, trying to contain himself. He knew, in that second, that nothing he said was going to make any difference whatsoever. The visitor was going to kill him. There was nothing he could say or do that might save his life. All he could do, by telling the man what he wanted, was prolong it perhaps a few minutes. Maybe only a few seconds.

The thought pushed panic through him. He pulled at the duct tape that seized his hands, but could not break it. In the silence in the room, he felt the man maneuver around him, like a wayward breath of cold wind on a hot day. He swallowed hard, the dryness in his throat as parched as if he'd held a red-hot coal on his tongue. And in that second, abruptly, surprisingly, an entirely different sensation settled over his heart.

Leroy Jefferson felt a sudden, complete calm settle within him. There was, he realized, no way out.

He could not fight. He knew no one would answer his call for help. And he knew no lie, nor no truth, could save him.

He thought he should be scared, but instead felt filled with an acceptance that bordered on defiance. He understood, in that second, that he had done precious little in his life that amounted to anything good or anything that anyone would have considered brave or even honest, and that now, facing his death, it saddened him to realize that no one would see him become these things. He would have liked it if someone like Walter Robinson or maybe Espy Martinez could have seen him change, in that moment, and that they realized that he had fought to protect them and maybe even had saved their lives. In that moment he hoped that when he was found, that they understood that he had died being something that he had never been before.

*"Who am I*, Mr. Jefferson?"

He finally knew the answer to this question: death.

But he decided he was not going to give the man and his knife the satisfaction of a reply. Instead Leroy Jefferson spoke out in a determined voice that pushed past the parched thickness of fear. "Old man, I don't know about all those other people. Maybe they told you what you wanted to know. Maybe they didn't. That be their business. But I know this: I ain't gonna tell you shit."

And then he quietly surrendered to the relentless agony that awaited him.

# TWENTY-ONE

## *HATRED*

**S**IMON Winter thought: I could have had him.

But then, in the next second, he realized: He could have had me.

"Stalemate," he whispered out loud.

The old detective sat deep in an armchair, heavy in thought, amidst the rows of books and periodicals of the Miami Beach Library. Fluorescent lights and steadily droning air-conditioning gave the room an independence from the blistering day outside. For a library, there was significantly less devotion to utter silence than one might have expected. Sturdy shoes clicked against the linoleum floor; an old man snored, a newspaper fluttered open on his lap; occasionally raised voices ruptured the still air as one elderly woman sought to explain something to another, defying the hearing loss that afflicted both. The room had a busyness to it that would have irked any true scholar; but it served a slightly different purpose, existing both as a place where information was gathered, and as a cool, well-lit world where some of the older people living on the Beach could meet and spend a few unconcerned hours surrounded by safety.

This, he recognized, was more or less the same reason he was there. In the twenty-four hours since the Shadow Man had fled from his apartment, Winter had decided several things. First, for the time being he was going to keep quiet about this new threat to himself. Secondly, he knew he was going to have to work harder and faster.

He had encircled himself with texts on the Holocaust, of which, understandably, there were many collected at the Miami Beach Library. He was riven with frustration. He was unable to shake the belief that somewhere in the past there was some bit of information that would open the door to the present. He was simply at a loss as to how to find that piece of history. All the books piled beside him, spread about on a small table and gathered at his feet, told him immense amounts about Nazis. They told him about what the Nazis did, and how they did it and where they did it and to whom they did it. He thought it an odd thing, to create, as they had, a world dedicated so completely to terror that it became commonplace and routine, and wondered if this were not amongst their greatest evils. But this observation did nothing to assist him in his pursuit of the Shadow Man; it told him nothing about what he felt he needed: some light that might penetrate the man's psyche. None of the books helped him in this pursuit. Some, admittedly, sought to examine the personalities behind the acts of the men in black uniforms. There were political explanations describing how men came to join the Nazi Party, how they decided to participate in S.S. actions, how they came to justify murder and genocide. These political explanations dovetailed with psychological profiles, but none of these even came close to touching the soul of the Shadow Man, because, as Frieda Kroner and Rabbi Rubinstein had pointed out, he was never a Nazi; he was supposed to be one of their prey. Yet he managed to reverse that equation somehow, and emerge from events that had left their marks on everyone connected to them. He was something entirely different, a unique player at the game of evil.

Simon Winter closed another thick history book with a snap that echoed in the large room.

If I do not understand this man, even if only a little bit, then he will slip past me again, Winter thought. He is not a man that has ever made the same mistake twice.

He slid deeper into his chair, dropping his head into his hands. He abruptly pictured himself standing outside his apartment, next to the trumpeting cherub, the night before, and he wondered what was it that had told him something was wrong.

Luck? Instinct? The old detective's sixth sense?

Winter exhaled slowly.

There had been no sound. No footstep. No tortured breathing.

There was not a light on that should have been off. No window open that should have been closed. He'd discovered the door ajar in the rear only after persuading himself that the Shadow Man was inside.

The night had been like every other. The darkness held the heat. The city pulsed on as it did every evening.

The only thing that was out of place was that a man with a knife had been waiting for him, and that if he'd not been overcome suddenly by some ancient sensation of dread and danger, he would no longer be hunting for the Shadow Man. He wondered where that sensation had come from, and did not know, but knew that he would be foolish to think that he would ever be fortunate enough again to have it come to his rescue as it had the previous night.

You should be dead, Simon Winter, he told himself.

He looked up suddenly, his eyes sweeping the room filled with old folks, reading books, magazines, newspapers. Some simply sat, lost in dreams of faraway times. His eyes widened and he felt a sudden surge of fear tumble through his body.

Are you here?

Am I hunting you, or are you hunting me?

He fought off the urge to rise and run, steeling himself inwardly, forcing himself to examine all the people within the range of his eyes. The man in the hat poring over the *Herald*. The wizened man who seemed to be studying the ceiling. Another man, wearing white socks and black oxfords beneath madras shorts, who walked slowly past, carrying a pair of detective novels, one in either hand.

Winter half rose and stared behind him, at the people gathered in other chairs, at other desks, partially hidden by the stacks of books and reading cubicles. Then he settled back into his chair. He took a moment to compose himself.

He smiled.

How did you know about me?

He knew the answer to that: Irving Silver.

But what did he tell you?

Just enough to make you decide to kill me.

But what do you really know about me? You weren't inside the apartment long enough, were you? There were no signs that you took the time to discover who I really am. Drawers weren't ransacked. Clothing untouched. You didn't find the gun, and you still don't know that I have it, and that I will use it, and that once, a long time ago, I was an expert with it, and that I doubt it will fail me should I call upon our old camaraderie. No, you were merely going to kill me because you thought I was a threat, and it was easier for you to do that than anything else.

Simon Winter nodded. You arrogant bastard.

But it wasn't as easy as you thought it would be, and now you're probably a little bit worried, and that's something I can use. And you probably want to learn more about me, don't you? Well, that might prove harder than you think. So, for now at least, you are in the dark. Perhaps not as much as I am, but still, you are groping about, and that may make you take a chance you wouldn't ordinarily consider.

Winter felt himself fill with harshness.

They were always easy, weren't they? Once they were young and scared or old and scared, but always they were lost and desperate, and you were never that way, were you? No, you were always in control. But you made a mistake when you killed Sophie Millstein because you never imagined her neighbor would rise up against you. You never thought that there might be someone out there in this great wide world who would consider finding you as immense a challenge as you consider staying hidden. And it never occurred to you that this man who decides to hunt you would come from a world you do not know. And I too know a great deal about the ways of death, and maybe just as much as you, and I too am old, and have not so much time left that I care about, so that makes me unpredictable and that also makes me a dangerous man, and you've never been faced by a dangerous man, have you?

Winter reached out and seized a ballpoint pen and a pad of yellow legal-sized paper and started to scratch some notes to himself.

What do I know? he asked himself. Then he answered the question: more than I think.

I know you are old, but appear perhaps younger. I know you are strong, because the years have been good to you.

Why do you kill?

To stay hidden.

Winter paused. That's not enough, is it? There's much more to it than simply staying safe, isn't there?

He smiled. You like it, don't you? You like the idea that some-one might recognize you? When Sophie Millstein spotted you outside the ice-cream store in the middle of the Lincoln Road Mall, it didn't send a shiver of fear through your body, did it? No, the shiver you felt was pleasure, because you were once again in the hunt, and that is what you like, isn't it?

An awful thought occurred to Simon Winter at that moment, and for a second his pen quivered above the yellow legal pad. Maybe Sophie Millstein didn't spot you by accident. May-be you'd been hunting her for some time. And the others too. How many?

He gritted his teeth. Everything seems to be one thing, then it turns into other possibilities. He admonished himself: Stick close to what you can grasp.

All right. He kept talking to himself, maneuvering through the maze of contradictions that might be the Shadow Man. All right, what else do you know? I know he doesn't fear the police, be-cause he came after me without much preparation. He was simply going to cut the life out of me, and then leave my remains for De-tective Robinson to clean up. So, he does not think he can be ar-rested. Why?

The answer to that question was immediately clear.

Because he is not a criminal.

If I were to discover your name today, what would it tell me? That you've never been arrested. Never fingerprinted. Never typed into any criminal data bank for suspicion of any crime. Never cheated on your taxes. Never made a late payment or de-faulted on a loan or returned a rental car late. Never pulled over for driving under the influence. Never even received a speeding ticket. You've led a quiet, unnoticed existence; an exemplary life with one small exception: You kill people.

Simon Winter breathed out slowly. He nodded to himself. That's what makes you feel safe. You know that the police operate in a world circumscribed by routine. He was reminded of Claude Rains's famous line in *Casablanca*: "Round up the usual suspects." But you'd never get caught in that corral, would you? Because you don't fit into what we were taught to look for. Leroy Jefferson did, and that was why Detective Robinson was so expert at finding him. But you're not some low-life, crack-addled junkie, are you?

He put the writing pad down on the arm of the chair. He wondered whether Walter Robinson had managed to get his composite drawing prepared. He was suddenly overcome with the desire to see the man he'd been so close to for those few seconds in the darkness of his apartment. I am beginning to understand you, Shadow Man, he whispered to himself. And the more I understand, the more light falls across your shadow.

He looked at the books gathered about him, and abruptly was struck with an idea. I'm looking in the wrong place, he thought. I'm asking the wrong people. The rabbi, Frieda Kroner, Esther at the Holocaust Center, all the historians—they're all the wrong people. They know only of the fear and the threat the Shadow Man created. I must find one of the men who helped create the Shadow Man.

Simon Winter picked up a book from the stack beside him titled: *The Encyclopedia of the Third Reich*. He flipped through it swiftly, until he found an organizational chart. He wrote down some numbers and designations on his sheet of notes, and then took a deep breath.

A long shot, he thought. But I've seen longer. And it's something you wouldn't expect, would you?

He collected his things and rose. There was a bank of telephones just outside the library, and he repeated the numbers for Esther Weiss at the Holocaust Center and for the historians he'd spoken with as well. For a moment he saw his reflection in the plate-glass window of the library front door and noticed his lips had been moving as he'd kept up his one-sided conversation. This amused him. Old people are forever talking to themselves, because no one else will listen. It is a part of the harmless madness that age brings. Sometimes they talk to absent children, or long-lost friends, or missing brothers and sisters. On occasion they converse with God. Often they speak animatedly to ghosts. Me, he thought, smiling to himself, I talk to a hidden killer.

Walter Robinson, too, was frustrated.

The composite drawing of the Shadow Man stared back at him from his desktop. The Identikit technician had drawn the face with a small, almost mocking grin, which irked the detective immeasurably. Not the drawing per se, but the smile, because it spoke of elusiveness and anonymity.

He had begun to perform several routine chores of detection, the sorts of tasks that detectives everywhere do, and which they are accustomed to meeting with some successes. But so far his own efforts had been fruitless. He had faxed the partial thumbprint taken from Sophie Millstein's throat to the FBI labs in Maryland, to see if their computer could come up with a match. The marriage of fingerprint technology and computers had been slow in developing. For years matches were performed by human eyes. This, of course, required the detective seeking a match to know who his suspect was, so that a technician could then compare the crime scene print with a properly taken exemplar. Only in the last few years had computer technology been created allowing an unknown print to be fed into a machine and an identity plucked from the millions of prints taken from the fringe population. Dade County's computer, a smaller version of one operated by the FBI, had already failed. Robinson did not hold out much hope that the agency would be any different. And, owing to the immensity of the FBI sample, the examination would take upward of a week, and he did not know if he had a week to spare.

He'd spent several irritating hours at a computer screen, searching through records for some sign of the Shadow Man. There had been two entries with the word *shadow* under known aliases, but one of these was a Hispanic hit man in his late twenties, presumed dead himself, a victim of the usual narcotics dispute, and the other was a rapist working in the Pensacola area, who had been given the sobriquet by the local newspaper. He'd tried some variations on the phrase, but without success. He'd even been clever enough to tie into the Miami Beach tax rolls, using the German *Schattenmann*, but this had been a dead end.

He had tried entering the national criminal computer data base, with key words such as *Holocaust* and *Jewish*, but the one had been negative and the other had produced a lengthy list of various synagogue and cemetery desecrations, also listed under *Hate Crimes*.

He had tried the word *Berlin* with an equal lack of success. Efforts with *Auschwitz* and *Gestapo* and other links were hopeless.

He had not actually expected any success, but every time his computer blinked the reply NO ENTRY FOUND, it renewed his frustration.

He had also gone back into the Miami Beach department's cold case file, wondering whether there might be other signs of the Shadow Man's work in ancient cases, but so far he'd been unable to find anything. Certainly there were unsolved homicides with Jewish victims, and probably some of these were Holocaust survivors, but whether they'd once come from Berlin, and how and where they'd survived the Holocaust, were not the sort of details contained in the files. Backtracking through cases five, ten, perhaps twenty years old, would take days. He had held the files in his hands and thought to himself that surely one, two, maybe more, could be the Shadow Man's handiwork. For an instant he thought of the men and women the Shadow Man had trapped in wartime Germany, and he realized the cases he held were as lost to him as those murders were.

The thought made him swear loudly, a torrent of obscenities, heard by no one.

Walter Robinson rose from his seat and started to stalk around the desks in the homicide office with all the intensity of a newly captured wildcat, hoping that motion might dislodge some thought that would lead him into a profitable electronic avenue. Every detective keeps in mind such salient memories, such as the Son of Sam case in New York, solved when someone finally checked on every parking ticket issued near one of the crime scenes. He moved from one side of the room to the other, stopping once to spend a minute or two staring out the window across the city, which baked beneath the midday sun. Then he hiked back to his desk, picked up the composite drawing, and holding it in front of him, continued pacing around the room.

He looked up only when he heard the voice ask him: "Is that our man?"

Simon Winter was standing across from him. Robinson nodded, covered the space between them in a quick step, and handed the old detective the picture. Winter held it in his hands for a moment, staring hard at the lines of the drawing. His eyes seemed to absorb every detail, imprinting them on his own memory. Then he smiled cheerlessly:

"Pleased to meet you, you sonofabitch."

What he did not say was: So, you're the man who tried to kill me.

"Now," Robinson said, almost offhandedly, "all we have to do is put a name to that face."

"A name . . ."

"Then I'll nail the bastard. You can take that to the bank. That's all I need. A name. Then his next stop will be the Dade County Jail. A brief stopover on the bumpy ride to Death Row."

Winter nodded. "Tell me, Walter, have you ever hunted a man involved in multiple homicides?"

"Yes and no," the detective replied. "That is, I busted a drug dealer once who'd killed four or five rivals. And I was part of the team that nailed that serial rapist who was working up in Surfside. We always thought there were probably some homicides that we could have made him on, especially up in Broward County, but nothing came of it, and he went away with a zillion-year sentence. But I know what you're really asking. You want to know about Ted Bundy and Charlie Manson and John Gacy and the Boston Strangler and all the others, and you're wondering whether I've ever participated in one of those investigations, and the answer to that is no, I haven't. Did you?"

The older man smiled. "I took a confession once, a guy sat across from me, smoking cigarettes, drinking Coca-Colas. That was back when they came in those six-and-a-half-ounce bottles, and you could polish off one of those suckers in a gulp or two. It was hot, and there was only this little fan running in a corner of the room, and it was late at night, and it seemed like every time I got that guy another Coke, he'd confess to another killing. Little boys, mostly. He liked little boys. This was down in the southern part of the county, not too far from where the Everglades reach down and touch the bay. Redneck country. He was a transplanted good old boy. Should have been humming 'Dixie.' Couple of scraggly tattoos, three-day-old beard, beat-up baseball hat. Could hardly read and write. He got up to maybe seventeen, eighteen confessed killings by the time the sun came up, and so we took him out. He was going to give us the tour, you know? I felt like a bus driver at a goddamn tourist trap, like some sort of nightmare sightseer, thinking about what sort of final hours those kids had had with this bastard. We used a Jeep at first, then that got stuck, so we had to switch to one of those swamp buggies, the ones they use for crossing the hammocks, with a big old airplane engine in the back roaring away. He was trying to show us where he'd left the bodies, but hell, there'd been so much rain and sun, and that place, well, everything looks pretty much alike, and he wasn't the brightest light ever either, so we didn't come up with much. Ended up just charging him with the one case that we'd made him on. He went to the chair, always claiming there were others out there. Lots of others. And, you know, every so often some hunter or fisherman comes across some bones out in the woods and muck, and I used to think maybe it was that guy's handiwork, but there was no way of telling."

Simon Winter shook his head as he ransacked the memory.

"It bothered me for years. It still bothers me. All I could think about was all the people out there, mothers, fathers, brothers, sisters, hell I don't know, who didn't get an answer from me. You know, that's one of the most important jobs a policeman can provide: certainty. When you can give it out, no matter how terrible it is, then you must do it, because it is a helluva lot easier for people to live with even if it's the worst certainty in the world, than to be left not knowing. Damn that swamp. It can cover up anything."

Walter Robinson nodded. "Now we could fly over those spots

in a helicopter, shooting the terrain with an infrared camera, and pick up the heat from a decomposing body."

Winter sighed. "Science is wonderful."

"So . . ."

"Well, I remember thinking, listening to this guy, wondering when he was gonna quit, and he never quite did. You get this sensation that you've been dropped down a well. It's dark and dank and you might never get out, and even if you do, all you'll remember is the nightmare. I think our guy is a little like that."

Robinson took a deep breath. "I'm having some trouble sleeping. Even with . . ." He paused and Simon Winter filled in for him:

". . . pleasant company?"

"That's right. Even with company. That obvious, is it?"

Winter grinned. "I was a detective once."

Robinson gave a small shrug. "I had nightmares the other night."

"What sort of nightmares?"

"Pretty much what you'd expect. Where you're watching someone drown and you can't do anything about it. That sort of thing."

"You know what used to frighten me the most?"

"What?"

"That there were other guys, like this good old boy that killed seventeen, eighteen, or maybe more kids, and that they were out there and not only could I never get them, but that they'd live and do these terrible things to poor children who never had a chance, and then they'd grow progressively more awful and get old and finally die peacefully in their sleep, never touched, never threatened, never anything other than one hundred percent evil. And now, I'm old too, and I worry that maybe there isn't a Heaven and there isn't a Hell. Because, goddamn it, it truly bothers me to think that if we can't catch these guys on this earth, they can just disappear into the great oblivion without being held in the slightest way accountable. That's what gives me nightmares."

Walter Robinson rubbed a finger across his forehead. "I hadn't thought of it that way."

"That's what makes this job so important, Walter. We like to think that there's a higher court. We hope there is, but there just might not be, and if there isn't, then it's completely up to us. Just us. Nobody else."

"You're a philosopher, Simon."

"Of course. All old men are."

"They *are* out there, you know. That's what we've learned, since you retired. Not just one or two, but more than we can count. Perverts of every stripe and color. Killers of unique styles and approaches."

"But this guy . . ." Winter glanced down at the composite drawing. "This guy isn't a sex fiend or a pervert or some star-crossed megalomaniac. He's not Bundy and he's not Gacy and he's not Charlie Manson. Something else motivates him."

"What do you think that is?"

"Hate."

"He hates his victims? But he barely knows them."

"No, he knows them well. Not them exactly, but who they are. But more importantly, he hates what they mean to him. They share a past. But I'll wager his hate goes back further. And what he wants to kill is history."

"What do you mean?"

"I mean, he has never known anything other than anger."

The younger man slowly bent his head to the picture. "That makes sense," he said after a moment. "Maybe that's what has me screwed up."

"How so?"

"I can understand perversion. I can understand blowing away the competition. I can understand shooting your husband for cheating on you. I've always been able to understand just about every reason for murder there is. But not this guy. Not yet. And that has me worried, Simon."

The old detective smiled. "I think," he said, "that perhaps I have not given you enough credit." Then he scratched at his head in a mock curious motion. "So, maybe if that is what moves this guy, don't you think we might try to find the source?"

"The source of his hatred?"

"Precisely."

Winter reached into a small backpack that he carried, which

contained some books and his notepad, and which made him think of himself as the oldest student walking the earth. He handed a piece of paper to Walter Robinson, who glanced at it quickly, then looked up with some confusion.

"What's this mean?" the detective asked. Then he read in a halting tone:

*"Geheime Staatspolizei Gbh. thirteen; Sec. 101."*

He looked up. "That's German, right?"

"Correct," Winter said. "That's my best guess at the military designation for the Jewish Bureau of Investigation. That's where the catchers worked. That was where our man got his training and discovered his vocation. I made a couple of calls too, over to the Holocaust Center and to a historian or two. They helped out. Now, what we need to do is find someone in Germany who has a list of the men who operated that section. Because someone else still alive will remember the Shadow Man, and maybe they'll know his name. The name may be changed, but it will be a start."

Robinson shook his head. "Do you think they kept a list of the killers they had working for them?"

"Yes. No. Maybe. I'll tell you what I've learned. I've learned that during the war the Germans kept lists and records of just about every damn crazy thing. They created this world that was completely upside down, where the laws protected the guilty and the criminals ran the courts. And because it was so bizarre, they became devoted to organization. Organization means paperwork. Sophie told me, right before she was killed, and I didn't hear her: *'Even when they were going to kill you, the Nazis had paperwork.'* So, I'd guess somewhere there is a list of the men who were in charge of the catchers. All the captains, lieutenants, and sergeants that handled all that paperwork. And now that there's no more East Germany, there are a lot of documents floating around over there. It's worth a try."

"But how . . ."

"Haven't you ever made an international inquiry before?"

"Well, sure. On that Colombian drug dealer I told you about. Contacted their police liaison . . ."

"So, let's do the same. In Germany. Same time, let's get in touch with the office of Special Prosecutions in the Justice

Department. You know, it seems like every so often an old Nazi turns up, and there's someone who deals with it. They would likely have a contact with the Germans."

"I don't know, Simon. Seems to me we should be concentrating here. . . ."

"Here, we're searching for a shadow. Over there, there's someone who knows this man as flesh and blood."

"Fifty years ago."

"But knows him, and that is something we will find valuable when we spring the trap."

"You're sure? They could all be dead. And they might not be willing to talk."

"Always possible, but if we don't try . . ."

"Then we won't know. Okay, I'm with you on that."

"Think of it this way. If you were a reporter at the *Herald* and you got a tip the Shadow Man was here, wouldn't you make those calls?"

"Probably."

"Well, we're not doing anything different. And we've got more resources. Why not get Miss Martinez to use her weight. State Attorney's Office will carry some impact with the German police. And remember, they're always sending those damn German tourists over here to Miami Beach. They might be eager to help."

Simon Winter smiled.

"The way I figure it," he continued, "when the Shadow Man walks into our trap, the spotlight we shine on him should be bright enough so that there is no way out."

Walter Robinson shrugged, and considered this to be an impossible idea. And then, just as swiftly, thought: Why not?

# TWENTY-TWO
## =THE EXPECTED CALL

**E**SPY Martinez worked the telephones steadily, doggedly, not altogether certain that she would find what they needed, but also not certain that they wouldn't.

As Walter Robinson and Simon Winter suggested, she had started with Special Prosecutions at the Justice Department in Washington, only to discover that this was a misnomer at best; she'd learned that Special Prosecutions was the smallest of offices, no longer manned on a full-time basis. It was more a designation assigned to whatever career attorney happened to be given a case file about a suspected Nazi. It had once been an actual office, but now had an accidental quality to it; as the years passed, it slipped out of the mainstream, dying out with the same ceaseless erosion that time had brought to the people it was supposed to hunt. There were only two active cases being handled: an allegation that a butcher in Milwaukee had once been a guard at the Treblinka concentration camp, and another, that a priest in a monastery in Minnesota had fifty years ago been a member of an S.S. Einsatzgruppen extermination squad in Poland. Both cases had been referred to the Immigration and Naturalization Service, where, as best as Espy Martinez could determine, they were shelved, awaiting the bureaucratic convenience that old age brings with death.

The State Department had been slightly more helpful; after a half-dozen calls, shuttling from office to office, a secretary had provided her with the police liaison number at the U.S. Embassy in Bonn.

She had persisted, working through the late afternoon and into the night, and finally was connected to a pseudomilitary type with an outgoing, friendly voice, who by happenstance was a native of Tallahassee, and therefore delighted to speak with someone from his home state. The liaison confirmed for her that German authorities would probably be willing, but hardly enthusiastic, to help her in her search—but only after she provided them with a name.

"These are Nazis I'm looking for," she said.

"Yes, ma'am, I understand that," the police liaison replied. "The police over here are cracking down on all sorts of neo-Nazi operations."

"I'm not interested in neo-Nazis," she said, thinking that somehow the long distance and the lateness of the hour were obscuring her words. "These would be real Nazis. Original Nazis, World War Two Nazis."

"Oh," the liaison answered. "Well, that might be a problem."

"How so?"

"Well, after the war the Allies, and then subsequently the West German authorities, designated a number of war criminals. But these were the upper-echelon types. The guys that had stuff to do with theory and planning. The people who carried out the orders, well, they were reassimilated mostly."

"You mean they just went back to doing whatever they were doing before the war?"

"Yes, ma'am. That was pretty much it. You see, if they'd tried to prosecute everybody who'd been a Nazi or worked for them, or helped in some way or another, hell, I guess they'd still be holding trials today. Now, of course, you got your exceptions to this. The concentration camp officials. People who participated in mass executions. That sort of thing. But I haven't heard of any of those cases being brought to trial, not for some time. You go through the Bundestag votes on this stuff, and you'll find a tangle of amnesties and pardons and redefinitions of what crimes were what. Then you'll find all sorts of statutes of limitations. Hell, they've even voted a couple of times on different laws trying to define what a murder was, during wartime."

The police liaison paused, then added:

"Memory's a funny thing, ma'am. Seems like the further we get from the war, the less people want to remember. Then you got all these new fascists demonstrating in the streets about foreigners, and committing assaults and even murders and waving swastikas and reading *Mein Kampf*. Authorities are pretty nervous about them."

"But lists . . . memberships, all the documentation . . ."

"Oh, you're right about that, ma'am. There's a list, somewhere. Probably one with all the names on it that you're interested in. But finding it, well, that's the problem. They have a huge document center here, but they're still sorting and cataloguing. Big job too, now that there are millions of other papers being sent over by the Russians and what used to be the East Germans. If you came over here, and if you were real persistent, I suspect you'd find someone over in that document center who could find what you needed. You get the names, then my police contacts would find them, if they're still alive. But that's a big job. You got some time on this, ma'am?"

"Not much."

The liaison seemed pessimistic. "You see, ma'am, the problem is, what you're looking for isn't considered a police matter. Not anymore. Now, it's a matter for historians. The world pretty much wants to get along and get ahead. Hell, you know over here it's a big damn issue what they say about that era in the classrooms. There's a significant percentage of people who either don't want it talked about at all or don't think it was all that damn bad. Except for the losing part, that is."

Espy Martinez sighed, wondering at what point murder slipped from the province of the police and prosecutors and became something for doctoral candidates.

The police liaison, with his slow North Florida drawl, seemed to hesitate, as if thinking.

"Well, miss, I'm not supposed to suggest this . . ."

Martinez sat up abruptly. "What is it?"

"Well, it seems to me you ought to try your questions on the only folks that are still real active in hunting Nazis. The kinda people who ain't all that interested in what the Bundestag says is a crime or not. I mean, there are a few people who think some crimes committed back then still deserve the world's attention."

"Who might that be?"

"I'm not giving you this number," the police liaison said. "I don't know you, and I will deny it should it ever come up. Politics, you know. We cooperate with the Germans. Best of friends about just about everything. But they get very touchy when it comes to former Nazis. Not what you'd call naturally forthcoming. Especially when the request comes from outside the borders. Don't like to be reminded of all those things much. And they aren't real fond of this old guy. He and his people have a way of reminding them about their, how shall we put it, uh, darker side."

"The number?"

"In fact, that's all they do. Remind people. Seems like an honorable thing to me, but then, anybody who's ever been a victim of any crime, much less the greatest crime ever committed, has a long memory."

"Who is it?"

"In Vienna. There is a place called the Simon Wiesenthal Center. Really just the old guy, who thank the Lord has a memory that will go on forever, and a few dedicated folks that work for him. But if anyone knows who operated that section in Berlin in 1943, well, they might. And they're gonna be a whole helluva lot more likely to help you when they learn what it is you're looking for. Then, maybe you get lucky, get a name or two, get back to me, and I'll get my police friends to provide us with an address before they get too suspicious."

The police liaison gave her a number and then disconnected the line. Espy Martinez thought, We all have memories of nightmare, and wondered why it was that the world was so eager to forget them. For an instant she was reminded of her murdered brother, and told herself that she would never forget what happened to him, no matter what arrived in her life. Then, just as swiftly, she wondered whether that was a wise thing. Then, be-

cause she did not like to examine herself as much as all that, she
stared down at the number and picked up the receiver.

As with most international calls, it took her some time to get
through, and then she was forced to leave a message, so that it
was nearly an hour before someone returned the call. The someone was a young woman, who sounded to be the same age as she,
although the woman spoke in English tinged with education and a
distinctive accent that Espy Martinez could not categorize. It was
not German. She identified herself as Edie Wasserman, and said
she was a worker at the center. The center's namesake, she said
quickly, was receiving an award in Israel, and unavailable.

"But what is it that you are interested in, Miss Martinez?"

"I am trying to find someone who worked in a particular section in Berlin, during the war."

"Do you have the section number?"

"Yes, as best as we can figure it out. Section 101, Geheime
Staatzpolizei . . ."

"The Gestapo. They were better at destroying records than
many other groups. The S.S. for example. Their cruelty sometimes seemed matched only by their arrogance. Yes. So, you are
interested in the Gestapo in Berlin in 1943. This is curious. A
prosecutor in Miami today wonders about the Gestapo in Berlin
long before she was born. Most unusual. What is this particular
section?"

"The Jewish Bureau of Investigation," Espy Martinez
answered.

There was a pause from the young woman on the end of the
line so distant. When she replied, it was slowly.

"Yes, we know of this section," she said. "The catchers?"

"Yes."

"A prosecutor in Miami, Florida, in the United States of
America calls us one day, how do you say? Out of the blue? Inter-
ested in the catchers? This is most intriguing, Miss Martinez.
What is it that you wish to know?"

"I am seeking information about an individual who was called
the Shadow Man. . . ."

"Der Schattenmann is dead, Miss Martinez."

Again silence slipped into the air in front of her.

"Why do you say that?"

"Because when a woman named Kubler who had been known as the Blond Ghost, who did much the same as Der Schattenmann, was arrested and tried, she was asked what became of some of the other catchers, and she said they were shipped east on the last few transports. You know what that meant, do you not, Miss Martinez? It meant you were dead."

"But you know of that section?"

"Yes. Much information came out of the records of Kubler's trial, which were only recently available, because she was tried and imprisoned in East Germany. Many names that we did not know. Some other documents are given to us privately. But Gestapo records are quite precious, Miss Martinez. And therefore, alas, not complete. But why is it that you are interested in this man who is by all accounts dead today? You are not a historian or a journalist?"

"Because I don't think he is dead."

"Der Schattenmann alive? You have proof?"

"I have deaths, Miss Wasserman. People who believe they saw this man here, and then were killed."

"People? Who could recognize Der Schattenmann?"

"A handful of survivors."

Espy Martinez could hear the young woman's sharp intake of breath, followed by a long silence, before she said: "I must know more. I will help you however I can, but we must know more. If this man is alive, then he must be found and punished. This is important, Miss Martinez. Critical."

"Names. I need names. If we can find out who he once was, then perhaps we can find out who he is now."

"Yes, yes," Wasserman answered. "I will do this now. I will call you back when I get some information. Names."

She hung up, leaving Espy Martinez to think that she was making some progress. She thought of calling Walter Robinson to update him, but decided to hold off until she actually knew something. So, instead, she paced about her small office impatiently, fiddling with other cases that she had pending that had been neglected and forgotten. This simply enervated her more, and before too long she thrust these files aside and simply sat at her desk, staring at the telephone. Time seemed to fray the edges of Espy Martinez's patience as she waited for the woman in Austria to call back.

It was past one when the phone finally rang.

"Miss Martinez?"

"Miss Wasserman?"

"I have some names for you, but I must extract a promise first."

"What is that?"

"That if this is true, if you succeed in finding the Shadow Man alive, that you will share what you learn with us. Not merely who he is, but how he escaped death in 1944 and how he arrived in the United States. All the details of his past, Miss Martinez. There is nothing that would not interest us." She paused, then added: "He sent many to their deaths, Miss Martinez. And there are some we believe he may have killed himself. This is a man who many will want to see brought to justice."

"That is what I'm trying to do, Miss Wasserman," Martinez said.

"I think we may not be speaking of the same justices."

"I will provide you with all the information I can, as long as I don't jeopardize my case here. You are interested in deaths that took place fifty years ago. But I want to prosecute him for killings that are here and now."

"I understand."

Again the woman hesitated. "There is a sensation, Miss Martinez, when you finally get close to one of these men. S.S. men, usually. Camp personnel. There is a special coldness about them. Perhaps it comes from living with such immense lies for so long that they come to not believe they did anything wrong. . . ."

There was another silence, before the woman concluded:

"Here are five names from our files, which is the best I can do on such short notice. I will keep working, though. Two men held the equivalent rank of major, which would have meant they were in their thirties or forties back in 1943, so I would not expect much from them, if they are still alive. The other three were a captain and two sergeants. They, perhaps, would have been younger, but of less importance. Good luck. I doubt they will cooperate, even if they do know something. But one never knows."

Espy Martinez wrote down the names. She stared at them, slowly drinking coffee, as she waited for morning in Berlin. At eight A.M. she dialed the number for the police liaison in Bonn overseas. To her surprise, he was at his desk.

"Any success, Miss Martinez?"

"Perhaps. You were right. They were eager to help. . . ."

"Good. I thought they might."

"I have some names. Could you get them run through some sort of data bank? Tax rolls? Driver's licenses? All would be elderly. . . ."

"Let me see what I can do. Stick by your phone. I'll simply tell the police these names have come up in a Stateside murder investigation. I'll tell them we're looking for some next of kin, or something. The police will be wary, but we'll see."

She rocked back in her seat and watched the second hand of her wall clock sweep about. Exhaustion began to cling to her thoughts, and she rubbed a hand across her face. She put her head down on her desk.

The ringing of the telephone awakened her. Startled, she almost lost her balance on her seat as she reached out for the receiver. She glanced at the clock and saw that it was nearly five A.M., and she felt a momentary dizziness as she answered the phone. It was the police liaison in Bonn.

"Miss Martinez?"

"Yes."

"Well, burning the midnight oil, I see. You must really want this guy something fierce. What's the weather like home in Florida?"

She shook the sleep from her eyes as quickly as possible. "Well, as best as I can tell, the weather is a constant sixty-eight degrees here in the Justice Building. I haven't been out for hours."

"I miss it, you know. No palm trees over here. None of that good old Florida sticky goddamn hot either. Don't know how nice it is until you land someplace cold, like Germany."

"I guess not."

"Well, here's what I have for you. Of those five names, only two seemed to produce any possibilities, when I factored in age and location. Those were the men you thought held the sergeant's ranks. One of the guys, Friedman, well, that's like Smith in New York. List ran into the hundreds. The other, well, Wilmschmidt, is a little less common. Still, got a couple of dozen names across the country. I can fax you the entire list for both."

"Okay," she said wearily. "That would be fine. I can start . . ."

"Well, I'll send you those, but there was one name that kinda jumped out at me that I figure you might want to start with."

Espy Martinez straightened up. "How so?"

"Well, age would be right, and he's still living in a Berlin suburb, but more importantly, the records check showed he's a retired policeman. On the force dating back to the 1940s. Remember what I said about assimilation during the Occupation?"

"Of course."

"Well, Miss Martinez, you got to understand what this country looked like in 1945. Just death and rubble. That was pretty much it. You remember your history? The Berlin airlift? Anyway, someone had to keep order, and so the Allies generally picked the people with experience. So, even if you were Gestapo once, it wasn't hard to make the leap to the postwar police. I'm just guessing now, but that would be my first choice for your mystery man. You've been pretty damn lucky so far, why not try him?"

She took the number down and gave the police liaison the fax number for the Dade State Attorney's Office. She looked at the number for a moment, trying to collect her wits, shaking the residual exhaustion from her consciousness.

Why not? she asked herself. Worth a try.

She dialed the number, not at all certain what she would say.

It rang a half-dozen times before being answered.

"Allo?"

"Hello. I'm trying to reach a gentleman named Klaus Wilmschmidt. Is this he?"

*"Vas ist das? Nich sprechen englisch. Eine minuten . . ."*

The phone was silent, then a hesitant, younger voice came on.

"Hello? What is this, please?"

"Do you speak English?"

"Yes. Who is this, please?"

"My name is Martinez. I am a prosecutor with the Dade State

Attorney's Office in Miami, Florida. I am in the midst of a murder investigation and I believe that a Mr. Klaus Wilmschmidt can provide us with some relevant information. I'm trying to reach him."

"Yes, this is his home. I am his daughter. But murder? What is this? He has never been to the United States."

Espy Martinez heard someone in the background asking a question in German, and the daughter hushed the man as she continued.

"The information we are searching for dates back fifty years ago. To Gestapo Section 101 in Berlin, during the war. Is that where your father worked?"

There was no reply.

"Miss Wilmschmidt?"

Again the line was silent.

"Miss Wilmschmidt?"

She heard a burst of German being spoken on the other end, a quick, snapping exchange before the daughter replied: "Those times are past. He cannot help you. I will not allow it." The woman's voice quavered.

Espy Martinez spoke swiftly. "I'm trying to find out about a man who worked in that section. A man who may have committed murders today. It's important. Your father may simply have some information—"

"He will not speak of those times. They are gone, miss . . . I did not get your name . . ."

"Martinez."

". . . Miss Martinez. He is old and those times are long ago in our history and he has lived a good life, Miss Martinez. He was a policeman and a fine man. I will not bring those times up to him. Now he is old and he is not well, Miss Martinez. He is not well, and deserves to live out his time on this earth in peace. So I will not help you, no."

"Miss Wilmschmidt, please, just one question. Just ask him if he knew of a man called Der Schattenmann? If the answer is no, then—"

"I will not. He is not well. He deserves peace."

"Miss Wilmschmidt . . ."

Before she could complete her plea, she again heard the gruff voice in the background demanding something in German, followed by a racking series of coughs. She heard the young woman angrily reply, and there was a sharp exchange of heated words before the daughter's voice once again came over the line.

"What was the name you spoke, Miss Martinez?"

"Der Schattenmann."

Martinez heard the woman turn away from the phone and utter the name. Then there was silence. After a considerable pause, she heard more German echo over the distance. Then the young woman came back on the line. There was an odd hesitancy in her voice, as if she had seen something she was unsure about, but that might be terrifying.

"Miss Martinez?"

"Yes?" She heard the policeman's daughter battle a sob.

"My father says he will speak with you, if you will come here so that he may see your face."

"He knows?"

"I am surprised. He has never spoken of those times, not at least with any—" She stopped, gasping a quick breath, before continuing. "You will come here? He cannot travel. He is far too ill. But he will speak to you."

Again the woman paused. In the background, once again, Espy Martinez heard German being spoken.

"This is the most unusual thing to say." The voice on the phone had a tremor within it.

"What is that?" Espy Martinez asked.

"He said he has been waiting every day for fifty years for your phone call."

# TWENTY-THREE

## *THE MAN WHO ONCE* ═══════*TAUGHT DEATH*

**W**ALTER Robinson was standing a few feet away from the bodies of an elderly man and woman. They were side by side, stretched out on their bed, inside an expensive, well-kept apartment that overlooked the ocean. The man wore a tuxedo, the woman a slightly dated, long, off-white satin evening dress, and they gave the appearance of a couple just returned from a New Year's Eve celebration. The woman's makeup was carefully applied, and diamond earrings glistened every time a police photographer snapped a picture. The man seemed to have trimmed his brushy, white mustache and slicked his hair down. He had taken care to fold a bright red silk breast-pocket handkerchief so that it splashed color across the black jacket, giving him a rakish, devil-may-care look even in death.

An empty vial of sleeping tablets was placed on a bedside table, next to two half-filled champagne flutes. A bottle of Perrier Jouet, with the etched flowers on the green glass, stood at solitary attention in a puddle of water inside a silver ice bucket.

He wished they'd left a suicide note, but couldn't find one. The couple, however, had taken the time to arrange all their important papers, insurance policies, copies of their wills, their mortgage, their bank statements, in a neat pile on the dining room table. He noticed that on their balcony there was a table with some potted plants, and he stepped outside and touched the dirt in each planter and felt that it was damp. He took a long, deep breath of the humid predawn air. He looked out toward the sea, feeling the darkness around him thin ever so slightly as the minutes crept toward morning.

He stepped back inside. In the bedroom, the lead detective was making notes on the double suicide, and Robinson approached him.

"They watered the plants too," he said.

"I guess they took care of everything," said the other detective. "They even left a stack of envelopes addressed to relatives, and a list of instructions for the funeral home."

"Any idea why?"

The detective nodded. "Right on top."

He handed Walter Robinson a manila envelope, and Robinson pulled out the papers contained inside. These were reports and a letter from a medical office clipped to a small booklet entitled *Understanding Alzheimer's Disease*.

"I guess they understood, all right," the detective said. "It wasn't too hard to see what was coming down the pike. Easier to go now, than try to fight that disease."

Robinson shook his head. "Can't see it," he said. "Can't see giving up a minute of life, no matter how lousy."

"Hell, Walt, what's so special about life anyway?"

Robinson was about to answer this question when the pager on his belt went off. He went into the kitchen to answer his call.

The Beach message center operator had a crass, businesslike voice. "Detective, I have two messages. They came in almost simultaneously."

"Yes?"

"You're to call A.S.A. Martinez at her office. And I have an urgent request that you meet with a Sergeant Lionel Anderson of the City of Miami police."

"Lion-man?"

"He gave me this address: King Apartments. Said you'd know which one. Said you have a problem with a witness."

"A problem?"

"That's what he said. He didn't say what sort of problem."

Robinson disconnected the operator and called Espy Martinez. When she picked up the telephone, he joked: "Isn't there some song about working hard just so's you can end up on the late shift?"

She smiled through her exhaustion. "I don't want to make a practice out of it."

"Any luck?"

"Yes. I think so."

His eyebrows shot upward and surprise curled around the edges of his reply. "Really? What have you got?"

"A man who knew the Shadow Man, way back, during the war."

"Where is he?"

"Berlin. And he's old and sick and he has a daughter who doesn't want him to talk to anyone about those times. He'll only talk face-to-face."

"Go," Robinson said impulsively. "Go right now."

Martinez breathed out slowly. "That's what I thought too."

"Just go and talk to the man. Whatever we learn—"

"I made a reservation. Could you come?"

"That would be nice. But I don't think so. The brass would never authorize this sort of potential wild goose chase."

"Do you think it is?"

"No. Because nothing in this case is as it seems. So, go find this old man and talk to him. Can you fly out today?"

"There's an afternoon flight that connects in London. I can sleep on the plane."

"Talk to him, then come back. Maybe you'll get a name, and all I'll have to do is look the bastard up in the phone book, get a nice arrest warrant, and everyone can go back to working normal hours."

"Nothing in the world is ever that easy. What will you do while I go gallivanting about Europe?"

"Well, right now, I'm going over to see our main witness. I got a message that there's some problem with Jefferson."

"Mr. Leroy fucking Jefferson. What sort of problem?"

"Won't know until I get there. He's probably complaining because crack cocaine prices went up while he was in jail and he wants to hold me personally responsible. Going right now. Let me know when your return flight arrives and I'll meet you. And let me know what this guy says. What was he, a Nazi?"

"A Nazi and a cop."

Walter Robinson smiled. "Hell. That's what every punk we arrest and every lawyer who represents them accuses us of being. It might be interesting to meet someone who actually was."

Early dawn light seemed to chase him across the causeway, dogging his steps as he drove from the Beach to Liberty City and the King Apartments. The routine fatigue of a night spent in the presence of unremarkable death made him feel as if his reactions had slowed and his thinking dulled, almost like a man close to the legal point of intoxication, but not quite. He had a certain light-headedness, which made his concentration wander. He wished he were joining Espy Martinez at the airport, but realized this was impossible. And he had a vague, unfocused fear that seemed to halo his thoughts whenever he worried about Frieda Kroner and Rabbi Rubinstein. He had only partially heeded Simon Winter's suggestion that they be left without police protection. He had ordered a pair of unmarked cars manned by officers out of uniform to watch their apartments. He did not know for certain whether the Shadow Man was stalking them, but he suspected he was, in a steady, unimpulsive way. Still, even if so, Robinson had the sense that he was making progress; he had a picture and a description and a witness and the partial thumbprint as evidence. Enough for a conviction. Now, all that remained was a name, and he thought that would arrive soon enough, especially after they set in motion Winter's scheme to flush the Shadow Man from hiding.

So, if not altogether confident, he at least felt things were in hand, and he yawned once or twice and rubbed his forehead as he rolled slowly down Twenty-second Avenue and turned toward Leroy Jefferson's home.

He saw the gathered police cruisers first; this made all the exhaustion flee from his eyes. Then he spotted the crime scene technicians' van, which gave him an electric shock of anxiety. He pulled his car to the curb sharply and pushed his way through a small gathering of the curious, the pale early morning light giving their skin a wan, lukewarm pallor. He waved at the uniformed officers holding the crowd back on the sidewalk and hurried toward the apartment building. He ignored the dilapidated elevator, choosing instead to bound up the exterior stairs.

He saw Juan Rodriguez and Lionel Anderson standing amidst a half-dozen other policemen outside the door to Jefferson's apartment. There were several plainclothes men working the area, one with a fingerprint kit, going over the door.

Sergeant Lion-man saw him first and directed a small, helpless gesture at the apartment.

"Where's Jefferson?" Walter Robinson demanded.

"Inside," Anderson replied. "What's left of him."

Rodriguez stepped aside, to allow him to enter the room. "Watch your step, Walt, amigo. There's blood pretty much every fucking place."

The light pouring through the doorway glinted off the tubular steel frame of the wheelchair. There was a thick, stifling sense of warmth and blood, a mustiness in the air as if the room had been superheated by both the tropical summer and murder. Robinson moved slowly toward the body; he forced himself to compartmentalize, to try to see every single detail inside the room in separate and complete fashion; Jefferson's eyes remained open; he'd watched his own murder. Robinson shuddered and stared hard at the duct tape that encircled Jefferson's wrists, and saw that a second strip had been placed across Jefferson's mouth, to keep him silent. The gray tape was streaked with vibrant red around the edges, caked up at the corners of his mouth. His eyes took in a sea of deep crimson blood that stained the floor beneath the chair. He saw that the bandages on Jefferson's ruined knee were ripped and torn, and he thought it obvious that Jefferson had known real pain in his last moments.

He felt an odd combination of sadness and anger. He wanted to curse at Jefferson, to grab him by the shoulders and shake him back to life. Instead, he swore beneath his breath, a quiet flood of obscenities as he took in the murder scene and felt all the confidence he'd had on the drive across the bay unraveling.

A flashbulb went off, and Robinson saw the medical examiner

lean down next to the body and gently lift the dead man's head, examining a long scarlet slice in the skin of the throat.

"Is that what killed him?" the detective asked.

"Maybe. Maybe not. Hard to say," the medical examiner replied, shaking his head.

"What, then?"

The medical examiner stood up slowly. "I think he drowned."

"Drowned? How?"

"Cut someone in the throat just right, tip the head back, and it just pours back down the airways, filling the lungs. Not a nice way to go. Takes a few minutes. Don't lose consciousness. But that's just an educated guess for right now. Look at this guy. He's been sliced up like someone took a Cuisinart to him. A lot of little cuts that won't kill you."

A detective moving near the side of the room looked up. "Sort of like one of those late night television commercials, you know? For the Veg-O-Matic. Slices, dices, chops—whatever."

A couple of cops laughed, and continued inspecting the room.

"Your witness, right?" the medical examiner asked.

"Yes."

"Not anymore. What was it, a drug case? I haven't seen this sort of thing since the late Seventies, when the Colombians and the Cubans were arguing about who owned the cocaine trade. They were partial to knives. Especially those electric ones—you know, the type your mother-in-law gives you for Christmas. They used to like to use those on each other. Slowly. Not exactly what your mother-in-law had in mind."

"No, not a drug case. A murder investigation."

"Really? I'd swear it was a drug case. You don't usually see somebody get tortured like this if the general idea is to shut them up. Usually just a nice quick bullet."

"This isn't the usual sort of case."

"Well, somebody sure took their sweet time about all this. Somebody who sure enjoys their work."

Before Robinson could reply, one of the other detectives joined in. "Hey, Walt, you know we found some crack cocaine spread around. Just a little, you know. And this guy had a long history of burning other dealers. I mean, maybe he was helping you, but he sure had a lot of bad-ass enemies out here in the real world. A lot of guys capable of carving up old Leroy there without too much thought and not a whole lot of concern over the poor slob. The guy he was helping you on, you sure that dude knew enough to come over here and do him like this?"

"I don't know. I didn't think he knew anything about Jefferson."

"Well, Jefferson made the paper the other day. Maybe that tipped him off."

"I still don't see how he made the connection. Shit."

"This guy you're looking for ... he a black guy? On the Beach?"

"No. He's a white guy. An old white guy."

A couple of the other detectives working the room stopped when they heard this. One shook his head in an exaggerated fashion.

"You think an old white guy came down here to the jungle in the middle of the night and did this? Not fucking likely," the detective said. "I mean, don't want to rain on your parade, Walt, but an old white guy? Down here? After dark?"

"No. I think he did."

"Well, maybe. Maybe once in a zillion years some old-timer could come down here and not get taken off himself. I'm not saying it couldn't happen, but hey, Walt, get real. My money is on the neighborhood crack distributors. This looks like the sort of thing they'd get hot for."

"Have you got any witnesses?" Robinson asked. "Anybody in the building see or hear anything?"

The detective smiled. "In the King Apartments? Somebody see something and then tell us about it? Forget it. And anyway, after what they did to Leroy, here, do you think someone else is going to be real interested in shooting their mouth off, and maybe taking *their* turn trying to explain why they talked to the cops to someone as handy with a knife as the psycho that did this?"

Robinson shook his head, and thought: It's useless.

He stepped away from the macabre tableau in the center of the room and leaned up against a wall, thinking that he was completely, totally certain that the Shadow Man had found a way into the apartment and was waiting for Jefferson, and that each slice in the junkie's body was like some exotic signature that only he could read. He recognized a fundamental truism in the responses of the other policemen: It didn't make sense that an elderly white man from Miami Beach would come to the center of the inner city to kill a low-life junkie and wannabe drug dealer, but he was certain that was what had happened. He also knew that anyone killing Leroy Jefferson was likely to get away with it. No one cared much about Leroy Jefferson either in life or death.

He took a deep breath.

Leroy Jefferson is merely dead, he told himself. The detectives working the case will shake a few informants, try to play one gang against another, see if they can't come up with a name that way. But they aren't really going to care, any more than I would. They'll maybe put in a little extra effort because he was a State's witness, but they understand the drill. You play on the fringe, you got to accept what's coming to you, and there was no one in the world who would say that, in a perverse way, Leroy Jefferson, Leroy fucking Jefferson, hadn't gotten precisely what the heavens were always expected to deliver to him. He'd only received it a little slower and more painfully than was the norm. A bullet in a drive-by shooting would have been statistically more appropriate. He thought there hadn't been much to like about Leroy Jefferson, but more, he hated how close they were, just as the murdered man had said. Could it have been me? Walter Robinson asked himself. If I'd taken a wrong step, made a bad decision, then I might have ended up like this: no suit, no badge, no lover, no future.

He looked over at the body and thought: No matter how far you travel away from this, it will always be there. It was like staring into a nightmare, one that was much closer to him than the vision the old couple lying peacefully on their bed had created earlier in the morning. He tried to imagine himself and Espy Martinez, old, together, and drinking champagne as they swallowed handfuls of sleeping tablets.

Walter Robinson let out a long, slow sigh.

He felt an abrupt chill, almost as if some bizarrely lost cold wind had singled him out from all the other policemen processing the room. He looked up toward the open eyes of Leroy Jefferson and thought: Was he waiting here for you when I dropped you off?

He knew the answer to this.

He remembered his offer to accompany Jefferson to the apartment, and in that second he imagined himself reaching for his weapon as the Shadow Man reached for him. He wondered: Would I have made it?

He did not think so.

He asked himself: Would he kill a cop too?

Again the answer was yes. He did not think the Shadow Man cared the slightest for the ordinary conventions of criminality, which held that killing a policeman was a considerably worse crime than eviscerating a drug-dealing State's witness.

He will kill anyone whom he perceives as a threat.

Robinson shuddered involuntarily, then looked around the room to see if any of the other policemen had seen the quiver in his shoulders. His eyes met Sergeant Lion-man's, and for just an instant the two of them locked, and the burly policeman nodded in understanding. Robinson breathed in hard, and saw the medical examiner hover again around the dead man's body.

One of the other detectives saw the same. "What's so interesting, Doc?" he called out.

The medical examiner was a small, bookish man, with delicate features and a bald spot on his head that glistened with sweat. He sometimes whistled while he worked on a body, a detail that caused no end of amusement amongst homicide detectives.

"I was just looking at this tape around the victim's lips," he replied. "Very strange."

"What's so strange?" the detective asked. The other men stopped working and looked his way.

"Well, for one thing, I don't understand all this blood caked up here and here. See, if the killer puts the tape on his mouth to shut him up, then cuts his throat so's he drowns, well, all the blood would be where most of it is. There wouldn't be any on his mouth. Gravity, you know. Liquid flows downhill."

"So, what are you saying?" Walter Robinson heard someone ask.

"I'm saying, something else caused this blood."

"Maybe he smashed him in the mouth before slapping on the tape?"

"Maybe. But no other external signs of a beating. Just signs of knife work."

The medical examiner whistled for a moment, a vaguely recognizable tune from a Broadway show. Then he reached out and put his fingers around the edge of the tape.

"Just can't stand waiting," he said quietly. "Never could, even when I was a kid. Birthdays. Christmas. Always wanted to see what was inside those packages." As he said this, he ripped the tape from the dead man's lips. It made a sucking sound.

The other men turned and looked. For a moment Robinson's vision was obscured by the medical examiner's body.

"I'll be damned." The medical examiner stepped back. "Well, I guess it's safe to say that someone was displeased with the victim's conversational style."

The doctor turned toward Walter Robinson, who saw that he held Leroy Jefferson's tongue in his hand. It had been sliced out at its roots.

By the time she was settled into her connecting flight from London to Berlin, Espy Martinez was snared by the inevitable tug of conflicting sensations: exhausted by erratic sleep and air travel, energized by the thought that she was doing something that might matter. She found her daydreams filled with successes; imagined headlines, envisioned the accolades from her officemates. She pictured herself and Walter Robinson linked by good fortune and public prosperity, and thought that high-profile triumph would allow her to force him upon her reluctant, antique parents, creating an avenue where even their prejudice would have to take a backseat to accolades.

She did not really think of the Shadow Man as anything other than a device for advancement. Ambitions in love and career were all she could concentrate on, as the jet engines droned outside and she sliced through the dark European sky. That she was thousands of miles from her home, and from the case in hand, was lost on her. She saw nothing unique in her destination, only that there was a witness that needed to be interviewed and that he might provide her with a name, and that might be all that she and Walter Robinson needed.

As the lateness of the hour settled on her, she worked on her list of questions for the old man she had traveled to see. She did not understand that she was somehow stepping into the history of nightmare. Simon Winter would have, as would the rabbi and Frieda Kroner. Walter Robinson might have begun to comprehend this, but as her flight began its approach into Berlin's airport, he was fighting nausea in a sterile autopsy chamber at the Dade County Medical Examiner's Office, watching as the physician carefully documented each of the dozens of slices in Leroy Jefferson's body, thinking, as each was noted on a form, that he could no longer underestimate the man he was hunting.

She exchanged some money at a kiosk inside the terminal and took a cab to the Hilton Hotel. She left instructions with the desk clerk that she should be awakened at eight in the morning, which was an hour before the police liaison from Bonn was scheduled to meet her.

For a moment, before crawling into bed, she looked out the window of her hotel room. What she saw was a modern city spread out under a night sky. She did not feel that far from home.

Timothy Schultz, the police liaison, was waiting for her in the lobby of the hotel. He was a thickset man, in his fifties, with close-cropped, military-style hair and a pleasant southern accent. As she exited the elevator, he rose from an overstuffed chair and advanced on her, hand extended.

"Well, hell, Miss Martinez," he said, "it sure is nice to meet someone from the great State of Florida, even if it is the wrong end of it."

"Glad to meet you, Mr. Schultz. Let me thank you again for all your help."

"No big deal. And anyway, most of the time I spend handling FBI queries about terrorists and international jewel thieves and all sorts of business scams. So, I got to admit, your request sure was a whole helluva lot more interesting than the usual thing come knocking over the telex. Wouldn't have missed this for the world."

"The daughter said she would translate for me. . . ."

"Well, then I'll just sort of back her up."

Espy Martinez nodded, her mouth open slightly, as if to ask something, but the police liaison anticipated it.

"I know, I know. I know what y'all are thinking. You're thinking how is it this good old boy from Pensacola lands over here, and he sure doesn't sound like he can talk one word of the lingo, ain't that right, Miss Martinez?"

"Well, the thought crossed my mind."

"Not too complicated. My grandparents were both German immigrants and I grew up in their house, 'cause my daddy ran out on us when I was still little. The old folks kept up the language, and so I learned it young. There you have it."

They started to walk across the lobby.

"You want me to give you the scenic tour, Miss Martinez? Or are you in a hurry to talk to this old guy before his daughter gets him to change his mind?"

"Mr. Schultz, tourism isn't what I'm here for."

He nodded and shrugged. "I'm thinking you're gonna get a different kind of tour," he said.

They drove through the city, and despite Espy Martinez's quiet attempts to focus on the upcoming interview, the police liaison kept up a steady travelogue, pointing out the sights of the city. Where the Wall once stood, parks, buildings, and a river flowed past the windshield. She found herself looking up occasionally when something he said spurred some memory. He drove her past the Iranishestrasse address of the Jewish Bureau of Investigation, but the building had been replaced by a modern office complex. Schultz explained to her that Berlin, like many European cities, had more lives than the proverbial cat; centuries of building had made it old and venerable, only to have the war turn it into a bombed-out world of rubble. The fifty years since the war had been filled with rebuilding, but hampered by the years spent divided between East and West. The result was an odd hodgepodge of architectures and ages. He laughed, and asked her to envision Miami fifty years earlier.

The old Nazi lived in tract housing outside the center of the city. It had a determined suburban feel to it, slightly alien, as if a poor model of an American concept. There was an insistent uniformity to the houses: white stucco, with dark slate roofs, trim gardens and shrubs, uncluttered streets. There was an orderliness to it all that made her feel uncomfortable.

Schultz noticed this, and said, "You got to remember, Miss Martinez. The Germans like things lined up and at attention. Everything in its place." He pulled to a stop in front of one of the homes. "Here we go," he said. "Should be interesting."

They were a few feet from the front door when it cracked open slowly, and she saw a striking woman standing hesitantly in the portal.

"Miss Wilmschmidt?"

The woman nodded. There was an awkward moment when she did not open the door, but then, as if still doubtful about what she was allowing to happen, the woman swung the door wide and gestured for them to enter. She was tall, in her mid-thirties, but thin-waisted, like a fashion model, with a wave of reddish-brown hair gently littered with gray, which only made her seem more elegant. She wore fashionable eyeglasses that hung from a retaining strap down onto an expensive white silk shirt. Her clothes, though, reflected her attitude: a chocolate skirt and dark stockings, a black blazer. Despite her stylishness, she had a spinster librarian's quality to her, a cold, tight, angry attitude. As Espy Martinez and the police liaison stepped into the small house, the woman said: "I wish you were not here, Miss Martinez. I wish that this was not happening."

"I'm sorry to intrude," Martinez answered. "I appreciate whatever help your father—"

"He is sick. I do not know the word in English. He cannot breathe. Because of the smoking. I do not know what you would call it."

"Emphysema?"

"Perhaps that is it. He is not supposed to become excited. That you understand."

"Of course. We'll try to keep this short."

"That would be good. I am supposed to return to the bank this afternoon. That is where I work."

"I'll try to be brief."

The daughter nodded, although clearly she did not believe this. At the same moment, there was a burst in German, which echoed from the rear of the house: *"Maria! Bring sie herein!"*

The woman hesitated. "Already he is too excited," she said.

*"Bring sie herein!"*

Maria Wilmschmidt swung her hand halfheartedly in the direction of the voice. Espy Martinez heard a series of painful coughs as they maneuvered through the narrow central corridor of the small, two-bedroom house.

The old Nazi lay in pajamas and dark dressing gown on a single, wooden-frame bed inside a still, cramped room. A sole window, framed by thick white curtains, allowed some gray daylight to enter the room. There were no pictures on the walls. The only other furniture was a beaten brown bureau and a bedside table littered with vials of pills and a water jug. A tall oxygen tank with a pale green mask stood next to the bed. In a corner a television set played soundlessly. The old man had been watching reruns of American television shows. In one corner, as if thrown there, was a pile of magazines and paperback books.

"Mr. Wilmschmidt, I am Espy Martinez. . . ."

She could see the blue tinge to his nose and the red flush of his cheeks caused by blood vessels starved for air. He wheezed harshly as he waved her into the room. She saw that he had large hands, with long, aristocratic fingers, though they were stained yellow at the nails. She realized that he had once been a large, thick man, but no longer; the disease that robbed him of air had gnawed away at his body as well, so that flaps of flaccid skin hung from his bones, giving her the impression that he was someone who was being devoured from within by his own illness.

*"Maria, bring Stühle fur die Gäste!"* Bring chairs for the guests! He coughed.

As the daughter responded, Espy Martinez thought him a man who never asked, only ordered. In a moment the daughter returned with three steel folding chairs, which she arranged by the bed.

Martinez sat down, nodded toward the daughter for translation, and said: "Mr. Wilmschmidt, I am investigating several murders that have been committed by a man once known here in Berlin as the Shadow Man. We do not know his current identity, so we are searching for anyone who might have known him and who can tell us about him."

The daughter dutifully translated.

The old man nodded. "So, he kills still, even today," he replied.

"Yes," Martinez said after listening to the translation.

"I am not surprised. *Er hat sein Handwek gut gelernt.* He learned his trade well."

"Who trained him?"

The old man hesitated, then smiled. "I did."

There was a momentary pause, and the daughter gasped and spoke rapidly to her father in German: "You should not speak of this! *Das bring nicht Gutes!* No good will come of it! You did only what you were told, nothing more! You did what others did, you were no different! Why should you help these people? *Das bring nicht Gutes!*" she implored.

Espy Martinez glanced at Timothy Schultz, but he was listening intently for the old man's reply.

"Just because I did what I was ordered, do you think it means nothing?"

The daughter shook her head, but didn't answer.

He turned to Espy Martinez: "My daughter is ashamed of the past and that makes her frightened. She worries what the neighbors will think. She worries what her employers at the bank will think. She worries what the world will think. I do not have so much time that I worry at all. We did what we did! The world trembled and rose up against us! And so, we were defeated, but the ideas, they have never died, have they? Whether they were right or wrong, they still live, do they not? You Americans should understand this better than anyone else. Do you understand, Miss Martinez?"

"Of course," she replied, after hearing the translation.

"*Nichts verstehen sie!* You understand nothing!"

The old man snorted, and this turned into a protracted cough.

"You cannot understand," he said, with a small snarl that maneuvered on his face into a twisted grin. "I was a policeman! I did not make the laws, only enforced them. When the laws changed, I enforced the new laws. If the laws changed tomorrow, then I would change tomorrow."

Espy Martinez didn't reply, other than to think that he had already contradicted himself.

He coughed again and reached for the oxygen mask. There was a hissing sound as he turned on the bottle and drew in several long drafts.

He peered at Espy Martinez over the edge of the mask.

"*Der Schattenmann lebt also noch und bringt noch immer den Tod.* So, the Shadow Man lives and still brings death. I knew this. Without you telling me this was so, I knew it. I have known this was true for years. I was the last of our group to see him, but I knew then that he would not die. Will it be you that kills him, Miss Martinez?"

"No. I merely want to arrest him and prosecute him in a court of law. . . ."

The old man shook his head violently. "There are no laws for the Shadow Man, Miss Martinez. For me, yes. For you, yes. But for him, no. Tell me again, Miss Martinez: Will it be you that kills him?"

"No. It will be the State."

The old man laughed. A brittle sound in the small room. "And so, it was the same with us."

"These are not the same things."

He laughed again, mocking her. "Of course not."

She stopped, eyeing the old man. "You said you would help me," she said after a momentary silence.

"No. I told you I would tell you of the Shadow Man. I have been waiting all these years for someone to come to me and ask of him. I knew that this would happen before I died. I did not know who it would be. Sometimes I thought it would be some Jews, perhaps the ones that still hunt for the old ones. I thought it might perhaps be a policeman, like I was. Or maybe a journalist, or a student, or a scholar, someone who studies these great and evil things. Someone who wants to know about death. This is what I thought. This I expected, every day. When the telephone rang, I told myself, this will be the one. If there was a knock at the door, I thought, now they have finally found me and come to learn. Even as the years passed, Miss Martinez, I knew someone would come. I knew this."

"How did you know?"

"Because a man like the Shadow Man cannot exist in silence."

"You taught him?"

Klaus Wilmschmidt stared hard at her. Then he slowly reached toward a bedside table, opened a drawer, and produced a long, thin, black-handled dagger, with a death's-head skull adorning the tip of the grip. He held the blade gingerly, letting his finger slide down the steel.

"This, this would be used for ceremonial purposes, Miss Martinez. A killer's knife would be thicker, double-bladed, with a wider grip, so that you can turn it more easily."

He stared at her.

"Do you know how many ways there are to kill a man with a knife, Miss Martinez? Do you know that it is different from behind . . ." He drew the blade slowly from right to left in the air in front of him. ". . . than it is from the front?" He suddenly jabbed the knife upward, twisting as it slashed the space between them.

She said nothing, and he laughed again.

"Will it not make you a better policeman, Miss Martinez?"

"What?"

"The more you know about death, the better you will be at detecting it. Is this not so? It was for me. And for many others, like me. I think you probably know some men like me, Miss Martinez. It is just that it is not always so pleasant to admit it."

He laughed again.

*"Sie glauben wohl ich bin ein böser alter Mann,"* he said. "I must seem to you to be a terrible old man." When his daughter hesitated in her translation, he grunted at her, gesturing with the knife. "And perhaps I am so. But I will tell you a story, about the Shadow Man, and then you may do with it what you will."

"Maybe it would be better if I just asked questions—" Martinez started, but the sick man's glare made her stop. The daughter managed to blurt out a few words in German, and then halted as abruptly.

*"Ich erzähle euch jetzt die Geschichte,"* he said. "I will tell the

story." He reached to his side and seized the oxygen mask, cupping it across his face, breathing deeply.

"It was 1941 when I was transferred into Section 101, and I had just been promoted to the rank of sergeant. Sergeant! Not bad for the son of a coal hauler whose wife had to take in laundry to help make ends meet. These people, my parents, my daughter never knows of them, because they die in an air raid in 'forty-two."

The old man stared at his daughter.

*"Du weisst ja was Seide ist,"* he said sharply. "You know silk. Silk and Mercedes cars, because of your international bank. You know money. We knew none of that! I was raised poor and shall die poor!"

The daughter did not translate this, but Schultz did, quietly, beneath his breath. Espy Martinez saw the daughter's face constrict, and she knew that she was glimpsing some longtime pain between them.

"You do not care," the old Nazi continued. "And so, I do not care either." He turned away from his daughter and back to Espy Martinez.

"The transports were running constantly then. Roundups daily. Sometimes twice a day."

"Roundups?"

"Jews. Transports to the East. To the camps." He smiled. *"Diese Züge waren immer püunktlich.* Those trains always ran on time."

Espy Martinez tried to keep a poker face. "The Shadow Man?"

Klaus Wilmschmidt turned away, just for an instant, his eyes searching out the window. He stared at the glass.

"I can see nothing," he said bitterly. "I lie here, and all I can see is a corner of the neighbor's house and a little piece of the sky past it. There is no light." He spoke the last words rapidly, and he reached across for the oxygen mask again, as breath started to wheeze from his chest.

In a moment he turned back to Espy Martinez.

"The Shadow Man was in the major's office. I was called in . . ."

On his bed, the old man lurched into a position approximating a man snapping to attention.

". . . The major knew something. That he was different. I only saw the boy sitting there. He was dressed like a workman. Heavy boots. Woolen pants and coat. He had a hat pulled down, so it was hard to see his face. The major says to me: 'This Jew will help us. He will catch other Jews for us. . . .' and I salute. This is something I expect. But what comes next is unusual, because the major, he turns to the Jew and he says, 'Willem, you are a Jew, are you not?' as if he is joking. And this boy, he is perhaps nineteen, twenty years of age, he makes a face like some beast in the zoo. Filled with anger and capture. And after a moment, he replies, 'Yes, Herr Major, I am a Jew!' and the major, he laughs and turns to me and says, 'Willem is not much of a Jew, Sergeant. Just the littlest bit. What bit is that, Willem?' and the boy, he answers, 'My grandmother, damn her.' "

The old man looked at Espy Martinez.

"You are a woman of laws, correct?"

"Yes. I am a lawyer and a prosecutor. . . ."

"*Ihr habt keine Gesetze wie wir sie hatten! Die Rassengesetze!* You have no laws like we had. The race laws." He laughed. "Poor Shadow Man! A half-Jewish grandmother who renounced her religion when she married before the first war. Who died before he was born. What a great joke that was, was it not, Miss Martinez? This woman whom he never knew put her blood in his veins, and because of that, he was to die. *Ist das nicht ein guter Witz?* Is that not a great joke? Can you not see the devil's own hand making sport of the poor Shadow Man?"

He paused, as if waiting for an answer, but she did not reply, so he continued.

"So, the major, he turns to me again, and he says, 'Willem can be a very useful boy. He will find Jews for us. And he will do other things too. For me. Is that not correct, Willem?' and the boy replies, 'Yes, Herr Major.' I do not know, but I suspect the major knows of this boy, and has experience with him in the past. I do not ask this, because the major gives me my orders: I am to train the boy. Surveillance. Pursuit. Weapons. Techniques of detection. Even some code work. Also forgery, which he has quite a fine hand for. *Der Junge soll das Geschäft der Gestapo lernen!* The boy is to learn to be Gestapo! A Jew! And so, I teach him, and do you know, Miss Martinez, no teacher ever had a pupil quite like him."

"Why is that?"

"Because he understands always, he can be on the next transport. And because he hates so fully and completely."

"The major, why did he . . ."

"Because the major was a smart man. A brilliant man! Still today, I salute when I remember him. He knew that finding Jews was his job. But he knew too that it would be useful to have a man like the Shadow Man always ready, always expert, for whatever task you might have. Did you want a document stolen? A rival murdered? What better man than the Shadow Man to perform any small, deadly task the major might have had. Because, Miss Martinez—*er war bereits tot!* He was dead already! All the Jews were. And he knew he owed his life only to his special capabilities."

Again the old Nazi smiled.

"We were killers together, Miss Martinez. He and I. Student and teacher. But he was far superior to me. . . ." The man on the bed rubbed a hand across his forehead. "I felt guilt. He did not."

Again he paused.

"He was our perfect killer, and you know what else, Miss Martinez?"

"What?"

"The Shadow Man truly enjoyed his job. Behind all his hate, he loved bringing death. Especially to the people he blamed for his own blood."

"What happened to him?"

Klaus Wilmschmidt nodded his head. "He was clever. He stole. Diamonds, gold, jewels, whatever. He stole from the people he found. Then he saw to their deaths. He knew, you see, Miss Martinez, he knew his own existence relied on his ability to detect Jews and to perform the major's special tasks. As the number of Jews to catch dwindled, in 'forty-three and 'forty-four, his own existence became more precarious. And so, he took precautions."

"What do you mean?"

"He took steps to survive, Miss Martinez. We all did. No one believed, anymore. When you can hear Russian artillery, it is hard to believe. But long before that, we knew. When you have helped create the lies, Miss Martinez, you would be quite a fool to believe them yourself."

"The Shadow Man?"

"He and I had an agreement. A mutual convenience. Of what he'd stolen, I was to receive half. And papers. He was quite the forger, Miss Martinez. And, of course, I was able to help obtain stamps and proper forms. So, when the time was right, we could disappear. Become something new. I was to be Wehrmacht. A soldier wounded on the Western front and disabled. *Ein ehrbarer Mann.* An honorable man. A soldier who merely followed orders and now wanted to go home in peace. Not Gestapo. And this, one day, when all was finished, I became. Handed myself in to the British."

"But the Shadow Man?"

"His task was more complicated. And, he was more clever than I. He searched for a man. Every day, he hunted. A man to become."

"I don't understand."

"A different identity. A Jew, like himself. Of close to the same age, size, education. With the same coloring. And, when he found this man, he did not put him on the transport, although that is what the records said. No, he killed him, himself. And he kept this man's person safe for his own use. He began to starve himself. . . ."

"Starved?"

"Yes. To become, you see! And he had his arm tattooed with a number as they did at the camps. And then, one day, he disappeared. A wise choice, that day."

Again the old man laughed, which prompted a coughing fit.

"It was wise, because that day the major, his protector, was drunk and asleep when the bombers came over, and did not awaken in time to go to the shelter, and so, when he did awaken—*er war bereits fest auf dem Weg zur Hölle.* He was already fast on his way to Hell!"

Wilmschmidt again choked on his laugh, reached for the oxygen, then smiled toward Espy Martinez.

"A good plan. I suspect he'd sewn his money into his coat. A rich man! He probably headed west, toward the Allies. I did. You did not want to be questioned by the Russians. But the Americans, like you, and the English, they still wanted to be fair. And if you landed with them, complete with a tale of escaping from a camp, starved and tattooed, would you not be embraced? *Zumindest man glaubte dir?* At least believed?"

Espy Martinez didn't answer. Her own throat felt tight and dry, and the small room seemed filled with an illness different from the one that racked the body of the old Nazi. She felt a thickness, a dullness, as if sorting through the story she'd heard would require a razor, and she had none.

"And so, he escaped?" she asked.

"He escaped. I was sure of it. I escaped, doing much the same." She stumbled internally, thinking hard.

"So that is how he came to be," she said. She abruptly reached down into her leather satchel and removed a copy of the composite drawing that Leroy Jefferson had created. She thrust it toward the old man, who held it in front of him. After a second staring at it, he burst into a harsh, raucous laugh. He shook the picture in front of himself and said: "*Es ist so gut, dich zu sehen, mein alter Freund!* It is so good to see you, my old friend!"

Then he turned to Martinez. "He has changed less than I would have thought."

Martinez nodded. "You've told me about the past," she said. "How do I find him? Now. Today."

Klaus Wilmschmidt lay back on his bed, eyeing her. He lifted a hand and gestured toward the vials of pills, the oxygen, and then toward himself.

"I am dying, Miss Martinez. I am in pain, and I can count the breaths I have left."

Maria Wilmschmidt sobbed slightly as she translated.

"*Gibt en einen Himmel?* Is there a Heaven, Miss Martinez?"

"I do not know."

"Perhaps. Perhaps not. So, once I was part of terrible things, Miss Martinez. Things you cannot begin to understand. I hear cries at night. I see faces on these walls. Ghosts in this little room, Miss Martinez. They are here with me. More every day. They call to me, and soon enough I will try to take a breath, but I will not be able. I will grab for the oxygen, but it will not work. And I will choke and die. That is what is left for me."

He paused, gathering himself.

"So, I wonder, can I die with what I know about this man? Tell me, Miss Martinez, will I now know peace? Now that I have spoken of him, and what we did?"

"I don't know," she answered, but she did.

The old man seemed to grow smaller, darker, as if night and fog had covered him like a coat. His breathing was raspy, erratic.

"Find the Shadow Man? That I cannot do, Miss Martinez."

"But—"

"But I do know the name of the man he became."

"Tell me!" she demanded quickly, as if she needed to know before the man on the bed coughed again.

He grinned, his face not unlike the death's head on the dagger he'd waved about earlier.

"Yes," he said. "I can tell you the name. And I can tell you something else."

"What is that?"

Klaus Wilmschmidt, the dying man, whispered his response: *"Ich weiss was für eine Nummer der Schattenmann auf seinem Arm hat. . . ."*

The old man's daughter paused for an instant, breathing once harshly, before she quietly translated: "I know the number the Shadow Man tattooed on his arm."

# TWENTY-FOUR
## THE HISTORIAN

SIMON Winter and Walter Robinson, standing slightly apart, watched as the rabbi and Frieda Kroner examined the composite drawing of the Shadow Man. The old people were quiet, studious, like a pair of scholars poring over some faded ancient hieroglyph, before they each sat back abruptly. Frieda Kroner had a slightly wild, runaway look on her face as she declared:

"That is him. Except for the chin. It should be much stronger. . . ."

"The eyebrows are not quite right. They should be more pinched, as if angry all the time," Rabbi Rubinstein said stiffly. "That would make his eyes more, I do not know, what, Frieda? Do you remember his eyes?"

"Yes." She nodded. "Narrow, like a vicious dog's."

"But the rest?" Robinson asked.

"The rest is the man we saw fifty years ago." Frieda Kroner said this in a firm, fierce voice. She turned to the rabbi. "Older. No longer young. Like us. Is this not so?"

"Yes. That is the Shadow Man," the rabbi agreed. He reached across and placed his hand on her arm. He turned to the detective. "I would know him in an instant."

"I also," Frieda Kroner added. She took a deep breath. "And, I am thinking, so would have poor Sophie and Irving. If our memories told us short or tall, thin or thick, dark or light, this was because so much was in there cluttered about and made it difficult to remember. But now, seeing this, I can say, that is him."

She shivered, but spoke in a firm, determined voice.

"So, Detective—and you too, Mr. Winter—you think he is out there tonight"—she gestured toward the windows and beyond—"searching for us, as he did the others?"

Simon Winter nodded.

Frieda Kroner laughed slightly, as if this were amusing. "So, perhaps it will be difficult to sleep. I remember this was the same, once before. A long time ago."

Walter Robinson had been controlling himself with difficulty, watching the old couple. "I've changed my mind," he said. "I think the risk is simply too great. This man is almost a professional killer. More than that. A homicidal psychopath. I think what would be wisest would be for each of you to visit relatives and let me use what information I already have to find him. That way you'll be safe and I won't have to worry about protecting the two of you. We can slip you out of town, and still trap him when he makes some sort of move toward the apartment here, or yours, Mrs. Kroner. But the important thing is, we won't have another death."

The rabbi curved an eyebrow up in surprise when he heard this. Simon Winter started to speak, but then held back. Frieda Kroner snorted.

"No," Robinson continued, holding up a hand to cut her off. "I think the first priority should be maintaining your safety."

The rabbi eyed the young detective and said: "Again, Detective Robinson, I do not think you are saying everything you know. Leave? Leave now? Why is it that you are suddenly so insistent?"

"I just want to keep you safe."

The rabbi shook his head. "That is not it," he said briskly.

Frieda Kroner had been watching Robinson carefully as he spoke. She suddenly smiled.

"I know," she said, like a child who has guessed which hand holds a concealed sweet. "I know why the detective is saying these things."

Robinson turned to face her. "Mrs. Kroner, I simply want—"

She shook her head, as if to replace the smile there with some iron-hard attitude.

"You have seen something, have you not? You have seen something about the Shadow Man, and you will not share it with us because you do not want to frighten us. As if there is something more terrible than what we have already seen. I have seen more of death than you, Detective, even if you live to be a hundred years old. You still do not understand us, do you, Detective?"

Walter Robinson was at a loss for an answer.

The rabbi spoke quietly then. "I think," he said slowly, "that sometimes this frightens me more than anything."

Frieda Kroner nodded. "You look at us and you see an old lady and an old man because you are young, and that means you are filled with all the prejudices of the young—" She held up her hand as Robinson started to protest. "Don't interrupt me, Detective."

He stopped.

"All right," she said firmly. "So tell me now. What is it you have seen?"

Robinson shrugged before replying. He thought, in that moment, that just as it was unwise to underestimate the Shadow Man, so might it be unwise to underestimate the old people sitting before him.

"I have no real proof—" he started.

"But, there is a but coming right here, correct?" the rabbi said with a slight sardonic smile. "There always seems to be a *but*."

"Yes. You remember the man who saw the Shadow Man in Sophie's apartment?"

"The drug addict? Mr. Jefferson?" Frieda Kroner said.

"He was found murdered early this morning in his apartment in Liberty City."

"Murdered? How?"

"Tied into his wheelchair and tortured with a knife."

Both the rabbi and Frieda Kroner were silent as they absorbed this news.

"The city police aren't certain that he wasn't the victim of the neighborhood drug dealers. In that part of the city revenge is frequent and it can be vicious, and there are indications that he was on many lists of people easily capable of murder. . . ."

"You do not think this?" the rabbi asked.

"No. I think we all know who is responsible."

"Mr. Jefferson, he was—" Frieda Kroner started, but again she was cut off by the young policeman.

"Jefferson died hard, Mrs. Kroner. Died hard and slow and in more pain than even he deserved. He was tortured, because someone wanted to know what he knew. And he was subsequently mutilated. I will not have either you or the rabbi in the same danger. Look at it from my point of view: It would mean my career, if something went wrong and this man reached either of you. And I could never forgive myself. So, no, I want the two of you safe."

Simon Winter had been startled by the news of Jefferson's death, but had hidden his surprise behind a poker face. He watched Robinson carefully and saw that he was genuinely shaken. So, when he did speak, it was softly. "You say Jefferson was mutilated? How?"

"I'd rather not go into the details, Mr. Winter."

"Well, he was tortured for a reason and then mutilated for a reason, because I think this man does everything for a reason, and so everything he does should tell us something and maybe help us think ahead as to what he will do next. So, I ask again, how was he mutilated?"

Robinson hesitated a moment, listening to the coldness in the older man's voice. "His tongue was cut out."

Frieda Kroner gasped and put her hand to her mouth. The rabbi shook his head.

"That is awful," the rabbi said.

But Simon Winter's eyes had narrowed and he was thinking quickly. He spoke in a low, confident tone.

"Well, I'll be damned," he said. The others looked at him. "You wouldn't have expected it of a low-life like Jefferson, would you? Not in a million years."

"What?"

"That Jefferson didn't tell the Shadow Man what he went there to learn."

"Which was?"

"What do the authorities know? How hard are you looking for him? How close are you to finding him? What evidence is there that he exists? I can think of a dozen questions that would take the Shadow Man out in the middle of the night."

Winter hesitated, shaking his head. "It also says this to me: that Leroy Jefferson didn't tell the Shadow Man about the composite drawing. So we still have that working for us."

Walter Robinson thought hard for a moment, then nodded. "I think you're probably right," he said. "Poor old Leroy." He hesitated another second, then added: "Of course, the mutilation could mean that the Shadow Man was simply angry at Jefferson *for* talking, and this was his way of showing it."

"Organized crime hit men have certain signatures," Simon Winter said quietly. "They do things that are supposed to leave a message. I don't think the Shadow Man does the same. His killings try for the concealment of routine. This time, I think he was frustrated. Frustrated, and perhaps you can see a touch of the racist as well. Leroy Jefferson wasn't anything to him other than an unfortunate obstacle. I think we should try to move quickly now. He is moving fast. So should we."

Walter Robinson thought hard about what Winter had said, and nodded. "Simon, I think you're correct. All the more reason to get Mrs. Kroner and the rabbi out of Miami Beach today. This minute. Right now."

When Winter looked blankly at him, Robinson added in an exasperated tone: "Damn it! The two of them are what holds it all together, right? Without them, what do we have? Herman Stein becomes a suicide again, forever. Sophie Millstein goes into the books as unsolved, assailant unknown. Just another goddamn statistic. And Irving Silver, he remains wherever he is. Missing. Period. Not even classified beyond disappeared, possible drowning. How many others are there out there in the same damn category? The only thing that points at one man and murder are these old folks! Without them, we never get into a court of law."

Winter took a moment before replying. "I know that." He was about to add to that statement, when Frieda Kroner interrupted.

She had paled slightly, and she was shaking her head vigorously back and forth. "I will not go," she said.

Robinson turned to her. "Please, Mrs. Kroner. I know your intentions are admirable, but this is not the time. I believe you are in great danger, and I believe you are essential to any ultimate prosecution of this killer. Please let me help you—"

"I can only be helped one way, Detective. Find the Shadow Man."

"Mrs. Kroner—"

"No!" she replied angrily. "No! No! *No!* We spoke of leaving before and decided against it." Her words drove her to her feet. "I will not hide! I will not flee! If he comes for me and I am alone, then I will fight him alone. He may kill me, but I will give him a battle he won't soon forget! I tried to hide from this man once and it cost me my entire family! Not again! Do you understand that, Detective?"

She took a deep breath.

"I am scared. That is true. I am old as well. And perhaps I am not as strong as I once was. But I am not so ancient and weak and feeble that I cannot make my own choices, and my choice is to stay whatever happens!"

She turned toward the rabbi. "Rabbi, this is simply me, the stubborn old woman speaking. You must make your own decision—"

He interrupted her. "And my decision is the same." He reached out and grasped hold of her hand. "My dear and old friend. Whatever there is that threatens us, we shall face together. You will pack a bag or two and move into the guest room here for a week or so or however long it takes for this to end. Then we can face whatever arrives together."

He turned to Walter Robinson. "We have lost much to this man. Families, and now friends, and there are but the two of us left. I do not know if together we can be stronger than he, but I am certain that we must try. So thank you, Detective, for your concern for our safety. But here is where we stay."

Robinson opened his mouth to say something, but Winter cut off his reply. "Listen to them, Walter," he whispered.

Robinson turned to the old detective, angry for an instant, but then he let the anger slip away, replaced by the advantage he thought keeping the two old people close would give him. "All right," he said. "But you will be protected. By me. I'm going to have an officer assigned here, around the clock."

He picked up the composite drawing.

"It's time to let this do us some good."

The plan was simple. That evening at services in two dozen different temples and synagogues, a brief, potent message was to be read:

A person known only as the Shadow Man, who is alleged to have committed crimes against our people in Berlin during the great darkness, is suspected of coming to live amongst us once again, here on Miami Beach. Anyone with any information about this individual is urged to contact Rabbi Chaim Rubinstein or Detective Walter Robinson of the Miami Beach police.

Nothing was to be mentioned concerning the murders. Simon Winter thought the announcement already too specific, and ran the risk of scaring the Shadow Man out of the territory, but Walter Robinson had insisted the wording be direct, half hoping that precisely that would occur, and then he could take his time to find the man wherever he went, leaving the two old people safe. He also did not think that the Shadow Man was likely to hear the message directly; he did not think the man spent any time observing any religious niceties. So, he thought, the Shadow Man will learn of the announcement secondhand. A conversation in a lobby, or on an elevator. Perhaps in a restaurant or at a newsstand. And just the reconstruction of the announcement, he hoped, would prompt the man to take steps without caution. That was all he wanted; for the man to act without thinking once, without preparing once. This time, Robinson was certain, he would be there.

More critically, both the old and the young detective agreed, the Shadow Man would still not know his anonymity was compromised. It was merely a question of putting a name to the picture.

Winter had suggested adding a further element to the plan, which Robinson had thought a wise one. The two of them were each to take the composite picture of the Shadow Man to the heads of several condo associations, including the one that Herman Stein belonged to. The idea was that by showing the picture quietly, someone might point them in the right direction.

When Walter Robinson returned to his office, before heading out on this task, he discovered that Espy Martinez had called. She had listed her arriving flight information and the cryptic message: "Some success."

He did not allow himself to speculate on what this might be, although he passed this news on to Simon Winter as the two of them drove north, up Miami Beach, into a world of high-rise apartment buildings.

"The name," he answered for the detective. "She got the name."

"He won't still be using it," Robinson replied.

"Maybe not. Probably not. But look, if he suddenly disappears, at least you'll have something to start with in records. Immigration records. Tax records. Records from relief organizations after the war. It'll turn you into a historian. My guess is, he rode that name into the States before changing it. Maybe there's something in social security. You never know."

"Sounds like a lot of work."

"And people think being a homicide detective is all glamour and glory, huh?"

Robinson laughed briefly. He had left the old couple in the rabbi's apartment, preparing tea for the uniformed Miami Beach officer assigned to watching them. What he had told the watchdog was simple: no one allowed inside unless authorized by him, personally, or carrying a recognizable badge. He had taken a copy of the composite drawing and taped it to the front door, next to the peephole. He had thought there were few advantages to high-rise condominiums, but one is that when one shuts the door, the apartments have the same safety characteristics as a cave. Only one way in and out. This allowed him to feel as if things were slightly under control.

"But," Simon Winter continued, "I don't think you find this guy through conventional methods. Never have. I think he finds you. What we have to do is beat him to the spot."

"That's a basketball term, right?"

"Precisely. When you're playing defense against a good player, you try to anticipate where he wants to set up on the court. And then you simply get there first." Winter paused, then added: "He's never experienced that sort of unpleasantness before."

"At least, not that we know of," Robinson said.

They entered into the concrete canyon sections of Miami Beach, where huge, ungainly high rises seemed to compete with the clouds at blocking out the sun. Like any city, the buildings give one the sensation of uniformity. Stack after stack of similar apartments, people living in vertical hives, their own identity and uniqueness competing against a world of identical shapes, angles, and sizes.

The first place they visited was Herman Stein's condominium, and the association head, a robust, bald-headed man, glanced at the picture they presented him with, but shook his head negatively. He pointed out that the association had over a thousand members, representing hundreds of apartments, and the picture, as best as he could say, didn't resemble any of them. This did not surprise Simon Winter. Nor was he surprised when the next two apartment complex association heads said much the same thing.

"Stein said he spotted the Shadow Man at a meeting," Robinson said, frustrated after several hours with negative results. "You know what we could do? Get lists from every building, find all the single residents, then go door-to-door until we come face-to-face with the bastard. He'll be on some list."

"Yeah," Winter said. "I thought he might be on a list too. But I couldn't find the right one. That might work."

The tone in his voice indicated that he didn't have any doubt that it wouldn't work.

Robinson glanced at his watch. He didn't want to be late for Espy Martinez's arrival. It was late in the day, and red streaks filled the sky to the west. Tendrils of night were already starting to creep through the shadows thrown by the high rises.

"I'm going to the airport," he said. "Want me to drop you someplace?"

Simon Winter was abruptly struck with an idea. He nodded

and gave the young detective an address. Then he folded up a copy of the composite drawing and slipped it into his pocket.

Walter Robinson pulled the car to the curb. "Something will happen soon," he said. "They read that announcement tonight." He looked down at his watch again. "Actually, any minute now. Should shake something loose in the next couple of days. And let's see what Espy found out."

"Call me when you know something. I'm going to be home after I stop in here."

"What's this?"

"Oh, a long shot," the old detective said, stepping back from the unmarked car. "And they've probably all gone home."

Walter Robinson eyed the older man. Overhead, a jet had turned on its final approach into Miami International Airport, and its route was carrying it over the midsection of the Beach. It was still too high for the engines to be heard, and the plane seemed to be floating across the darkening sky.

"How long a shot?" he asked.

Winter had started to turn away, but when he heard the question, he faced about and made a slightly dismissive gesture with his hand, as if to say not worth the detective's time and effort. Robinson saw this, saw precisely what the motion was supposed to create within him, fought off the urge to pull the car out into traffic and head to the airport, which was where a large part of him eagerly wanted to go. Instead, he slipped the car's gearshift into park and jumped out from behind the wheel. Simon Winter, a few feet away on the sidewalk, paused and grinned.

"What, don't trust me?"

"It's not that," Robinson said as he caught up with the older man. He didn't add to that statement. Instead, he asked, "What is this place?"

"This is the Holocaust Center," Winter answered. "But more importantly, it's the only place I've been to, since all this started, where the past meets the present. Other than over several dead bodies, that is."

He pushed his way into the office building, trailed by the younger detective.

The receptionist was collecting her things when they came

through the door, frowned impatiently, but was impressed when Robinson flashed his badge. It only took a few seconds for them to be swept into Esther Weiss's office, where the young woman stood beside her small desk. She greeted Simon Winter rapidly, with both familiarity and crispness. She too had been preparing to depart.

"Mr. Winter, have you had any success? Are you still persuaded this man is here?"

Winter introduced Walter Robinson, and Esther Weiss asked: "Are the police now believing the Shadow Man is here?"

Robinson answered this swiftly. "Yes."

The center director shuddered slightly, placed her small briefcase on her desk, and sat down. "This is a terrible thing. I never thought such a thing possible. He must be found and brought to justice. There are courts in Israel. And Germany . . ."

"I'm more interested in a court across town," Robinson said.

Esther Weiss nodded. "Of course. He must be brought to justice." She seemed about to add to that statement when Simon Winter stopped her.

He had had that conversation with the young woman before, and part of the advantage of old age, he thought, was insisting that roads once traveled did not need to be traversed again. So, following his instincts, he reached inside his jacket pocket and unfolded the composite picture of the Shadow Man. He thrust it across the desk at Esther Weiss without saying anything. She reached out, spreading the picture on the desk in front of her. She stared hard at the drawing, just as everyone else had, but when she looked up, there was a slight twitch at the corner of her right eyelid and a tremor crept into her words:

"But I know this man," she said slowly, as if confused. She recoiled from the drawing as if it were a current of electricity. "At least, I have seen him once, twice, a few times before. . . ."

Espy Martinez was surprised that Walter Robinson wasn't at the International Arrivals terminal to meet her. She was in that unsettled state caused by traveling across large time zones; she was uncertain whether she was exhausted or energized. She went directly to a telephone and called his office, only to learn that he had not checked in since he was at the rabbi's apartment.

She debated whether to head home, the thought of a shower and a change of clothing, and perhaps a nap as well, being a powerful attraction. But she had the sensation that things were taking place, and she felt slightly on the forgotten side of events, which surprised her; written on a piece of paper inside her briefcase were a name and a number and, she thought, maybe all they needed to find the man they hunted.

She took one last quick glance around the airport terminal, but did not see Walter Robinson. She insisted to herself that she shouldn't feel irritated, that after all there were higher priorities than being met at the airport, and she wondered if perhaps he hadn't received her phone message, or that the arrival time could have been garbled. She filled herself with excuses, which made her forget, momentarily, any fatigue, and headed outside.

She stood, waving for a cab, amidst the noxious combination of exhaust fumes and syrupy evening heat that filled the half-enclosed waiting area. She climbed into the backseat of the taxi, gave her home address, and leaned back, letting the tropical air slide around her. But before the cab managed to reach the airport exit, she changed her mind, and pitching forward, speaking in rapid-fire Spanish, told the driver to take her to the rabbi's apartment on Miami Beach.

Simon Winter had grasped Esther Weiss by the arm. With his free hand he thumped hard on the composite drawing.

"Who?" he demanded. "Who is it!"

Walter Robinson had jumped forward, gesturing, his voice urgent with a cold, harsh hope. "Where have you seen this man?" he asked, his words trampling the same furious questions by the older detective.

Esther Weiss stared crazily at the two men. "This is him?" she asked, high-pitched.

"Yes," Robinson replied. "Where have you seen this man?" he repeated.

Esther Weiss's mouth opened slightly in astonishment, and Simon Winter could see the formulation of fear behind her eyes. He released his grip on the woman's arm, and she slid into her desk chair, still wide-eyed, staring at the two men.

"But here," she answered slowly. "Right here . . ."

Winter was about to speak, but Robinson beat him to the punch. The young man's words were measured, slow, still colored with a cool appreciation of good fortune. "When, how, tell me what you know, right now," he said. "Leave nothing out. Not the smallest detail. Anything could help us."

"This is the Shadow Man?" the woman asked again.

"Yes," Simon Winter said.

"But this man is a historian," she replied. "With impeccable credentials . . ."

"No, I think not," Winter said quietly. "Or perhaps he is both. But this is the man we are searching for."

"Start at the beginning," Robinson said. "A name. An address. How is it you know him?"

"He studies the tapes," she said. "We allow scholars to study the tapes privately. Scholars and historians and social scientists . . ."

"I know that," Simon Winter said impatiently. "But this man. Who is he?"

"I have his name on file." Esther Weiss coughed as she spoke. "I have it written down. And an address. I have these things. A résumé too, I think. We keep all these things in the confidential files. You remember, Mr. Winter? I gave you some names once before. . . ."

"Yes. I remember. Was he on that list?"

"I can't recall," the young woman said. "I gave it to you. I just don't remember."

Walter Robinson interjected himself smoothly. "But now you can go to the file, correct? You can go to the list of scholars and pick this man out? Is he on a Rolodex? In an address book? Now, Miss Weiss, if you please."

"I can't believe—"

"Now, Miss Weiss."

She hesitated, then acquiesced: "Yes. Of course. Right away."

The center director unsteadily moved to a black, lateral file cabinet tucked into a corner of the small office. She rolled the top drawer open and began searching through the collected papers. After a moment she muttered, "There are more than a hundred people authorized to examine the tapes."

As she continued to search, Simon Winter asked: "Is there a procedure for getting this authorization? I mean, does somebody get checked out?"

"Yes and no," the young woman replied. "If someone's credentials seem in order, then approval is pretty much routine. The scholar must submit a statement as to why they need access to the tapes, and describe any use they intend for them. They must also sign a waiver and a confidentiality clause. We are strict about prohibiting any commercialization of the memories we have on tape. But what we're mainly interested in avoiding are the revisionists."

"The what?" Robinson asked.

"The people who deny the Holocaust ever took place."

"Are they crazy?" Robinson blurted out. "I mean, how can someone—"

Esther Weiss looked up, a small manila folder in her hand. "There are many people who want to deny the existence of the greatest crime of history, Detective. People who would explain away gas chambers as delousing units. People who would say that ovens were for baking bread, not people. There are those who think Hitler was a saint and that all the memories of his terror are so many conspiracies." She took a deep breath. "Rational people would say these views are madness. But it is not so simple. Surely, Detective, you can understand that?"

He could not, but he did not say so.

Esther Weiss put her hand to her forehead for a moment, as if shielding her eyes from something she did not want to see. Then she handed the manila envelope to Simon Winter.

"This is the man that resembles your drawing," she said.

The old detective opened the file and drew out several sheets of paper. The first was a form requesting access to the tapes. Attached to that was a letter, a curriculum vitae and waiver forms, signed.

At the top of the résumé was a name: David Isaacson.

Beneath that was a Miami Beach address.

"What do you remember of this man?" Robinson asked.

"He was in, I don't know how many times. He was very quiet and not outgoing in the slightest. I only spoke to him once, the first time. He told me that he too was a survivor, and I asked him to contribute his own memories to the tapes, and he agreed, but said it would have to wait until he finished his memoir. That's what he was working on. His memoir. He said it was to be privately published. After his death. He said it was for his family, so there would always be a record for them to remember."

She hesitated, then added: "I thought this was admirable."

"Is there a log, showing numbers of times visited?"

"If we collect the staff, perhaps we could piece that together. But once someone has access, they are given their privacy with the materials."

"How did he get approval?"

"See the other letter?"

Winter and Robinson both looked down at the letter clipped to the file. It was from the Holocaust Memorial organization in Los Angeles, and it was signed by an associate director. It asked that all scholarly perquisites be permitted for Mr. Isaacson, who had done similar work with materials in Los Angeles.

"You called? Checked this out?"

"No," Esther Weiss said hesitantly. "It was signed by the associate director."

Walter Robinson nodded. "Don't worry," he said slowly. "It makes no difference."

Simon Winter looked up. "So, these other things on the résumé. The degrees from New York University and the University of Chicago. The publications, and all that. You didn't check. . . ."

"Why?" she replied. "Why? It was clear he wasn't a revisionist! He even showed me the tattoo on his arm!"

Winter held up his hand. He could see the young woman's face was drawn. She had paled and seemed to be teetering on the edge of panic.

"I didn't know," she said. "How could I have known?"

Winter didn't answer that question. All he could think about was the Shadow Man. Polite. Quiet. Doing nothing to draw

attention to himself, examining tape after tape, looking for anyone who might have known him.

Hunting, the old man thought.

The same thoughts filtered through Walter Robinson. But he
took the time to answer Esther Weiss's question. "You were
never meant to know," he said. He paused, and added firmly:
"But don't worry. This is ending now."

He looked down at the address. Then he reached across the
desk and picked up the telephone. He dialed the Beach police
headquarters, identified himself briskly, and demanded to speak
directly with the captain in charge of the special weapons and tac-
tics squad.

# TWENTY-FIVE
## THE TATTOO

**B**OTH Simon Winter and Walter Robinson under-estimated the impact that the announcement would have on the community of survivors. As evening passed into night, telephones throughout Miami Beach were ringing. At the few old Deco-style hotels that had not been taken over by the youth movement and still catered to the elderly, knots of people up past their usual bedtimes stood in the lobbies, or on the wide, outdoor porches, loudly discussing what they had heard. At Wolfie's Restaurant, not far from the Lincoln Road Mall, there was an argument going, which turned abrasive and strident. It caused some of the younger people and several foreign tourists visiting the landmark to turn their heads, wondering why the ordinarily quiet, placid old folks were raising their voices. A stranger overhearing the heated talk would have seen anger in several faces, but had they looked closer, would have seen fear as well. A deep, blackened fear, rising through long-held memory; although there were precious few who had ever heard of the Shadow Man, every man and woman was scarred by a recollection of a similar terror, whether it was Gestapo or S.S. or merely the awful knowledge that they had done what they were ordered to do, and voluntarily delivered themselves to the machine of evil.

And so, the idea that a piston in this machine was living among them created an unsettled sensation, a step or two on the road to panic, that summoned remembered nightmare in all their voices, sounds that went unheard and unrecognized by the young and the trendy occupants of the Miami Beach scene on their way to the dance clubs and night spots, but which fairly shouted to those older people.

Espy Martinez was peripherally aware of the stir that had been created. She sat in the living room of the rabbi's apartment and listened as he and Frieda Kroner handled phone call after phone call. She quickly understood that these were not calls containing information, but pleas for reassurance. This, the rabbi handled expertly, speaking in a soothing, practiced voice, listening, letting memories drop around him like so many invisible petals from dying plants.

She listened as she overheard him say:

"No, Sylvia, it is just this one man . . ."

"Yes, the authorities are searching for him. We will find him . . ."

"I agree. This is a terrible thing. Who would have thought it?"

And then he hung up, turned toward her as if to say something, and the telephone rang again. He picked it up, smiled wanly, and said: "Of course, Mr. Fielding. Of course I remember you. Ahh, I see. You heard as well. Is there something you know? No? Oh, I see. Of course. Of course . . ."

The rabbi shrugged, and continued to speak with his caller.

Martinez turned to where the uniformed Beach police officer was busy reading the Sports section of that morning's paper. She opened her mouth to say something, then stopped. Instead, she rose to her feet and walked to the patio doors, staring out for a moment. The horizon seemed to glow with a dull silver intensity created by the city's lights. She wondered where Walter Robinson was, and wished she were with him.

He and Simon Winter were sitting in a briefing room at the Beach police headquarters, discussing arrest procedures with the SWAT captain and his nine-man team.

"In and out. I don't want to give this guy even one second. Full restraints as soon as we have control, I mean hands pinned, and legs too."

"No problem," replied the SWAT captain with an offhand wave. He seemed singularly unimpressed with the need for a tactical squad to arrest one elderly man. "You have a judge sign a warrant?"

"Got it right here." Robinson paused. "I had trouble with my last arrest," he understated.

"Heard that," the SWAT captain replied. "But you followed established procedure. These things happen." He was an experienced policeman, who wore his military training every waking minute and probably snored in his bed at night to a marching cadence. Square-shouldered and close-cropped, he was the type of person who considered discipline a virtue beyond intelligence and who was forced to quit coaching his son's Little League team because of too insistent an approach to victory.

"The man we're arresting should be considered armed and extremely dangerous."

"Everyone we arrest fits that category," he replied matter-of-factly. "Automatic weapons?"

"No. I don't believe so."

"Well, there you have it. Likely to surrender when confronted?"

"Hard to say."

"Likely to run?"

"More likely to disappear," Simon Winter added softly, but with just enough force for the SWAT captain to hear him. The captain turned to him.

"That would be a first for me, old-timer," he said condescendingly.

"This is a case of firsts," Winter replied.

The captain unfolded himself from the briefing chair, and as he did, the nine members of his team rose with him.

"Whenever you're ready," he said confidently.

Walter Robinson nodded. He went to a wall telephone and tried Espy Martinez's home for the tenth time, only to once again get her answering machine. Then he dialed the number for the rabbi's apartment. This was the fourth time he'd tried this number, only to be frustrated by the busy signal. He had the authority to get the phone company to interrupt, but he was reluctant to use that. He merely wanted to inform the rabbi they'd had a break in the case, thinking that even without a lengthy explanation, this news would reassure the old couple. Simon Winter had concurred in this view.

He was surprised when the phone rang and the rabbi's voice was immediately there.

"Yes, this is Rabbi Rubinstein. Who's calling, please?"

"Rabbi, it's Detective Robinson."

"Ah, Detective. Your announcement has had some effect. The phone is ringing off the hook."

"I've been trying to get through. Any information?"

"No. Only people upset, which is understandable. But I am still optimistic someone will know something. It seems as if they will be calling all through the night."

"Look, Rabbi, Mr. Winter and I have found something out, no, don't interrupt, I don't want to go into detail right now. I will call you later, but we may have made some progress. Just sit tight, you and Mrs. Kroner, okay? Is the officer still there?"

"Yes."

"Make sure he stays alert."

"Of course. But you say you have discovered something? This is good news. What sort of progress?"

"Really, I'd rather discuss it later, in case it amounts to nothing."

The rabbi hesitated. "All right," he said after a moment. "Do you wish to speak with Miss Martinez? She is here."

Walter Robinson smiled and felt his stomach leap. "Yes," he said rapidly. There was a momentary pause before he heard her voice.

"Walter?"

"Espy, I've been trying to reach you. I'm sorry I missed the flight, but we've had a break. I've got a name and address—"

"Are you heading there now?"

"Yes. Stay there. I'll call you when we're finished."

Espy Martinez felt a surge of excitement. She wanted to accompany the arrest team, but she was also aware that Walter Robinson had not asked her to.

"I want to be there," she said firmly.

"Espy, last time I allowed you to go on an arrest in the middle of the night, I nearly got you shot. Not this time."

She started to protest, but stopped.

"Your trip—" he started to ask.

"I learned some things," she said. "Fascinating things. I mean, I never knew. You study history in high school, college, but you don't really know it until you come face-to-face with it. That's what happened. This guy, Walter, the Shadow Man, he was carefully trained by the Gestapo. All sorts of techniques. Surveillance. Forgery. Murder. You name it. A mean customer, Walter, be careful."

Robinson had a vision of Leroy Jefferson in his wheelchair and thought: *beyond* mean. He realized that Espy Martinez knew nothing of what had happened to their witness, and was about to tell her, and then decided against it. He could see the SWAT team strapping body armor into place, stamping their feet like a collection of quarterhorses before a roundup, and he realized he had to go.

"They trained him?"

"Made him into an expert. Can you imagine that? And these guys, Walter, they were the best, if you could call it that, and the man that told me all this says that he was the best of the best. So, play it safe, okay."

"Of course."

He was about to hang up, but she stopped him, lowering her voice. "There's one other thing, Walter. It might be helpful. . . ."

"What?"

"He had a death camp number tattooed on his arm. That was one of the ways he disguised himself near the end, when all hell was breaking loose over there and all the rats were leaving the sinking ship. I have the number. He may have changed his identity a million times, but I don't think he'd change that number. If you get your hands on him—"

"What is it?"

"A26510," she said.

He wrote this down.

A block from the address of the man who said he was writing his memoirs, the SWAT team captain transferred from the van carrying his squad and into the unmarked patrol car that Walter Robinson drove. The SWAT captain hurriedly tossed himself into the rear seat, moving as swiftly as his body armor would allow.

"All right, Walt," he said. "Let's drive by."

Walter Robinson wordlessly put the car in gear and they slowly drove down a dark, small side street in the midst of a modest residential area. The section of Miami Beach around Forty-first Street is an odd collection of houses; some, which abut the waterway that carves through the Beach, are million-dollar homes. Others are large, elegant, two-story designs, with Deco touches, and red barrel-tiled roofs, eagerly sought after by many of the young professional types moving back to Miami Beach. But interspersed with these, on streets with less imposing palm trees and pockmarked, gravelly roads, are far humbler houses, low-slung, with flat brick tiles, old jalousie windows, and a depressing uniformity. They were often what realtors liked to term "starter houses," which meant they could be afforded by couples just starting out and not being bankrolled by a parent, or the old and finishing-up people who still wanted to call the Beach home, and who had not yet been chased by fear of crime into the high-rise condos. Many were in that realtor's euphemistic category of *handyman's specials*, which indicated that years of constant heat and sun pounding away each day had caused the wooden floors to buckle and warp—or the cement foundations to crack and sway. It was not unusual for one of these houses, as old as their occupants and suffering from as many of the ills and pains of age, to lurk in the shadows thrown by some large, landscaped, remodeled home housing a doctor, a lawyer, or a well-heeled businessman and his family, sitting on the backside of progress like a poor reminder of neglect.

The address that Walter Robinson held in his hand was for one of those houses.

He slowly crunched the car to the hard coral-rock curb across the street. The house in question was set back from the street about twenty yards, with a desultory pair of scraggly bushes guarding the front door.

"Window bars," Simon Winter said.

He'd been silent most of the ride, thinking hard about the man they were narrowing in upon.

"Probably around back as well," the SWAT captain said. "And dead-bolt locks on the doors. There'll be a side door, or one in the rear, but most likely by the side where those garbage cans are located. But that's it. Two bedrooms, two baths, no central air, so those window units are on and going strong, and making a racket that will cover any noise we make. See any signs of an animal?"

"No fence. Hold it . . ."

The three men froze in position as they saw a figure cross in front of a front window. A tall man. Moments later a shorter shape followed. In a moment the front room of the house filled with the unmistakable glow from a television set.

"He's got a wife," Winter said. "I'll be damned."

"You want her taken as well?" asked the SWAT captain.

"Yes," Robinson said. "She may have helped him."

"She may also know nothing," Winter said.

"Well, we can find that out back at headquarters."

The SWAT captain took another long look, and then gestured for Walter Robinson to move the car ahead. He did this, not flipping on the headlights until they were a half block away from the target house.

"No sweat," the captain said, leaning back in his seat. "Two in back, two at the side, then the rest of the team goes in through the front door. He won't know what hit him."

"That's what I thought would happen the last time," Walter Robinson said.

"So what happened to that guy, the one that gave you the trouble before?" the SWAT captain asked.

"He ran into the guy in that house," Robinson replied.

Simon Winter listened with half an ear to the SWAT captain brief his team one final time about the layout and the approach. He realized that Walter Robinson was allowing him along on the arrest as a courtesy, and realized as well that he had to stay in the rear, away from the actual action. A part of him wished that it were he going through the door first, but he realized this was simply his own ego speaking to him. He felt an odd mix of emotions: an excitement that the man that had dominated his thoughts was so close, but a bittersweet recognition that once handcuffs were slapped around the Shadow Man's wrists, his own participation in the event would fade. He thought that he should be pleased, that it was his work that ultimately provided the connection between composite drawing and name and address, and he understood that in all likelihood he would get the instant attention and notoriety that newspapers and television bring. But this would diminish as the days went past, and he had the unsettling thought that a few weeks after the Shadow Man was arrested, he would inexorably return to precisely the same position he was in when Sophie Millstein had knocked on his door with terror in her eyes.

He remembered that position wryly: sitting on his couch with his revolver barrel in his mouth and finger on the trigger.

Without thinking, he lifted his hand to his left, where the pistol now rode in his old shoulder harness, concealed beneath a light windbreaker that was making him sweat as if nervous, which he hoped had so far gone unnoticed. He did not think that Walter Robinson realized he wore it. He did not care. The weight beneath his armpit was as reassuring as an old friend's handshake.

He turned away from the SWAT team as he heard the clickings and clackings of men checking weapons, and stared up past the dingy pale green streetlight glow toward the wide expanse of night sky, and tried to think what it was that he had learned that would speak to him in the days to come. For an instant he turned toward the young detective and measured him, finding a bit of envy reverberating around within himself. He wanted to have it all to do over again. Every moment. Every frustration. Every pain.

He thought he would not trade any of it, and he bit down on his lip at the thought that in a short amount of time he would once again be finished, useful to no one again, and alone.

"Simon? You all set? Ready to get this guy now?"

He turned toward Robinson's voice. He saw an enthusiasm in the younger man's eyes.

"Absolutely," he said.

"Good," Walter Robinson said, putting his hand out and grabbing the older man by the arm, a gesture he recognized sprang in part from excitement, and perhaps affection. "Tomorrow, maybe we can go fishing. Or the day after. You promised, remember?"

"I'd like that," Winter said quietly.

They moved the unmarked car.

"This bring back memories?" Robinson asked.

"You get to be my age," Winter replied, smiling slowly, "and everything brings back memories. Spend more time looking backward than forward."

"Not you," said the younger man. "Come on, Simon. Let's finish this guy now. Put the cuffs on him and the fear of God inside him. You and I. Show him he ain't so goddamn smart after all."

"I'd like that," the old detective replied, although he did not know whether he was lying or not.

They chose a vantage point around the corner from the small house, shielded from sight by an eight-foot-high stucco wall that enclosed the target's neighbor's small estate. The SWAT captain made one final check, adjusting the earpiece on his intercom set, made the men count off, and then, with a small chopping motion of his hand, sent the team into action.

The squad barreled around the corner and swooped down the street. Their black jumpsuits blended with the inky midnight air. Robinson, poised just behind the SWAT captain, waited like a sprinter at the start of a race, muscles tightening while listening for the starter's gun.

The SWAT captain listened, hunched over, then repeated out loud in a soft voice: "Back door team in place. No sign of activity. Side door team, ready. Okay, here we go!"

The front door group swung out and down the street on the run, their boots slapping the sidewalk like a drummer beating a reveille.

Walter Robinson held out his hand to restrain Simon Winter for a moment or two, then the two of them lurched forward, just behind the quick-moving dark shapes. The ground beneath their feet seemed to evaporate, and Robinson was hardly aware of the energy he was expending. He had a flash, a momentary memory of his own, cutting down the center of a football field, reaching for the ball suspended in the air, the roar of the spectators dull and distant in his ears. But then this passed and he found his own vision tunneled in on the front door, where a burly SWAT member was readying a door-buster.

"Police! Freeze!" the SWAT captain shouted.

And as Robinson watched, the man swung the thick black steel door-buster and there was a resounding crash and splintering of wood.

A few feet behind Robinson, Simon Winter moved swiftly, his breath coming in jagged pulses.

He immediately heard a high-pitched scream of shock and panic, and glass breaking, and he heard the SWAT captain yelling, above the sudden cacophony, "Go! Go! Go!" and he saw the team members pouring through the shattered door into the house. Robinson had surged ahead as well, trailing the team by a few feet, gun in his outstretched hand. The air was filled with voices, all shouting commands, and he pushed himself toward the entrance of the house and the light that was pouring out into the night like a dam that had sprung a leak.

Simon Winter heard Robinson screaming: "Get down! Get down on the floor! Hands behind your head!"

These words mingled with the woman's frightened cries, sounds that resembled nothing human other than the emotion of fear that engendered them.

Winter vaulted through the door and saw the SWAT captain and one of his men bent over a large man on the floor of the modest house. Robinson, gun pushed up against the man's ear, was shouting commands. To the side, two of the SWAT team held a small, thin, elderly woman. Her white hair had been pinned back and had come loose, so that it flew around her face. She was crying piteously, "What have we done? What have we done?"

The SWAT captain watched as Robinson snapped handcuffs around the supine man's wrists and then half rose.

"We're clear," the captain said with satisfaction. He turned to

Robinson. "Told you so. Piece of cake. So this is the tough old killer you've been hunting?" In a corner of the room the television set was blaring loudly, a late night talk-show host was making jokes. The SWAT captain gestured for one of his men to shut it off.

Walter Robinson jerked the man to his seat and spoke rapidly. "David Isaacson, you're under arrest for murder."

Simon Winter saw the man's face for the first time. Light seemed to slice across the fear in the man's eyes, leaving a scar.

"What have I done?" the man asked.

"Shadow Man!" Robinson fairly spat the words as he jerked him up to his feet. The detective seemed to rattle the man, pushing his face right up to the suspect's. Then he thrust him into a nearby armchair. "You're going away. I'm going to see you on Death Row."

Simon Winter stepped forward then and stared hard at the man in the chair.

"Oh, my God," he said slowly, softly. He reached out and seized Walter Robinson's arm. The young detective turned briskly, irritated at being stopped, and then hesitated when he saw Winter's eyes.

"What is it?" he asked angrily.

Winter felt his mouth grow dry, and the words he spoke seemed to crack and splinter like the door to the house. "Walter, look at him, goddamn it!"

"What?"

"Look at his face! The damn picture! He doesn't look a thing like the goddamn composite!"

For the first time Walter Robinson turned back to the man he'd arrested and stared hard into his face. "No," he said slowly, "Simon, you're wrong. The build is the same, the hair—"

"Look at him! That's not the man Esther Weiss picked out!"

Walter Robinson, a man who sometimes arrogantly prided himself on remaining calm under the most difficult of situations, felt a touch of panic soar through him, unwanted, unwieldy, and almost out of control. His eyes widened as if trying to take in the contradiction between the picture and the man sitting before him.

"Who are you?" he demanded.

"I am David Isaacson," the man stammered in reply. "What have I done?" he asked again.

"Where do you come from?"

The man looked confused, and so Simon Winter stepped forward.

"How long have you been here?"

"On Miami Beach, some twenty years."

"Before that?"

"In New York City. I was a furrier."

"And before that?"

"From Poland, once, many years ago when I was young."

The man's wife finally managed to pull loose from the SWAT team members and threw herself next to her husband. "David, what is it, what is it?" she cried, clinging hysterically. She turned to the policemen and shouted with bitter anger: "Gestapo! Nazis!"

The room grew quiet for an instant, save for the woman's sobs.

"Are you a survivor?" Simon Winter asked abruptly.

The man nodded. "What is this?" he asked, as if sliding into shock.

Robinson stepped over to David Isaacson, grabbed his forearm, and pulled it forward, rotating it slightly. He ripped the man's shirt as he pushed it up. In almost the same motion, he reached into his pocket and pulled out the paper on which he'd written the number Espy Martinez gave him. He thrust the paper down next to the purple-blue tattoo on the man's wizened forearm, and saw immediately that the two numbers were different.

"Oh, my God," he said slowly.

"Gestapo!" the wife cried out again.

Simon Winter saw the same and turned, staring back through the smashed door, out into the night, which seemed to mock them with every shadow.

You're close, he thought. You're close. But where?

# TWENTY-SIX
## THE TEAKETTLE

**T**HE Shadow Man stood silently in a darkened space at the edge of an alleyway, just past the lip of light tossed onto the sidewalk by the fluorescent sign of a vacant pharmacy. He looked up at the sixth floor of the rabbi's apartment building.

The side of him that usually spoke of caution argued that he was unwise to stand there, even for a moment, even if unseen and undetected. He sometimes thought listening to this voice within him was like having some overly protective angel perched on his shoulder. This time, the voice was shrill, insistent, and it demanded that he leave, and leave that instant.

Pack a bag. Check into a hotel by the airport. Fly out on the first plane in the morning.

He shook his head.

I have unfinished business, he argued to himself. It awaits me up in that building.

What business? Stay safe. You have used up this life, as you have used up others before. These years on Miami Beach have been pleasant and profitable, but they have finished now. You knew this time might arrive, and now it has. Too many people are circling around, looking under rocks, checking behind doors, searching for you. You have heard people speaking about the

Shadow Man as if they knew you. It is time to fade away and become someone new.

He leaned back farther into the darkness of the alleyway, pushing his back against a dingy gray wall.

Los Angeles will be nice, he told himself. There was an apartment, bank accounts, and a different identity awaiting him there. Chicago would be acceptable as well. The groundwork for a similar arrangement was established in that city. In Los Angeles, I will have to get a car. Everyone there drives. But in Chicago, that won't be necessary. In Los Angeles, he was to be a retired businessman; in Chicago, he was already known as a retired investor. He considered the two situations, unable to make up his mind. It made no difference, really, he told himself. As soon as he took up either one identity or the next, he would start in building the framework for a third in some new city, so that there was always more than a single option awaiting him. Perhaps Phoenix or Tucson, he thought. Someplace warm. He did not like the idea of a winter in Chicago. He realized he would have to do some research. He did not know whether either of those cities had the type of elderly Jewish community he could tap into. Were there survivors there? he wondered.

Deep in the distant night, an auto-alarm-system klaxon horn severed the still heat. He listened for a moment, until it abruptly disappeared.

He spat on the ground, suddenly furious.

I have enjoyed it here, he whispered to himself. All these years, I have been comfortable. He liked the way the tropical nighttime had a richness to its darkness that seemed to cloak all his angers.

He considered the list of enemies arrayed against him. He dismissed the policeman and the prosecutor swiftly, making a small, involuntary motion with his hand, as if carving a piece of the dark air in front of him. He never feared the police. He believed they were too stolid and unimaginative to catch him. They searched for evidence and clues, and never understood that he was more of an idea. Although this was perhaps as close as they had ever been—as close as anyone had been since 1944—he still considered them too many steps behind him. But his cautious side reminded him: Never before had the police actually known he existed. This made him pause, until his arrogant persona recalled that this was precisely the reason he'd taken so much trouble over the years to always have at least two different identities available. That he'd infrequently needed to hurry was testimony to his careful planning. And, he thought harshly, this is really no different.

But then he pictured the old detective, the neighbor, which made him hesitate. This man worried him more, mostly because he did not completely understand why he was in the picture at all, and because he was neither official nor someone like his usual quarry. The Shadow Man conjured up a vision of Simon Winter and made a quick assessment. He seems dogged and intelligent. He has instincts that are formidable. But he is not here tonight, and will be left clutching at emptiness in the morning. So, the Shadow Man thought, he is perhaps dangerous, but he will remain too slow and out of step. And what really are his resources? A cleverness and some experience. Enough to find me? No.

Still, he shook his head and told himself: You should have killed him that night in his apartment. He was lucky.

He won't be lucky again.

The Shadow Man took a deep breath of air and pictured the old pair up in the apartment.

They are the real danger, he told himself. They always have been. They always will be.

A star shell of fury burst within his chest, stoked by long memory.

They have always been to blame. Since the very beginning.

They are the only ones who remember.

They are the only ones who can pick me out.

For a moment he shifted his feet, then forced himself to remain under control, although he felt withering rage resounding throughout his body. How many were left? he wondered suddenly. These two? Others? How many more can there be, who can recall the Shadow Man?

Perhaps none.

He allowed himself a small smile.

Maybe these are the last two who ever saw the Shadow Man. He had spent much time, in archives and memorials, among documents and videotapes, reading books and studying faces.

Years of work. Killing work. It was inevitable, he told himself. Inevitable that someday you would find the end of the line. The last Jews from Berlin. And perhaps they were right there in front of him, waiting in that sixth-floor apartment.

This thought filled him with a familiar and welcome desire.

And so, even if his cautious side told him that escape was wise, and had been insisting this since earlier in the evening, when he'd first overheard someone say "Shadow Man" as he'd stepped onto the elevator in his own condominium and had patiently listened to the conversation beside him and learned of the announcement made in those places of worship, his sense of fury told him that he could not depart for any of the other lives he'd so carefully established knowing that those two old people were left behind to bedevil him on some future date.

Inwardly, he smiled.

I will enjoy ending them, he thought. Perhaps it will be a beginning for myself.

The Shadow Man collected himself. He compromised with his cautious side: I will leave by midday. I will finish this and then I will not hesitate, I will depart.

He told himself that truly there was not that much to worry about.

I have prepared this well. There has been no hurry to this collection. I have been inside the rabbi's building three separate times, been to the roof and been to the basement. I have examined the electrical system and the circuit breaker box, and I have stood outside the rabbi's apartment. I have even checked the old microfilm of the architect's plans filed with the City of Miami Beach, showing the layout of the rooms inside. I have prepared a plan and it will work.

It has always worked.

He remembered a time, many years earlier. It came back to him slowly, a memory that seemed like a dream that faded in the first moments of awakening. He could picture a family, and he could picture the upstairs, attic flat that he knew they hid in. Two small children, who cried when the bombers came over; a mother and father, grandparents, a cousin; all jammed into two little rooms. He tried to remember their names, but was unable. He re-

membered they had pleaded hard for their lives, and paid hand-
somely. And then they had died, like all the others. They were
like rats, he thought, holed up in some deep crevasse. But he
knew how to bring them out into the open.

He looked up at the apartment building.

I have done this many times before.

He reached down and picked up a small bag at his feet that held
several important items. Hefting this, he once again stared up at
the building.

*Judenfrei,* he thought to himself. That was what the Reichs-
führer once had promised to the entire world. And that is the same
promise I made to myself. Perhaps tonight I will finally be
*Judenfrei.*

He visualized the old woman and the old rabbi.

His face seemed to slide then into a cold, frozen visage, one of
determination and duty. He stepped slightly forward. From the
edge of the alley, he carefully searched the empty street. There
was some traffic a few blocks away, but nothing that overly concerned him. And so, moving from darkness to darkness, he eagerly crossed toward his targets.

They do not know it, he reminded himself. None of them ever
knew it. But they have already been dead for days.

Simon Winter watched wordlessly as Walter Robinson tried to
sort through the confusion caused by the arrest of David Isaacson.
The elderly man and his wife sat on a bench in the corner of the
homicide offices, alternately scowling, threatening to call their attorney—though clearly they had none, especially one who would
arise in the middle of the night to help them—and grudgingly of-
fering up the occasional morsel of information. These came more
readily after Walter Robinson assured them that the city would
pay for the repair of their front door and any items broken in the
mistaken arrest. This back and forth between the angry couple
and the detective went on for some time, moments that drove Simon Winter toward frustration.

It was deep into the night and heading toward morning when
Robinson finally slipped away from the couple and approached
Simon Winter. Behind the detective an overly solicitous,

cloyingly polite, uniformed officer was helping the Isaacsons to their feet, ushering them out of the offices and to a squad car and a chauffeured ride home.

"Well?" Winter asked.

"Well, shit," Robinson replied, sitting down heavily in a seat next to the old man. "Aren't you tired, Simon? Don't you want to go home and go to bed and wish maybe this mess would just get up and disappear while you slept?"

"That sounds unlikely," Winter replied, though he smiled through the lateness of the hour.

"No shit," Robinson said. He laughed, self-mocking. "Man, have I made a pile of crap here that's gonna take me a month to straighten out. . . ."

"A month in triplicate," Winter said. The young detective snorted another laugh.

"You're right about that. Man, Simon, you don't have any idea the forms I'm gonna be filling out. And then I'm gonna get my butt hauled in front of every brass-assed superior officer in need of chewing somebody out. And that's a big number. And then there's the department lawyers. Gotta give them their shot . . ."

"He planned it, you know," Winter said softly. "He knew somebody might make the connection, and so instead of making up a phony name and address, he used a real person. He had a choice between creating a fiction that maybe we could backtrack from or that might have drawn someone's attention, and a confusion that would create a mess, and he selected wisely, I think. And he picked out someone that resembled him, if only slightly. What do you think? Think he saw Isaacson at some meeting? On a videotape? Strolling on the beach? In a synagogue? Grocery store? Restaurant? Picked him out of some crowd without the guy even having the slightest idea what he was contributing to?"

"Somewhere, you're right about that. Maybe Isaacson will be able to figure it out for us after he's calmed down. But I doubt it. Anyway, it ain't gonna happen tonight."

Walter Robinson let slide a long, deep breath. "The Shadow Man seems to have a good idea how bureaucracies like the police department work. Think he was a cop once?"

"Remember who trained him. Where could you find a more devoted bureaucracy than Nazi Germany?"

"Maybe right here on Miami Beach," Robinson said bitterly, pushing haphazardly at some forms on his desk. "Ah, hell, that's not true. But I see what you're driving at. The fucker's smart, isn't he?"

"Yes. And you know, all that preparation tells me something else."

Robinson nodded, not listening for an answer, but providing one himself: "That the Shadow Man has an exit door all ready and open, and once he walks through it . . ."

"He's gone."

"That occurred to me as well." Robinson leaned back. "I made a call," he said slowly, "just wanted to check something out. While the Isaacsons were stewing over there. I called out to Los Angeles and got the director of the Holocaust Center out there on the phone. You know the letter that Esther Weiss had? Signed by an associate director?"

"No such person, right?"

"Right. Letterhead was proper, though."

"That's easy enough. Just write them a letter, requesting any old thing, get something back on their nice official stationery, head to a copy machine and bingo, there you have it. Hell, you could take it off a fund-raising letter."

"That's what I thought too."

"So," Simon Winter said slowly, "where does all this leave us?"

Robinson paused. "Maybe the old folks will turn up something. Or maybe he'll make a move for them. Or something. The phone was ringing off the hook at the rabbi's earlier. Maybe the announcement will do some good, other than scaring the hell out of everybody. Otherwise, well, we're not exactly at square one, but what the hell square we're on, I don't know."

Winter nodded. He held his hand out and grasped a piece of the air between them. "He seems close, and then, nothing," he said. "We just have to grab faster."

"We have to find someone to grab at," Robinson said.

He leaned back, rocking in the swivel chair at his desk.

"All right, Simon. Tomorrow, you and I, we start in again with the composite." He smiled. "Instead of going fishing. That still seems our best chance. What do you think?"

"Legwork never hurts a case," the old detective replied, though he doubted he had the time and energy for it.

"We should head home now," Robinson said. "I'll drop you off. And tomorrow, don't wear that gun, okay? I'm trusting you that you've got a proper license somewhere. But I sure as hell know you haven't got a permit to carry a concealed weapon."

Simon Winter managed a small grin. He rose. The thought of sleep wasn't unattractive, and there, within the brightness of the police headquarters, any sense of urgency dissipated slightly as fatigue nibbled at his imagination.

With an effort not unlike a diver launching himself from a high board, Robinson kicked himself up and out of his seat. "Let's go before the sun comes up," he said.

The two men rode the elevator down to the ground floor in late night silence, each filled with his own thoughts. When they stepped outside the cocoon of the police building, a wet warmth seemed to drape over them, as if there had been a storm nearby that had deluged some close area but just missed them. They walked through the lights to the detective's unmarked car and slid into their seats, staying just the smallest step ahead of exhaustion. Robinson slowly ground the starter on the car and gunned the engine twice, as if that could invigorate him as well. The police dispatcher's voice scratched through the radio speaker, and Robinson leaned forward, reaching for the knob to shut off the irritating, tinny sound, only to have his forearm seized by Winter.

He looked up at the old man, whose eyes had abruptly widened, and in the same moment, Robinson felt a surge of electric energy race through his own body, past all the frustrations and weariness, rendering him abruptly and completely alert.

Winter's voice was hard-edged, but almost breathless. "That was the rabbi's place, goddamn it! That was the rabbi's address she just gave. I heard it! She just moved a goddamn hook and ladder company to the rabbi's apartment building!"

Robinson thrust the car in gear and smashed down on the gas pedal.

"Who's there? Goddamn it! Who's there?" Winter shouted, as if he couldn't remember.

Walter Robinson didn't reply. He knew. Two old people, one young and probably inexperienced police officer, and Espy Martinez.

And one other.

Espy Martinez had fallen asleep on the living room couch shortly after the two survivors had departed for their respective bedrooms. The police officer detailed to watching over them had repaired to the kitchen area, where he sipped coffee, tried to read a novel that the rabbi had recommended, and half dozed while counting the minutes before his shift changed and someone else would get assigned to a task he considered slightly glorified baby-sitting, and which had bored the interest out of him within five minutes of his arrival.

When the ringing of the condominium's fire alarm system had suddenly creased the air, he'd been on the verge of sleep, and he shot to his feet unsteadily, cursing in surprise.

Espy Martinez also rose up, a fear falling through her stomach, thrashing about in the semidarkness and disorientation of awakening in an unfamiliar room.

In the guest bedroom, Frieda Kroner had been having an unsettling dream, one that touched the shores of nightmare, where she had seen herself in a space she couldn't recognize and that seemed to grow increasingly smaller around her. Every time she tried to find the exit door, it seemed to move, just as she reached for the doorknob. The alarm bell sliced across this sweat-soaked sleep, and she awakened, shouting in German, "Air raid! Air raid! Get to the shelters!" until a few seconds passed and she remembered where and what year it was.

The rabbi, as well, awakened abruptly, shivering as if cold, the ringing bell beating on him like a fighter's flurry of punches. He reached for his dressing gown and hurried from his bedroom.

The four people came together in near-panic and surprise in the living room.

The young officer spoke first. His voice was slightly on the high edge and rapid, as if the words were trying to keep up with his heartbeat. "Look, everyone stay calm, just stay calm." He said this, but of course his tone implied the opposite. "Okay, stay together, and we'll head out, right now. . . ."

Espy Martinez took a step toward the door, only to be stopped by Frieda Kroner grabbing her arm.

"No!" the old woman shouted. "No! It is him! He is here!"

The others turned to face her.

"It's the goddamn fire alarm," the young policeman said. "Let's stick together and get the hell outside."

Frieda Kroner stamped her foot. "It is him! We are being attacked!"

The policeman looked at her as if she were crazy. "It's a fire, damn it! We may not have much time!"

The rabbi spoke then, his voice quavering, but filled with calm. "Frieda is correct. It is him. He is here." He turned toward Espy Martinez. "Do not move, Miss Martinez."

The young policeman stared at the old people. He tried to force reason and calm into his voice, but these emotions were frayed. "Look, Rabbi, goddamn it, these old buildings are fire traps! They can go up in a second! I've seen it! I've seen people get trapped! We've got to get out, and get out now! What floor are we on?"

The rabbi looked oddly at him. "The sixth."

"Goddamn it, don't you know that there's not a piece of fire-fighting equipment on the Beach that can reach this high? We've got to get downstairs, and do it now!"

The ringing continued, filling the air around them with insistence. They could hear voices penetrating through the apartment walls and door, and muffled sounds of feet in the hallway outside. They all stopped and listened, all hearing several panicked screams as well.

"See! Damn it!" the young policeman shouted. "Everyone else is getting the hell out! Come on, once a fire gets going in these old buildings, boom! They just go! There's just not that much time! We've got to get to the stairway now!"

Frieda Kroner sat down abruptly on a sofa. "It is a trap, yes. But it is him that has set it." She folded her arms. Her voice rattled, but she managed to force the words out: "He is coming for us now."

The rabbi sat next to her. "Frieda is correct," he said. "We open that door and we will die."

"We stay here, we're gonna get cooked!" the young policeman insisted. He stared at the old couple as if they were completely out of their minds.

"No," Frieda Kroner said. "I will not leave."

"Nor I," said the rabbi. "It is how he caught so many of us once. Not this time."

"You're out of your minds," the policeman said. "Look," he pleaded. "I'm right with you. Even if this crazy old fucker is out there, he's not going to try anything with me by your side. Come on, let's go!"

"No," Frieda Kroner repeated.

The young policeman raised his eyes, imploring the heavens to force reason on the obstinate old people.

"We're gonna die!" he shouted. "Miss Martinez, help me."

But Espy Martinez just stared at the old couple.

"All right," the policeman said unsteadily, after letting a short silence speak for them. "Look, let's do this: I will go out and check it out. I'll see what's happening, and I'll come back for you as soon as I know the coast is clear. If I can, I'll bring a fireman. Got that? Okay? You sit tight, and I'll be back with help. Miss Martinez, you come with me, at least then you'll be safe and out, okay? Now let's go!"

He hurried to the door, and Espy Martinez took a single step behind him, then stopped.

"No, you go. I'll stay here with the rabbi and Frieda."

The policeman turned around. "Don't be crazy," he said.

"Go!" she answered. "I'm staying."

The young policeman hesitated, then thrust open the door and disappeared down the now vacant corridor toward a nearby stairway.

At first the two men did not speak as the unmarked car, headlights flashing, siren wailing, hurtled through the diffuse city lights. Simon Winter gripped the door until his knuckles whitened with the strain. The city seemed to race past them, like a film in accelerated motion.

Walter Robinson steered the car with death in his heart.

As the engine surged and the wheels squealed in complaint, as the force of motion pinned him to his seat, he realized that he was in real trouble. Everything that meant anything to him seemed suddenly to be threatened by the Shadow Man: his love, his career, his future. This knowledge drove him to desperate fury. He threw the car down the street with an urgency beyond anything he'd ever known, gasping for air as the speed seemed to rob him of wind.

Winter spoke first, groaning as the car spun briefly out of control, then righted itself with an anguished machine complaint.

"Hurry," he shouted.

"I am," Robinson replied between gritted teeth. He shouted out an obscenity as some red-flash sports car started to pull out in front of them. There was a blaring of horns as they swept past.

"Two blocks, hurry," Winter urged.

Walter Robinson could see the building looming ahead. He saw the beat of the police and fire strobe lights twisting and turning in the night. He slammed both feet on the brake pedal, and the cruiser swerved to the curb.

The two men thrust themselves out of the vehicle. Robinson stood by the door, peering toward a melee of people in nightgowns, bathrobes, and pajamas, milling about in front of the apartment building, dodging out of the way as firemen started to string hoses to a nearby hydrant, while others lurched into air tanks and seized axes.

"Espy!" he shouted. "Espy!" He turned to Winter. "She's not there," he yelled. "I'm going up after them."

"Go!" Winter replied. He waved the young detective forward with a sweep of his hand.

But in that second, as Robinson turned, Winter had another idea, a cold-steel thought that took no affection or devotion into its equation. He did not follow Robinson, as the frantic policeman dashed across the street and, ignoring the cries of protest and danger that suddenly rose from the fire department personnel, burst forward into the building. Instead, Winter slid slowly to the side of the street, stepping back into a shadow of his own, in the lee of a building, only a few feet away from where the Shadow Man had stood himself a short time earlier, although he did not know this. He searched out a vantage point from where he knew he could see almost everything. The panorama of firemen and trucks, policemen and rescue workers, spread out before him. But he kept his eyes on the clutch of people who'd emerged from the condominium and who were standing about nervously, frightened, pushed by the equipment and fear just off to the side of the building, wearing bathrobes and worry.

The ringing in the hallways continued. Espy Martinez turned toward the old people. But Frieda Kroner rose.

"We must get ready," she said.

But before she was able to move, the lights in the apartment abruptly quit, throwing the room into complete darkness.

Espy Martinez gasped, and both old people cried out.

"Stay calm!" the rabbi shouted. "Where are you, Frieda?"

"I am here," she said. "Here, Rabbi, at your side."

"Miss Martinez?"

"I'm here, Rabbi. Oh, my God, I hate it! Where are the lights?"

"All right," the old man said evenly, "this is what he will do. He is a man of darkness. We know that. He will be here any second. Frieda?"

"I'm ready, Rabbi."

The three of them stayed in the center of the room, listening for sounds other than the ringing of the alarm bell. Then, after a few moments, penetrating behind that noise, they heard the distant wail of sirens heading toward them. But these were overcome by a pungent, frightening odor that began to seep around them like the fear they all felt.

"Smoke!" Espy Martinez choked.

"Stay calm!" the rabbi insisted.

"I am calm," Frieda Kroner said. "But we need to get ready." Her voice seemed to trail across the room, and Espy Martinez heard her disappear into the kitchen. There was the sound of drawers opening and closing, and then steps as she returned. At almost the same time, the rabbi seemed to move about the living room, and Espy Martinez heard a desk drawer open and then slam shut.

"All right," the rabbi said. "Let's wait for the policeman to return."

The smell of smoke, not strong, but still insistent, swirled around them.

"Patience," the rabbi said.

"Strength," Frieda Kroner replied.

Espy Martinez felt the darkness seep over her and through her, wrapping itself around her like some graveyard mist. She tried to tell herself to remain calm, but slowly she felt the tug and twist of panic searching around within her, seeking a handhold. She could hear her breath coming in short, sharp bursts, almost as if each intake of wind wasn't enough to fill her lungs, and like some drowning person, she wanted to thrash for the surface. She did not know, in that moment, what she feared the most: the night, the fire that lurked somewhere in the building, or the man the old people were certain was moving toward them steadily. All these things became tangled in Espy Martinez's imagination, along with ancient and unresolved fears, and she stood stock-still in the black room, feeling as though she was spinning in some terrible centrifuge.

She coughed and choked.

Then she heard another sound, muffled, close yet not too close, an urgent pounding.

"What's that?" she whispered. Her voice was cracked.

"I don't know," the rabbi said. "Listen!"

The pounding sound seemed to vibrate in the room. And then they heard a loud, demanding voice: "Miami Beach Fire Department! Anyone in there?"

The pounding continued, and then the voice and the sound came closer. Espy Martinez realized instantly that it was a fireman, moving down the apartment corridor, knocking on every door, searching for anyone who might have stayed behind.

"It's a fireman," she said loudly. "He'll get us out! He's looking for us!"

And before either of the old people could react to this, she jumped across the living room, half stumbling in the darkness over some wayward piece of furniture. She seized the door and pulled it open as behind her both the rabbi and Frieda Kroner shouted: "No! Don't open up!"

She did not hear them, instead flinging the door wide and calling out: "Here! Here! We need help!"

She heard a man's voice from close by in the darkness and could just make out a shape heading toward her.

"Who is it?" the voice asked.

"It's me," she said, "and the rabbi and—"

The blow caught her around the shoulder and across the jaw, knocking her almost senseless and spinning her around. She fell back into the apartment with a half scream and groan. She did not black out, though she could feel her grip on her consciousness loosened, and she was suddenly aware that she was on the floor and that there was a shape hovering over her. A shaft of light sliced across the room, and in her dizziness she saw the rabbi had a flashlight in his hand. She saw too that the figure looming above her had a knife and he was slashing down at her, just as the rabbi hit him in the face with the beam of light. The glare seemed to cause him to alter his swing, and she felt the blade carve through the air just above her.

The Shadow Man straightened up, lifting his arm as if to block the light that coursed from the rabbi's hand, and he did not see Frieda Kroner, who had jumped to where Espy Martinez lay on the floor and who was swinging an odd black shape toward him with a great grunt of exertion. The shape thudded fiercely into his arm with a dull, iron noise, and he screamed in unfamiliar pain.

The old woman was shouting then, in her native tongue: *"Nein! Nein! Nicht dieses Mal!* Not this time!" And she swung the weapon again, and again it found flesh.

The light in the rabbi's hand wavered, flashing about the room as he too sprung toward the Shadow Man from the opposite side, so that the attacker was bracketed as he straddled the fallen young woman. In the rabbi's free hand he held a large brass menorah, which whistled as it cut the air. His first blow smashed the Shadow Man's shoulder, and the rabbi roared a deep wordless battle cry with his effort. The flashlight fell to the floor, and for just a second Espy Martinez saw the rabbi standing like a baseball batter in the hitter's box, readying a second swing. Her head pivoted dizzily and she tried to push herself up, only to be knocked down by the force of the Shadow Man's leg as it passed by her. His foot caught her chest, and for an instant she thought she'd been stabbed.

She wondered in that moment whether she'd been killed, then realized she hadn't. She pushed herself up again, straining to hear past the guttural cries coming from Frieda Kroner, until she heard the rabbi say, quietly, breathlessly, like a man who had won a hard race: "He's gone!"

And she realized this was true.

She felt as if the world was suddenly quiet, although in reality the room around her was still being riveted by the continuing sounds of sirens and alarm bells.

She turned in the darkness to Frieda Kroner, who was speaking to her in German. "*Horen sie mich? Sind sie verletzt? Haben sie Schmerzen?* Are you all right? Are you hurt? Are you in pain?"

And oddly, she thought she understood every word, and replied: "No, no, I'm fine, Mrs. Kroner. I'm fine. What did you hit him with?"

The old woman laughed suddenly. "With the rabbi's iron teakettle."

The rabbi picked up his flashlight and shone it into their faces. Espy Martinez thought they all must look pale, as if death standing so close to them had left a bit of his color behind, but Frieda Kroner, at least, had a wild, Valkyrie look of triumph in her eyes.

"He ran! The coward!" Then she stopped, and said in a much quieter voice: "I suppose no one ever fought back before. . . ."

The rabbi, however, was direct: "We must get him! Now! It is our chance!"

Espy Martinez gathered herself, nodding her head. She reached out and seized the flashlight. "That's right, Rabbi. Follow me."

And grabbing them both, she led them out into the corridor, like a pilot flying through a thick fog, pushing through the darkness for the stairwell.

Walter Robinson, battling an unfamiliar panic, unable to see, trying to feel his way in the blackness and run at the same time, raced up the emergency stairs, his feet making a drumroll of urgency against the concrete steps. He could hear his breathing, forced, harsh, punctuated by the distant sirens and the continual ringing of the alarm system.

He did not see the body until he tripped over it.

Like a blind-side block, it sent him spinning forward, pitched out of control, smashing his hands against the stairs as he fell. He shouted out in surprise and fought to regain his composure. He gathered himself and reached down, almost seized by some emotion beyond fear at the thought that his hand would find the wizened skin of either the rabbi or Frieda Kroner, or worse, the soft touch of Espy Martinez. When he felt the bulk of the body, he was initially confused. Then, as he groped in the darkness, he touched the policeman's badge. He drew his hand back sharply and realized that it was covered with blood.

He bellowed then, as loud as he could, "Espy! I'm coming!" anything, he hoped, that might distract the man he was certain was ahead of him. Anything that might make him hesitate in his deadly task.

He still could see nothing, and anything he might have heard was obscured by the inner cacophony of fear. He seized hold of the stair railing and bounded ahead, racing again for the sixth floor.

He called out again: "Espy!"

And then from within the darkness, he saw a shaft of light, and heard a reply: "Walter!"

He cried a third time: "Espy!"

And then he saw the three of them as they flashed the light toward him.

"Are you okay?" he called out.

"Yes, yes," she shouted. "But he's here!"

Walter Robinson reached out and grasped hold of Espy Martinez, who wrapped her arms around him, and whispered, "Jesus, Walter, he was here! He was here and tried to kill me. The rabbi and Mrs. Kroner, they saved me, and he ran. He ran away when she hit him. But he's here still, somewhere."

Robinson pushed her back and looked at the old couple. "Are you all right?" he asked.

"We must find him," the rabbi replied.

The detective removed his weapon.

"He's here somewhere, right in this darkness," the rabbi said. "In the building somewhere."

But Frieda Kroner shook her head. "No, I think he ran. Maybe down the other stairwell, at the other end of the building. Quickly, quickly, we must go!"

Trying to hurry their pace, Espy Martinez clinging to Walter Robinson, and the rabbi and Frieda Kroner walking with the gingerness of age but the urgency of need, the four of them began their retreat down the stairwell. Robinson took the flashlight and led the way, pausing only at the third floor to briefly examine the body of the policeman. The old woman gasped when the flashlight's beam caught the red stain of blood across the man's throat. But what she said was: "Faster, faster, we cannot let him get away!"

Simon Winter clung to his spot of darkness, watching the scene in front of the apartment building. There is a moment when one is fishing in shallow waters that one spots just the slightest ripple of motion, as an unseen shape beneath the surface pushes water in a direction different from the wind and the currents and the tides, and one recognizes the closeness of their quarry. It was that subtle shift in the hurried movements outside the rabbi's home that Winter searched for. He thought: There will be one person here whose presence has nothing to do with fire and alarm and being forced from the comfort of one's bed in the early morning hours, and everything to do with killing.

So he let his eyes scour the scene, looking for that small push against the flow.

When he saw it, he straightened up sharply, dark excitement filling his core.

What he saw was this: a thickset man, dressed in simple, dark clothes. The man was hunched over slightly, emerging from the building, allowing himself to be directed by a fireman who had better things to do, toward the knot of displaced people gathered by the side of the street.

Simon Winter took a step or two parallel to the man.

He saw him disappear into the midst of the crowd, picking his way from the front to the rear. The others were all staring ahead, up toward their homes, searching for smoke and flames, but seeing none, impatiently waiting for some signal or information from the fire personnel who were hurrying in and out of the building.

But this one man seemed to have none of the same concerns.

Instead, he maneuvered slowly through the throng of anxious people, head down, obscuring his face, working steadily toward the back and the darkness of the street behind them.

Simon Winter picked up his pace.

He could not see the man's eyes, could not see his face, but he knew. For a moment he twisted about, trying to spot Walter Robinson or any other officer who might help him. But he could see none. He realized that he had stepped from the shadows himself, onto the sidewalk, and was caught in a shaft of light thrown by an illuminated store sign. Winter took a step into the street just as the man looked up for one second and saw him, standing out, staring at him.

Both men froze, in recognition.

Then, suddenly, from behind them, in a sound that defeated sirens, alarms, and the noise of the fire-fighting machinery, Simon Winter heard a voice. It was raised high, but not a scream, more a sentry's great shout of alarm.

The words were in German and they fractured the night: *"Der Schattenmann! Der Schattenmann! Er ist hier! Er ist hier!"*

Winter turned abruptly, for just an instant, and saw Frieda Kroner stepping out into the center of the street. The rabbi was beside her, and he too shouted: "Der Schattenmann is amongst us! Find him!"

He waved his arms wildly.

Simon Winter saw Espy Martinez and Walter Robinson, clutched together, a few feet behind the old couple. The detective had his weapon drawn, his face set, as his eyes roamed the area. Winter saw him shouting directions at the fire personnel and at the surprised uniformed officers gathered at the scene. Then he quickly spun back to the crowd of people, and saw that the Shadow Man had turned and run. He just caught a glimpse of the man's shape as he plunged down a darkened side street, heading in the direction of the beach. The people in the crowd were suddenly buzzing, talking, a hundred different voices all battling for prominence, faces bent together in shock and astonishment. He thought he should try to signal Walter Robinson, and in that second realized he had no time.

So, instead, he forged ahead, alone, in pursuit, the words "He is here! He is here!" ringing loudly in the night behind him.

# TWENTY-SEVEN
## ═══════════*MORNING*

**S**IMON Winter ran with a speed he'd not felt in years.

The street around him seemed a tangled maze of parked cars, shrubbery, garbage cans, and city debris. He swept forward with the energy of a man much younger, settling into a dogged, quick pace, thinking that this was not a sprint he was running, but a marathon. He could just make out the solid shape of the Shadow Man as the killer darted from darkness to murky gloom, dodging the shafts of light thrown by street lamps and the occasional store sign.

He had nearly a block-length lead on Winter at the start of the race, but by the time the Shadow Man emerged from the side street onto Ocean Drive, the old detective had cut a third of that away and left it behind him. He could hear the slapping sound that his basketball shoes made against the brick-red sidewalk, and he stretched his stride farther, so that his long legs rapaciously chewed up the distance.

The streets were empty in the predawn darkness.

The young people that were so prevalent everywhere on the Beach had slid away in assignation or frustration, leaving the night spots quiet, lights dimmed. The usual thump of iron-hard music had evaporated into the night. No fast cars squealed their tires and accelerated in youthful posturing. No giggling, alcohol-smeared voices called out to each other. No crowds jammed the walkways searching for adventure. It was the dead time of the night, when fatigue even afflicts the young, just before night loses its grip on the city and daylight slowly fingers the horizon, searching for the morning.

Even the police and fire trucks that jammed the street outside the rabbi's apartment seemed suddenly to be nothing more than ancient memory to Simon Winter. If there were city sounds of sirens and urgency, they were distant, like childhood recollection.

He was alone as he ran, save for the specter ahead of him, dodging across the width of Ocean Drive, leaving behind the meager lights of the restaurants and bars that were only a short time earlier jammed with people.

Winter breathed in hard, and listened to the ocean.

It was off to his left, running parallel to his course as he pursued the Shadow Man. He could hear the waves beating their eternal tattoo against the shore.

He swept past the last of the night spots, slicing now next to high rises like so many huge monumental blocks that obscured the beach and ocean from the street. He could feel a stitch forming in his side, but he ignored it and ran on, letting the pounding of his feet fill him, keeping his eyes on the man ahead, who had settled now into a steady, fierce pace of his own.

I will run him into the ground, Winter told himself.

I will chase him until he turns gasping for air, exhausted.

And then I will have him, because I am stronger than he.

He bit down hard on his lip and then let air burst out from his lungs in a great gasp.

Other small pains tried to force themselves onto his consciousness—a blister that erupted on his foot, a dull ache in his leg—but he ignored these, then negotiated with them. If you do not cramp up on me, calf muscle, then I will soak you for a long time in warm water, which you will enjoy and which will restore you. So I make this promise to you: Give me this race and I will repay you tenfold, but just do not cramp up now. And as he said this to himself, the pain seemed to subside, and he picked up his pace slightly.

He saw that the Shadow Man no longer dashed from darkness

to shade, that he now ran straight ahead, arms pumping, an arrow seeking to simply outdistance his pursuit. This encouraged Winter, and gave him some new strength. He thought: Now, perhaps finally, after all these years, you too know a little bit of the fear that arrives when someone relentless is on your heels. Now, perhaps, you know a little bit of what it was like for so many others. It's hard, isn't it, when you want to hide but you have no time, and the pursuit at your heels is striding closer with every yard?

Now, you've felt panic for the first time.

And I hope this feeling hurts.

He ran on, letting all the world around him slide away, until he saw only the Shadow Man's back as the killer fled, block after block, straight down the island toward the southernmost tip of Miami Beach.

Simon Winter saw the Shadow Man glance back once and then increase his speed, and he recognized this for what it was, the precursor to evasion; so when he suddenly shifted direction, like an athlete on a field of play, slicing off into a walkway that cut next to the end of a condominium building, Winter was ready, already sprinting hard, so that the change in direction wouldn't give his quarry even a moment to hide in some dark corner. The Shadow Man must have felt the distance between them diminish, because he did not hesitate. Instead, he raced down the walkway and smoothly vaulted over a fence, heading toward the wide stretch of beach and the ocean beyond. Winter was prepared. The fence was chain link, about eight feet high, designed to keep people walking on the sand out of the condominium's property. He tried to take it in stride, grasping hold of the metal links and clambering over the top. He tossed a leg forward, but one of the sharpened wire links on the uppermost rim caught the cloth of his pants and he tumbled forward, momentarily losing his balance.

For a sickening instant he felt himself suspended in the air, and then he pitched out, falling hard to the solid packed sand beneath him.

Pain rose up and grabbed him.

Red hurt filled his eyes and he felt like a fighter who takes a blow to the chin, unsure whether he was still standing or had fallen to the canvas.

He lost his wind, and a momentary head-spinning dizziness wrapped around him. He had a taste of gritty sand in his mouth, and he forced himself to one knee, shaking his head to clear his thoughts.

He peered down the beach unsteadily. In the gloom of light thrown by the apartment building, he could just make out the shape of the Shadow Man running on the hard gravel and coral sand a dozen yards from the edge of the white-rimmed surf. His fall had lost him his advantage, and he pushed himself up, making a quick inventory of his body, searching for broken bones, and found none. Shaken, he stepped ahead unsteadily.

Simon Winter took a deep breath, gritted his teeth, and started running again. First one hesitant stride, then another, squeezing speed past pain, recovering the pace that he hoped would shorten the distance between them. He could feel a trickle of blood at the corner of his lip and a contusion forming on his forehead, and he thought he'd cut himself when he fell to the earth, and then, slotting these with the other stiffnesses and pains that were abruptly shouting for attention, he pushed on, ignoring them all.

The crash of waves against the beach was stronger now. He ran, keeping cadence with the rhythm of the ocean.

Night seemed to be loosening around him. He was suddenly aware of where he was: racing through the spot at the very tip of Miami Beach, where they'd come across poor Irving Silver's clothes, past the small, empty park across from Government Cut, with its huge schools of tarpon, heading out the long rock jetty that reached far into the ocean.

As he ran, Winter thought: The Shadow Man has been here before and he is comfortable in this darkness. He thinks he owns it, but he does not know that I have been to this place as well, and so it is as much mine as it is his.

He clambered up onto the rocks and then to the wooden walkway that the fishermen used. You're here, he thought, somewhere straight ahead.

The old detective peered into the vaporous night. His eyes searched over the dark, hunched shapes of the black boulders that made up the jetty. And he thought: One of those figures breathes and waits.

From where the fishermen's platform ended, the jetty pushed more than a quarter mile farther into the sea. Winter stopped and reached slowly beneath his jacket, removing his old service revolver.

Then he stepped to the end of the fishing platform, still staring out at the haphazard jumble of jagged rocks. White spray slapped at the slick black shapes.

Did you know, he asked carefully, you were running to the end of the earth?

He nodded to himself. He ran to the darkness. He ran to where he knew there would be no light.

Simon Winter's hand rested on a wooden barrier constructed at the limit of the platform. I have fished here, he thought. It is time to fish again.

He knew a cautious man would simply wait there until light slid up over the horizon. He lifted his eyes and looked to the east and thought there might be just the smallest graying at the edge of the world. If he waited, he realized, soon enough a police car would come along, and soon enough dawn would mold shapes out of the blackness of night. But even as he thought of patience and delay, and recognizing that he'd pursued the Shadow Man into a corner, he clambered forward, over the wooden barrier, onto the glistening, wet jetty rocks. He continued searching for the man lurking in the remaining darkness, somewhere ahead of him. He thought: Do not give him time to think. Do not give him time to catch his breath. Don't give him the time he needs to gather himself and prepare for you. Let the fear of the chase work hard for you. No one has ever growled at his heels the way you have this night. Take him now, when he is being hurt by this uncertainty. Although he did not say this to himself, it was almost as if Winter was afraid that by waiting for the morning half-light to show over the horizon, his quarry would somehow evaporate and disappear in the brightness of day.

This is our time, he thought. Now.

Moving slowly, trying not to lose his balance and slip on the wet rocks, he slowly worked his way toward the end of the jetty. He was alert, on edge, fighting to keep himself steady and knowing that somewhere, amidst the blackness, the Shadow Man had turned, hunkered down, and was waiting for him.

He said a small prayer, wishing that perhaps a stray light from the rich man's development on Fisher Island would slap the jetty, just enough so that he could see the Shadow Man, in whatever crevasse he hid. This prayer, however, went unanswered. Muttering an obscenity, Winter pushed forward gingerly, trying to be certain of each step he took. The basketball shoes that had served him so well in the race down the street now threatened to betray him. They gave him little purchase on the satiny surface of the jetty rocks.

He felt his foot sliding, and he thumped down, catching himself before slipping into the sea waters. The edge of a rock creased his knee, sending a sharp pain through his leg. He cursed quietly, beneath his breath, and rose again, slightly unsteadily, pausing to search ahead, narrowing his eyes as he looked down the length of stone shapes.

But in that moment's hesitation, the Shadow Man surged from the darkness between two rocks, grunting with a great burst of force, driving his knife blade at the old detective.

Winter pivoted at the sound coming at him, lowering his shoulder to absorb the force of the assault. It was as if a piece of the night had risen up against him. He tried to bring his weapon to bear on the shape that thrust at him, but could not find the human shape in the grip of black that charged at him.

He shouted out, some crazed sound of fear, knowing that it was probably a knife slicing the night, hunting for his flesh. He grabbed out with his free hand to ward off the blow. For a second he felt a razor's breath jab through his palm, and he grabbed at the pain before it could find his chest, wrapping his fingers around the Shadow Man's wrist.

He realized that the same slippery dark world that had bedeviled him and had made his feet slide on the rocks had compromised the force of the Shadow Man's attack. Instead of striking out like some deadly feral snake intent on the kill, he had scrambled, slithering, losing some of his strength and forcing the knife slightly astray. Despite Winter's grip on the Shadow Man's arm, it bore down, slicing into the loose folds of his windbreaker, fraying his shirt, where, for an instant, it was caught like a fish in a net.

The momentum of the assault tumbled Winter backward. He felt himself falling, twisting like a drunk on the ice, slamming down hard against the rocks. He could feel the thickly muscled forearm still in his grip—he knew he could not let it loose and expect to live—and he dug his fingers into the man's flesh, holding the knife at bay, still struggling to bring his pistol around. The Shadow Man grabbed at him, and Simon Winter felt his own right wrist encased by a powerful hand.

Locked together, the two men thrashed on the rocks, strength against strength, trying to gain an advantage that they could turn into death. Winter pushed a knee forward, locking it against one boulder, and he used this to create leverage, jerking himself around, feeling a momentary weakness in his assailant. Both men groaned hard with exertion, saying nothing, but letting their grip try to speak for them.

The Shadow Man's breath was hard against him, and Winter bellowed in pain as the man's teeth tore into collarbone. The Shadow Man drew back, and Winter smashed a shoulder toward the man's nose, hearing a thudding grunt as he connected. But the force of the thrust threw them both off balance. Like an old tree battling a hurricane wind, they swayed, then toppled hard. Still clasped together like a pair of murderous dancers, they rolled from the jetty, crashing once, then twice, against the sharp rock edges, and then tumbling into the thick, warm salt water.

For an instant they plunged beneath the surface, still entwined together, still struggling. Then they burst upward, their heads breaking the ink-black surface simultaneously.

Winter gasped for air as the two men twirled amidst the waves. There was no longer anything beneath his feet, nothing to push against. They both dropped beneath the surface again, then rose, kicking, back into the air.

He could feel the Shadow Man pushing the knife inexorably toward his ribs, seeking to cut out his heart. Again he tried to bring the revolver, still locked in his grip, to bear, but the man's hand was too strong. The pistol wavered just inches away from where a bullet might do some damage, while all the time the point of the Shadow Man's knife sought to end the struggle.

A third time they slid beneath the dip and sway of the waves, the weight of water punching him like a fist. When they burst through the surface again, Winter realized they had thrashed their way farther from the beach and the jetty. For an instant, as they churned in the blackness that enveloped them, he could just make out the Shadow Man's eyes.

And what Simon Winter saw first, in the final darkness of this last night, was something both awful and simple. They were gripped in an odd stalemate of strength, and there was only one way to break it. He knew, right in that second, what it was he had to do.

He understood: The only way to kill him is to let him kill me.

And so Simon Winter suddenly pulled the Shadow Man's knife hand hard toward his side, letting the blade find the flesh above his hip, just beneath his ribs and away from his stomach, in what he hoped would not be a fatal stab. The sudden pain was sharp, a wet, horrific hurt as his body absorbed the blade.

The motion took the Shadow Man by surprise, throwing him off balance, and in that small time, he did not drive home the advantage that Winter had given him. His training and instincts, which should have caused him to raise the knife point up hard, killing the old detective, for the first time perhaps ever, failed.

As the knife hesitated in his body, Winter savagely reached across and grabbed his gun with both hands. Doubling his strength, he jerked the weapon up against the Shadow Man's chest, and shouting a great bellow of pain and rage that rose above the crash of the surf, he called on the old gun that he'd worn for so many years to answer for him one final time.

The water muffled the shots as he fired. But he felt the revolver buck in his hand and he knew that each bullet was smashing home.

He pulled the trigger five times.

A wavelet splashed in his face, and he felt the Shadow Man abruptly, almost gently, release his grip and slide back away from him. Winter gasped for air.

In the last darkness of night, Simon Winter saw a look of confused surprise on the killer's face. He felt the Shadow Man's hand drop from the knife, and then the blade fell away from his side, falling into the warm water. The old detective saw death just begin to seize hold of his adversary, but a final outrage soared within him, pushing past all the pain and shock. He reached across a wave, grasped hold of the Shadow Man's white hair, and he pulled it toward him, jamming his revolver into the man's mouth, open in the astonishment of dying. He whispered harshly, "For Sophie, God damn you, and for all the others too." He held the pistol steadily for just a half second to let his words crease the last moment of the Shadow Man's life, and then fired his final shot.

The sound echoed briefly across the waves, then was lost in the noise of the surf.

Walter Robinson drove the squad car slowly over the loose coral rock and sand of the access road adjacent to the ocean. In his left hand he held a powerful spotlight, which cut through the last of the night gloom like a rapier through loose folds of cloth. He swept the light in an arc across the expanse of empty beach, the beam dancing across the waves as they rolled toward land, following it with his eyes, searching for the old detective.

"Do you think he's here?" Espy Martinez asked quietly.

"Yes. No. Somewhere," Robinson replied hesitantly. "They both are."

She did not respond to this, but continued to peer through the graying darkness. The rough stone of the road crunched beneath the tires of the policeman's car, and she cursed the noise it made. She tried to sort through all the sounds of the end of the night: the car engine, the tires against the road, Walter Robinson's harsh breathing so unlike the softer sounds he made when he slept by her side, the nearby rumble and slash of the surf against the shore. She thought if she could simply pigeonhole each sound, identify it, qualify it, assess it, and discard it, then she would finally come across a single tone that was different, and that would be Simon Winter.

Or, she thought swiftly, the Shadow Man.

She had watched Walter Robinson plunge like a diver into the

crowd of elderly people outside the rabbi's apartment, demanding, shouting questions at the gathering, a wild man, possessed.
"Did you see an old man? Did you see a man with a knife?" The
rabbi and Frieda Kroner had accompanied him, rapidly speaking
in several languages, like a pair of simultaneous translators. The
people surrounding the detective had looked skittish, riveted by
the suddenness of fear, unable to speak, until one ancient woman,
clutching at the arm of an equally ancient man, had tremulously
raised her hand.

"I saw," she had said. "I saw something."

"What?" Robinson had demanded.

"A man. Not a man with a knife. But a tall man with white
hair."

"Yes, yes, where?"

"He ran," the old woman had said. She had lifted her arm and
Espy Martinez had seen a bony finger quiver in the air as if fighting a gust of wind, pointing to the ocean beach. "He ran that way
as if he were chasing after the Devil. . . ."

She no longer knew how long they had been searching for the
old detective. Ten minutes that seemed to be a thousand. A half-
hour that was longer than any day she'd known. It seemed to her
that each minute that slid past them laughed cruelly, mocking
their hunt.

"He could be anywhere." She cursed beneath her breath. "We
don't even know if they came this way. . . ."

"I think they did," Robinson replied, still swinging the flashlight's beam toward the beach and the waves beyond, his head
halfway out the open window of the police cruiser. "If he'd gone
north, he would have been turning toward all the downtown
lights. No, he would come this way. He'd run for the darkness."

"And Simon?"

"Simon would chase after him."

Espy Martinez took a deep breath. "It will be daylight soon,"
she said. "Maybe we'll spot him then."

"That will be too late," Walter Robinson replied. His hand
clenched the steering wheel tightly. He wanted to gun the engine,
surge forward, anything that would make him feel as if he were a
part of the pursuit and not simply wandering about aimlessly.

Espy Martinez looked at the set of Robinson's jaw, saw the frustration tightening the muscles of his forearm. She felt helpless, like a physician standing at the bedside of some terminal patient. She turned away and continued sorting through the sounds again. A distant siren. A breaker finding the shoreline. Her own heartbeat in her ears.

And then, at that moment, something different. A single cracking sound, like someone far away stepping on a dry branch. A noise that rode the air directly to her like a lover's whisper.

"Stop the car!" she shouted.

"What? What? Did you see something?"

"Did you hear it?" she asked.

"What?" Robinson replied. "Hear what?"

But Espy Martinez was already jumping from her seat, slamming the door on the still-rolling vehicle. As her feet hit the sandy road, she cried back over her shoulder, "A shot, I heard a shot. . . ." Robinson jerked the gearshift into park and leapt after her.

Simon Winter rocked on the top of the waves like a child in a cradle. He could feel his life's blood slipping through the knife wound in his side and it seemed to him as if he was wrapped in an immense warmth.

He thought of Frieda Kroner and the rabbi, and he spoke out loud to them: "You are safe now. I did what you asked." In the same moment, he pictured his old neighbor and thought: Sophie Millstein, I have paid my debt.

He did not feel any pain and this surprised him. All the deaths he'd known over so many years had always seemed to him to be so many rippings and tearings, he had always assumed that violence was the bridegroom of pain. That he felt only a slight light-headed dizziness intrigued him.

The weight in his free hand reminded him that he still held his empty revolver. He leaned back, as if reclining on the waves, and considered for an instant that he should simply let it slide from his fingers into the black water beneath him, but he could not bring himself to do this. Inwardly, he told the weapon: You did what I asked, and I am grateful. It was what I expected and you do not deserve to be abandoned and thrown away after such service, but I do not know if I have the strength to lift you up.

Still, he tried, failing the first time, then coughing back some seawater, and succeeding in slipping the weapon back into his shoulder harness, which gave him an immense sense of satisfaction.

Simon Winter took a deep breath. He clasped one hand over the bleeding wound, and with the other, he took a single, great overhand stroke, swimming for an instant.

He thought to himself that it would be nice to die on the beach, that when he slid away from life it would be good to have solid ground beneath his feet, so that when he had to face death alone, he could do so squarely. But the long stretch of sand was more than fifty yards distant, an impossible trek, and he could sense the tug of the tide, pulling him farther from the shore. He swept through the water again with his free arm, but exhaustion abruptly filled him, and he told himself that choosing the site of one's own death was something of a luxury that few people could afford, and that he should pay this no mind, but accept what the next few minutes had in store for him. But, even with this thought ringing in his head, he found his arm pushing past the fatigue brought on by the chase, the fight, and the wound, and he struggled again against the current.

This made him smile.

I have always been stubborn, he thought. I was a stubborn child, and I became a stubborn young man and years passed and I turned into a stubborn old man and that is what I am now and fighting is a good way to die.

He kicked hard with his feet, trying to swim with the last bit of strength that he had. He gasped for a breath of air, and saw something that astonished him, coming from the beach, piercing the gray hour. It was a shaft of light, and at first he thought it was death coming for him, and then he realized it was nothing so romantic; instead, it was something temporal searching for him, and he lifted his free arm above the waves as the beam probed the air about him, and finally fastened on his hand lifted high.

* * *

"There!" Espy Martinez shouted. "Jesus, it's him! Simon!" She cried out to the old man. "Simon! We're here!"

"Do you see ..." Walter Robinson began, but she finished, "... No, he's alone."

He handed her the light as he started to strip off his jacket, his own weapon, socks and shoes. "Hold the light on him," Robinson insisted. "Don't lose him."

She nodded and stepped into the wash from the breakers, trying to get closer to the old man, the tropical waters encircling her knees. "Go, Walter," she said. "Help him now!"

But she did not have to say this, as the detective was already thrusting himself headlong into the surf. He disappeared for an instant in a burst of white water, crashing through a breaker as it rolled onto the beach, emerging on the far side, his arms and legs stabbing furiously into the body of the ocean.

She kept the light riveted on the old man struggling far from shore. She could just barely make out Walter Robinson's dark form, darker even than the waters that gripped them both. She saw Winter's outstretched hand wobble and then dip out of sight, although she could still just see his shock of white hair like a whitecap on the waves. "Go, Walter! Go!" she cried, although she didn't think her words would carry above the surf. Swim hard, she whispered to him. Swim fast, Walter.

He could feel the tidal pull helping him leave the shore in his wake, but he knew the fickleness of the ocean, for what was helping him this second, would turn on him treacherously when he reached the old detective. He kept his head down, rotating it only to grasp immense drafts of air and to check his bearings. His swim had none of the usual steady rhythm of exercise, but was filled with a fierce wrestling against the warm dark that encapsulated him.

Walter Robinson pierced the water rapidly. He was aware that the beam from the flashlight seemed to be dissipating, and realized that gray dawn was creeping across the horizon. He paid this no mind, but swam on, each pull with his arms straining his muscles. He called out once: "I'm coming, Simon! Hang on!" but the effort to lift his head and shout disrupted the fury of his progress, and so he pushed his head into the waves silently, listening only to the splash of his hands and kick of his feet and the hoarse sound of his wind as he bit air from the last of the night.

Simon Winter put his head back, and glanced up once into the sky, before he was smacked in the chin by a wavelet, and he coughed out briny salt water. He tried to tread water with one arm while keeping his hand pressed to the wound in his side, but this was difficult, and he felt suddenly as if there were hands beneath the surface of the ocean pulling at him gently, coaxing him to relax and slide down under the surface. He kicked his feet again, keeping his head barely above water and thought for the first time that night, through the entirety of his pursuit and fight, that he was old, and that the years had left him with little except loose muscles and quick fatigue.

He breathed out slowly, and then he heard Walter Robinson cry to him. He tried to reply, but it seemed to him that the ocean surrounding him was filled with an insurmountable noise, and he could not. Still, he managed to raise his hand once and gesture, and he saw a flurry of explosions across the top of the waves as the young detective hurtled toward him.

"I'm here!" Simon Winter managed to say in what he thought was a shout, but was barely a whisper.

"Hang on!" he heard Robinson answer, and he did. He closed his eyes for an instant, thinking he was a little like an exhausted child fighting sleep, and then he was aware of the young man in the water beside him, and he felt Walter Robinson's furious grip on his arm.

"I've got you, Simon, just hang on!"

He opened his eyes and felt Robinson's arm encircling his chest.

"It's over, Walter," he said quietly.

"Just take it easy, Simon. What the hell . . ."

"We fought, and I won," Winter said. "You make sure they know. . . ."

"Are you hurt?"

"Yes. No." Simon Winter wanted to say: How could a man like that hurt me? But he did not have the strength.

"The Shadow Man?"

"Gone. I got him."

"All right, Simon, you just lean back. I'll take you in. Just breathe easily and relax. You're gonna be okay. I promise. We'll go fishing tomorrow after all."

"I'd like that," Winter replied softly.

"It's gonna be okay," Robinson continued. "I'll save you."

"I am saved," Winter answered.

The old detective felt the young man's strength lifting him up to the top of the waves, and he leaned his head back and felt himself being carried forward, steadily, powerfully, toward the shore. He closed his eyes and let the rhythm of the swim rock him gently. He thought: I have become a tiny child again, cradled in my mother's arms.

Simon Winter sighed once, and opened his eyes. He looked back to the east and saw a vibrant red and gold band of light streaking urgently across the horizon.

"It's morning," he said.

Robinson did not reply, but swam on, fighting the tide and the waves that slapped and pulled and insulted his every thrust, as he had so many times before. He was not precisely sure when the old man died, but he knew this was true as he staggered through the breakers, and felt Espy Martinez's hands reach for him, and gently lower them both to the beach, where, for an instant, the three of them all lay, side by side.

The sun rose hard, fast and insistent as if bored and impatient and eager to begin the day's work. It filled the beach with painful glare and an uncompromising heat that danced in waves above the chalky sand. The tropical sky was an iridescent blue, a Chamber of Commerce sky, marred only by an occasional puffed-out white cloud or two that would meander lazily across the perfect palette like an unwelcome visitor.

Walter Robinson and Espy Martinez sat shoulder-to-shoulder in the middle of the beach, their clothes drying stiffly on their skin. She had a blanket tossed over her shoulders, and she shivered once, though she wasn't cold and the air around her was building with the day's heat. Behind them a half-dozen police vehicles crowded the access road, and several uniformed officers were holding back a small crowd of the curious, gathering to watch the activity. A quarter mile offshore, a Coast Guard cutter and two Miami Beach police patrol boats wandered back and forth through the blue water. Martinez could see two divers readying equipment on the stern of one of the patrol boats.

"Do you think they'll find him?" she wondered out loud.

"I don't know," Robinson replied. "The tide was running out pretty fast." He turned toward where a white-jacketed medical examiner was helping a pair of technicians enclose Simon Winter's body in a black vinyl bag. He caught one last sight of the old man's white basketball shoes as the zipper was sealed shut.

Robinson watched the medical examiner lurch across the sand. A light breeze ruffled the man's jacket as he approached.

"The old guy didn't drown," he said. "There's a knife wound in his side. How'd he get that, Detective?"

"He had a busy night," Robinson replied.

The medical examiner huffed once, then moved off to supervise removing the body.

"Who was he?" Martinez asked quietly.

"The Shadow Man?" Robinson shook his head. "I don't know. I doubt we'll ever know. He was someone once, but he probably changed names and identities so many times since the war, that whoever he truly was was lost."

She nodded.

"And now?"

"And now, nothing."

She hesitated, then she placed her hand on his forearm. Walter Robinson picked her hand up and placed it to his forehead, as if it were ice that would cool his brow. Then he returned it to his own arm and smiled.

"Well, not exactly nothing," he said.

In front of them, the technicians were lifting the body bag. Slowly, they started to struggle across the beach, their shoes digging down into the loose, chalky sand, as if the weight of the old man they carried had somehow grown and expanded and was almost greater than they could manage.

"Were you friends?" Espy Martinez asked.

"We were beginning to be," Robinson replied. "I thought he could teach me something."

Martinez considered this statement for a moment, then said, "I think he did."

They sat quietly for another minute, until she heard her name called from the road behind them. They both turned and saw the rabbi and Frieda Kroner being restrained by a uniformed officer. The policeman turned toward the detective, and Robinson signaled him to let them pass.

"It's all over," Robinson said, as they approached. "You can thank Detective Winter for that. You won't have to worry about the Shadow Man again."

"Poor Mr. Winter," Frieda Kroner said. She wiped at her eye. "I shall thank him in a prayer and I will say one for all the others, as well."

Rabbi Rubinstein nodded his head.

"One can never destroy every shadow, Detective," he said. "Not from such a great darkness." He reached over and grasped Frieda Kroner's arm in his and quietly added: "But to destroy one, is a great enough achievement."

Then the old pair of survivors turned and arm in arm, started back up the beach toward the city and their homes. For a moment, Walter Robinson and Espy Martinez watched them slowly pick their way across the beach as if memory itself were as loose and crumbling as the sand beneath their feet. Then he reached out and linked her arm in much the same way, and the two of them together followed.

# JOHN KATZENBACH

## Terror awaits.

Look for these tales of suspense at a
bookstore near you:

# IN THE HEAT OF THE SUMMER
# THE TRAVELER
# DAY OF RECKONING
# JUST CAUSE

Published by Ballantine Books.